LETTERS TO
PENTHOUSE
V

I0939419

Published by
WARNER BOOKS

LETTERS TO PENTHOUSE

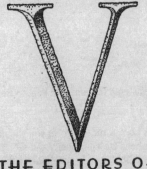

THE EDITORS OF PENTHOUSE MAGAZINE

WARNER BOOKS

A Time Warner Company

Penthouse® is a registered trademark of Penthouse International, Limited.

WARNER BOOKS EDITION

Cover design by Don Puckey

Warner Books, Inc.
1271 Avenue of the Americas
New York, NY 10020

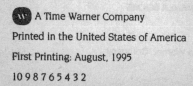 A Time Warner Company

Printed in the United States of America

First Printing: August, 1995

10 9 8 7 6 5 4 3 2

Letters To Penthouse V

CONTENTS

Letters To Penthouse V

Contents

The great thing about sex is that there are so many ways to enjoy it, so many twists and turns on the road to orgasm. Many of our readers travel the reliable, tried-and-true highway on their journey to the ultimate pleasure. More daring folks delight in discovering the more challenging but perhaps even more satisfying routes to their final carnal destination. This collection of letters includes everything from the traditional to the outrageous. There's something for everyone. So fasten your seat belt and get ready for a ride you're not likely to forget.

John Borrelli
Senior Editor
Penthouse Special Publications

Domination & Discipline

WHEN THE "BABY" MISBEHAVES, THE SITTER MUST PUNISH HIM

Reading your magazine has prompted me to write about something that happened to me when I was eighteen. My parents worked, so we had a female college student living with us. In exchange for a place to stay, Amanda did housework and "baby-sat" me. Amanda was a pretty girl with large breasts.

During my summer vacation, I started hiding in the closet of her bedroom while she was in the shower. When Amanda would come out, I'd watch her get dressed.

One day I must have made some noise, because she caught me in the closet with my dick in my hand. Was she mad! She threatened to tell my parents when they got home, and I was so scared and embarrassed, I started begging her not to tell.

After she cooled off a little, Amanda got me to agree that I deserved to be punished, and said that we could work something out.

Amanda ordered me to get undressed and lie across her knees so she could give me a spanking. She spanked my ass until it was red and sore, then laughed at me because my dick was rock-hard. That was just the beginning.

Amanda proceeded to make me her "little slave boy." I had to put on her silky panties and do all the housework. To make sure I didn't tell my parents, she took pictures of me wearing her panties and pushing the vacuum. She swore she'd give copies of the pictures to all my friends if I spoke a word to anybody. Later that day she made me eat her pussy and lick her asshole. She also spanked me again, and this time I came in her panties, so she made me eat my own come.

The rest of the summer, while my friends were partying at the beach, I spent most of my time serving my mistress. On Saturday nights, when my parents went out to dinner, Amanda made me model her lingerie for her friends. By the end of the evening, I would have eaten the girls out, been spanked at least once, and led to the bedroom, where the girls would tie me up and take turns sticking dildos up my rear end.

When Amanda finally graduated from college, she fucked me once, burned the pictures and said it had been fun. I haven't seen her since, but I actually miss being her slave. I've dated a lot of women since then, but have never been in a relationship that was as satisfying. I will continue to look for the right woman to be my next mistress.—*K.D., Portland, Maine* ⊙┼▣

A GIRLFRIEND ENSURES THAT THE PUNISHMENT FITS THE CRIME

After reading about guys who were forced by their wives or girl-friends to suck cock, I thought I would relate an experience I had a few years ago.

I was dating a girl named Dana who was absolutely beautiful. She was thirty-two years old, five feet nine inches tall and one hundred twenty-five pounds with thick, flowing brown hair, sparkling blue eyes, a perfect smile and a body that would make a centerfold jealous. She was a definite head-turner, and she knew it. We had been dating for about a year when I made the mistake of having a fling with a sexy girl I had met at work. Dana found out and called me at home to tell me that I had humiliated her by sleep-ing with this girl and that she didn't want to see me any more. I told her I was sorry and begged her to give me a second chance. She said that she would think it over, and told me to come to her house the next evening at seven o'clock for her answer.

I knocked on her door at seven o'clock on the dot. When Dana let me in, I saw that her friend Charles was visiting. Charles is very openly gay.

Dana called me into her bedroom and told me that she would give me one more chance, but that I would have to be punished. She said that since I'd humiliated her, she was going to humil-iate me. If I wanted to get back together with her, I would have to have sex with Charles while she watched. I just stood there in disbelief. Dana said she would give me until the count of ten to make up my mind.

When she got to ten, I still hadn't said a word, so she grabbed me by the arm and told me to leave. I pleaded with her, but she held firm. She then informed me that she was going to call one of her friends from work, go over to his house and fuck his brains out. She knew that would get to me, so I agreed to her terms. She said that because I'd hesitated, I would have to ask her permission to have sex with Charles. She ordered me to get on my knees and beg to suck his cock. Dana told me that she was going to teach me a lesson I'd never forget. She wanted to watch Charles fuck me up the ass, and wanted to watch me kiss, lick and suck his cock.

I was led back into the living room, where Dana ordered me to do a striptease. Once naked I was told to dance around the room and pose for them. Dana then put lipstick, makeup, a wig, a garter belt and stockings on me. Then I was instructed to undress Charles. He had blond hair and a muscular build. But as good-looking as he was, I was not at all interested in having sex with him.

Once Charles was nude, Dana ordered me to kiss and lick every inch of his body, starting with his toes. I was told to save his cock for last. When I got up to his chin, Dana made me French-kiss him. Charles put his hand behind my head and shoved his tongue down my throat. Dana told me to kiss and lick his cock. While I did it, Dana taunted me, and really making the most out of the situation. Then she told me to beg Charles for permission to suck his cock. I paused for a few seconds, and Dana yelled, "Do it!"

I dropped to my knees and said, "Please, sir. May I please suck your cock? Please? I beg of you, sir, please let me suck your big cock."

Dana really got off on this, and made me plead for about ten minutes. Then she said, "Okay, you can suck it, but first I want to watch him fuck you in the ass."

They bent me over a chair, and Charles stuck his cock up my rear and pounded away. Dana asked me how it felt to be fucked up the ass. "You like it, don't you?" she yelled.

"Yes, ma'am, I like being fucked in the ass."

Dana told Charles not to come, because she wanted him to come in my mouth so she could watch me swallow it. Charles pulled his cock out of my ass. After running to the bathroom to wash it off, he came back and shoved it in my mouth. Dana told me to suck it until he came. She was incredibly aroused, and really turned up the verbal humiliation. She said, "Suck that cock!"

I stopped sucking his cock momentarily. Dana was quick to slap my cock and start yelling at me again. "Put that cock back in your mouth and start sucking it. Suck it until he shoots his load in your mouth. You better swallow it all."

I felt Charles's cock start to throb. Dana saw the scared look on my face and put her hand behind my head, ordering me to swallow every drop. Charles exploded in my mouth, and I tried to back away, but Dana kept me in place.

Before the evening was over, Dana forced me to masturbate for them. I had never masturbated in front of anyone before, and it only added to my embarrassment. She had me ejaculate on Charles's cock, then lick it all off. While I was licking my own come, Charles got hard again. Dana smiled and said, "Suck him off. I don't think you've had enough come tonight."

I sucked Charles's cock until he shot his load into my mouth.

Dana informed me that if I ever pissed her off again, I would receive the same kind of punishment. I dated her for two years after that incident, and the punishment was repeated at least two dozen times during that period. I was so infatuated with her, I couldn't stand the thought of her leaving me.—*J.M., Indianapolis, Indiana* ⊙╾▪

SHE PROMISED TO HONOR AND OBEY—IT'S NOT NICE TO BREAK PROMISES

I am a twenty-six-year-old man who has been married for over three years. When I was in college and masturbated frequently, I had elaborate fantasies about complete domination over women.

Before getting married, sex between my wife Gina and me was frequent and passionate, but stayed pretty much on the normal side. Occasionally we experimented with ice cubes or whipped cream, but these episodes were far too infrequent for me.

Things continued this way until about a year and a half ago, when we hit a dry slump. To pick things back up, I suggested that we talk dirty to each other in bed. Gina took to this better than I'd expected, and soon we were talking trash to each other during every sex session we had. This excited me very much, and perked our sex life back up. It also seemed to make Gina more uninhibited and experimental. We even ordered a sex toy through a catalog! Then, about six months ago, it happened!

We were getting ready to fuck and leafing through *Penthouse Letters* to get ideas for something different to do, when we read a letter about a woman tied spread-eagle to a bed. "It's a shame we don't have any rope. We could try that," Gina said.

It surprised me to hear her say that. "Would you really want to do that?" I asked.

She just shrugged and said, "Sure."

That night while we fucked, I imagined that Gina was tied down, and I came like never before. Afterward, when we were getting dressed, I told her that most of my fantasies concerned bondage, domination and discipline. I thought that comment would be soon forgotten. Boy, was I wrong!

The next night while lying in bed, Gina told me that it had always been her fantasy to be completely under my control. I couldn't believe my ears! "I'll do anything," she said. "I'm your little girl."

My heart was pounding rapidly, and I didn't know what to do at first. Finally I stood up, walked over to the wall and leaned against it. "Come here," I said.

Gina came over and stood in front of me, waiting for my next command. "Get on your knees and rub my cock all over your face," I ordered. Gina has an adorable face, and watching her rub my cock all over it was driving me wild. She was panting like a slut in heat. I could tell she was really enjoying it. I then told her to begin sucking my cock. When I had her pick up the pace, I told her that right before I came, I was going to pull out of her mouth and come all over her face. "Would you like me to do that?" I asked. She nodded. I told her to beg for it, "Oh please, Daddy. Let me suck you until you squirt your come all over me. I'll be a good girl, I promise!" she whimpered. After I came, she looked up at me and smiled, my come dripping all over her.

After wiping her off, I instructed her to lie on the bed and not to move, make a sound or come while I played with her. I spent about twenty minutes playing with and sucking her tits and cunt until she could take no more and began moaning and squirming around on the bed. I told her what a bad girl she had been. "And what happens to bad girls?" I asked her.

"They get punished," she replied.

"Well, then get up on all fours," I ordered.

I then got my belt and began spanking her ass. I started off lightly because I didn't want to hurt her, but when I saw she didn't mind, I began spanking her in earnest.

After tiring of this, I stopped. I told her she was a good girl for taking her punishment, and now it was time for her reward. I plunged my tongue into her delicious pussy. She was so wet and hot, I had her coming in no time. After she came I decided it was time to explore some more new ground. I had fantasized before about eating her sweet ass, but was afraid she would think it was weird. Now I didn't care, because I knew I was in control. I started tonguing her butt. "Do you like this?" I asked her.

"Do you?" was her reply.

When I told her I did, she said, "Then so do I. I want whatever you want. I'm here to be your plaything." I was in heaven!

I decided that I wanted to have my ass eaten. I got up on all fours and commanded her to lick my asshole. There's nothing like having a woman's tongue up your ass! Unfortunately, I couldn't enjoy it for too long, because I was ready to fuck.

Gina got on all fours, and I plunged my cock in to the hilt and fucked her harder than I'd ever fucked her before. While we fucked she yelled, "Oh yes, Daddy! Beat your little girl! Make it hurt, I love it!" Needless to say, this sexual encounter was a huge success!

Since that night I've ordered bondage equipment through the mail. I have tied Gina up and treated her like a slave countless times. Once I left her tied to the bed with a dildo in her cunt and a vibrator up her ass while I went downstairs, smoked a cigarette and watched television for twenty minutes. The whole time she was sobbing for me to come upstairs and eat her pussy.

Sometimes we have "normal" sex, but even then we both know who's in charge, and if she gets out of line, I'll remind her.—*Name and address withheld* O╾▪

HE STARTED THE DAY A SIMPLE MAN—NOW HE'S A FANCY NANCY

I'm writing to tell you about my transformation from a simple man to a submissive slave. It all started when I fantasized about what it would be like to dress as a woman. I had never worn women's clothing before, but I really wanted to try it, so one day I worked up the nerve to go into a lingerie store.

As I entered the store, I was really nervous. I made sure no one was there except me and the saleslady. She walked up to me and asked if I needed any help. Her name was Annabel. She was unbelievably beautiful and dressed very sexily. I couldn't take my eyes off her. She was tall and slim with long blonde hair and blue eyes. I blushed furiously.

Annabel smiled and said, "Can I help you pick something out for your wife or your girlfriend?"

I said, "No, thanks. I'll just look around." I had no idea what I was looking for, and my hands were sweating from nervousness.

After about ten minutes, Annabel came over to me. I was looking through the panties and bras, trying to figure out what size would fit me. Annabel asked, "What size do you need?"

I said, "I don't know."

She asked, "How big is she?"

I gulped and said, "About my size."

At that point I thought I would die of embarrassment. Annabel just smiled, looked right at me and said, "Are these for you? Tell me the truth, because I can help you find the right size."

I looked into her eyes and said yes. Annabel said, "This is your first time, isn't it?" Again I said yes. Annabel just took my hand and said, "You've come to the right place. We're both going to have fun with this."

Then she said, "If you listen to me and do what I say, you're going to look great. Now go to the dressing room, and I will bring you a few things to try on."

I went to the dressing room without saying a word. I couldn't believe I was in a ladies' dressing room, ready to try on lingerie with a beautiful saleslady just outside the curtain. I was afraid someone might come in, but she said, "Don't worry, it's almost closing time."

She handed me a pair of sexy black lace panties and a matching bra. I put them on—they fit perfectly. Annabel said, "Let me see," and opened the curtain.

I felt a bit humiliated, yet excited at the same time. Annabel giggled, "Don't you look sexy. Let me see what else I can find for you." When she walked away, I left the curtain open.

She came back holding a pair of lacy black nylons and a matching garter belt. Then she went to the storage room and returned carrying a blond wig. She smiled and said, "Try this on."

The hair came down to my shoulders, long and silky. I told her I felt like a complete woman. Annabel said, "I think I will rename you Nancy. Step out here, Nancy, and let me get a good look at you."

I stood in front of her, waiting for her approval. She could tell how excited I was by the size of the bulge in my panties. "By the looks of things, you're having as much fun as I am. There are a few things missing, but unfortunately, I don't have them here, I will have to go next door to the dress shop."

With that she walked out the door. A few minutes later, she returned with a bulging shopping bag. She pulled out a sexy red minidress, matching pumps and a black belt.

I put the garments on right there in front of her. I felt so at ease with her by that point. She said, "Now sit down and let me apply your makeup."

First she applied foundation, then blush, eye shadow and bright-red lipstick. When she was through, she said, "Now look in the mirror and see what a pretty young thing you have become." I felt so feminine.

Just then two ladies entered the store. I didn't know what to do. Annabel said, "Don't worry, they're friends of mine," before calling them over. I was so nervous, not knowing what they would think when they got closer. Annabel introduced them as Tatiana and Babette. Babette smiled and said, "And who is *she*?" To my utter dismay, Annabel told them the entire situation. Tatiana and Babette seemed to take it in stride, but I decided it was time to leave.

When I went back to the dressing room, I found that my clothes were gone. I looked over at the ladies. Annabel said, "If you are going to leave without my permission, then you will have to leave as Nancy."

I walked over to Annabel and asked permission to leave. She said, "You must learn to listen to me. Now, as your first punishment, I want you to take off your dress and show Tatiana and Babette what you are wearing underneath."

As I slowly took off my dress, I became excited and had no way to hide it. Annabel said, "Put your hands on your hips and turn around so we can see all of you. Do it now." In a loud voice, Tatiana said, "Look how sexy she is in her garter belt and nylons."

Babette said, "Annabel, I think she should be punished for getting so excited in her panties. Just look at that bulge!" Tatiana agreed.

Becoming more nervous, I said that I couldn't help it if my cock was hard. Annabel said, "What was that I heard you say? From now on that is your pussy. Have you got that? Now I want you to ask Babette if you can pull your panties down and rub your pussy."

I couldn't believe what I was doing, but I looked at Babette and did as I was told. She smiled and said, "Yes, but only pull them down to just above your knees. Do it slowly."

Annabel pulled a camera out of her bag and said, "Here, Tatiana. As Nancy rubs her pussy for us, take some pictures."

I slowly pulled my black lace panties down and my hard cock—I mean pussy—popped out. I started rubbing it slowly. I was so excited, I knew it wouldn't be long before I came. Soon huge globs of spunk were landing on the floor. The girls laughed the whole time. Annabel said, "Now didn't that feel good? I think you need to thank Babette for letting you come."

Still holding my pussy in my hand, I thanked Babette for letting me masturbate. She smiled and said, "Annabel, I think you've won this one over."

Annabel then stroked my cheek and said, "There are going to be some rules. Do you want to be my live-in maid? Answer yes or no."

I said, "Yes."

Holding up my "man" clothes for me to see, she said, "Take one last look, because you won't be needing these any more." With that she threw them in the garbage.

Annabel continued, "From now on you will wear what I tell you to wear, except when you go to work, but you must wear pretty lingerie under your work clothes." Babette and Tatiana watched me intently to see if I would agree to Annabel's terms.

I said, "Yes. I will do as you say."

"Good!" she exclaimed happily. "Now go put your dress back on and fix your lipstick. We need to buy you more clothes and makeup of your own."

Babette added, "And she will also need a razor to shave all her body hair."

"Yes," Annabel said. "I expect your legs, underarms, chest and genitals to be smooth. You got that?"

I moved in with Annabel that very night. One day she told me that she had told her boss, Vince, about me. He wanted to meet me, so I had to come to the store and hang around all day. Annabel even made me assist some of the customers. I looked pretty good, but I think some of them could tell I was really a man.

Near the end of the day, Tatiana and Babette came in to see if Vince had arrived.

Just then he walked in. He was big and well-built with dark hair. Annabel locked the doors and brought Vince over to me. He said, "I hear you suck a mean dildo." I was so nervous, I couldn't respond.

Annabel turned to me and said, "Nancy, the girls and I set this up for you. Now do as you're told. Kneel in front of Vince and ask permission to undo his pants and suck his cock."

I assumed the position, knowing there was no going back. Vince gave me a big smile and said, "Get to it, Nancy." Babette squealed and said, "I've got to get this on videotape."

I pulled Vince's pants down to his ankles. After I removed his underwear, his big cock nearly hit me in the nose. As I was about to suck my first cock, Babette yelled, "Hold it! Annabel, make Nancy fix her lipstick"

Annabel handed me a tube of bright red lipstick. I applied it slowly as Babette got it all on film. By that time pre-come was dripping from Vince's cock. Annabel said, "Go ahead, take it in your mouth."

And that's just what I did. I couldn't believe how natural it felt. Before long I had so much of his cock in my mouth that my nose was nestled against his balls. Vince grabbed my hair and said he was ready to come. Annabel said, "Nancy, I want you to swallow it all."

Just then Vince started shooting his load down my throat. I swallowed as much as I could, but some dripped out the corners of my mouth. After Vince left, Annabel said, "Girls, I think Nancy is one of us now. And even if she doesn't think so, we have the tape to prove it."—*N.E., Roanoke, Virginia*

BORED WITH MARRIAGE, A HORNY LADY BECOMES A NASTY MISTRESS

I'm a thirty-year-old, married female. I am considered very attractive, with long red hair, a cute little ass and firm breasts. My husband works all day, then spends the evening getting drunk in some bar. He is usually so drunk by the time he gets home, I haven't set eyes on his cock in over two years.

Because I am a very horny woman, I fell in the habit of fingering myself several times a day. Recently, however, I've found a new way to satisfy myself, and my new lovers are more than eager to satisfy my lust for sex.

I got into domination about six months ago after I started reading your magazine. Now I am treated like a queen by my sex slaves. I've known Ned and his foxy wife Erica for many years. I've always wanted to fuck both of them, so I put a plan into action.

Erica is a hairdresser with short blonde hair, tits nearly as big as mine and a knockout body. I called her at her salon, told her I needed a haircut and asked if she would stop by my house on her way home. She said she'd be by around six o'clock that evening. My next task was to get Ned to come over to my house before six. That was no problem. I called him up and asked him to help me move some furniture. He arrived at my house at four in the afternoon. I was wearing a pair of tight shorts and a skimpy tank top. Ned gave my body a good once-over as I led him down to the rec room in the basement. "What do you need moved?" he asked.

"Me," I replied, removing my top, freeing my juicy tits and grabbing his crotch.

Ned said, "I'd like to, but I don't screw around on Erica."

I pushed him onto the bed and tied his hands to the posts with the ropes I had placed there for this occasion. Then I pulled down his jeans and ripped off his shorts, exposing his tasty dick. All the while Ned was begging me to let him go. "Not until I fuck your brains out," I said before ravaging his cock with my mouth. It didn't take long to bring his cock to attention.

I took off my shorts and lowered my aching pussy onto his cock. As I fucked him I told him that his sweet wife was coming by shortly, and that soon she would also be my prisoner. Soon Ned shot his load deep into my pussy. "I wonder what your beloved Erica will say when she finds your come inside me," I teased.

"Please don't say anything," Ned asked. I just laughed. Then I took one of my dildos, greased it up and stuck it deep inside Ned's tight ass. "That better be there when I get back," I warned, "or your wife will get a good whipping."

I took a bandanna and gagged his mouth with it. "See you soon, big boy," I said as I headed upstairs. I put on a robe, hid a pair of handcuffs under a sofa cushion and waited for Erica. She showed up shortly after six.

Her skilled hands and fingers gave my scalp a good massage as she washed and conditioned my hair. When she admired my beautiful red hair, I said, "It's all natural. Here, see for yourself." With that I opened my robe and let her gaze at my flaming-red pussy. "Very nice," Erica cooed.

After Erica was through styling my hair, I told her to have a seat on the couch. "I really need to get home," she said, looking at her watch.

"Just a few minutes," I begged.

We both sat down and made small talk. After a few minutes I told her that I've always wondered which of us had the biggest tits. "Let me check yours out," I said.

Erica was more than willing. She unbuttoned her shirt and removed her bra. I pulled her close and gave her a wet kiss on the lips, then bent down and sucked her sweet nipples. "Let me show you something, baby," I cooed as I took her hand and slipped one of her fingers up my cunt. I said, "Your dear husband was kind enough to give me just what I needed."

"That bastard!" she yelled, getting up. "Just wait until I get home!"

"Not so fast," I said, pulling her hands behind her back and handcuffing her. "I've got Ned tied up downstairs, and now you too are going to be taught a lesson," I said as I marched her downstairs.

Once in the basement, I had Erica suck her husband's cock. "Get it hard, baby. I want to fuck him again," I whispered. Erica quickly bobbed up and down on Ned's cock. I could tell by the look on his face that he was about to come. "Enough," I said, pulling Erica away. Then I noticed that the dildo had slipped out of Ned's ass. "Bad boy!" I yelled at him. "You know what this means."

He just nodded. I went over and removed the gag. "Yes, Nicole," he said.

I grabbed his balls and barked, "That's Mistress Nicole—to both of you. Erica, get over here and bend over. I'm going to whip your ass."

I grabbed a belt and whacked her ass until it turned beet red. "Please," she begged, "I'll service your every desire, my beautiful mistress."

"Good girl," I said as I licked her tingling ass. Because you have been so good, I have a special treat for you."

I called out to my gardener, Derek, who is over six feet tall and very well-hung. Derek took his big black monster and rammed it deep into Erica's cunt. He gave her a savage fucking before filling her with his juice.

I untied Ned and had him fuck me up my ass while Derek made him suck his dick. "Get it hard so I can fuck your wife's delicious ass," Derek screamed.

After Ned had made Derek's cock as hard as a flagpole, I coated it with petroleum jelly and guided him into Erica's tight ass. The two of them fucked like animals in heat. Finally he exploded deep inside her asshole.

I am now divorcing my husband and moving in with Ned and

Erica. Not only do I keep them in line, but Ned has a foxy secretary who's in need of a little discipline. She's next.—*N.G., Battle Creek, Michigan* O+ ⚿

BEWITCHED, BOTHERED AND BUTT-FUCKED BY A YOUNG BLACK BUCK

I'm a thirty-eight-year-old woman who was divorced a few years back. I'm about one hundred fifty pounds, five feet six inches tall, and I have large tits that always get plenty of attention.

I live in a small apartment building near a university, close to my job. Recently, a young black guy named Stephen moved into the complex. He is very handsome, and I found myself fantasizing about him. This embarrassed me, as I hardly knew him and I was sure he could read it on my face.

One day when I was coming home I bumped into Stephen. He's only twenty-three years old, and a part-time student. He smiled and started making small talk. After a few minutes I asked him in for a drink. I don't know where I got the courage. He immediately accepted my offer.

After several drinks it was obvious that he knew what was on my mind. He suddenly said, "You'd really like some black cock, wouldn't you, bitch?" I was shocked, because he had been so kind and quiet before, but I found myself also wildly excited at his change of manner. Still, I didn't know how to respond. He sneered a little, and said, "You need me to tell you what to do, don't you?"

I had to look down before I could answer. "Yes, please. It's been a long time for me. I'm not sure I'll know what to do anymore."

He didn't hesitate. "To start off, you need your fat ass spanked, just to let you know who's in charge. So get that nasty bubble-butt over here now!" I looked at him while I considered. He looked at me with a softer expression, and added, "You don't have to, you know. We could play a different game."

That made up my mind, and I slowly walked over to him. He became stern again, and told me that if I wanted my plump bottom reddened I was to take off my skirt and panty hose and get on his lap fast or he'd leave. I trembled a little as I dropped my skirt and slithered my panty hose down to the floor. I bit my lip and climbed onto his lap.

Stephen started spanking, slowly at first, watching my reaction, then faster and harder when I didn't complain. After only a few swats the tears were streaming down my face, and I felt really turned on. After fifteen or twenty blows he stopped. My butt was really tingling, and it hurt—but it also felt wonderful. To say that I was confused is an understatement. Stephen started roughly kneading my flesh. Soon he was fingering my cunt, still slapping my ass from time to time with his other hand. I was so wet and worked up! I just closed my eyes and enjoyed the pleasure and the pain that were coursing through my body.

Stephen stopped before I could come. He turned to me and said, "You like having a big, black buck dominate you, don't you? Don't just look ashamed—if it's true, tell me!"

I turned to look Stephen straight in the face and see if I could still find the gentle part of him in his eyes. I couldn't see it anymore, but I said, "Yes. I want you to dominate me." He smiled and told me to get off his lap and finish undressing so he could see my fat tits. I did. I stood naked before him. He didn't touch me at first, just continued staring, a wicked grin on his face. It sent shivers down my spine. I was his emotional hostage.

He finally spoke. "I think you like being degraded and pushed around, and you want to serve me in any way I want—is that right?" The words shook me to my very core. I didn't speak. He yelled, "Fuck you! I guess I'll just leave."

Through the mist of my indecision I heard myself say, "No, Stephen, please don't go. You're right."

"Right about what?" Stephen drawled. He wanted me to say it myself.

I answered, "I want to please you, and I'll do exactly as you say." The cold smile came back to his face. He told me to get on the floor on my hands and knees and crawl over to him. I did. He undressed, and I was face to face with his half-hard prick. I knew what he wanted, so I started sucking.

When his cock was hard, he pulled away from my mouth, walked behind me and started to fuck me. I was dripping cunt juice down my legs by this time, but it wouldn't have mattered how wet I was. He rammed into me so suddenly and so hard that it felt like he'd cut me. After a few strokes, though, I was pushing back at him fiercely every time he drove his dick into my pussy.

Stephen didn't want me enjoying myself quite so much, though. After a short time he pulled out and leered, "Now I'm gonna ream your ass."

I hadn't counted on anything like that, and yelled, "No, it'll hurt, it won't fit."

Stephen smacked me on the ass and said, "Of course, it'll hurt—but I'll make it fit." I thought I'd die as he slowly pushed and wiggled his prick inside me. Tears of pain, humiliation and intense pleasure streamed down my cheeks. He rocked back and forth for what seemed like forever. From time to time Stephen smacked my ass. The intense feelings and emotions were incredible. It was like nothing I'd ever experienced before. I didn't even know I could feel like this. It wasn't like having an orgasm, but the pleasure was almost as intense, and continued as long as he was in me, not rising and falling the way an orgasm does.

Finally Stephen came, and the two of us fell in a heap on the floor. As I lay there I realized that he'd never even kissed me. He got up, sat on the chair and asked me my name. I said, "Helen." He turned to me and told me that for an older, fat, white slut I was "better than average."

He ordered me to get dressed as slutty as possible right away, because he was going to show me off to some of his friends. He said that my need to be used, abused, degraded and dominated would be truly fulfilled. I got dressed and we went out.

His three friends spanked me, fucked me, shoved their dicks up my ass and slapped me while I gave them blowjobs. I loved it all. Stephen routinely has me gang-banged by five or six guys. Recently he tried charging for a bunch of these guys to fuck me. He only charged a dollar, because he said that's all an old, fat, white slut is worth. I had reached my limit, and I told him that he'd gone too far and I was leaving.

To my amazement, he threw the guys out and spent the rest of the evening comforting me. He told me that anytime I didn't want to do something, all I had to say was, "Enough!" and it would stop. Until any scene reached that point, though, he would never give a sign that his disdain was anything but real. I spent most of the night crying tears of relief, and we went to sleep in each other's arms.

The next morning his smiles were gone, and everything was back to normal. Stephen called me a bitch and a whore and threw me out of his apartment, knowing I'd be back at sunset. I don't know how this will end, but right now I have exactly what I want.—*H.W., Dallas, Texas* ⊶ ▪

ALL THE WAY FROM ANTI-GAY TO THE BELLE OF THE BALL

My name is Sue. I'm a thirty-eight-year-old black woman with a pretty face and a once-sexy figure. I played varsity sports while growing up, but have since become extremely overweight. I'm five feet nine inches and two hundred seventy-five pounds.

I've been dating a fellow named Harlan who is white, twenty-eight years old, five feet ten inches tall and about a hundred fifty-five pounds. After dating Harlan for a short while I revealed to him that I was bisexual, which didn't go over very well. I should have known his reaction wouldn't be great, because he has made taunting comments concerning some of my male friends who are openly gay. Harlan had also made fun of my weight, but it was his taunting of gays that made me decide that he needed to be taught a lesson.

Harlan is very shy and conservative in his lovemaking. Believe it or not, he insists on covering himself up when undressing near me. I have often fantasized about having him masturbate and then eat his come in front of me or, better yet, watching him suck a cock. I knew he would never do either of these things for me voluntarily.

I decided that the best way to punish him would be to humiliate him. I came up with an idea that I was pretty confident would work. If it did I would finally get to see him masturbate, suck cock and eat come. The thought of watching him eat a man's come gave me chills up and down my spine.

Harlan, among other shallow notions, thinks a woman's place is in the home. He has always resented woman being allowed in the military. Discussing this always gets him fired up. Even though we had never wrestled, I knew that I could tie him up in knots. Well, it was easy to get him up on his high horse. All I had to do was say that women have served in combat all over the world for thousands of years. When he said that woman were physically weak, I told him that I could whip his ass.

Harlan laughed and said, "I could pin you and make you say uncle in about twenty seconds." That's when I knew I had him.

I sneered, "Oh really? Do you want to bet on it?"

He laughed again. I was going to enjoy this more than I had thought. Harlan said, "I'll bet as much as you like."

"Oh, I didn't have money in mind." It was the Friday evening of a long weekend. I told him that the loser had to do whatever the winner wanted for the next three days. The loser had to be completely obedient. Harlan began to look doubtful at that, but I called him a chickenshit and a welcher. He couldn't take that and agreed to the bet.

I told him, "Honey, you're gonna lose this bet. And when you do, I'm going to make you masturbate in front of me, and I'm going to make you dress in women's clothing. Then we're heading for a black gay bar I know, and you're going to learn to suck cock." I asked him if he had ever eaten a man's come before, and of course he said no. I replied that I was going to make him eat a lot of come. "It's an acquired taste. Pretty soon you'll be begging for it." The thought of him eating come made me laugh out loud, which really got to him.

Harlan said, "No way."

I said, "A bet is a bet. It sounds like you're afraid you're going to lose."

He growled, "Okay, the bet's on. I'm not concerned because I'm going to win anyway. I just can't believe you'd sink low enough to imagine those things. Of course, it gives me some ideas about how to treat you when I win."

We faced off in the middle of the living room, and I had Harlan pinned before he knew what happened. It was so easy that I decided to have some more fun by wrestling around on the floor with him, putting him in one uncomfortable hold after another. After about fifteen minutes of being thrown around the room he was beaten, but hadn't yet said uncle, to end the bet. I thought it was time he did, so I threw him down on his back, jumped on him and stripped him naked. I moved behind him, put his arms behind his back, put my legs around his and spread his legs wide open while pulling up on his arms.

He started begging me to stop, and yelled uncle repeatedly. I made him say that I was stronger than he, and that he would pay off the bet and be my slave. I also made him say that he would masturbate and also suck cock. Not only did I make him say it, I made him beg to masturbate and beg to suck as many cocks as I wanted. When it got to the part about sucking cock he hesitated, but I said, "Come on, sweetie, it could be worse. I licked my middle finger and jammed it up his ass. He got the point, and started begging to be allowed to suck cock and swallow sperm.

I had an orgasm just listening to him begging to eat come. I let him up, directed him to kneel in front of me on top of the coffee table and made him beg for permission to masturbate. Harlan said, "Please let me masturbate for you. I want to stroke my cock for you and eat my hot come." I told him to start masturbating.

Every time it seemed that Harlan was almost coming I made him stop, lick the drops of come that had collected on the end of his cock and tell me how he wanted to suck cock. I finally let him come, catching it in my hand. After he begged to be allowed to eat it, I made him slowly lick up every drop.

Having planned this event for some time, I had already purchased women's clothing, makeup and a wig for him to wear. I dressed him up in his sexy new attire—garter belt, stockings, bra—the whole nine yards, except that I wouldn't allow him to wear panties.

I took him to the gay bar, where we met up with a gay black friend of mine. I enlisted my friend's help, and before the night was over he arranged for Harlan to suck off five guys in a back room of the bar, including sucking off my friend twice. It was the greatest sight watching Harlan, on his knees, kiss, lick and finally suck a cock. I made sure everyone came in his mouth, and that he swallowed every drop.

For the rest of the weekend I either kept him naked or in a frilly French maid's outfit that kept his ass, cock and balls exposed. On the second night I invited three girlfriends over (Cleo is actually a transsexual, but she looked hot, especially her cock, which I saw for the first time that night). I dressed him in a French maid's outfit for the evening. I made him masturbate for us and eat his come, but only after begging.

Then I was ready for some real fun. I told the girls how much Harlan liked sucking cocks, and they wanted to see Harlan work on Cleo. Since they all knew of Harlan's previous taunting of gays they were going to have some real fun. Cleo dropped her dress and stood there wearing only a pink garter belt and stockings. With her firm tits, small waist and tasty cock hanging between her legs, she looked great.

The girls told Harlan to kneel in front of Cleo and beg to suck her cock. We all loved watching his humiliation and made it as embarrassing as possible for him.

I had never seen my girlfriends this excited before. They said that if his begging wasn't good enough, they were going to spank him. He begged and pleaded to suck Cleo's cock, but the girls decided to spank him anyway. While begging he said, "Please let me suck your big, beautiful cock, please, I beg of you, let me suck your big, hairy cock, please let me suck your cock and taste your hot, sweet come." After some more begging we had him kiss and lick every square inch of Cleo's cock. Then the girls told him to take Cleo's cock in both his hands and suck her off. When Cleo came, she shot part of her load in his mouth and the rest all over his face, spreading it around with her cock.

I made Harlan swallow the come in his mouth, but had him leave the rest on his face for the entire evening. One of the girls told Harlan that for the privilege of being allowed to suck Cleo off, Harlan should show his appreciation by kissing and licking Cleo's asshole.

The girls told me that that was the most exciting and sensual night of their lives. They loved watching Harlan's humiliation, and they all asked if they could return for some more fun with the "sissy." Of course I said they could use Harlan anytime and any way they wanted to, and the girls have been over frequently, especially Cleo.

Since that first weekend, Harlan has been my slave. Being able to live out my fantasy took some initiative and careful planning, but it was well worth it.—*L.M., Biloxi, Mississippi*

YOU'RE NOT TOO OLD TO BE TAKEN OVER MY KNEE

I moved here from England ten years ago, when I got married. My wife Liz had a nine-year-old daughter. England has a long history of spanking for discipline. My wife didn't believe in it.

My stepdaughter Bonnie is now nineteen and has been away at college for the past year. She came home on break recently, and brought her roommate Moira. On Friday night they stayed out until three in the morning. Saturday my wife and Bonnie had a fight, as her curfew is one o'clock.

I told her that, regardless of whether she was right or wrong in her argument, she had to control her temper or she'd get the spanking she was so long overdue for. She said I wouldn't dare.

Bonnie normally sleeps in just a T-shirt and panties, so when I grabbed her and pulled her over my lap, she had little protection. When I gave her her first spank, she really started cursing at me. I stopped (keeping my hand on her panty-covered bottom) and calmly said, "If you don't stop, I'll take your panties down and really let you have it."

Again she told me I wouldn't dare, adding, "You're not my

father." That stung, and I was determined to sting her in return. I pulled her bikini panties right off, exposing her round little bottom. She squeezed her legs together so I couldn't see anything, but I knew that a few well-placed swats would soon change that.

I lectured her first, and then really began spanking her. After about a dozen slaps she started crying and kicking her legs, begging me to stop. Her bottom was turning a pleasant shade of red, and I was really getting turned on by all her squirming. It had been a long time since I'd administered a good spanking, and I was enjoying myself immensely.

I was equally enjoying the sight of her pussy lips, which were now in plain view, as red and swollen as her white cheeks were becoming. As I continued to spank her, I noticed that her lips were getting moist, as I had hoped they would, and she was moaning. Just when I was getting well into the game, though, she started to apologize. It was unbearable to me to stop, but there was really no excuse for going on, so I withheld my hand, and stood her in the corner.

While all this was going on, her friend Moira had been yelling at me and calling me names, saying she'd have me arrested for assault. I told her if she didn't mind her own business she'd get the same treatment, hoping of course that she would ignore my warning. I wasn't disappointed. She continued swearing at me.

When I finished with Bonnie I grabbed Moira, a small blonde, easy to turn across my knee. Moira was wearing a nightgown, and when I pulled it up to her waist, I found she wasn't wearing any panties. As I began spanking her, her pale white skin quickly turned red and she continued to twist and wiggle, trying to escape. Nonetheless, it was soon clear that she too was aroused by my efforts, as the very strong smell of her pussy juice told me.

She was much more stubborn than Bonnie, and ended up being spanked much longer. At first Moira didn't want me to know she was enjoying herself, but after a while she abandoned her attempt to hide her pleasure and began openly humping my knee. She continued crying and kicking, but her hard, fat clit was pressed against my leg and she bounced up and down instead of twisting and trying to get away. Before I finished she had an orgasm, and her juices flowed and left a wet spot on my pants.

I stood her in a corner also, and told them I wouldn't release them until they stopped crying and apologized. The sight of these two shapely young girls rubbing their sore, red bottoms was a sight to behold. Bonnie asked me very humbly if she could put her panties back on, but I told her no. They both held out a little longer, but soon Bonnie, and then Moira, apologized very contritely. I let them go about their business, while I ran back to my bedroom to release my own pent-up tension.

Later, Bonnie and my wife went shopping. Moira stayed home to rest. I was out by the pool when Moira came out wearing a skimpy black bikini. She asked me to rub cold cream on her tender bottom and suntan lotion on her back. She managed to lie in the sun, but only on her stomach, as her bottom was so sore.

Since this first episode, they have both come to visit again, and both have found ways to force me to give them spankings. Not that I need forcing, you understand, but there's something to be said for maintaining the illusion. My wife now agrees that we should have used spankings to punish Bonnie years ago. Barebottom spankings have become the standard punishment in our home.—*G.W., Galveston, Texas*

TWENTY-FIVE LESSONS ON HOW TO BE A BETTER HUSBAND

I'm thirty years old and have been married to Reggi for seven years. Recently Reggi found out that I have been fucking my twenty-four-year-old secretary. Reggi is exceptionally beautiful, and we have a great sex life, but I couldn't resist Liza, and had been fucking her for about eight months when Reggi found out.

Reggi and I make love about four times a week. Reggi loves sex, will always try new positions and never refuses to suck my cock. When she found out that I was fooling around, she went crazy and threatened to leave me. I begged her to stay, and told her I would never do it again. After a lot of begging, Reggi said she would stay, but insisted that she first had to get even. I was to be punished by having no sex for thirty days. In addition, since I really need Liza as my secretary, Reggi said that I could keep her, but Reggi wanted a little chat with her. She also told me that if it happened again she would be gone immediately. The expression on her face let me know that she wasn't joking.

My punishment started. I was forced to sleep in our extra bedroom away from Reggi. In addition, Liza couldn't speak to me except about business. During that month, Reggi was often not home when I got home from work. She usually arrived home at two or three o'clock in the morning. In addition, Reggi told some of my co-workers about my situation, and I was the butt of their constant jokes. My affair with Liza was well known in the office, and I suspect one of my co-workers was responsible for Reggi finding out.

The night that my month of punishment was over, Reggi handed me a large box. I opened it, and inside were about twenty-five videotapes. Reggi sat down with a smirk as I put on the videotape. The tape showed Liza, completely nude, lying facedown on a bed, and Reggi standing over her, fully clothed, whipping her ass with a riding crop. Liza was telling Reggi she would be good and never fool around with me again.

When Reggi stopped whipping her I was very surprised to see three of my co-workers—Glenn, Stevie and Billy—appear on the screen. They started to strip, and Reggie told them to fuck Liza up the ass. Liza was begging them to please be gentle, as she had never been fucked up her ass. Reggi smacked Liza again with the riding crop and told her to beg to have her tight asshole fucked. Liza was facedown with her butt in the air when Glenn got behind her and started to penetrate her asshole. It took at least twenty minutes of Glenn's thrusting for him to get his cock all the way in. I could see that Liza was finally starting to relax and had begun to enjoy her reaming. Glenn stroked on until he shot his come all over her back.

Stevie was next. He was able to slide his cock right into her ass. He talked a lot, telling her how tight and hot she felt. He said he'd wanted to do this for a long time, and had been saving a load for her all week. When he came, you could see that it was indeed a big wad. By now Liza was begging for more.

When Stevie was finished, Billy had his turn. Liza was begging for his attention, and before he stepped up to her there was a shot of her asshole, which had remained wide open after Stevie was finished, come dripping out of it as she panted, thrusting her hips back. Then Stevie plugged her hole, and in a few minutes Liza received her third dose of sperm of the evening.

In the final scene, Liza was in between Glenn, who had his cock in her pussy, and Stevie, who had his cock in her ass, while

Billy shoved his dick in her mouth. All of Liza's holes were filled, and she was mumbling for them to fuck her hard. After they came, the camera zoomed to a shot of Liza's very red asshole with four loads of come dripping out. The tape ended, and I realized that I had a huge hard-on. I was also grateful that Reggi had kept her clothes on. It would be hard to go to work if my wife had let my co-workers fuck her.

Reggi told me to put in the second tape. My joy about Reggi keeping her clothes on was short-lived. The second tape began with Liza, lying on my desk naked, and Reggi, completely nude, wearing a huge strap-on dildo. Reggi looked right at the camera and said it was her turn to fuck Liza's tight little ass. She positioned Liza so that her ass was facing the camera and pushed the dildo halfway in. She stopped and asked Liza, "What do you want?"

Liza shouted, "I'm a slut, and I want my ass fucked." Reggi accommodated her, ramming the rest of the dildo to the bottom in her asshole. Reggi was giving Liza a tremendous fucking, which actually caused Liza to have a wrenching orgasm. After Liza came, Reggi withdrew from her ass. She took the riding crop and whipped Liza a few times on the butt, then told her to get her sorry ass out of there. Reggi lay down on my desk and spread her pussy for the camera.

That's when my co-workers appeared on the screen. My worst fears had been realized. There was Reggi getting the fucking of her life from three guys on my desk in my office. Glenn, Stevie and Billy each took turns fucking her pussy. She also gave them each a blowjob, letting them come on her face and in her mouth.

All of this had a strange effect on me. When the tape was over I was so horny that I went over to Reggi and ripped off her clothes. When I got to her panties I saw that she had completely shaved her cunt. I wanted her pussy so much I didn't stop to think about it. I rammed my dick into her bald hole and came very quickly.

After I came, she sat on my face and had me eat my come out of her. I continued to lick her for almost two hours, during which time she had half a dozen grinding orgasms. We finally calmed down and went to bed. Before we went to sleep she told me that over the next few days I would have to watch every single video, including the one where her pussy had been shaved.

When I got to work the next day everybody knew that I had seen the video. I was invited to Glenn's office, where six of my co-workers told me how good a fuck Reggi was. I was very humiliated. Liza was brought in, and she repeated her performance, letting the guys triple-penetrate her. She said she was sorry that I couldn't fuck her, but Reggi wouldn't allow it. The guys also suggested that I watch the rest of the tapes and see how much Reggi loved being fucked.

When I got home that night, video number three was in the machine. Reggi again sat on the couch while I watched. This tape started with both Reggi and Liza naked on my desk. Both women were masturbating themselves with vibrators. Reggi pulled hers out and inserted it into Liza's ass. Liza was on her back with her legs spread wide while Reggi worked one vibrator in her ass and one in her pussy. Liza was soon bucking all over the desk, moaning, "Oh, God! Here it comes! Oh, Reggi, fuck me!" Compared to this, Liza had been laid back when we had sex together. Now she was screaming and throwing herself around as she had a tremendous orgasm.

Liza left the picture. She was replaced by a guy named Ben, also from the office. He stripped, and stuffed his cock in Reggi's cunt. He came quickly, but Reggi went to work on his softening cock with her mouth. Glenn appeared, and fucked Reggi while she sucked Ben's cock. I watched three tapes that night. In the first five tapes, Reggi had fucked six different guys from my office. Still I was monstrously turned on by it, and that night I again ravished Reggi's pussy.

The next day was Friday, and my co-workers all had a good laugh trying to guess what tape I was up to. I was humiliated all day and I was glad it was Friday. I was prepared to go home and spend the weekend seeing what was on the rest of the tapes, to get it over with. That night Reggi and I watched three more tapes. In one tape Reggi had four of my co-workers jerk off on her face. In the last tape that night, after three guys fucked Reggi, Liza appeared again and sucked the come out of her pussy.

When we went to bed that night I sucked on Reggi's shaved pussy until she came twelve times. We spent the entire night in a 69. We awoke early Saturday morning, and Reggi served me breakfast while I watched more tapes. The tapes were of more of my co-workers with Reggi.

Around noon Reggi left me alone to watch more tapes. One tape was made in a hotel room, with just Liza and Reggi. They were fucking each other with a double dildo. At the end of the tape Liza shaved Reggi's pussy, then Liza got on the phone and called a guy named Carter. Carter was a friend of Liza, and he was the first to fuck Reggi's newly shaved pussy. On the next tape Carter and two of his friends fucked Reggi silly. It was very exciting to watch my wife being serviced by so many different studs.

When Reggi got home, around eight, I was ready for more fucking. When I asked where she had been, she asked me what tape I was up to. I said I had viewed twenty of the tapes so far. She said she was with the guys on tape number twenty-four, and suggested I skip to that one.

I put the tape in. There were Reggi and Liza, in a room with many men. First they did a striptease, then they went over to each guy, opened his pants and sucked his cock. Eventually they lay down on a blanket in the middle of the room and masturbated for the crowd. Occasionally, guys would come over to them and jerk off on them. I recognized some of the men from my office and others from previous tapes. At one point Liza was surrounded by eight cocks. She was sucking some while others were fucking her. The camera moved to Reggi, who was fucking one guy and blowing two others. At the end of the tape Liza had several of the men fuck her in the ass.

When the tape was over I turned to Reggi, who was now naked. She told me she had just been gang-banged and asked if I would like to fuck her also. I was a little upset that my wife was fucking so many different guys, but I was so horny that I just stripped and fucked her. Her pussy was still loaded with come from her adventures earlier in the evening.

When I asked her if she felt that she was even with me, she told me she really enjoyed slutting around, and if I wanted to stay married I shouldn't complain. In addition, she told me that, since I had started this, I was not to be allowed to fool around with other women.

Recently Reggi invited some of her boyfriends over to our house. While I watched from the couch, Reggi got fucked in her asshole for the first time. She was telling the guys how much she liked it and each took his turn in her rear. Glenn and Billy were there that day, and when I saw them at work the next day they really humiliated me. They had brought in pictures of my wife letting them fuck her ass. Of course, they showed anyone who they could get to look.

I protested to Reggi that I couldn't take any more. She said she was bored with all those guys anyway. I was thrilled. We went to the bedroom and I fucked her up the ass. Since then, neither of us has fooled around. But I am looking for a new job, as it is hard to work in an office where almost every guy has fucked

wife. We often watch her videos. Now that I feel safe again in our
relationship I get really turned on, and we end up fucking like
bunnies.—*L.J., Tampa, Florida* O┼▪

DOES SHE OR DOESN'T SHE? JUST ASK EDDIE, VINCE, MILT, ALAN . . .

Angie and I have been married for twenty-two years, and for
about twenty of those years we have been using domination to
spice up our sex life. Angie is a true submissive who enjoys
being tied up, humiliated and exposed. She is forty-two years
old, has blonde hair, blue eyes, long legs, a great ass and nice tits.

After our first two years of marriage, things started to become
routine. Angie read an article about women who like to be slaves
to their men, and said she wanted to try it. We started slowly,
with me demanding that Angie be naked whenever we were
alone in the house. I would order her to cook and serve my dinner, dance for me and kneel at my feet while I watched television,
all in the nude. From there we progressed to bondage. At first
Angie loved being tied spread-eagle to our bed. But soon she
learned to enjoy being tied up in different places throughout the
house and, finally, outside.

Over the years we've met several other couples who played
the same sex games we do. We'd get together a few times a
month. The wives were always the slaves, and the husbands their
masters. All the slaves were required to service any master who
demanded it. Usually the night would start with the wives stripping and putting on their slave collars and wrist and ankle cuffs.
One of the games the wives seemed to like best was when one
wife would serve all four masters at once. This happened about
once a month, usually on a Sunday afternoon while the masters
watched sports on TV.

One hot July afternoon last summer, it was Angie's turn to be
our slave. She spent the afternoon naked, serving four of us
snacks and drinks whenever we asked for them. Best of all, she
gave each of us at least one blowjob (I got two), and fucked two
of the other husbands. To cap off the afternoon's activities, we
tied her facedown to the dining room table and took turns spanking her ass-cheeks. When her behind was all hot and pink, one of
the masters, Eddie, butt-fucked her. After that, we called it a day.

Angie was sitting next to me while I drove home. Her dress was open, and she had nothing on underneath. She said, "I'd love to do all the things I did this afternoon again, but with three guys I've never met before."

I gave it a little thought and came up with an idea. We have a small campsite in the Adirondacks in New York State. Angie and I have spent many wild weekends there with her as my full-time, nude come-slave. The camp is at the end of a dirt road. About a quarter of a mile down the road is another camp, owned by a group of guys who come from the city to hunt and fish.

The next day I called one of the guys, Milt, and found out that he and two of his friends were going up that weekend to do some fishing. It was the perfect arrangement for what Angie wanted. That night when I got home, I told her I was in the mood to head up to the country. "It could be the weekend your wish comes true," I said. She was so excited she could hardly speak.

We arrived about noon on Friday. We spent the afternoon in the woods, with me leading my naked Angie through the underbrush, tying her up in several different places. At one point I trussed her spread-eagle between two trees, then found a branch and whipped her butt, tits and pussy. She climaxed from the moment the branch first made contact with her skin.

That evening, Angie and I went to a restaurant and bar in a small town not far from the camp. At nine o'clock, the guys from the city showed up: Milt, Vince and Alan. I introduced them to Angie, and we sat around and had a few drinks. Then Angie announced, "I'm my husband's come-slave for the weekend, and will do anything he wants." The guys fell silent—they must've thought Angie was drunk and out of control. But I assured them that what she'd said was true.

The five of us left together. In the parking lot, I decided to show the men I meant business. "Take your blouse off, Angie!" I commanded. She did so immediately, revealing a skimpy black bra. "Take off your shorts," was my next order. Angie obeyed, stepping out of her shorts. The men stared at her in her black bikini panties. Seeing my wife there in the parking lot, wearing just her underwear, gave me a raging hard-on. I was sure the other guys had erections too. I decided to go for broke.

"Take off your bra!" I ordered. Angie unhooked the garment and let it fall to the pavement. "Now your panties!" I continued. She slowly peeled the bikinis down her long legs. When they were off, she draped them over the end of her finger and offered them to Milt.

"We'll be down to your camp to pick those up in a little while," she said to him. With that, she strutted off to the van and got in.

We drove to our camp and stayed there long enough for me to get Angie ready for the night's fun. I attached her slave collar, wrist and ankle cuffs, and secured her hands behind her back with a light chain that looped between her legs and up to the front of her collar. Angie said she wanted to walk to the men's camp. She was quite a sight walking through the woods in nothing but her sandals and slave regalia.

When we got to the camp, the guys were ready and waiting. When they saw Angie, they couldn't believe their eyes. I unhooked her hands, and we sat around and downed a few brews. Vince asked, "Will she dance for us?"

I said, "She'll do anything you want." Vince put on some music and Angie began to dance in a very provocative way. After a while, I hooked her hands back together, then raised her arms above her head and attached them to an overhead beam. Angie continued to sway to the music, and I told the guys to start feeling her up. They ran their hands over her body and pumped their fingers in and out of her pussy. Milt even shoved a finger up her ass.

I let Angie down, and Milt ordered her to crawl over to them and start sucking their cocks. With her hands behind her back, she made her way to them and sucked them off, one at a time. It was fantastic to watch her filling her mouth with one hard dick after another. Angie sucked all the guys to creamy climax and drank their sperm, leaving me with a hard-on that wouldn't quit. She then sat in a chair, her legs spread, and played with herself. "My wife loves being a sex slave," I said. "It was her idea to be a slut for men she'd never met, which is why I brought her up here to meet you. Do anything you want to her. Believe me, she loves it."

The rest of the night was filled with one erotic display after another. We all fucked Angie while she was tied spread-eagle to a cot. For the night's final activity, she bent over a chair and blew me to orgasm while Vince fucked her in the ass and Milt and Alan masturbated onto her face. We made arrangements to meet the guys the next day and videotape the proceedings, and then Angie and I went to sleep.

She woke up about noon, and put on the only things I allowed her to wear that day: makeup, sandals, and her slave collar, wrist and ankle cuffs. At one o'clock Milt, Vince and Alan showed up, and off we went into the woods. They took turns leading Angie by her chain. I got some great footage of them on videotape. We spent the afternoon tying up Angie in as many ways as we could think of. Each time she was strapped down or trussed up, we'd all fuck her cunt, mouth and pussy. Whenever one of us blew a load, we shot it all over her skin, but didn't clean it off. Before the afternoon was four hours old, she was coated from head to toe with a layer of sperm you could smell a mile away.

Milt really got into it, making Angie crawl through the woods, ordering her to pose in a number of raunchy positions for my camera and constantly reminding her that she was the come-slut of four horny, demanding men. The afternoon ended with Angie being tied over a fallen tree. This time she sucked three of us off at the same time, moving her mouth from cock to cock as Milt drove his prick up her ass.

That night I asked Angie if she'd had enough, but she said she still hadn't had her fill. She told me she wanted to go off by herself with the three men, but that I could watched them if I kept my distance. Within the hour she was again stripped down to her chains and restraints, and walking away with Milt, Alan and Vince. As they headed off, I could hear her say, "Remember, boys, I like a little humiliation."

I watched from a distance as my wife was led to their camp. I moved closer to their cabin so I could look inside and see what was going on. Milt started things off by having Angie finger herself to a climax while sucking each of them off. He made her rub their come all over her tits, then lick it off.

Next he took a chair and put it in the middle of the floor, then made Angie stand on it and dance while he drank a beer. When his bottle was empty, he ran the lip of it up and down the puffy slit of her pussy.

"Do you want to come, slut?" he asked.

"Yes! Make me come."

"No, we want to see you make yourself come," Milt said. He handed her the bottle and told her to masturbate with it. She pumped it in and out of her pussy, bringing herself to orgasm in a matter of minutes. I could see the pussy juice pouring down her legs. Unable and unwilling to control myself, I masturbated at once, soaking the side of the cabin with a thick blast of spunk.

As the night progressed, Angie was used in many ways, including being tied to a cot and fucked in the pussy, and tied face-down and fucked in the ass. But the thing she seemed to enjoy most was when she was forced to give each of the men a head-to-toe tongue-bath. Her hands were tied behind her back for this, of course, so she had to please the men entirely with her mouth. From what I could tell, she did a good job. She started with Milt, sucking his fingers, then nibbling her way up his arm, across his chest, his belly, and then on to his cock, which she pumped a few times with her teeth.

Then Milt turned over. This time Angie started by nibbling on his toes, sucking them clean, then licking his feet, calves, knees and thighs. Once again she ended up at his cock, which was hard and throbbing. Angie took it down her throat, sucking an orgasm out of Milt that made him tremble all over.

She did the same for Vince and Alan, with one slight variation: Alan made her fuck his asshole with her tongue. She's done that to me on many occasions, so I know the pleasure she brought him was intense.

By this time it was getting late, and Angie said she had to go. The guys said they wanted to do one more thing first. They had her lie on the floor with her hands tied behind her back. Then each man knelt in front of her and commanded her to suck him off. As each one was about to come, he pulled his cock out of her wet mouth and aimed it at a different part of her body. Milt soaked her face with his come, while Vince painted her breasts with his white load, and Alan pulled his prick out of her, pumped it a few times and shot his sperm all over her stomach. They then lifted her to her feet and told her what a great time they'd had.

As Angie was leaving, she saw her panties from the previous night and asked if she could take them with her. Milt said sure, but instead of handing them to her, he used them to wipe the come from her pussy, legs, tits and stomach. Then he rolled them up in a little ball, told her to open wide, and placed the panties in her mouth.

I met her on the road and walked behind her, enjoying the sight of my wife walking naked through the woods, gagged, tied and reeking of sperm. When we got back to our camp, Angie's last duty was to fuck me one more time before we went to sleep. We had fantastic sex. I was very worked up from seeing her with those three men, and was abe to come twice without losing my erection. Angie, although she'd done enough fucking and sucking that weekend to occupy a houseful of whores, couldn't get enough of my dick. She probably had ten orgasms before finally telling me she was too exhausted to go on.

The next morning I got up late. Angie was already awake and freshened up. She put on a wraparound dress and a pair of red thong panties. As usual, she was braless. As we were leaving, we came upon Milt, Vince and Alan loading their car. We stopped and talked for a while. Just as I was about to drive off, Angie said, "Wait a minute." With that she untied the sash on her dress, took it off and tossed it into the van. Standing there in broad daylight, in just a pair of panties, she looked great. She slowly peeled the panties down her legs, handed them to Milt and, looking him in the eye, said, "I'll be back for these someday, if you'll promise to humiliate me again."

"I promise," said Milt. Angie got back in the van, naked, and re-mained naked for the entire ride home!—*F.D., Burlington, Vermont* O⊢▣

PARTING THOSE CUNT LIPS IS SUCH SWEET SORROW, TEACH

I want to tell you about the sumptuous, erotic humiliation I recently received at the hands of a gorgeous high school fellow. I've already described the whole affair to my husband, who found it shocking but stimulating.

I am a former actress who recently took a job as drama teacher in a large, suburban high school. I am extremely attractive and slim, and while I'm not especially well-endowed in the breast department, my legs are long, tawny and elegant. In my younger years I always landed the part of the dewy-eyed ingenue. But it's hard to play seventeen when you're forty-one, which is why I'm now teaching.

Since I began last fall at Southton High, I've frequently worn a certain short red minidress to my classes—"that damned red dress," my sweet husband calls it, because of the distraction it has caused him over the years. It barely covers my hips, and shows off nearly every inch of my thighs. I like it because it makes me feel free and youthful. I'm quite proud of my legs, and I suppose I thought the dress would help me bridge the age difference between me and my students. I hoped it would put me more in touch with them. Little did I realize what kind of touching it would ultimately lead to.

We're doing *Romeo and Juliet* this semester, and Romeo was being played by an incredible young hunk named Chris. He's a curly-haired, strapping young eighteen-year-old outlaw with a face to die for, and a reputation as the most sought-after lover at school. Girls swoon over him, boys envy him, and even we female teachers must do our best to keep our thoughts on a professional level when we deal with him.

But it all came unglued for this teacher last week. I was directing a scene in which Romeo kisses Juliet, trying to help Chris and his co-star, a lovely girl named Margaret, turn the scene into something truly passionate. It was increasingly evident to me that neither Chris nor Margaret needed any help making the scene catch fire.

I suppose I was hovering a little too closely over them—out of jealousy—because suddenly Chris released Margaret and turned to me. "Here, Mrs. Hellman. I'll show you how we kiss," he said. To my astonishment, he swept me into his strong, enveloping arms. Before I knew it, I was a limp dishrag, a melting pillar of female flesh having the blazing hell kissed out of me—all in full view of my students; mind you! I felt Chris's ripe, young mouth force mine open (it didn't take a lot of forcing, actually). His delicious tongue snaked its way into my mouth.

By reflex, I closed my own lips over it, sucking it deeply into my mouth. My clipboard slipped from my hand and my notes scattered across the stage floor. All my dignity was gone. I was scarlet with embarrassment, completely under this boy's spell. The kiss went on and on. Chris was fucking my mouth with his tongue, kissing me into a trance. I tried to whimper a weak protest, but it got caught in my throat, under his sweet tongue, and came out instead as a meow of pleasure.

My students were shocked. I could hear them whispering, "What a slut," and maybe they were right, but I couldn't seem to control myself. I could feel the hem of my red dress rising above my black bikini panties, coaxed ever upward by Chris's strong, young hand. The teacher's white ass-cheeks were in full view to all who cared to look. "He's gonna fuck her right here!" came the hum from the other students, and I wasn't so sure they were wrong.

Chris brought a hand to my thigh, curling his fingers into the wet, soft inside of my cunt. To keep myself upright, I clamped my thighs around his hard leg. This increased the friction of his fingers against my overheating clitoris. I wondered if I was going to thoroughly disgrace myself by climaxing against him. I needed him to fuck me—I wanted his hard, teenage dick inside me. I didn't care whether it would cost me my job or even my self-respect. Those things seemed trivial compared to the passion I was feeling at that moment.

Just when I thought I couldn't take it any longer without coming, Chris released me as suddenly as he'd taken me. My legs were liked cooked spaghetti, and I dropped clumsily to the floor. I struggled to my hands and knees as the entire cast erupted into whistles, catcalls and mocking applause. Looking up, I could not bring myself to make eye contact with my conquering young stud.

Still on my knees, I dismissed the cast. When the last student had filed out, ogling me over his shoulder, I finally looked up at my teenage god. "If you have any compassion," I whispered as I looked into his eyes, "you will finish what you started. Come now, you animal, and fuck your teacher."

Bless his young heart, he did. He had the tact to take me to the darkened area behind the rear curtain. There he propped me against a costume trunk, pulled my black panties halfway down my legs and filled my soaked, willing vagina from behind with the longest, hardest, silky-smooth cock I'd ever taken in twenty-five years of lovemaking. When this boy erupted in me, I cried out and wept. I was full of shame, but still powerfully aroused. I turned around and covered his mouth with kisses. Then I dropped to my knees again and cradled his fabulous cock in my hands, nuzzling and kissing it gently before drawing it into my mouth to suck the nectar of our combined juices.

The experience was as humiliating as it was magnificent, and I hope it's only the beginning. As attractive as I am, I know I can't compete for Chris's attention forever against the likes of the high-school cuties who are always hanging around him. But I have persuaded my dear, long-suffering husband into serving as a one-man audience for a special performance starring Chris and myself, this coming Saturday night, in the bedroom of our home.—*Name and address withheld*   O┼▪

SIMON SAYS . . . WELL, HE DOESN'T SAY MUCH— THEY WON'T LET HIM!

I am a twenty-year-old woman, and share an apartment with my best friend Rita who, like myself, is a college senior. I work out with weights at a gym every couple of days, so I am fairly well-muscled. I've had intercourse with men, but for the past couple of years most of my sex has been with Rita. Until last semester, I hadn't had a dick in me for nearly two years, and I don't think

Rita had either. Well, that changed when Simon moved into the apartment next to ours.

Simon was a small, lightweight freshman who'd probably never fucked anything in his life but his hand. Rita and I thought he was pretty cute, though, so we became friendly with him. Late one Saturday night Rita and I were sitting around watching television and drinking beer, when we heard Simon walking up the stairs. We were both pretty loaded, and all we had on were panties and T-shirts that barely covered our butts. I jumped up, opened the door and said to Simon, "Come in and have a beer with us. No excuses, kiddo. We're having a party!"

He said he'd just come from the library and had to study, but there was no way I was going to let this adorable little guy spend Saturday night with his books. I grabbed his arm and pulled him into the apartment. He was wearing a T-shirt, gym shorts, socks and tennis shoes, and was all embarrassed about the way we were dressed, but Rita got him a beer to help him relax. We had him sit between us on the couch. Simon was shy and red-faced, and tried to avoid looking directly at our scanty attire. He attempted to keep his eyes glued to the TV, but when I looked down at his crotch, I could see he had a huge erection. It was sticking straight up in his shorts, which started my pussy leaking and made my nipples poke through my shirt.

Rita had also noticed his erection, and I could see we had the same idea. "Rita," I said, "come into the kitchen with me. Let's make our friend something to eat."

In the kitchen, Rita and I took a roll of duct tape from the drawer. We went back to the living room, and I lay down on the floor and told Simon to rub my back. I couldn't believe it, but he did so without putting up a fuss. Then I told him it was his turn, and made him take off his shirt and lay facedown on the floor. I think he was happy to do that, because it enabled him to hide his hard-on.

"Close your eyes," I said to him, and he did. That's when Rita and I pinned his arms behind his back and taped his wrists together. He was helpless, and although he kept struggling and trying to get up, Rita straddled his head, sat on his face and pinned down his shoulders with her knees. She rubbed her pussy over his face while I took off his shoes, socks and gym shorts, leaving him in just his underwear. I pulled off his briefs, exposing his cock and balls. His hard little peter continued to bounce around as he struggled.

He had a six-inch hard-on, nice tight balls and a cute little patch of pubic hair. Rita started to play with his nipples, and I ran my fingers lightly over his genitals. I don't think I'd ever seen a cock that hard before!

Simon was telling me to stop, but I asked him, "Why should I? Aren't you having fun?" I kept fondling him just to the point of orgasm, but would not allow him to come. Poor Simon probably never had had a woman touch him before, because all of a sudden his cock spasmed and he started to shoot his spunk. He erupted so hard, it actually hit Rita in the face. Pretty soon there was come everywhere—on his hairless chest, his pubes, my shirt. I know a drop or two even landed on my lips.

Rita got up and said to Simon, "You got come all over me. Now I have to take these off. She pulled off her T-shirt, exposing her tits to him. She also slipped out of her panties, giving him his first view of her shaved pussy. While I undressed, Rita got up to get a wash cloth and a ball of string. When she returned, she washed Simon off, then tied the string tightly around the base of his cock. Then she pulled him up to a kneeling position and made him crawl on his knees to a chair.

She sat down in the chair and told him to lick her pussy. It's not like he had a choice, but he didn't seem to mind either. He tongued her salty box until she came, which didn't take long, as Rita climaxes easily. I was so hot that I was playing with myself, and as soon as Rita was done with Simon, I took her place. His tongue felt good in my pussy. Although he didn't really know what he was doing, he managed to hit all the right spots, and pretty soon I came too. He was pretty shocked when my cunt exploded and my juice leaked all over his face!

I pulled Simon up by the string around his cock and then untied it. His cock sprang free and stiffened completely in about three seconds. "Time for your reward for being such a good boy," I said. I grabbed his butt, slipped my mouth over his hard peter and started to suck him.

I was getting too much of his pubic hair in my mouth, though, so I got another idea. I took him to the bathroom and made him lie on the floor. "What's going on?" he asked, but I told him to keep quiet and enjoy himself while I clipped his pubes with a scissors. I'd never seen a guy with a shaved crotch before. Simon was going to be my first. After clipping all the hair off, I got shaving cream and spread it over all his pubic area, including his asshole, and shaved him completely. Soon his totally bald boner was throbbing right in my face.

I grabbed him by the dick, led him back to the living room, and made him stand in front of me with his legs spread as far apart as possible. Then I sucked his beautiful cock. I licked and nibbled the head and shaft while Rita worked on his balls. His smooth skin felt warm and slippery in my mouth, and I feasted hungrily on his little pole. I dug into his ass-cheeks with my long nails, and that's when his cock really began to throb. He plunged his cockhead down my throat, and I got ready for his load. When he blasted off, I swallowed most of his come, and made him lick the rest off my lips.

But we had a problem: Simon's cock was soft again, and Rita and I were really turned on. I could tell she wanted to fuck him as badly as I did. We made him go to the bedroom and lay down on his back. Then we spread his feet apart and tied them to the bedposts. Rita held Simon's cock and balls, and I taped his hands to the bedposts.

He didn't even put up a fight this time. He was such a cute sight, this young, hairless boy spread-eagle on his back, with his beautiful, soft cock aching to be played with. Rita started to suck on it, and then moved up and rubbed her pussy against it.

It looked like it was going to be tougher than we thought to get him hard again. Rita sat on Simon's face and told him to eat her out. Meanwhile, I got out a tube of KY jelly, lubed my finger up and slipped it into his ass. He bucked a little, and I moved the finger back and forth inside him. Sure enough, his cock began to stiffen, but it still was only semihard. I removed my finger, took out my vibrator, coated it with jelly and inserted it in his asshole. He tried to resist, but I told him to keep quiet. I slowly worked the vibrator in and out of his ass until the hole had loosened up enough to accommodate the whole thing. As my fuck-toy buzzed away in his ass, his peter responded, growing to full hardness.

He had such a nice dick that I hated to cover it with a rubber, but cover it I did. Rita mounted him first because she was really hot. She slid down his pole, rode him for about two minutes and came. It's such a turn-on watching a woman come so quickly! When she was done, I pushed her out of the way, put a fresh rubber on Simon's shank and impaled myself on his hot cock. I bounced up and down on him, sticking a finger in my pussy and massaging his dick while we fucked.

Simon began to thrust his hips up, really fucking me hard. Rita took advantage of his movements and began to fuck his ass with the vibrator. I could feel his cock swelling in my pussy, getting bigger and harder by the second. When he came, it pushed me over the edge too. Rita crammed four fingers into her pussy and worked them feverishly, uniting us in a wild, three-way orgasm.

Our shy little Simon was shy no more. He was insatiable that night, and moved in with us the next month. We made him our love slave. He had to fuck us, suck us and do anything else Rita and I told him to do. Occasionally we would bring a woman friend over for dinner, and if he got an erection in her presence, we made him jack off for her.

A few weeks ago Simon went to Europe on vacation, but he'll be back in a month or so. Rita and I can't wait. We've thought of a few more things to do with our slave. Maybe we'll order him to write to you and tell you all about them.—*Name and address withheld* O⊢⬛

SOUNDS LIKE THANKSGIVING WITH ALL THAT DARK MEAT AROUND

For a long time I tried to get my sexy wife Gina to fuck a black man. We used to swing and pick up young male hitchhikers for her to fuck and suck while I watched, so I knew she wasn't a prude. But for some reason she always turned me down on this particular request.

I work nights, and don't get home until about one o'clock in the morning. The other night when I came home, I found my wife doing her thing with three young, big, black studs. They were all naked and fucking like mad. I was amazed to see this, and my cock was hard in a flash. One of the guys came over to me and told me to take off my clothes. I said, "No, I just want to watch."

The man grabbed my arm and yelled, "You'll watch, all right. Now strip!"

I got undressed, and he tied me to a chair to watch the show. All the guys were very large in the cock department—one of them was nearly a foot long! He was fucking my wife doggie-style, pounding the hell out of her hot cunt for all he was worth.

"How do you like seeing your bitch fuck a black man?" he asked. "I love it."

"Yeah," he replied, "she said you would. Well, keep looking. She'll be getting plenty of it."

My wife was having a super time. She had one cock in her cunt and one in her mouth. The third guy was jacking off in her face.

The guys told me that after they were done fucking Gina, I'd have to suck them clean. Then they were going to fuck me in the ass. I didn't know what to do, but the look on his face assured me that they weren't going to let me out of that room without getting a piece of me too.

When one of them came in Gina's pussy, she climaxed, screaming like mad. I knew she was loving it. He pulled his cock out of her. It was dripping with his come and her cunt juice. He stuck the cock in my face and said, "Suck my dick." I couldn't refuse. I opened up wide and he stuffed it in. It felt like a log in my mouth, but I found I loved the taste.

By this time one of the other guys had shot his load down my wife's throat. He too wanted a piece of my white ass. My wife urged him on. "Go on and fuck my husband," she squealed. "Get on all fours for him and take it up the ass like a man, Jim." I got on my hands and knees, my mouth still wrapped around the twelve-inch meat-stick I'd been sucking.

"Use some Vaseline and go easy on me," I said.

"Yeah, right," the man said with a laugh. "Why don't you just shut up and let your ass do the talking." He stuck his big thumb up my rump and primed the tight hole a few times. I knew I was in for a heavy fuck. My wife was laughing and looking on, sucking a pair of big black balls while I got ready to be split open.

The man grabbed my ass cheeks, spread them wide and eased his big cock up my ass. It hurt at first, and my eyes began to tear. But as it went in deeper, I relaxed my muscles. He started to fuck me deep with long strokes. It felt great. To my amazement, I went wild. I began pushing back hard, to get the giant penis all the way up my ass. He was really getting into it too, fucking my ass like it was a cunt.

"I love fucking!" he bellowed. "Ass, pussy, man, woman, black or white—I don't care!" Then he turned to Gina and said, "I'm going to fill your pussy-ass husband with a load he'll never forget!" When he came, it felt so good that I shot my load too.

I loved being fucked so much that I begged the other two me to cram their dicks in my ass. They were only too happy to oblige. My wife was getting off watching them fuck me. When they pulled out of my ass, they had me bathe them clean with a wash cloth, then suck them back to hardness so they could fuck my wife some more.

It went on like that until four in the morning. When the three men left, I asked my wife what made her finally decide to fulfill my fantasy and do it with a black man in front of me. She told me she worked with the three men, and had been fucking them for years without my even knowing it! I'm glad she finally let me in on her secret. I would've never known the pleasures of being humiliated and fucked up the ass by such a trio of studs.—*J.V., Boston, Massachusetts*

<u>Three-For-All</u>

THAT'S ODD—MY HUSBAND NEVER SUCKS COCK AT HOME

Last weekend my wife Gloria and I traveled east for a convention. Artie, a friend of ours, had moved to the city we were visiting, and insisted we stay with him for the weekend. As we'd missed him terribly, he didn't have to insist too strenuously. We all eagerly looked forward to a fun weekend.

Artie met us at the airport. He took us out to a great Mexican restaurant, where we all got reacquainted. We laughed and talked for hours, but soon Gloria and I were tired and we had to call it a night.

After dinner we went back to Artie's apartment. Even though Gloria and I protested, he insisted we take his bedroom while he slept on the couch in the living room. We said our good nights and went to bed.

While lying in bed, Gloria and I discussed Artie. We'd never seen him with or heard him talk about any women. We've always wondered why. Then Gloria shocked me by saying she would like to see me go down on him. I've always considered myself straight, but I told Gloria I'd try anything once. I had thought about giving another guy head before, but it never crossed my mind to actually do it. And certainly not with one of my closest friends!

I reached under the covers and found that all this talk had gotten Gloria extremely wet. I told her that I didn't know if she'd ever see me go down on Artie, but that she was going feel me going down on her! We ended up having incredible sex until we were both too exhausted to keep going. We drifted off to a deep, contented sleep, wrapped in each other's arms.

I woke up a few hours later, and after pondering the idea for a while, I decided to give Gloria the treat she wanted. I quietly got out of bed and walked into the living room. I startled Artie out of a deep sleep and asked him if he'd like to help me give my wife a big surprise. He was hesitant, but I told him that if anyone felt uncomfortable, we could stop. He finally agreed to help me.

Artie turned on the light, and was a little shocked when he saw I was naked. Once he got a look at my clean-shaven crotch, he smiled. It was at that moment I decided that we were going to have some fun.

Artie undressed, revealing an incredible body. I couldn't believe it—I was getting turned on by seeing another man naked. That had never happened to me before.

We walked into the bedroom, where Gloria was still sleeping. I put the light on in the bathroom so we could all see what was going on. Artie climbed into bed on one side of Gloria, and I on the other. I gave her a kiss. She was a bit groggy, but when she felt Artie's hands on her, as well as mine, she quickly came to life!

We took turns kissing her and fondling her breasts. Then Gloria and Artie locked in an embrace and I slid down between her legs. Her pussy moistened almost immediately and she let out a soft moan.

I feasted on Gloria for a while as Artie's and Gloria's tongues became acquainted. Then I decided to go for broke. I reached over and grabbed Artie's cock. I felt them stop embracing to watch. I was trembling as I took the head of Artie's cock between my lips. I licked up and down his shaft, then took him as far into my mouth and down my throat as I could. The feeling of a cock in my mouth excited me so much—more than I ever could have imagined! He tasted great.

I started really going to town on him, then all of a sudden he told me he was going to come. I was ready, and couldn't remember ever wanting anything more. I caught all of his come in my mouth and swallowed it down. I loved it! Artie and I locked in a tight embrace and kissed. It felt very different to be kissing a man, but it also felt right.

The next thing I knew, I was inside Gloria. When I was ready to come, I pulled out, and Artie took me into his mouth and swallowed my come. By then he was hard again, so he mounted Gloria. The three of us made love to one another all weekend, not worrying about who was doing what to whom. It was the wildest weekend I've ever had.

I don't know if I'll ever have sex with another man again, but I am glad that I did with Artie. It was a totally unforgettable experience. Now Gloria wants to bring a friend of hers, June, into our bedroom so she can have a same-sex experience!—*R.Y., Dallas, Texas* O⊢▥

THE FOOTBALL GAME WAS OKAY, BUT THE HALFTIME SHOW WAS GREAT

A few weeks ago I went to a local sports bar to watch a football game. At about three o'clock, a man and his wife walked in. He looked to be in his mid-fifties, and she looked to be around forty. The wife had an incredible body.

I caught the woman looking at me a few times. She would smile, then start watching the game again. A few times she said something to her husband, then he looked over. I'm five foot eleven and one hundred ninety pounds, with black hair and blue eyes. I've been told I'm gorgeous, and I'm inclined to agree.

The game was almost over, so I called the bartender over to settle up. He put a fresh drink in front of me and pointed to the couple. I lifted my glass in thanks. The man walked over, introducing himself as George and his wife as Denise. He said, "My wife finds you quite attractive. Would you like to have a nightcap with us back at our hotel?"

I said, "Sure, what the hell?"

On the way up to their room, Denise reached over and rubbed my crotch. When we got there, she went into the bathroom. When she came out, she was stark naked. Her 34C tits were beautiful. She said, "Come on, guys, what are you waiting for? I'm all ripe and ready for the taking. Let's get started."

George was almost completely naked before I'd even gotten started. He dove between his wife's legs and started eating her pussy. My cock was fully hard when I took off my shorts. Denise said, "Oh yeah, baby. Come over here and let me have some of that. Your cock is incredible. I need it."

I knelt by her head, and she started licking my cock. I put my hands on her tits and started rubbing her nipples. She said, "That's it. Play with my nipples. I love the way you do that."

Denise started sucking my cock, taking as much as she could. She started grinding her cunt against her husband's mouth and moaning. She clamped her lips around my cock as her orgasm took over. Denise then got on her hands and knees, turned to me and said, "Okay honey, fuck my pussy hard." I put my cockhead at her entrance and slid my eight inches in. She yelped then, low, throaty sounds that came from deep in her chest. Suddenly she screamed, "Fuck me deep! Fuck me harder! Harder! I'm coming!"

I did as she asked. All of a sudden I felt a tongue on my balls. That did it—I started to shoot my load into her cunt. When her cunt finally stopped milking my cock, it slipped out. George took my cock into his mouth and licked it clean. He then started licking and sucking his wife. I sat back and watched until George finally shot his load down Denise's throat. She went into the bathroom to clean up.

When she came back out, she stretched out next to me and started playing with my cock. It didn't take long for it to get rock-hard again. I played with Denise's tits, and she started sucking me off again.

George started finger-fucking her, and she moaned around my cock. After a few minutes of this, I told her I was about to blow, so she stopped and straddled my hips.

She spread her cunt lips, and George grabbed my cock and put the head in her hole. She eased her cunt down until I was in up to my balls. Denise's cunt felt like a tight velvet glove, and every time I licked her nipples, her cunt muscles would contract around my cock and she would moan real loud. I couldn't believe how good it felt.

Denise humped my cock quickly. Her juices ran down my balls as she had one orgasm after another.

When she climbed off me, George said, "Let me clean you up."

George was a major come freak. My crotch was never licked so thoroughly. I rested for a few minutes, then looked at my watch. It was close to three o'clock in the morning, and I had to be at work at eight, so I got dressed and said good-bye.—*C.P., Terre Haute, Indiana* O⊢▬

GENEROUS ROOMIE SHARES EVERYTHING WITH HER LONELY FRIEND

When my wife Penny and I were still dating, she shared an apartment with a girl named Betty. I spent just about every weekend staying at the girls' place. I practically lived there.

Because the apartment only had one bedroom, I usually ended up sleeping on the couch, because I didn't really know Betty that well, and things were rather awkward at first. It wasn't long, though, before Betty felt comfortable enough to start walking around in her bathrobe in front of me, or just a T-shirt and panties when she was getting ready for bed. I found it quite arousing to catch glimpses of her cleavage when she reached for her coffee in the morning, or to see the dark shadows of her nipples through her T-shirt before she went to bed.

Betty had tits the size of grapefruits, and she couldn't walk across a room without them jiggling around. I couldn't help but look, no matter how many times Penny elbowed me in the ribs. Most of the time Betty's robe hung half open, and I frequently found myself shifting position so I could get a good look at them when we were sitting around watching television. I'd always keep a pillow handy to cover my aching cock at times like that.

Because of the lack of privacy, whenever Penny and I fucked, we were restricted to a late-night rendezvous on the living-room floor. We tried to be discreet about it—at least at the start—but once we got into it, it was difficult to be quiet. Our breathing became uncontrollably heavy and ragged, we grunted and moaned, and Penny couldn't help but whimper as I slammed my cock in and out of her cunt. Penny loved to take it from behind as she leaned against the coffee table, gripping the sides tightly in her hands, her tits pressed flat against the wood, her nipples so hard you'd think they might scratch it. Half the excitement was trying to keep quiet so Betty wouldn't hear us, but I admit that sometimes I rammed it into Penny harder than usual, trying to make her cry out loud enough that Betty *would* hear and come catch us in the act. Unfortunately, Betty never did come out.

Later on in our relationship, Penny didn't think twice about having us sleep together in her bed. Just sleep, though. Sometimes I'd wake up fresh from some hot dream and press my stiff dick between Penny's legs, but she almost always put me off—or if she did want it, she'd lead me out into the living room and fuck me there.

Soon, though, it became a game to try and fuck without waking Betty, who was sleeping only five feet away. Penny would reach back and give my cock a squeeze to let me know she was interested, then she'd raise her nightgown and pull me toward her wet and waiting fuck-hole. I'd press it in slowly, careful not to make any noise, burying it deeper and deeper with as little movement as possible. With my left hand I'd play with her nipples while chewing on her earlobe. Once I'd gotten all seven inches of my meat deep inside her, I'd just keep pressing into her, gyrating my hips ever so slightly while she worked me with her powerful cunt muscles. In no time my throbbing cock would be emptying its load, and we'd lie there panting, spent and satisfied, certain that Betty had no idea. We were dead wrong.

One night when Penny had come over to my apartment for dinner, she told me that Betty had confessed to hearing our lovemaking several times. In fact, she had stayed awake on several occasions just waiting for us to go at it. She told Penny it made her hot to hear us fucking so close to her there in the darkness, and that she never resisted touching herself while she listened. Jamming her fingers into her pussy, she'd lay there quietly masturbating, trying to come at the same time we did. It was all she could do, she told Penny, to keep from climbing into bed with us and joining in.

Hearing this, my cock twitched, needing some attention. Penny obliged, knowing how much the story had turned me on, and took me into her mouth, working her lips over me and stroking my balls until I'd blown my load down her throat, all the while pretending the lips that were wrapped around my cock were Betty's.

"Do you really want to fuck her?" Penny asked afterward.

"What do you mean?" I replied hesitantly. Penny then told me her plan, guaranteeing that we'd all be satisfied when the night was finished. She said she'd set everything up for the following Saturday. I could hardly wait.

When that night came, the three of us rented a movie, and Penny made drinks for everyone, making sure they were a little stronger than normal to loosen everyone up. We were all fine-tuned before we hit the sack. As soon as the lights went out, Penny spread her legs invitingly, and once between them I began pumping my hard cock in and out of her. She moaned and bit her lip, and then began to whimper as she always does when she's aroused.

"Do you like it?" I asked. "Do you like my hard cock, Penny?"

"I love it," she breathed. "Fuck me."

That was the prearranged signal. We both fell silent and held our breath. We couldn't miss the rasp of Betty's labored breathing and the moist sounds of her fingers working away between her legs. We heard a sudden, frightened intake of breath. I got out of Penny's bed, went over to Betty's, and drew back the sheet. She froze. She was lying on her back, her nightgown hiked up around her waist. Caught in the act, she could only giggle nervously and blush.

"Looks like someone else needs a cock," Penny said. "Go ahead, give her what she wants."

Betty bit her lip and stared at my rock-hard cock, still sticky with Penny's juices, then reached out to touch it. Her hand shook in anticipation as she pulled me toward her waiting pussy. As she rubbed the head against her clit, rocking her hips up and down, I removed her nightgown and freed her giant boobs. The nipples were as big as silver dollars. I rolled them between my thumb and forefinger before working them over with my tongue. At that point she couldn't take it any more. Grabbing me by the hips, she pulled me into her and, because she was so lubricated, there was hardly any resistance.

"Oh yeah, oh yeah, oh yeah!" she said. "I've dreamed of this so many times. Penny, you're so lucky!"

Betty's tight, wet cunt felt as if it were on fire. I kept pulling all the way out, then jamming in again so my balls slapped against her ass, keeping time with our frantic movements.

It was Penny's turn to watch and listen. She lay on her side, playing with herself and teasing her nipples. "Shoot your come in her mouth," she moaned. "Come on, do it!"

Betty threw back her head and licked her lips, moaning, "Oh, yeah. Come in my mouth, yeah!"

Hearing them telling me what to do sent me over the edge. I pistoned in and out of Betty's juicy cunt a few more times, then pulled out and shoved my cock into her mouth.

When I was empty, I presented my still-hard cock to Penny for her to lick clean. She did so with lovingly wet kisses and strokes of her tongue. I was in heaven.

Penny and I got married the summer after that. Betty frequently visited and I serviced her on a regular basis—even when she had a boyfriend. I guess you just can't get enough of a good thing.—*E.N., Sault Ste. Marie, Michigan* ○┼▣

AILING MAN LEARNS WHY WOMEN ALWAYS TRAVEL IN PAIRS

This event took place six years ago, but is burned in my memory as though it happened yesterday. I was single at the time, playing the field, and seeing four or five girls from work. An old friend with whom I'd shared an apartment in college was coming to visit me. Her name is Meryl. And man, was she hot. When it came to fucking, she was the best. She definitely made my experience at college more enjoyable.

While Meryl was visiting, one of the girls I was seeing, Lisa, showed up at my apartment. To say I felt a bit uneasy would be putting it mildly. I told Lisa I wasn't feeling well, and really didn't feel much like going out. To my surprise, Meryl spoke up and said, "No problem. Lisa and I will go out. Don't bother waiting up. We'll be gone for a while."

With that, they left. The whole time they were gone, I worried that they were telling each other everything. It was getting late, so I headed off to bed and figured I'd deal with the situation in the morning.

Some time later I was awakened from a dead sleep by Meryl. She was shaking me and laughing. Both she and Lisa were taking their clothes off and giggling. I asked what they were doing, and Meryl replied, "We're going to give you what every man fantasizes about! Get ready for the night of your life!"

Lisa straddled my cock and slowly lowered herself down onto it. She's a bodybuilder, and she worked her finely toned body up and down my pole like a piston engine. Meanwhile, Meryl positioned herself over my face and mashed her beautiful pussy against my lips. I cupped her beautiful ass in my hands as I tongued her delicious hole. Her clit was standing at attention, and I lashed at it until she filled my mouth with juice. She tasted absolutely heavenly—even better than I'd remembered.

As soon as Meryl came, she immediately asked Lisa to switch places with her. Lisa then moved up and parked her wet slit where Meryl's had been. I did the same to Lisa as I had to Meryl. Lisa bucked and rocked and shrieked and moaned.

Meryl was busy sucking my cock when Lisa released her nectar into my mouth. She then joined Meryl, and the two of them sucking me was a sight to behold. One would take my balls into her mouth while the other sucked my cock down her throat. Then they'd switch. Pretty soon they were both licking my cock up and down, one on each side. I knew I couldn't last much longer at this pace. I was glad when Meryl climbed up and lowered her steamy cunt onto my throbbing member. Lisa resumed her position astride my soaking-wet face.

Meryl began bucking like a bronco—a familiar sign that she

was ready to come. I started thrusting my hips upward to fuck her harder as her hips gyrated. When she let out her loudest moan and I felt her juices running down my hips, I lost it. My hands grabbed Lisa's thighs as I jammed my tongue deep into her pussy. My balls spasmed as they shot a huge load into Meryl's heavenly sanctuary. We all collapsed. I wanted a repeat performance the next morning, but Lisa was gone before I got up.

Since then I've moved closer to where Meryl lives, and I'd sure like to repay the favor with a friend of mine.—*S.W., Winston-Salem, North Carolina* O⊢▪

HOT, STEAMY WATER IS THE PERFECT BACKDROP FOR HOT SEX

One day my friend Richard invited me over for a dip in his hot tub. Our wives were out of town, and the company was welcome. After several drinks our conversation turned to sex, and Richard commented that his wife Kara had always fantasized about threesomes, and was particularly attracted to me. Kara is a cute brunette with perky breasts and a fine ass. She always gave me lingering hugs or brushed her hands on my ass, and now I knew why! The thought of making it with Richard and his lovely wife Kara made my cock swell to mammoth proportions.

The conversation then turned to my wife Maureen's attributes. Richard thought that she was one of the most attractive women he had ever known. The thought of Richard slipping his cock between her legs and sucking her nipples had my imagination running wild. I told him that I didn't know how she'd react, but that I would definitely encourage it.

Over the next couple of months, I would suggest to Maureen, while we were having sex, that she fantasize about what it would be like to have four hands caressing her. Or how wonderful it might feel to have both of her fabulous tits sucked at once while she held a cock in each hand! Maureen never said anything, but as the weeks went by, our sex life got better and better. We were fucking with a passion we hadn't shared since the early years of our marriage.

We had made plans to spend an evening hot tubbing with Richard and Kara, but Richard called that afternoon to tell us that Kara had been called in to work a night shift. Maureen really loves hot tubs, so we decided to go over and hang out with Richard anyway.

Soon the three of us were sipping our drinks and chatting away amid the bubbles of the hot tub. Maureen was sitting between me and Richard, her pink-tipped breasts bouncing. Richard became increasingly preoccupied with Maureen's gorgeous tits, and our conversation began to lag. It was time for me to get things started.

Maureen was leaning back with her eyes closed when I reached over and stroked her nipples. She gazed at me through half-open eyes as her breasts heaved. Her nimble fingers toyed with my cock. One of Richard's hands was parting her thighs, and he gently sucked one of her breasts as I nibbled on the other. My cock felt as if it were going to burst. With her other hand, Maureen brought Richard's cock to full mast. It was quite impressive.

As Richard and I caressed, kissed and stroked her, her breathing (and ours) became labored. Her brown eyes glazed over. "Enjoying yourself?" I murmured as I kissed her. Her reply was a long moan. She was grinding her hips against our fingers as we took turns working her cunt and clit.

Maureen turned and kissed Richard, thrusting her tongue deep into his mouth as she stood up. She positioned him on the edge of the tub and slid his cockhead between her lips. I moved behind her, sliding one hand over her hot sex and cupping a breast in the other. Her nipples became as hard and firm as the cocks she had been stroking. She took all of Richard's seven inches down her throat. He held the back of her head as she literally devoured his cock. I watched her mouth work its way up and down his shaft, her tongue teasing the underside of his manhood. Watching my wife give head was an incredible turn-on. I slid my cock into her hot, steaming cunt from behind. Richard was getting close to coming, and was now furiously pumping his cock into Maureen's mouth. She stroked his balls and moaned in pleasure. My cock felt as if it were melting against her velvet walls of love.

The heat from our fucking had my come boiling deep within my balls. I knew I couldn't last much longer—I was ready to explode. Richard started coming and let out a guttural groan as Maureen hungrily gulped down his jism.

Then, in a voice I hardly recognized as hers, she cried, "Fuck me hard! Deeper! Yes, yes, yes, yes!" as I drove into her. Then I started to explode in the most incredible orgasm I'd had in years.

We all rested a few seconds, too spent to move. Our bodies were still trembling from the aftershocks of our respective orgasms. Then Maureen turned around and sat back, drawing my hips to her face as she did so. She took my still-stiff cock into other mouth, nursing the last of my come onto her tongue. She took Richard's cock in her hand, then took turns engulfing us. Smiling, she said in a hoarse whisper, "I hope Kara enjoys you two tomorrow night. I have to work . . ."—*M.O., Houston, Texas*

HOWDY, NEIGHBOR! CAN I BORROW YOUR WIFE FOR A FEW HOURS?

I am twenty-nine years old and my wife Carly is twenty-seven. We bought two townhouses five months ago. The townhouse we live in shares a wall with the other. Not all the rooms have the common wall, but the master bedrooms do. Our tenants are Brad and his wife Ellen. Ellen is slim, with small breasts and long, dark hair. She is also very shy. We have only heard them in bed twice since we moved into the place.

Carly and I work very hard, and we don't always have as much time to spend together as we would like. My wife is very sexy, and we do try to fuck at least once a day. Normally we do it in the morning before we go to work, because at night we are too tired. During the weekends we fuck often. In fact, on some weekends we only get out of bed to eat or use the bathroom. We have fucked in every room in the house, in our backyard, in our car and other places too numerous to mention. Carly frequently walks around in the nude, and loves to display her body. She is five foot five and weighs one hundred ten pounds. Her blonde hair is very soft, and I love to wrap my cock in it. Her 36C tits are firm enough that they do not need any support, so although she wears a bra to work, at home or when we go out, she goes braless. This is great because I always have access to her tits. Her pink nipples are so sensitive that at my slightest touch they become as erect as little cocks.

Last Saturday we went to a party at my boss's summer home, about forty minutes from our house. About halfway through the evening, Carly whispered to me that she wanted to fuck. We finally left the party and, during the ride home, Carly lifted her dress so her pussy was exposed. Every so often she would insert a finger, then run it under my nose and on my lips. I could smell and taste her pussy. I couldn't wait to get home and fuck. Neither could she. She started playing with my cock, and when I was hard as a rock, she told me to pull off the road. She climbed onto my lap and sank down onto my raging hard-on. Her pussy was incredibly wet, and I slid in without any trouble. Carly lowered the top of her dress so I could suck her tits. It didn't take us long to come.

We drove home with Carly playing with my cock and me playing with her tits and pussy. We were still half-dressed when we entered the house, so we took off the rest of our clothes and fucked until we were exhausted.

The next afternoon Carly went outside to sunbathe while I did some paperwork. About two hours later she came in and told me that Ellen had come out to join her and had started crying. When Carly asked her what was wrong, Ellen said that Brad only makes love to her about once a month. Ellen heard us fucking many times, and wondered why Brad did not want her as often.

The next weekend Brad went on a fishing trip, and when I got home from work I found Carly and Ellen drinking cocktails and discussing sex. Carly had invited Ellen to have dinner with us so we could cheer her up and talk about her problem.

After dinner we ended up in our bedroom, with Carly stroking my cock and kissing Ellen at the same time. I unbuttoned Ellen's blouse to reveal a sheer white bra. I wanted more, so I unhooked the bra, removed it and gazed at the smallest tits I have ever seen, although her dark-brown nipples were quite large in comparison. I put one hand on her tits and the other down her slacks to feel her hairy cunt.

The three of us finished undressing, and I compared the two nude women in front of me. One had very small tits and a hairy cunt. The other had beautifully molded tits and a shaved cunt. Ellen admired Carly's bald pussy, so I ran to the bedroom for a razor and shaving cream. I had a great time removing all the hair from Ellen's snatch. In no time at all she was bald as a baby. Her pussy looked beautiful.

After being shaved, Ellen looked great and was ready to be royally fucked. She and Carly lay down on the bed and spread their legs. I looked at two cunts with thick red lips, just waiting

for my mouth and cock. Ellen's cunt was burning with desire, so
I spread her lips and licked her slit. Carly played with my ass and
balls while my hands wandered over Ellen's tits, belly and pussy.
I flicked my tongue on her clit, which was stiff and red. She liked
it so much, she pressed her cunt against my face and flooded me
with her juices. Her cunt was now well moistened, so I stretched
myself over her body. Carly directed my cock to Ellen's cunt and
rubbed the head up and down.

She gradually inserted the head until I had about two inches in.
Ellen was afraid that it would hurt, but Carly stroked her and told
her it would be wonderful. I increased my efforts, thrusting
harder into Ellen's cunt. I got all the way in, then stopped.

Ellen started moving her hips, and I could feel her tight sheath
pulsating around my hard cock. I felt my semen boiling up from
my balls, through my cock and into her pussy. I squirted until her
cunt overflowed and the sperm oozed out around my prick and
dripped onto the sheets. What a mess!

I finally withdrew. Carly sucked my cock clean while I fingered Ellen's pussy. Carly moved her head faster and faster, her
mouth working its magic on my cock. When I was hard again,
Carly got on her hands and knees, and I fucked her doggie-style.
I pounded into her hard and fast while her body shook in orgasm.
I slammed into Carly's pussy as I released another load of burn-
ing-hot semen into her tight channel.

After a while I pulled my shrinking dick from her well-fucked
pussy and lay back on the bed between my two naked females.
Ellen crawled between Carly's legs and used her mouth to clean
her up. Finally Ellen straddled me, her newly shaved pussy over
my mouth, and said, "Lick me again. I really love it."

I began sucking and licking Ellen's smooth pussy. At the same
time, Carly took my balls and cock into her mouth. After I came
in my wife's mouth, I was too tired to continue. I watched as both
women faced each other and felt each other's breasts and pussy
while they kissed. We ended up spending the entire weekend engaged in sexual activity.

Brad came home Sunday night, and Ellen showed him her
pussy. We could hear them fucking through the wall, and we felt
proud. Ellen came over after Brad had gone to sleep. She couldn't
thank us enough. We fucked her again, and she went home, very
happy.—*T.D., Cincinnati, Ohio*

HURRICANE ANDREW WAS NOTHING COMPARED TO TROPICAL STORM MARY

I am a thirty-one years old, six foot one and one hundred ninety pounds. I work out four days a week and am in fairly decent shape. I work for a large insurance company, and was one of the first people sent down to the hurricane-damaged Miami area last year. One of my assignments was a house that hadn't been hit too hard.

The owner was a thin blonde woman. Her name was Mary, and it was obvious that she spent a good deal of time working out. She was not, however, built to the point where she lost any of her femininity. In short, she was one hot-looking woman.

After introducing myself and explaining what I would be doing, I proceeded to itemize the damage to the house. After completing the downstairs, Mary led me by the hand up the spiral staircase to the second floor. Her hand was warm, and I felt a surge of electricity pass between us when we touched. As I had been cut off from my normal outlets of sexual release for almost one week, my mind couldn't help but turn to thoughts of sex, particularly considering Mary's beauty and warm, inviting personality.

As she led me down the hallway toward the damaged terrace, I happened to glance into an open bedroom door. I saw a young Asian girl lying on a large waterbed. Mary said, "That's my roommate, Caroline. I'll introduce you properly later."

Several times, while bending over to measure the terrace, I caught Mary looking at my tight, firm buttocks. I caught her licking her full, pouty lips in what I correctly surmised was intense sexual anticipation. My cock soon became as hard as a rock.

She came toward me and, while lightly rubbing her long, superbly manicured fingers up and down my denim-clad crotch, looked intently into my eyes and said, "Caroline and I need a hunky stud like you to make us feel good. Can you do that? Can you make us feel good?"

There was no way that I could refuse this beautiful lady's request. She could have given a dead man a hard-on. I did ask that she allow me to take a quick shower, as I had been outside for a good portion of the day, and my body was not in any condition to be shared with anyone, especially not these lovely ladies. I wanted everything to be perfect.

Mary directed me to a shower that had three nozzles. As I began to strip, Mary brought Caroline into the bathroom.

I turned to face a beautiful girl of about twenty-two. She stood about five foot five with a dark tan and firm, round breasts capped by thick, half-dollar-size nipples that were begging to be sucked.

After we had soaped one another's body, Caroline knelt down and took my cock into her hot mouth. As I hadn't had an orgasm in about a week, it was all I could do to keep from shooting my juice into her warm, wet mouth. It was very visually stimulating watching Caroline's lips engulf the smooth crimson knob of my hard-on again and again as the water cascaded over her face and caused her silky black waist-length hair to stick to her voluptuous body. I somehow garnered the willpower to gently pull her mouth from my raging unit before I came. Her lips left my engorged glans with an audible pop, and she followed me out of the shower to towel off in the spacious bathroom.

Mary, who had been furiously fingering her juicy slit while watching this outstanding display of fellatio, wrapped her arms around me from behind and proceeded to run her strong right hand up and down my dick. Her left hand was firmly but gently squeezing my full, heavy testicles. This caused a thick, clear drop of pre-come to appear. I then began to work my way up Caroline's thighs to her dripping-wet cunt lips. As she enjoyed the stimulation I applied to her clitoris, she began to moan. Suddenly she screamed as she came with wild abandon. I then pulled my tongue from Caroline's sweet box and replaced it with the tip of my rod. This caused her hips to buck up and down. She moaned, "Oh, baby. Shove that hard, big, wonderful cock deep inside me. I need it so bad. Give it to me."

I began slamming her with long, full strokes. After about fifteen minutes of this, Mary said, "It's my turn. I want him now."

She faced me and spread her long legs wide so that her gorgeous slit was at my eye level. I had to taste that golden box. I grabbed Mary's lovely hips and licked her from slit to clit. She began to scream and buck against my face as she had the first of several orgasms she would have that day. Caroline scooted under me and applied suction to my log with her talented mouth. After about ten minutes of this, I could no longer control myself, and while Caroline sucked my bursting head and tongued the gaping slit, all the while rhythmically stroking the shaft, I felt the rush that always precedes my orgasms. I moaned, "Oh baby, I'm gonna come," but the amount and force of that first shot must have come as a surprise, because her head jerked back. My cock slipped from between her lips, causing the second shot to jet in a thick, ropy strand across the floor. She quickly stuffed me back into her mouth so she could finish me off by stroking me tenderly while spurt after spurt surged down her throat. She sucked and licked me until I began to soften. Mary scooped the sperm off the floor and daintily licked it from her fingers. I collapsed in a satiated heap, but I knew that I was not finished, not by a long shot.—*E.C., Madison, Wisconsin* O⊢▪

WHERE THE BOYS ARE—IN OTHER WORDS, IT TAKES ONE TO BLOW ONE

My live-in boyfriend David had been complaining about my blowjobs, and was always trying to get me to give him better head. Though I enjoyed sucking David's dick, it's true that I considered cocksucking to be strictly foreplay and not the main course. I suppose I was always so anxious to feel his prick in my pussy that, after a few minutes of licking, I would pull him out of my mouth and coax him between my legs. No matter how often David told me that guys really love a good blowjob, I always found a way to keep it short and get right to fucking.

I came home from the beach one Saturday afternoon—I had gone alone because David was at work. I was about to go in the bedroom when I heard David's voice coming from there, moaning and groaning in ecstasy. Thinking he had one of our sexy female neighbors in our bed, I was tempted to barge in and give them both a thrashing. Instead I kept my head and tiptoed to the door. It was slightly ajar, so I slowly stuck my head in for a peek.

What a shock! My boyfriend was in bed enjoying himself all right—but with a guy! David was kneeling on the bed as a well-muscled, blond-haired guy was sucking his stiff pole. The two of them were so occupied, they didn't even see me. David's eyes were glazed with lust as he begged the blond guy to suck harder. The guy was on all fours, munching David like a high-priced whore. His own stiff cock bobbed between his legs as he moved his mouth up and down my man's dick. They must have been making love for some time, because both of them were sweating, and as I looked at their glistening bodies, my jealous anger began to turn into horny desire. I stuck a finger into my bikini panties and started to play with my moist crotch.

The two horny studs kept at it, in total ignorance of me, as I continued to watch. I couldn't believe how sexy and dirty they looked together. David was shouting in ecstasy as the blond licked his huge purple cockhead and squeezed his balls. The sight made the juices drip freely from my vagina.

The blond guy slathered his tongue all over David's glistening cockhead, coating his tongue and lips with David's pearly pre-come. I could tell David was on the verge of coming. But as I inched my head through the doorway for a better view of the moment of truth, the blond man suddenly saw me out of the corner of his eye and stopped.

Standing there very embarrassed, all I could manage was a weak, "Hello."

David and his friend grinned at me broadly, and then David said, "You caught us. I hope you're not angry."

"A little jealous," I replied. "But mostly I'm really turned on."

"Come into bed with us," the blond said, "and we'll both fuck you. My name's Josh."

I wasn't going to pass up an opportunity like that. Josh and David carried me to the bed and pulled my bikini and T-shirt off. I could feel the warmth of their sweaty bodies as I slid in between them. I was so horny, I didn't know who to touch first.

David was soon behind me on all fours, licking my ass-cheeks as the muscular, blond Josh licked my swollen nipples. I could feel my clit poking out from my cunt as I reached down and grabbed Josh's huge cock. I had a wild desire to suck this stranger's dick—and I was determined to do it better than I'd ever sucked anyone else before.

I slid my tongue down his sweaty chest, past his navel and to his sexy cock. I licked the pulsing head into my mouth as his hairy balls swayed under me, brushing my chin. David had moved from behind me and was urging me to suck his friend's cock. "That's it, lick it good. Taste it and make him come."

His friend moved from his kneeling position to lie on his back, and I glanced at his sexy body while I temporarily let his member slip from my mouth. I leaned over him, licking his stiff little nipples as he moaned in delight. I could smell the sweaty aroma seeping from his damp armpits as I moved back down to his cock.

David lay beside me as I grabbed Josh's meaty penis. The two of us began to move our tongues up and down the shiny shaft. I was so sexed up as we took turns sucking this guy's beautiful cock, my cunt was really drooling! While David sucked Josh's pole, I toyed with his blond pubic hair and licked his heavy balls. Then David and I switched positions, and he licked the guy's sac while I fed on his shank.

Josh was mumbling incoherently, gasping and sighing, ensnared in our web of lust and loving every minute of it. I could tell he was going to come any minute, so I yanked his trembling cock as I tongued it, eager to make him blast a monstrous load into my mouth. David could see the wild desire in me as I slurped and sucked. He fingered my itchy pussy, bringing me to the peak as well.

David also massaged Josh's thigh as he urged me on. "Make him come. Come on, honey, make him shoot. Give it to her, Josh. She's dying to swallow a big load."

Right at that moment the guy shouted, "Oh, God—here I go!"

I moved with electric speed, pursing my lips for the arrival of his spunk. Josh screamed as loads of semen poured from his cock. I sucked and gulped and swallowed, feeling the thick liquid bolt down my throat. His cock pulsed and pulsed, shooting a quart of come into me. It was the first time I'd ever tried to swallow sperm, and I had no choice but to let a lot of it leak out of my mouth and dribble onto the bedspread.

Finally the stud stopped erupting. I pulled away so that David and I could both lick his friend's come-soaked cock clean. Josh moaned how great he felt, and I said the same thing. David looked at me without a word, conveying with a single smile the thing he'd been telling me all along: there's nothing like a good blowjob.

By now I had to have a cock in my pussy, so I straddled Josh, taking his cock into me with one quick downward motion. Despite just having come, his prick stayed totally erect and he started fucking me hard. My cunt felt those electric charges of ecstasy again as his big, thick tool moved back and forth, in and out, pleasuring my hungry gash. David knelt beside me, masturbating feverishly. He then moved so that his hard cock was hanging over his friend's mouth. Josh stuck out his tongue and started to mouth David's prick. I felt my first orgasm rip through me as I rode Josh, watching with delight as he treated David's cock to several long licks.

Josh then began to suck David in earnest again, taking his trembling flesh into his mouth and letting David fuck it like a pussy. David was moaning deeply as I watched his cock slide in and out of this man's obviously talented mouth. The three of us were moving in unison, pleasuring ourselves with each thrust and wiggle.

I heard David cry out, "Oh, man, that's so fucking good," as his friend licked away at his throbbing shaft. David's cock jumped and pulsed as he shot streams of come all over Josh's chest. I leaned over and licked David's sperm off Josh's hairy chest, and continued to grind as he fucked me silly. Minutes later, he and I came together.

The three of us spent the rest of the afternoon fucking and sucking until we were exhausted. Now David wants me to bring another woman into our bedroom. I already have a good idea who it's going to be. You can expect another letter from me soon.—*V.S., Boston, Massachusetts* O⊢▫

DRIVE-IN DIDDLING GIVES WAY TO AFTER-HOURS TRIPLE FEATURE

One night last summer I went to the drive-in with my girlfriend Aileen, her friend Paula and two other friends, John and Chris. It's the only drive-in around, so we spend a lot of time there partying and getting wild.

About halfway through the movie, Paula got out of the car and went to the rest room. Then John and Chris got out to get some popcorn. The second they'd all left the car, Aileen was ripping my pants open and giving me the handjob of my life, pumping me so fast I'm surprised she didn't sprain her wrist. In response, I slid my hand up her skirt to play with her hot little box. I fingered her pussy, which felt like warm pudding, and we really started getting into it.

Just as Aileen and I started working our hips, masturbating ourselves into each other's hand, Paula came back to the car. It was an awkward moment, but there was nothing we could do. I just put a blanket over our laps so Paula wouldn't be able to see what was going on. She probably knew anyway, but who cared? It felt too great to stop.

Then Aileen whispered in my ear, "I want to suck your cock right now!" Who was I to argue?

"Go ahead," I told her. "Blow me."

By now Paula was listening to every word we said. She just giggled and watched the movie. Or tried to, that is. Aileen pulled the blanket away and slid her hot, wet mouth onto my cock. I rarely get blowjobs from her, but when I do, they're great. I looked over to see if Paula was still watching the movie. She wasn't. Her eyes were fixed on us.

Suddenly Paula leaned over and gave me a very wet kiss. Aileen looked up for a moment and smiled, still pumping my cock with her hand and licking the spongy head. It looked as though something might develop between the three of us, but then Chris and John came back, and we had no choice but to stop. I buttoned my pants and sat through the rest of the movie with a cock as hard as a diving board.

But the night didn't end there. We dropped off John and Chris after the movie, and then Aileen, Paula and I all retired to my apartment. Clothes were flying off as we walked through the door. We hit the bed immediately, and within minutes I had four tits draped over my face. I started with Aileen's huge globes, licking each soft expanse of flesh, sucking each nipple to hardness. As soon as I switched my attention to Paula's tits, Aileen had my cock in her mouth. It was hard as steel. I couldn't believe it—my fantasy of a threesome was finally coming true!

I lay Aileen on her back and buried my face in her shaved, tight, very sweet pussy. I licked and sucked her to three orgasms, feasting on her clit as if it were a full-course meal and drinking her juices. She writhed and screamed loudly on the first two orgasms, but on the third, her cries were quiet, almost muffled. I looked up to see that Paula was straddling Aileen's face, pumping her pussy up and down on my girlfriend's mouth. I almost came just seeing that happen. Moments later Paula shuddered and came, her hips pivoting back and forth, drizzling a shower of female nectar all over Aileen's face.

Aileen and I next took turns eating Paula's pussy. Between licks we would kiss deeply, sharing Paula's sexy juices. When Paula had experienced a few orgasms, they switched places and Paula and I sucked away at Aileen's snatch.

My biggest surprise came when Aileen said to me, "I want to watch you slide your cock into Paula. Do it, fuck her for me." I had always dreamed of balling Paula, and now that I had Aileen's blessing, it was going to be better than I'd ever dreamed.

Paula got on all fours, with Aileen underneath her. As Aileen licked Paula's clit, I slid into her dripping pussy from behind. I could've come at once, but I held off, determined to make it last. I pumped slowly, but as Paula came closer to orgasm, Aileen urged me on more and more. "Fuck her good, baby," she exclaimed. "Fuck that pussy as hard as you can." She was rubbing her own clit and licking my dick as it slid in and out of Paula. It had to be the best sexual experience of my life.

Moments later the two women trembled all over and had intense orgasms. With a shout I emptied my load into Paula's pussy. I pumped so much cream into her that most of it came out of her cunt and flowed down her legs.

I recovered quickly and soon fed my raging hard-on to Aileen's pussy. Her legs, raised high in the air, were soon wrapped around my neck. She put her hands on my ass and pulled me into her deeper and deeper. I pumped her as fast as I could, while Paula sucked on her tits and shared many kisses with her. With my cock hammering into her, and Paula rubbing her clit and licking her nipples. Aileen came repeatedly, screaming and gasping. Her hot little pussy was dripping all over my cock.

Paula licked Aileen's clit while my cock continued its onslaught. This brought her to her greatest orgasm of the night. She squirmed so much that my cock almost fell out of her. I rested her heels on my shoulders and positioned us at an angle that kept my cock buried inside her while I fucked her wildly. With Aileen screaming in pleasure as I humped away, I shot my hot come into her hungry box. Then we all collapsed on the bed, too tired to move—for a few hours, anyway.—*Name and address withheld.* O╾▪

SHE ALREADY HAS TOM AND HARRY, SO WHY NOT SOME DICK TOO?

The night started innocently enough. My husband Thomas and I had gone to dinner with Harold, an old college friend of ours who was in town for the weekend. As he'd done in the past, Harold would be staying in our guest room.

We'd been at a local pub for dinner and had each had several drinks. After returning home, Thomas, Harold and I sat around talking and polishing off a bottle of wine. I have a nice figure and consider myself an attractive woman, and I must admit I was enjoying the attention of these two attractive and very masculine men. Thomas and I have a good marriage. He'd been my only lover in fifteen years of marriage, but I have always had fantasy lovers. Harold had been one of them.

It may have been the drinks, or my secret fantasies, or both, but I realized I was getting extremely horny. I was flirting heavily, making sexual comments and taking every opportunity to be an exhibitionist. My skirt was knee-length, but sitting across from the two men was giving me the opportunity to show off my long legs. Thomas has always complimented me on having a sexy butt, and I was showing that off too.

It was nearly midnight when we decided to go to sleep. Although the idea of having Thomas and Harold in bed with me had been darting through my mind for hours, I was sure Thomas would never allow it to happen. I excused myself to go into the bathroom, feeling the wetness between my legs. I wanted the two of them to join me for a night of wild sex, but didn't know how to ask.

When I returned to the bedroom I saw Harold and Thomas standing at the foot of the bed. The sheets were folded down—a hint of things to come. I walked directly up to Thomas and kissed him. "I'm nervous," I said to him, "but this is what I want." Then I turned to Harold and kissed him passionately. I was frightened to turn and look at Thomas for fear of how he was taking this, but all at once his arms were around my waist and his hard cock was pressed up against my rear.

Thomas undid my skirt and Harold unbuttoned my blouse. It was Harold's hand that first slid down my stomach to play between my legs. By this time I was so wet that his fingers slid in easily. I was freely humping Harold's hand as Thomas removed my bra and began to suck on a nipple. They were already hard and pointing out as Harold took the other nipple into his mouth.

I undid Harold's trousers and held his cock. It was nice and hard, just like Thomas's. The men lay me on the bed. Harold knelt in front of me and brought his mouth between my legs. It was wonderful. He sucked on my clit as I squirmed and moaned and pulled him close to me.

The two men stripped and joined me in bed. I wasn't sure where to start, but Thomas and Harold knew just what they wanted: pure sex. As Thomas and I kissed, Harold spread my legs apart and moved into position to slide his cock into my wet hole. Needless to say, my cunt was filled by him on the first thrust. For the first time since Thomas and I were married, another man had buried his cock in me. What made it even better was that it was happening while my husband was kissing me!

Harold slid in and out of my pussy, slowly at first. He began to pick up speed and power. Soon enough, as Thomas sucked my nipples, Harold was pounding me with all the strength he had. I couldn't hold still. I was lifting my ass high off the bed to meet his every powerful stroke. He was able to keep it going for what seemed a heavenly eternity before coming with a loud groan.

After Harold pulled out of my hole, Thomas's cock slid into me. My cunt was hot and sopping wet, thanks to the large load Harold left behind. Thomas didn't last as long as Harold, but his thrusts had the same power behind them, and I had at least two more orgasms.

By the time Thomas was finished screwing me, Harold was hard again. He rolled me onto my stomach and had me get up on all fours, hungry to push his cock back into my vagina. As Harold pumped me from behind, Thomas sat in front of me and put his rod in my mouth. It stiffened as I sucked it. It was probably the greatest experience of my life, being fucked and sucking a cock at the same time. I think every woman should do it at least once in her lifetime.

As Harold plunged in and out of me with all his might, I was giving my excited husband the best blowjob he'd ever had. With the constant slapping of Harold up against my ass, it wasn't easy to concentrate on my husband's cock, but I did the best I could. Both men were able to keep their erections a very long time before coming. I have no idea how often I climaxed in that position, but believe me, it was a lot.

The three of us continued to have the wildest sex imaginable, in many different positions, until long after the sun came up the next morning. We are already making plans for an encore weekend this fall.—*C.C., Montgomery, Alabama* O⊢▪

SHE MAY BE JUST A POSER—BUT JUST LOOK AT THOSE POSES!

I got a pleasant surprise when I showed up at work this morning. A girl I'd known in college was hired as an assistant on our floor. Although we were never friends at school, I knew she was wild in the dorms. I hoped that she hadn't cooled down much. She was beautiful and sexy, and I was itching for a taste.

I walked up to her desk and said, "Hi, Sharon. Long time no see." Close up, she was even prettier than I'd remembered. Her hair was longer now, and framed her face in a seductive way. She had a very sexy face, and was wearing a red dress that was tight in all the right places.

"Dean!" she cried out with a huge smile. "What a surprise. How've you been? You look great." We chatted for a few minutes, then she asked, "What are you doing for lunch today?"

"Actually I have an errand to run at lunchtime, but I'll come back and we can talk again later this afternoon if you want."

"Sure," she said. I turned and walked back to my office.

Now, you may be wondering why I passed up a lunch date with a sexy woman who was definitely coming on to me. You see, the errand I had to run involved Sharon. I was going home to get some pictures of her I'd been holding onto for years. A friend of mine who'd dated her for a while in college had taken them. He was bitter when they broke up, and told me to take them off his hands. They showed Sharon in many sexy poses and in various states of undress. Most of them were taken from behind, but in a few, her tits, and definitely some of her snatch, were in view. I knew that if she was as open about sex as she'd been in college, she'd get a kick out of seeing the pictures again. If not, she'd at least be happy that the photographs would now be in her possession.

When I got back to work, I went straight to her desk. She was eating a Whopper and fries. I dropped an envelope containing the pictures on her desk and headed for my office. Before I could get there, she shrieked and called me back.

"Where did you get these? Did Gary give them to you?" she asked breathlessly, but with no anger in her voice.

"A long time ago. But don't worry. I only looked when I first got them. They've been sitting in my drawer for years." I thought it best not to tell her the truth, which was that I'd probably jerked off to those pictures a few hundred times.

"Are you mad?" I asked.

"No, you just surprised me is all. He told me he'd burned those pictures. It's kind of flattering actually, knowing you've had them all along."

She couldn't keep her eyes off the pictures. I could tell by the look in her eyes that she was getting turned on just thinking about her randy college days.

"Listen," she said, leaning forward and giving me a quick view of her cleavage. I swallowed hard and leaned forward too. "I want to play a little joke on Gary, but you'll have to help me. I know where he's living, and I want to send him some more pictures like these. He'll go crazy wondering who took them. He's married now, but he was always really jealous. You'd take some pictures of me naked, wouldn't you?"

I could barely believe my ears. Sharon really was the wild woman I remembered hearing about. I said, "Uh, sure. When do you want to do it?"

"How about tonight?" she asked.

"Okay. We can go to the fax room and do it there. No one stays here late except me, and we'd have total privacy. I'll just run home and get my camera."

She thought it over for maybe a second, then agreed to be there at seven o'clock. Just for the hell of it, I blew her a kiss as I walked away. Out of the corner of my eye, I saw her give me a wink. It was fucking incredible! I might actually have a shot at fucking this beauty.

The rest of the day passed pretty quickly. I left my office a few minutes early and went home for my camera. When I returned, I went to the fax room and waited for Sharon. Just after seven o'clock I heard a knock on the door, and let her in. She looked great, and I told her so.

"You're sure there's no one here?" she asked with doubt in her eyes. I assured her that everyone had gone home, and offered her a chair.

"So what kind of picture should we start with?" I asked. "You decide."

She got up and, without another word, started to undress. She asked me for a hand with the zipper on her dress, and I quickly stood behind her to help. The zipper came down smoothly, and the dress slipped off her shoulders and down her shapely body. She stepped out of her dress. Her butt was big and beautiful. I'd seen it many times in those photographs, but in the flesh it was something else. Being this close to it was quite exciting. I tried to tell myself not to reach out and squeeze it—but I did anyway. She let out a little whoop of surprise and gave me a big, sexy smile.

Sharon ran her tongue over her lips. Looking down, she saw

my cock growing to hardness. She started to unzip my pants. I was stunned and delighted by this turn of events.

"I thought these pictures were going to be of you," I said.

"Can't a girl have a little encouragement?"

Was I in heaven or what? She bent over at the waist in her bra, panties and high heels—all red—as she released my cock from my underwear. She made a purring sound as she wrapped her tongue around my shaft and slurped me into her hot mouth. Gary had told me she loved to give head. He used to say she could drink sperm like water. I was amazed at how good she sucked, her big eyes looking up at me as her head slowly bobbed up and down on my swollen dick.

She increased her suction and her pace, making dirty little slurping sounds the whole time. It was such a rush! Then she started tickling my balls, which made me come like crazy. She deep-throated my cock for the explosion, letting my sperm blast straight into her stomach.

"So, how was that for starters?" she asked as she used my handkerchief to wipe her lips.

"Better than I could've done," I joked. "Too bad we couldn't get it on film for Gary."

Sharon sat on a desk and said, "Let's make this the first shot." She had on red bikini panties that accentuated the curves of her butt. I was starting to harden again already. I quickly picked up my camera and started snapping pictures of her hot ass and legs.

After a few more ass poses, she coolly removed her bra and stepped out of her panties, smirking at me as I took in the sight of her in nothing but high heels. I took some more pictures as she moved around the room, showing off her great bod.

I told her to get on her hands and knees. She giggled, "I'm used to that position, Dean. I love to do it doggie-style." I snapped some shots of her in her favorite position, and a thought occurred to me. "Maybe you *should* have a partner in these pictures," I said.

"You mean you want to be in them too?"

"No," I said. "But my friend Lenny lives across the street. I can call him up and let him in. He's a good-looking guy. You'd be great together."

She seemed unsure at first, but her resistance quickly gave way to approval. "All right," she said. "Call him up and we'll see what happens."

It took a few minutes to convince Lenny over the phone that I wasn't joking with him or setting him up for some big practical joke. Finally he agreed to come over. I let him in the freight entrance and brought him upstairs. His first look at Sharon was of her sitting on a desk with her feet on a chair, still naked except for her high heels.

"Pleased to meet you, Lenny," she said, her interest growing when she saw how well-built he was. "You're quite a big guy. Your muscles, I mean." Lenny just smiled.

I said to Sharon, "Why don't you do the same thing to Lenny that you did to me a few minutes ago, and I'll shoot some pictures of that." She gave me a nod and said to Lenny, "Come here, big boy. Let's see what kind of cock you have."

Lenny was quiet, but he wasn't shy about whipping out his prick for Sharon's approval. She got more then she bargained for, and even I was surprised that he had such a huge shank.

"All right, Mr. Big Dick!" Sharon said eagerly. She began to suck at once. I shot two whole rolls of film of her feeding on Lenny's big schlong. I was so hard and worked up, it seemed as though my cock might explode without even being touched. Sharon and Lenny probably forgot I was even there. Sharon was munching wetly, moaning all over Lenny's dick, tugging his balls and working her mouth—she was born to suck cock. Big Lenny just kept feeding her his tube, fucking her mouth with a velocity I didn't think was humanly possible.

As much as he was enjoying the blowjob, though, Lenny wanted more. He lifted her up while she was still attached to his prick, then pulled her away and said, "Time for something new." He bent her supple body at the waist and lay her facedown across the desk. "You like to fuck as much as you like to suck?" he asked.

"What do you think, stud?" she replied, spreading her cunt lips for him. "If you know where to hide it, I know how to ride it." Lenny slipped his swollen hose into her and began to fuck her doggie-style, just the way she'd said she loved it. It was like an X-rated video. As I took pictures, they really went to town. He was pounding feverishly into her, and she was screaming in pleasure.

I finished off the last of my rolls of film and considered the aching state of my poor, neglected boner. "I hope you're still hungry, Sharon," I said, putting the camera down. I walked over to her, my hard prick sticking out like a weather vane. Sharon grinned at me when she saw it dangling in front of her mouth. God, did she love dick! Even though Lenny was humping her silly, she didn't miss a beat, and quickly stuffed my penis into her mouth.

Lenny said, "Fuck her mouth, dude," and slammed into her hard and fast. A few minutes later he pulled out and came all over her rear end.

When he recovered from his spasms, he stood next to me and we took turns sticking our cocks in Sharon's busy mouth. Lenny's did not get hard again, but Sharon didn't seem to mind. She alternated between his limp sausage and my hard prong. It seemed that as long as her mouth was filled with something, she was content. So we did our best to keep her happy.

When it was obvious that Lenny wasn't going to get another erection for a while, however, he tucked his cock back in his pants and waved good-bye. I was afraid she was going to quit now that Lenny was gone, but she stayed right on me, giving me a blowjob that defies description, and draining another big load of come out of my shaft. Just like last time, she took it all down her throat, swallowing every blast that shot forth from my dick.

When I was through coming, she licked her lips and got up off the desk. I almost had to hold back a tear when she reached for her dress. It was over.

"Well, Sharon, it's certainly been an eventful day," I said. "I hope you had as much fun as I did. Maybe we can get together again sometime. Tomorrow?"

"We'll see," she said. "Just let me have that film. Won't Gary be surprised."

We left the room, which still smelled strongly of sex. As we rode down in the elevator, she made breezy small talk—as though she hadn't spent the last hour sucking my cock and fucking a stranger. Amazing!

We went our separate ways, and I said, "See you tomorrow." She walked to her car and said, "Thanks for everything, Dean," and licked her lips one last time for me.—*Name and address withheld* ○┼▪

Head & Tail

NEOPHYTE BENDS OVER TO LAND THAT FIRST BIG CLIENT

When you're first starting your own business, you'll do just about anything for that first big account, right? Well, a while back I learned just how far I would go. I'm a thirty-two-year-old male, struggling through the trials and tribulations of owning my own business. I had been working for three months, trying to land one special account. That account alone would easily set me up for the next two years. I met with the owner of the firm and took him to a very expensive restaurant for dinner. After dinner he wanted to have drinks at a nearby bar. This turned out to be lots and lots of drinks. I was feeling very loose, when all of a sudden he asked me how badly I wanted his account. I told him I would do "anything" to get his business. He just smiled and said, "Good. That's definitely good to know."

We had several more drinks, and the conversation turned from business matters to sex. He kept remarking how horny he was, and I offered to line up some local girls for his pleasure, but he refused without giving me a reason.

At midnight I gave him a ride back to his hotel, and he invited me in for a drink. As he handed me my drink, his hand lightly touched my ass. Then he told me to get comfortable and helped me remove my suit jacket. He again remarked how hot he was, and said he might see his way to signing with my company if I could get him some release. Again I offered to get some girls, and he just laughed. "Get more comfortable," he said. "Slip into the things I have laid out for you in the bathroom, and you'll be much more comfortable."

I went into the bathroom, and saw what he had in mind! My client wanted me dressed as a woman—he had laid out a lacy teddy, a garter belt, crotchless panties and nylons . . . all in sheer black lace! As I saw it, I had two options—either tell him no and leave, or don the sexy garments, satisfy my customer and land a million-dollar account. Mama didn't raise no fool, so I hurriedly removed my clothes and put on the lingerie.

When I stepped out of the bathroom, he just stared. "Black's your color," was all he said. He had removed his clothes while I was changing. He led me to the bed, laid me down and started feeling every inch of my lace-covered body. I had never been with a man before, but I let him have his way with me. After feeling my body, he gave me a deep French kiss. Strangely enough, I felt myself getting hard! He then maneuvered us into a 69 and took my stiffening cock into his mouth. He rubbed his cock over my lips until I finally opened my mouth and took him in. He pumped my mouth for several minutes, and I could tell that he was about to come. He didn't pull out—he just unloaded his hot come down my throat, gagging me slightly until I managed to swallow the entire load. It was slightly salty, but not as bad as I thought it would be.

He rested for a few minutes, then climbed on top of my cock—lowering himself until I was buried deep in his ass. He then rode me hard, pumping like a madman. His asshole was so tight, I exploded in just a few minutes, filling his hole with my hot juices. As he climbed off my cock and repositioned himself between my legs, I noticed that he was hard again.

He took some come and lubricated my asshole, then lifted my legs and spread them wide. He penetrated me slowly, but soon was fully buried inside me and humping me as if there was no tomorrow. He finally came and filled me with his spurts.

By that time we were both exhausted. He lay next to me and went to sleep. I waited about half an hour, put my clothes back on and left. True to his word, a signed contract was delivered to my office the next day. There is, however, a clause in it, requiring that we meet every three months to personally discuss the "relationship" of our two companies.—*C.H., Salt Lake City, Utah* ○┼▪

HIRED SHUTTERBUG FINDS SOME INTERESTING DEVELOPMENTS ON PAYDAY

I'm twenty-five years old with black hair, brown eyes, a dark complexion and a five-and-a-half-inch dick. I recently had a fantastic sexual experience that I would like to share with you. My girlfriend's friend was having a birthday party for her son. The friend knew that I owned a video camera, and wanted to know if I would videotape the party. My girlfriend's friend Lori is thirty-five years old and pretty good-looking, with a nice, large ass on her. That ass always gets me hard.

While my girlfriend was at work, I went to Lori's apartment to get paid. When I got there, she asked me to come into the bedroom so she could get the money for me. She sat on the edge of the bed and motioned me to come closer. That's when Lori told me she didn't have the money, but would be willing to compensate me in other ways. I asked, "In what other ways?" even though I already knew the answer to the question.

Lori smiled and pulled my shorts down—my cock popped out right in front of her face. She put my dick in her mouth and caressed my balls with her hand. As she sucked my dick, she took her clothes off while I removed my own. Lori sucked me until I couldn't hold back any more. I shot my load down her throat until my knees went weak and I could barely stand.

She then pulled me on top of her, and we made out for a while. As soon as I was hard again, she said, "I want you to fuck my pussy from behind."

Lori got on all fours, and I started pumping her pussy. Large asses like Lori's have always turned me on, and seeing my cock disappear into her was great. She then surprised me by saying she wanted my dick up her ass. I asked if she had any lubricant, and she said, "Forget that shit. Just ram me with all you've got."

So into her asshole my cock slid. Lori squeezed my cock with her inner muscles. It felt wonderful. After some more humping, she told me to tell her when I was ready to come. I told her I wasn't going to be long. Lori pulled away from me and lay on her back, saying, "I want you to eat me."

I stuck my tongue deep inside her pussy while she tenderly cleaned my dick and jacked me off. I felt her pussy contract as my licking intensified. At that moment I couldn't hold back anymore, and I busted my nut all over her hand.

We lay there exhausted for a while, then put on our clothes. As I was leaving, she said, "I can't wait to do this again." Trust me, we didn't wait that long.—*Name and address withheld.*

AN UNEXPECTED RESTROOM ENCOUNTER LEADS TO FORBIDDEN PLEASURES

The park was dark—I think they turn the lights off because of all the nightly action. There is a light on outside all the restrooms, which are easy to spot from the parking lot. I looked around carefully to ensure that no one was hiding close by. Parked in front of one of the restrooms was a pickup truck—since it was the only vehicle around, I figured I was safe.

I rushed into the restroom. As I went in, I noticed that all the stall doors were closed, and it seemed as if no one was there. After I'd finished tending to my needs and turned around to tuck my cock back into my ladies' panties and raise my feminine jeans, I looked up and saw him. His pants and briefs were down around his ankles. With one hand he held the door to the stall open—the other was wrapped around the thickest cock I had ever seen. It was about eight inches long, and I knew instantly that I wanted it. As sexily as I could, I lowered my jeans to expose my panties, trying not to appear too cock-hungry. He flexed his finger and beckoned me closer.

With my jeans at my hips, I was barely able to walk without making a fool of myself. During the whole encounter, not a single word was spoken. There were a lot of grunts and moans, a couple of sighs and plenty of heavy, fast breathing.

His left arm went around my waist, and my left hand replaced his on his cock. We kissed deeply as I started jerking his thick cock. His hand soon dropped to my ass, and he rubbed it through the silk panties. As we finally broke the kiss, I dropped to my knees and started licking his cock from base to tip. I kissed the whole thing before taking it into my mouth.

I worked his cock as I never had worked a cock before, using everything I had ever learned. I reached into my pocket, pulled out a lubricated condom and lovingly stretched it around the thick cock that was inches from my mouth.

Once it was on, I stood up, lowered my jeans and panties, then turned around and bent over from the waist. I offered myself to him as I relaxed the muscles in my ass.

He rubbed his cock up and down the crack of my ass, then put his thick head against my tiny hole and held my hips. With a combined effort, he pushed forward as I pushed back. We both moaned as he popped in. His thrusts were slow at first, which drove me crazy with desire. As his speed increased, I pushed back to meet his thrusts. I shot my load on the floor as he kept fucking me faster and faster. All of a sudden he moaned and forced his entire cock inside me. I felt it pulse and jerk as he shot his thick load. I came again.

He held me for a long time and then slowly pulled out, much to my disappointment. As he cleaned his cock, I cleaned my ass. He raised his trousers and walked out first. I followed a few minutes later, and it was then that fear gripped me, thinking about what I had just done. But I got over it quickly, and ultimately was glad I'd done it.—*S.F., Carson City, Nevada* O┼ⲙ

DRESSING UP FOR FUN GETS THIS GUY MORE THAN HE BARGAINED FOR

I'm a twenty-three-year-old lesbian. I've just recently read my first *Penthouse Letters,* and I got so turned on from reading the letters about two women getting it on, I want to share the first, but certainly not last, experience I had with a woman.

I've always been turned on by the sight of a woman in nylons and heels, but I was too shy to make a move. So up until about a year ago, when I ate my first pussy, I'd make my boyfriend Chris wear nylons, pumps, dresses and makeup. This helped to satisfy my lesbian desires. After making Chris dress like a woman every day for almost a year, I still wanted to eat a pussy.

One Saturday night Chris and I went out dressed up as hookers. He did his makeup extra heavy that night and painted his fake fingernails bright red. When we got to the nightclub and went in, several guys hit on him, telling him how much they'd love to fuck him.

Chris grabbed my hand so we would look like lesbians, and we walked in. Now, since Chris makes a great-looking girl and the two of us were acting like lesbians, this beautiful woman walked up to us and asked if we wanted to party with her. I quickly said yes.

To make a long story short, Chris, Rory (the lady we met) and I ended up at our apartment later on that night. I talked Chris into letting me handcuff him to the bed and letting Rory watch me fuck him. Little did he know that he was literally going to get fucked for the first time.

After cuffing his hands, Rory and I sat down in front of him and began kissing and caressing each other's legs, quickly moving our hands under each other's skirt. I finally touched my first pussy. After stripping down to nothing but our nylons, Rory lay down beside Chris and I began caressing her satiny-smooth legs while sucking the crotch of her hose. My fantasy was coming true.

I then pulled her hose down to her knees and began tonguing her pussy and fingering her asshole, quickly bringing her to orgasm. Chris was so stunned he was at a loss for words, watching me eat a pussy right in front of him. After Rory did the same for me, she pulled an eight-inch dildo out of her purse and strapped it on. She then moved beside Chris and started caressing him, telling him she was going to fuck his tight asshole.

Chris started ordering me to uncuff him, so I pulled my hose off and sat on his face, forcing him to eat my pussy, while at the same time Rory pulled his stockings down to his knees, lifted his legs up, sank that eight-inch dildo in his asshole and began fucking him. Chris was moving his head from side to side, and the movement was making me come. Even though he had initially protested, soon he was coming as hard as I had.

After fucking Chris for about ten minutes. Rory pulled the dildo out of his ass, lay on top of him and gave him a long French kiss.—*E.R., Atlanta, Georgia* ⊙━▦

WORKOUT BUDDIES INDULGE IN SOME IN-HOME, AFTER-HOURS PUMPING

Like most of your readers, I never thought I would have an adventure to write. But just a couple of weeks ago, one of the most exciting sexual experiences I've ever had occurred at my friend Peter's apartment.

Peter and I both work out together at the local gym. I'm twenty-six years old, five foot eleven and weigh one hundred eighty-five pounds of solid muscle. I work for an accounting firm, and the exercise allows me to work off the frustration of sitting at a desk all day. But most important, I like to keep myself in shape for when I take my shirt off for the ladies. But, while the women love my muscles, they also adore the seven-inch love-muscle that dangles between my legs. Peter is the same age as me, six feet tall and two hundred pounds. His muscles are well-defined, each one cut and sharp. He is absolutely ripped. From what I have seen in the shower at the gym, his dick is about the same length as mine, only a little bigger in circumference. Peter does not lack for female companionship, having bedded several different women throughout the four years I have known him. His sandy-blond hair, blue eyes and laid-back personality, coupled with his muscular body, keep the women clamoring for him.

On one particular night, Peter and I had been working out late in the evening. After a hard workout, we showered, dressed and prepared to leave. As we were going out the door, Peter invited me over to watch a couple of movies. As I had nothing else planned, I readily agreed. On the way to the apartment, we stopped and bought a couple of six-packs. Little did I realize what was about to happen to me.

The air-conditioning in Peter's apartment was broken, and the temperature hovered around eighty-five degrees. A small fan helped somewhat, but soon we were both sweating from the heat. Peter took off his shirt to get a little more comfortable. His back glistened with sweat. Soon we settled down to watch a movie and drink some beers.

The first movie Peter put on was an X-rated one I hadn't seen before. The ladies were gorgeous and demonstrated some great cocksucking talent. In the next scene, the girls went down on each other, and my dick sprang to attention. I love to see women suck each other's cunt. All the fucking and sucking on the television screen had me horny as hell. Damn, I sure needed a pussy to slam into right about then. Peter was also horny as hell—I could tell by the outline of his hard dick in his shorts. The movie ended, and I went to the bathroom while Peter put on another movie.

The second movie started with a couple of gorgeous broads licking each other's cunt. They were soon joined by two good-looking guys who were ready to fuck them into delirium. After some heavy-duty fucking, the guys came, spraying their jism onto the girls' stomachs. Each girl rubbed the jism into her skin, then licked the excess off their fingers. The guys rested and watched the girls go at each other's cunt again. The girls went at it hot and heavy, which again had my dick straining in my shorts. Suddenly the girls stopped what they were doing and started watching the guys. I couldn't believe the scene unfolding before my eyes. The men got into a 69 position and went after each other's dick. Seeing this was a new experience for me, but surprisingly, it had me hornier than I'd ever been before.

I was mesmerized by the action on the screen. After sucking each other's dick for a while, the guys began to masturbate one another. While watching the steamy action, I felt a hand massaging my knee. The hand soon moved to my upper thigh. I couldn't believe Peter was making a move on me like this. I was both scared and excited. Because I did not protest, Peter assumed everything was okay. Soon his hand was massaging my dick through my pants. Then his hand moved underneath my T-shirt. Peter rubbed my chest with his firm, strong hands while I, almost without thinking, removed the T-shirt. My naked chest was soaked from sweat and excitement. I could feel myself shaking, and Peter lowered his hand to massage my rock-hard dick once again.

My hand moved toward Peter's arm, and I massaged it slowly, encouraging him to continue manipulating my tool. I massaged his arm and slowly worked my way to his massive shoulders and then to his chest, which felt as sweaty as mine. I turned slightly toward him to get more comfortable. I gradually moved my hand down his body, finally reaching the monster that was squirming to get out of his pants. I had never touched another man's dick before, but I wanted to feel it in my hands. I could see the head poking out of the waistband of his shorts. Pre-come was oozing out and pooling on his stomach.

Peter pushed me back onto the sofa and told me to relax. He gently but firmly massaged my shoulders, moving down to my chest. Then he moved even lower, kneading the tight muscles of my stomach before finally reaching my shorts. Peter unbuttoned my pants and pulled down the zipper, letting my prick, which felt as if it had grown to ten inches, spring out. Peter pulled my shorts the rest of the way off. He stood over me, his massive frame looking gorgeous as sweat continued to drip from his body, and removed his own shorts. I couldn't believe the size of Peter's swollen cock. It stood hard and erect, pulsing with every beat of his heart.

Peter knelt down beside me and began to lick my chest and suck my nipples. I couldn't believe it. I massaged his back as he made his way toward my crotch, never touching my dick, then back up to my neck. I reached for Peter's bursting cock, and for the first time in my life, I held another man's dick. It felt great. I slowly moved my hand up and down the long shaft. Peter's dick was covered with pre-come, so there was no friction. My hand just glided up and down his massive pole. From the sound of his low, guttural moans, I knew that what I was doing made him feel good.

Peter took my hand away from his dick and climbed back onto the couch, hovered over me as if he was about to do pushups. I reached up and felt his rippling chest. He then lowered his hips slightly until our dicks were touching. I couldn't begin to explain the sensation. We slowly moved against each other, humping our dicks together as if we were fucking the finest piece of pussy on earth. The pleasure I was feeling was so intense, and I knew I would come much too soon. By this time Peter was howling like a wolf. We pumped and mashed against each other for about ten minutes until the excitement became too much to control. We exploded in simultaneous orgasm. I never dumped as much come as I did then. Exhausted, Peter lowered himself onto my body, and I could feel our come spread between us as he lay there and gulped air, his chest heaving into mine with each breath.

As I came back to reality, I could hear the movie still playing. One of the guys onscreen was fucking the other in the ass. With Peter still lying on top of me, the action on the television had me hard again almost instantly. I massaged Peter's sweaty back and then asked him to trade places with me. His cock was also coming back to life, and I knew much more fun was in store.

I gave Peter a body rub, ignoring the part of him that needed the most attention. I kneaded and massaged every muscle of his body. The excitement and anticipation he was experiencing was evident from the expression on his face. After massaging his feet and calves, I slowly moved back up to the object of my desire. Peter's cock appeared even bigger than it had earlier. I lowered my mouth and planted soft kisses on his penis. I knew Peter was loving every minute of this treatment, as he often gasped for breath. I was hesitant to take his cock into my mouth. I had never believed that I would or could do something like that, but I did do a lot of things that night I never imagined I would do.

Finally I closed my eyes, inhaled his masculine musky scent and took his dick into my mouth. I wrapped my tongue around his dick and slowly massaged it by moving my head up and down. Peter was in seventh heaven, and that familiar howling sound returned. His hips were bucking as if he were riding an untamed horse. I stopped, as I did not want him to come too soon. I wanted the sensation to be prolonged as much as possible. Peter had introduced me to a new aspect of sex, and I wanted him to enjoy it as much as possible.

I spread his legs and gently massaged his balls, giving them an occasional lick. Soon I was licking his cock again with the gusto of a cheerleader on prom night. After a few minutes of this treatment, I engulfed Peter's dick. He grabbed the back of my head, pushing his dick deeper down my throat, and started slowly pumping his hips. His excitement continued to grow, and he began fucking my face even faster. I held on for all I was worth. Finally he could take no more. I felt him shooting his salty jism down my throat. I can't believe how great it tasted.

At that point Peter went wild, consumed with a raw passion for sex. Incredibly, he remained hard after the treatment I had just given him. Peter threw me onto the floor and sprawled over me, humping and grinding his dick against mine. He worked his way down my body, beginning at my nipples, which he sucked and bit. He was a pure, raw, sexual animal. He moved down my body and, as I had done to him just moments before, took my throbbing dick into his mouth. His warm, moist mouth surrounding my dick shot waves of pleasure through my body. Every inch of me tingled. It felt so great! I knew I would come any second, but somehow I managed to hold back, enjoying every glorious minute. Peter's animalistic desires were tamed somewhat by his need to give me as much pleasure I had given him.

Peter's head bobbed up and down on my pole, slathering every inch while he continued making his guttural animal sounds. Never would I have believed that two men could have such an intense sexual experience without a pussy to stick their cocks into.

Finally the moment of truth came. I grabbed Peter's head and pulled it farther down onto my dick. I could feel his slight beard scratching my upper thigh. I exploded so hard, I thought I would pass out. Peter swallowed every drop of my jism. Totally spent, I just lay there for a few minutes trying to recuperate.

Peter, however, had other ideas, as he still had a raging hard-on after the blowjob he had just given me. Sweat dripped from his muscular body onto mine as he massaged my dick and tried to bring it back to life. His hands felt great on my body, but at that point there was no bringing my dick back to full mast. Peter continued to massage my body, relaxing me for further pleasure. He turned me over and climbed on top to massage my backside. It felt great, and I wished it could have gone on forever. Peter licked my back, slowly moving down to my ass. He then lifted my ass into the air, positioning me on all fours. I knew what was about to come, and I was scared as hell, but also excited. This had been an evening of many firsts, and I had been so turned on that I wanted to experience everything there was to possibly experience.

Peter placed his dick at the entrance of my netherworld. He continued to massage my back and ass to get me to relax. Suddenly he broke through. The pain was exquisite. Peter remained motionless for a few minutes to allow me to accommodate the snake in my ass. After a while he began a slow in-and-out movement. His cock felt great in my ass, and as he pulled back, I would move to try to keep him in. After several minutes of rapid fucking, Peter exploded deep inside me. He remained there for several minutes, as my sphincter muscles did not want to let his wonderful cock loose.

As a thank-you, Peter jacked me off, bringing me an incredible third climax that evening. Finally, Peter's dick withered and withdrew from its dark hiding place. After lying there for a while, Peter and I got up and took a shower, where we explored each other's body some more. We let our stiff cocks rub together and later sucked each other off. Our sexual experience lasted five hours. We wanted more, but sheer exhaustion took over.—*I.V., Louisville, Kentucky*

TRAVELING SALESMAN FINDS OUT THAT HIS WIFE IS THE OFFICE "IN" BOX

My wife Jenny and I have been married for six years. Jenny is a small, slender woman with long black hair. She is attractive, although not really beautiful, and has a spectacular body. During her high school and college years, she tells me, she was extremely self-conscious about the size of her breasts, which are firm but incredibly large for a woman her size. On her petite, slender frame they are impossible to ignore. Her nipples are so huge, they are completely obvious through any kind of light clothing.

For years she did her best to hide her breasts, and dressed very conservatively, always complaining about being "top heavy." Of course, I've always loved her tits. The great thing about them is that, in addition to their size, they are incredibly sensitive. If her nipples are played with, she immediately turns to Jell-O. It's like her nipples are directly connected to her pussy. She can have an orgasm just from having her tits played with—especially if I am a little rough with her nipples. She simply goes crazy.

However, I have to admit that our sex life is probably not that great. I work very long hours, so I'm tired a lot. I have never felt completely adequate in bed with Jenny. She always tries to make me feel everything is fine, but when we have sex I don't last too long and my penis, I'm afraid, is smaller than average.

I realized Jenny secretly wanted more out of sex a couple of years ago when I rented an X-rated movie for us to watch together. This film had several big, muscular guys with huge cocks making it with a small, thin woman. They all used every orifice of her body several times. I looked at Jenny during one particular scene, where the woman was being taken in a number of different ways at once, including anally. I thought she would disapprove of such fare. Instead her eyes kind of glazed over, and she used one hand to slowly rub her upper thighs while the other tweaked one of her nipples.

I asked her what she thought about the scene, and she confided in me that one of her longtime fantasies has always been to be dominated by several men with very large cocks. We had some hot sex after that—but I knew from then on that I would never be able to satisfy her in the way she desired.

Jenny, now in her late twenties, has become more confident. She's stopped hiding her figure and has started wearing clothing that actually shows off her big breasts. I find this exciting, but it also worries me because of all the male attention she now gets.

It all came to a head at a large pool party my boss George recently threw at his house for our entire sales staff and their partners. George is divorced, about thirty-five years old, and lives in a huge house on several acres of land. He has a very large built-in pool, a hot tub and a patio with an outdoor bar. His house sits up on a big hill, with a three-hundred-yard driveway leading to it that keeps the place secluded. It's a real mansion. George inherited the business from his father and really throws his money around. He played college football and is still in good shape, standing about six and a half feet tall and carrying well over two hundred pounds of rock-solid muscle.

I suppose it all began with the bathing suit Jenny bought for the party. It was a tiny bikini that barely hid anything. Her breasts are so big and full that the bikini top only covered about half of each breast. From the side, in fact, you could see nearly her entire breast. The bikini bottom left most of her ass exposed too—it was no bigger than a thong. I told her that there would be over fifty people I worked with at this party, and I didn't want them seeing so much of her body. But Jenny wouldn't budge. She told me that her new suit was "in style," and that I was being ridiculous, whereas I should've been happy to be with such a sexy woman.

When we arrived, Jenny had on a short terry-cloth robe that she wore over her skimpy suit. As I looked around, I realized that most of the other salesmen hadn't brought their wives. They were helping out tending bar, keeping the food stocked and so on. Jenny walked over to the hot tub and slipped off her robe—she looked simply unbelievable. She began rubbing oil on her body, and those big tits of hers were just swaying and bouncing around. In a matter of minutes a small crowd of guys had silently taken up strategic positions around her just to ogle her body.

She was on a chaise longue, with her knees slightly up, when I walked over and realized that, in this position her bikini bottom was completely inadequate: there were large expanses of pubic hair visible for everyone to see. Jenny has a very hairy pussy, and she obviously hadn't shaved before putting on this suit. So imagine me standing there, asking her if she'd like me to get her a drink, knowing that about ten guys I work with were staring at her nearly naked body all afternoon long, knowing I couldn't do a thing about it.

I just tried to enjoy the party, but it was tough. After we'd all been drinking and catching rays for about two hours, my boss came up to me and told me it was my turn to be bartender—all of the salesmen were putting in shifts of about two hours each. He put his arm around Jenny's waist and said, "Don't worry. I'll keep your wife entertained." She'd already had several drinks, and I could see by the look in her eyes that she thought George was attractive.

I went over to the bar, about thirty feet from the hot tub, and did my best to keep the guests supplied with drinks. I could see Jenny moving around, talking and laughing with George, and realized again that her bathing suit was way too small. Her breasts and ass were all but completely exposed.

While I was bartending, someone put on music so people could dance on the patio. I looked up and couldn't believe my eyes—George and Jenny were locked in a slow dance. Instead of keeping a polite distance, he was holding her so close that her breasts were flattened against his chest. I could tell she'd had too much to drink, which always makes her horny. As they danced, George stroked the small of her back and the top of her ass. I couldn't bear to watch.

About that time, we ran out of white wine at the bar. Someone directed me to the basement, where there was supposedly a large supply of wine and liquor. I went downstairs and saw that George had a large wine cellar. I was in the back, looking for white wine, when I heard my wife's voice.

"George, where are you taking me?" Jenny giggled. George told her he wanted them to cool off for a minute out of the hot sun, and thought she might enjoy seeing his wine collection. I crouched down behind the farthest wine rack—I was only about fifteen feet away from them. Jenny said that she didn't know anything about wine, except that she liked to drink it. George laughed, came up behind her and put his arms around her waist, grinding his crotch against her ass.

"You have an unbelievable body," he said. "Do you know you've been driving all the men at this party crazy?"

My wife just giggled and stood there with her eyes closed. Instead of pushing him away, Jenny leaned back into him and said, "My husband is really mad at me. He thinks my bathing suit is too small."

George realized that Jenny was responding to his moves and said, "Your husband should be proud of your body. You like men looking at you, don't you?" As he asked her this question, he slowly brought his hands up and took a breast in each one, squeezing them gently. He repeated the question. "You do like men looking at your body, don't you?"

Jenny's eyes were closed and she was rocking slowly back and forth, rubbing her ass against his cock. George pulled her around and kissed her. She momentarily pushed him back and said, "My husband is right upstairs—I shouldn't be doing this."

George took her hand and placed it on his cock, which was now pushing the front of his bathing suit out a couple of inches. "We can leave right now if you can honestly tell me you don't want to see this," he said. He held her wrist while she rubbed his cock through his suit. He leaned forward and kissed her again, and this time she opened her mouth, sucked on his tongue and began making little moaning noises.

George let go of her wrist, but she kept rubbing his erection. She said, "Oh my God, George, it's so hard!" I could see George smiling. He told her to wait a minute, then walked over and locked the door. He said, "Don't worry about your husband. He'll be busy bartending for at least another thirty minutes, and nobody would dare come down to the wine cellar without asking me."

George took Jenny by the arm and led her to a sofa about twenty feet away from where I was hiding. He slowly peeled off his suit. His cock was truly awesome—about nine or ten inches long and very thick, with a huge head. He sat on the sofa and asked Jenny to take off her bathing suit. She stood up in front of George, pausing momentarily. "Do it Jenny, right now," he told her. "You know you want me to see your body."

I couldn't believe it—she reached up and unsnapped her top, and there were her big breasts, in the flesh, dangling before George's eyes, the huge nipples completely erect. She then peeled off her bottom and stood there quietly. George said, "Rub your tits for me. Play with your nipples." Jenny followed his orders obediently. She began to rub her breasts, then took her nipples between her thumb and forefinger and began pulling and twisting them.

A few moments later George said, "Get down on your knees and suck my cock." Jenny fell to her knees and slowly licked his dick from his balls to the tip, rubbing her tits as she did so. While she blew him, George talked to her, telling her she was beautiful and how much she excited him.

He then helped her to her feet and told her to sit on the sofa. He stood in front of her and slowly rubbed his big cock all over her face, saying to her, "Tell me you love it. Tell me you're my little suck slave and that you'll do anything I tell you to do. Tell me I can have you anytime I want. Tell me, Jenny."

Jenny sat there with her mouth wide open, taking the thrusts of George's immense penis. George really knew how to work his dick. He teased her with it as she sucked, putting the head of it between her lips, then pulling back and rubbing it all over her face, which was getting red from the friction.

Suddenly Jenny said, "Please don't tease me anymore. Just let me suck it. Let me feel it gush down my throat."

He smiled down at her and said, "First tell me you'll do whatever I say. Tell me you love being my sex slave."

Jenny sighed and said, "I'll do anything you want, just let me have that beautiful cock."

George leaned forward, and I watched, openmouthed, as my wife sucked and slobbered over his cock for a good ten minutes. George then said, "I don't want to come in your mouth. I want to fuck you so you can spend the rest of the day feeling my come dripping out of your pussy."

He told her to slide her ass to the edge of the sofa, then knelt down and pushed her knees up to her chest so that her cunt was spread wide. He said, "Rub your pussy for me. Get yourself hot."

I couldn't believe it—Jenny reached down and began to rapidly rub her clit. "Fuck me, George," she said. "Give me that giant dick." George couldn't hold out any longer. He began to rub his cock up and down the sopping wet entrance to Jenny's pussy. She began to moan and shake and plead with him to enter her. With a single thrust, he pushed his full ten inches into my little Jenny and began to pound away, fucking her very hard. Jenny immediately had a violent orgasm, moaning and grunting as she climaxed, bucking her ass up to meet his cock.

My boss then began to tease her again, fucking her hard, then stopping suddenly. Jenny frantically reached up and began pulling his ass toward her, saying, "No, George, please don't stop. Make me come again . . . please!" George continued to fuck away, playing very roughly with her breasts as he screwed her into submission. I couldn't believe his staying power—he must have fucked her hard for twenty minutes. Jenny had four wild orgasms in that time. Finally she reached down and began milking his balls. "Come for me, baby," she urged. "Come in my juicy pussy." George grunted loudly and had a tremendous orgasm, driving his big cock into her as deep as it would go and filling her cunt with his juice.

He pulled his prick out of Jenny's vagina, stuck it in front of her face and said, "Clean it for me with your pretty mouth." Jenny didn't even hesitate—she began licking the come off his cock, not stopping until it was soft again.

George told her to get dressed and go back to the party. "I'll be up there in a minute," he informed her. Jenny put her bathing suit back on. But before she could leave, George grabbed her and asked, "Are you my fuck-slave?" She nodded her head yes. "Do you want more of this cock?" Again she said yes. He told her that later on in the evening they would have another opportunity to be alone. My wife looked at him and smiled, then left.

I was completely stunned by what had just happened. I'd just watched my wife become a complete slut for my boss, doing things for him that she'd never done with me, and loving it. I was hurt and angry, but also strangely excited—my cock was hard as a rock. When my erection had gone down to where it was no longer noticeable through my bathing suit, I got a few bottles of wine and went back upstairs to the bar.

My bartending shift ended a few minutes after I got back, at which time I went to find Jenny. She was stretched out on a chaise longue with a worried look on her face. She was probably wondering if I'd noticed that she'd been absent for thirty minutes. I told her I hoped she'd been having a good time, as I'd been too occupied behind the bar to spend time with her. She said, "George kept me busy meeting people, and we also danced a few times."

I tried to erase the truth from my mind, but I couldn't. The music was turned up, and men kept asking me if I minded if they asked Jenny to dance. Jenny loves to dance and I don't, so I couldn't really say anything but yes.

The party was really getting cranked up. I watched Jenny on the patio, sweating in the hot sun, covered with baby oil and just about naked. She was totally uninhibited, grinding her hips to the music, her big breasts bouncing with every move. All of the salesmen were loving it. On the slow songs, she'd always end up with some guy grinding his crotch into her. As she'd been drinking all day, she was so horny that she just ground back, eventually dry-humping pretty much every guy there. I could see the guys whispering to each other and nodding in her direction. They all seemed to believe that they had a good chance of fucking her before the party ended. And from the looks of it, they were right.

Her rear end was totally exposed, her bikini bottom bunched up between her ass-cheeks. Her nipples were also clearly outlined through the top of her suit. She danced with about eight different guys. The last dance was the worst. Henry, one of our top salesmen, had her in a slow dance, and in front of everyone he actually put his hand between the cheeks of her ass and rubbed. Jenny just giggled and kept grinding her crotch into his.

When the song ended, I asked her to come with me into the house. We found an unoccupied room to talk. My heart was pounding. I was angry and embarrassed, but again, my cock was like iron. I told Jenny I was tired of seeing her flaunting her body in front of all these men, but she just laughed and said that I was being ridiculous. As she spoke, she put her arms around my waist and rubbed up against me. She must have felt my erection, because she asked, "What have we got here?" She pulled my cock out of my suit and said, "Oh, I think you liked seeing me with those men, didn't you, honey?" She began stroking my cock. "I think watching those guys rubbing my butt got you all worked up."

I couldn't speak. I felt like I was going to explode. Jenny knelt down in front of me, said, "Let me make it all better for you," and began to suck on the head of my cock while pumping it with her hand. I came in about ten seconds, shooting a tremendous load into her mouth and down her throat, something she'd never let me do before. "You taste so good," she said, and continued nursing on my cock as I calmed down. She then told me that she'd just been flirting, and that I should be proud that all the guys thought she was sexy.

We went back to the party, and soon it started to get dark. I was thinking about George telling Jenny that they would have another opportunity to be alone, when he came up to me and asked me to be the designated driver for a few of his guests who were too drunk to drive. I had no choice but to agree. George said, "Don't worry about Jenny. We'll keep the party going until you get back."

I had five people to take home, the farthest one living about twenty miles away, so he figured I'd be gone for at least an hour. I drove like a wild man and, when I got back about forty minutes later, parked about a block away and walked up the driveway so as not to make a sound. The pool area was surrounded by hedges and was extremely well lighted. I could see in from about fifteen feet away, but they couldn't see me in the dark. When I looked in, I quickly realized that almost everyone had gone home. Jenny was reclining on a chaise longue and looked half-asleep. George was saying good-bye to some people. There were two other men, Kurt and Ted, from my sales group, standing at the bar.

When the others had left, George came back to the pool area, helped Jenny out of the chair and began to dance with her to a slow song. I could see Kurt and Ted closely watching to see what George was going to do. Kurt and Ted had been among those dancing with Jenny earlier in the evening, and had taken advantage of every opportunity to fondle her body. With the rest of the guests gone, George wasn't even subtle with Jenny. He gave Kurt and Ted a "thumbs up" signal, and they came over and sat down on a lounge chair, watching him.

Jenny had her arms around George's neck, and he was holding her ass-cheeks in his hands, whispering in her ear. He stopped dancing, turned her head toward him and began kissing her right in front of the other guys. I could see Jenny's mouth open to welcome the movements of George's tongue. He played with her breasts and squeezed her buns.

"Please, George, not in front of these other people," Jenny moaned. "Anyway, my husband will be back any minute."

George took her hand, put it on his cock and said, "If you want this again, baby—and I know you do—my friends get to watch. Anyway, it's not like we haven't done this already today. Now, take your suit off for us. Your husband won't be back for at least half an hour, and we'll be able to see his headlights from down the driveway."

Jenny stood there just looking at George, but she kept her hand on his cock, stroking it through his suit. George peeled off his bathing suit. His erection was enormous. Jenny immediately put her hand around it and said, "I know I shouldn't be doing this again—please don't let my husband find out." George smiled over at Ted and Kurt, then reached out and pulled Jenny's top off. He turned her around and, standing behind her, took one of her breasts in each hand. He said, "Gentlemen, little Jenny here is going to make us all very happy. Isn't that right, honey?" As he said this, he took her nipples between his thumbs and forefingers and she began moaning with desire.

Kurt and Ted stood up. It was then that I noticed Ted had a small video recorder in his hand. George led Jenny to the chaise longue, and she lay back as he pulled off her bikini bottom. Ted began to tape the action as George pushed her legs up and began working his cock into her pussy. Jenny was groaning and bucking her ass up, saying, "Yes, yes—fuck me George. Give me that big cock. Do it, baby. Do it." She was acting like a complete slut, and my coworkers were getting it all on tape.

Kurt knelt by her face and began rubbing his cock over her lips. Jenny didn't even hesitate. She opened wide and began to noisily suck his hard prick. Kurt told Ted to come in for a close-up as he fucked her mouth. "Suck that dick, Jenny," he moaned. "Tell me you love to feel it on your tongue."

"Oh, God, do I love it," Jenny said between licks. "It's so hard, so . . . big!"

George was fucking her really hard, slamming his big cock into her over and over again. He gave Jenny several huge orgasms. She was starting to shake incessantly, yelling, moaning and holding her legs up high so she could feel every inch of George's penis inside her.

After George came, he climbed off Jenny. She kept her legs completely spread open and continued sucking Kurt's cock. He suddenly stiffened and said, "I'm coming. Suck it down, little lady." Jenny was groaning and slobbering all over his big dick, totally out of control with lust. He pulled his cock out of her mouth and came all over her face. Kurt smiled at the camera, reached down and scooped up a large puddle of spunk from her chin. He told Jenny to suck it off his fingers, which she immediately did.

Ted had seen enough. He handed the camera to George and told Jenny to roll over and get on her hands and knees. Her ass was up in the air. Ted squirted baby oil all over her butt as he took off his suit. I couldn't believe the size of his dick. It was bigger than George's—bigger than any cock I'd ever seen. "Does your husband ever fuck your pretty ass?" he asked.

"No," she answered, "but I wish he would." I was shocked. Why hadn't she told me? I would've been glad to ass-fuck her. But now it looked as though the privilege of having first crack at it would go to Ted.

"Please don't hurt me," Jenny said. Then she reached back and spread her asshole wide open. Ted began to fuck her ass with his thumb, as George moved in with the camcorder for a close-up. Jenny was moaning, slowly grinding her ass against Ted's hand. "Oh, I've got to have it!" she suddenly blurted. "Fuck my ass with that big dick." Ted began to rub his cock across her asshole, then pushed forward and began to shove it in. Jenny was grunting and moaning louder and louder as he buried his prick in her ass. I couldn't believe it—he forced that gigantic cock all the way into my petite wife's tight ass!

Once it was all the way in, he began to shove it in and out with tremendous force. "You like that, baby?" he asked. "Push back against me. Feel my cock in there. Give me that ass." He was too excited to last very long, and in a few minutes had a tremendous orgasm. When he pulled out of her ass, he pried apart her ass-cheeks wide so George could get a shot of his big cock sliding out of the tight channel.

And they still weren't done with their fuck-fest! At her urging, Kurt flipped Jenny over on her back, straddled her chest and began rubbing his cock between her tits. I couldn't watch anymore, and went down to the car. I drove up the driveway slowly to let them know I was on my way back.

When I walked to the pool area, George said Jenny had taken a nap and was getting dressed. In a few minutes she came out with a dazed look on her face. George put his arm around her, told me I had a great wife and that he hoped we'd had a good time at his party. Kurt and Ted were both standing there smiling at me, their cocks still smelling of my wife.

On the way home, Jenny didn't talk much, except to say that she needed to take a shower. When we got home, I made sure to be in the bathroom when she emerged from the shower. I couldn't believe the way her body looked. Her nipples were red and swollen, and she had red marks on her breasts and thighs from all he rough sex she'd enjoyed. When we got into bed, I asked her if she'd had fun at the party. She said, "You know I did. I just hope you're not too mad at me for flirting with those guys."

I never did tell my wife that I knew exactly what happened at the party. Nor did I tell her that thinking about her sucking and fucking other men got my cock harder than it had ever been. But as a result of what I saw that day, Jenny and I now have fantastic sex. George now schedules me to be out of town about two times a month, and I know that during these intervals Jenny goes to his house for wild sex with him and his horny friends. She always tells me she's out with her girlfriends, but I know where she really is. When I think about her with George's cock in her mouth, or Ted's cock crammed up her ass, I can fuck like a thoroughbred.—*Name and address withheld*

PILOT COMES IN FOR A LANDING WHERE THE SUN NEVER SHINES

I am a thirty-three-year-old female who has just divorced after a fourteen-year marriage. My body isn't that great, but I love to use it. I am an avid crotch-watcher, something of an exhibitionist, and I love to make love!

About two months ago, I began noticing a friend of my ex-husband. What I began noticing, actually, was the hard bulge in his pants whenever I was around. Neither of us being the aggressive type, it wasn't until we got drunk together that we finally ended up in the sack. Neither of us had ever been with anyone other than our spouses. Since then, we have had an incredible love affair. We have made love in so many places—his plane, his hangar, his office, on the road, in his truck, in parks . . . we've managed to have sex just about everywhere we've been alone together. The best part is we are also the best of friends.

When we first met, he was still married, but I couldn't help myself. He has the kind of body women crave. I could just sink into his broad shoulders, slim waist and firm butt. His cock is long enough to touch bottom when we fuck, and also quite thick. He is uncircumcised, which has proved to be a lot of fun for me. I love playing with his foreskin. And does he have endurance! Oddly enough, he doesn't realize how sexy he really is, the result being that he's modest and doesn't try to act like a stud.

Mike is an airline pilot, which causes him to be out of town for long periods of time. Recently he was gone for two and a half weeks. While we were able to talk and fantasize for hours each day on the phone, it just wasn't the same as being in the bed together. The sexual frustration was building up in both of us.

Finally one morning he called to inform me that he would be back in just thirteen hours. His wife was out of town, so the night would be ours. It was the Fourth of July weekend, and as I watched the fireworks from my front yard, I grew wet with anticipation thinking about the fireworks that would take place in my bedroom that night.

He got to my house at five minutes to midnight. I met him at the door and gave him the biggest kiss and hug he'd ever had. We made our way to the kitchen so I could fix us a drink. He couldn't keep his hands off my body! I managed to get the ice and bourbon into our glasses while he stood behind me kissing, sucking and biting my neck and shoulders. My neck is extremely sensitive, so this was driving me nuts.

While his mouth was busy on my neck and shoulders, his hands roved under my shirt and kneaded my braless tits. I was grinding my butt against his incredibly hard dick. We were still standing in the kitchen when I turned around and undid his pants, pulled out his dick and began playing with the hard, swollen flesh. He unbuttoned my shirt and started sucking on my tits.

We decided to move to my bedroom. We grabbed our drinks and literally ran up the stairs, tugging at each other's clothes on the way. Mike quickly stripped off the rest of my clothes—but I removed his clothes even faster! He kept commenting that it was going to be a long night without sleep, which was all right by me. We are both very oral, and couldn't keep our mouths off each other. He was sucking and biting my tits and nipples, while I kissed and sucked anything I could reach. He knows I love to suck his cock, so we finally ended up in a 69.

I was devouring his meat, balls and butt-cheeks while he kept himself busy sucking and licking my pussy and tonguing my asshole. He has a very talented mouth! Butts are a major turn-on for both of us, so we always spend as much time as we can probing them with our fingers and tongues getting the most out of our lovemaking.

After getting him close to orgasm, but not letting him come just yet, I rolled him on his back, straddled his cock and gave him a ride to remember. He loves coming with me on top, and I usually climax three to four times this way myself. I pumped up and down on his stiff-as-a-board cock, and seemed to come on every downstroke! After two and a half weeks without my man, it felt fantastic. It didn't take long before he exploded deep inside my pussy.

One great thing about Mike is that once he's come, it takes him just a couple of minutes to get hard again, and then he can fuck for hours. We shut off the lights and got down to some serious lovemaking. I pulled him on top of me and let him use that beautiful tool on me in a way my ex-husband never could. I wrapped my legs around his waist and he proceeded to stroke deep and hard, filling me completely with every thrust.

While he's thrusting into me, I like to finger-fuck his butt. It makes his dick throb and gets him so horny that he pumps into me a mile a minute, guaranteeing me a fantastic climax or two. This night he surprised me by asking, "Do you want me to fuck your ass?" Although we always played with each other's asshole, we'd never gone that extra mile. In fact, I'd never had a cock in my anus. But with Mike, I knew it would be fantastic.

"Yeah," I said. "Stick it right in my virgin hole."

Mike seemed especially delighted that I'd never been butt-fucked before. He reached into my nightstand and took out some baby oil. I massaged it all over his cock and balls, as well as on my asshole. After lubing us up, I fingered his bunghole and said, "That's where I want you to give it to me."

I stopped finger-fucking and got on all fours. We both grunted loudly as, inch by inch, his fat dick sank into my asshole. What an intense feeling—it was like being fucked for the first time. I loved it!

My asshole was so tight that I could feel every vein and curve of Mike's dick as it traveled in and out of my chute. The orgasms I experienced as he did this were unlike any I'd ever had before. They seemed to start from deep within my gut and explode outward until every part of me was tingling—even my scalp!

Mike couldn't hold back his climax for long. "I have to come!" he announced breathlessly.

"Pull out and soak my ass," I told him. He took his cock out of me just as the first blasts of semen spewed forth, bathing my buns in a creamy coating of sperm that he rubbed into my skin like lotion.

After some cuddling, we got up, showered and then sat up all night drinking and talking about his trip. I'm sure that in the years to come I'll have plenty more to write about the time Mike and I spend together. For now, let me just say that my ass, pussy and tits have never been happier.—*A.P., San Jose, California*   O⊢▣

<u>Pursuit & Capture</u>

SEX-STARVED MARINE IS GUNG-HO FOR LOVING
AFTER BOOT CAMP DEPRIVATION

I am a young marine stationed at a base in the South. I come from a small town in Iowa, where I have a very sexy young lady waiting for me. Her name is Jenny. Before I was stationed at this base, I attended boot camp on Parris Island. While I was in boot camp, the only thing I could think of was my beautiful hometown honey. There were many times when thoughts of making hard, passionate love to her were all that kept me going. At least once a week I would have a wet dream in which she was the star attraction. She has an excellent body and an awesome pussy, so you can understand how horny I was most of the time.

I was thrilled when graduation day finally arrived. Although boot camp had seemed like it would go on forever, it was finally over and I knew I'd get to see my honey again. I could hardly wait! Jenny accompanied my mother and stepfather to the Parris Island graduation ceremony. She wore a beautiful floral print dress that showed just enough skin to tease me. Of course I couldn't look at her very much during the ceremony for fear of my madman drill instructor jumping all over my ass, but I snuck a peek at her whenever I thought the coast was clear. There I was, standing ramrod straight in the scorching heat with a huge hard-on in front of hundreds of people. I couldn't wait to get the fuck off that island and sink my cock into my baby doll's hot, wet pussy.

Immediately after graduation, Jenny and I headed for home. I had a two-week furlough before I would be shipped off to my first assignment, and I was really looking forward to having some time off. Since Iowa is a long drive from South Carolina, we planned to stop off at a motel to spend the night. When we arrived at the motel, I felt myself getting extremely nervous as well as excited. After all, it had been a *long* three months without any sex in boot camp! I was dying to feel Jenny's mounds of flesh in my mouth and to feel her tight pussy engulfing my cock. Although on one hand I couldn't wait, I was also feeling some performance anxiety. After all, we hadn't been together in months.

When we got to the room and slowly started to kiss and caress each other, it was like our first time all over again. After about fifteen minutes of foreplay, I slowly started to take off her dress, which I had been dying to take off for hours anyhow. First I exposed her tits. Her nipples were hard as rocks. Let me tell you, they were a sight for sore eyes!

It wasn't long before I had her completely undressed and lying on the bed. I immediately started to run my tongue all around the hot lips of her sex. She squirmed in ecstasy under me. She was so wet, and her juices tasted so good, that I licked up every drop of pussy juice that I could get from her.

She begged me to fuck her, and by this time I had the biggest throbbing hard-on that I'd ever had in my life. I slowly took off my pants and exposed myself to tease her a little. I stood there for a minute to show off my new, hardened Marine Corps body. She was quite horny, so she just grabbed my ass-cheeks and pulled me down on top of her.

I ran my cock up and down her slit to stimulate her a little more. When she couldn't handle it any longer, she grabbed my cock and guided it into her pussy. Her tunnel was so tight I could hardly believe it. It felt so good, I came almost immediately. I shot a huge load of come into her.

My cock continued to stay hard, so I kept on going because it felt too awesome to quit. Besides, she was loving it, and I didn't want to let her down. After about half an hour of steady pumping, I blew my second wad into her. By this time she had had several serious orgasms and was squirming all over the bed. I love it when she does that. I actually enjoy her orgasms more than my own, because it gives me a great deal of pleasure to know that I have satisfied her completely.

The sex we had that night was probably the best we've ever had. We have been lovers for almost two years, but that night was simply awesome. After all, they do say that absence makes the heart grow fonder! I'd like to add that it also makes the dick grow harder! You never forget the first time you and the woman you cherish make love, and you never forget the best time either.—
C.J., Cedar Rapids, Iowa

WHEN YOU CAN'T SLEEP, HERE'S SOMETHING TO DO BESIDES COUNTING SHEEP

I'm lying in bed naked. You're all I can think of. It's so lonely here. I can't sleep. I wish you were here with me. I pretend that you are lying next to me in bed. I imagine that I can even hear you breathing.

I turn to lie on you, resting my head on your chest. You put your arm around me and pull me closer. I start to play with your nipples. My tongue slowly circles your left nipple as my fingers caress your right nipple. You moan lightly. I slowly suck on your left nipple as I move my hand down your stomach.

My hand reaches the waistband of your briefs. As I start to lick your neck, I slowly slip my hand into your underwear. I gently touch the tip of your penis, and you moan and pull me even closer. I tilt your head toward me and press my lips against yours. Our mouths open and our tongues begin to dance a slow dance. My hand strokes your penis and your balls. Our kiss grows more passionate. Your penis becomes hard and erect. I run my fingertips lightly up and down the shaft, hearing you moan with passion.

I pull away from your lips and start to nibble on your ear. You reach over and cup my left breast, squeezing it lightly. You tease my nipple with your fingertips and I squeeze your penis. Then I push your hand away and lean over to suck your nipples. My tongue playfully moves from the left one to the right one. Next it travels down your stomach to your underwear. I pull off your briefs and move down to the foot of the bed to suck your big toe. Then I start licking my way back up the inside of your leg.

When I reach your scrotum, I gently suck your right ball and then your left. My mouth moves up and I take your penis into my mouth. My head bobs up and down while my tongue dances around your penis. I caress your inner thighs with my hands as I suck, suck, suck your penis.

I lift my head and dangle my breasts over your penis and balls. I move my body up onto yours and we kiss hungrily. You roll me over and suck on my tit. Your fingers play with my nipple. My legs are spread wide with desire. Your hand moves down and you slowly play with my clit. You push a finger deep inside me. You remove it and bring it to my lips to suck dry.

Then your head goes down to suck the sweet juices out of my cunt. Just when I feel as if I am going to explode with passion, I lift your head. I position your penis between my breasts and slowly tit-fuck you, pressing them tightly around your cock. Suddenly you explode, bathing the sheets with your semen. I scoop some up and massage it into me like an exotic oil, making my breasts sticky.

As I turn over to kiss you, I realize you are not there. It was only a dream.—*L.M., New York, New York* ⚷

SIXTIES REVIVAL CONCERT HELPS BRING BACK THE SUMMER OF LOVE

Last summer my brother dropped by one evening to invite me and my roommate to a sixties rock 'n' roll revival concert he had tickets for. When I heard who was going to be playing—Hot Tuna, The Band and Iron Butterfly—I knew I had to go! I had never had the chance to see these groups in concert when I was younger, and I didn't know if I'd have the opportunity again. I was especially looking forward to seeing Iron Butterfly because they'd always been one of my favorite groups. In fact, their song, "In-A-Gadda-Da-Vida," was my absolute favorite song. So we headed for the club they were to play at that night.

We got there much too early, so we had to wait to get in. Fortunately we came prepared with some beer and several joints, so the time passed quickly as we partied and hung out. Finally they opened the front door, and we got seats at a table on the second-floor balcony. It was a small club, so no matter where you sat you had a great view of the stage.

The first group soon took the stage and started jamming, and shortly after that I lit up another joint and passed it around. By this time we were all having an excellent time and feeling pretty mellow. We were really getting into the music, and seeing so many foxy ladies—many of whom were wearing miniskirts or short shorts—made it even more enjoyable. After the first group left the stage, I got up from the table to take a walk around the club and check out some of the babes.

The place was packed, and by the time I had made my way to the other side of the dance floor, the second group had come on. I walked out toward the middle of the floor, where the crowd swelled up in front of the stage, to get a better look at the band. I started dancing in place along with the music, trying to be careful not to bump into anyone. Every once in a while some beautiful creature just passing by would stop for a minute to dance a few steps with me before continuing on.

By the way, I'm about six foot three and weigh about one hundred seventy-five pounds, so I'm on the slender side. I'm a relatively good-looking (and freckleless) redhead, with wavy, shoulder-length hair, blue eyes and a neatly trimmed beard. That night I was dressed rather nicely in blue jeans, a white shirt and a blue-and-white striped jacket. After the second group played their set, I went back to our balcony table to tell my brother and my roommate what a good time I was having even though I didn't have a lady friend along with me.

Before I could say a word, my roommate told my brother to check out the foxy chick in black shorts. He pointed toward a girl who was standing on the right side of the stage in front of the speaker column, and handed my brother the binoculars. Now the place was rather small, so the binoculars really weren't necessary, but when I spotted this babe I borrowed them next. She definitely deserved a close-up look!

What I saw was a gorgeous, well-rounded ass sitting on top of the best-looking pair of legs in the entire club. These luscious charms belonged to a petite blonde who was wearing black shorts and a black halter top. Her hair fell gracefully past her shoulders. I handed my roommate the field glasses and said to myself, "Now instead of just sitting here, why don't you give these guys a lesson in the art of picking up girls. Just light up a cigarette and walk down there. If you stand by that chrome pole you'll be able to see whether or not her face matches the rest of her." To be honest, I was feeling a little nervous about it, but the next thing I knew I had a lit cigarette in my hand. So I got up and went back down to the dance floor. When I had made my way to the chrome pole, I moved over next to her, trying to act nonchalant although my heartbeat was beating a hundred times faster than the music. My heart rate slowed considerably, though, when I saw she was talking to a guy standing next to her. I figured that he must be her boyfriend, so I resigned myself to just seeing Iron Butterfly up close. They came on soon after that, and were totally hot. They even played some new material and really kept the tempo going. I play the guitar myself, so I appreciate the smooth transition a good group can make when segueing into the next song.

This dynamite lady was dancing in place right at the edge of the stage, and I thought to myself, those boobs of hers are going to be sore by the end of the night if they keep hitting the stage that way. She wasn't very tall, so her perfectly rounded boobs were just an inch or so above the stage, and she was bopping around so much that her tits kept bumping into the stage. I started dancing to the music too and really began to get into it. She and I even did the Bump together for a few minutes. I tell you, that really picked my spirits up!

When she wasn't dancing, she'd prop herself up on the edge of the stage with her arms, her feet off the ground, and bend over onto the stage from the waist up, seemingly trying to get as close to the band as possible. Every time she did this, I was offered a tantalizing side view of her exposed ass-cheeks. After a bit of these gymnastics, her arms were obviously getting tired. I noticed that no help was being offered by the guy she had been talking to, so I wondered what would happen if I gave her a helping hand to stay up there. As I placed my right hand on the stage and caught a whiff of an excited female's odor, I suddenly realized what this chick was doing. I could feel the stage vibrate under my hand, and she was obviously using it as the world's largest vibrator.

Well, instead of giving her a helping hand, I simply shifted my left leg behind her (I had been pressing my body against her for some time now and she hadn't given me any signs that she wanted to move away), allowing her to straddle my leg. It was a little awkward, but since she was so light I was able to easily support her weight. Now she could freely lie down and get back up without taxing her arm muscles. Can anyone guess why this had me looking more and more to my left and less and less at the band? Well, while taking all this in, I noticed another couple on the other side of the stage. The guy was holding the girl up, and he was right behind her, his crotch pressed firmly against her ass-cheeks.

A couple of times the lead guitarist came right in front of us, and each time this lady I was holding up would reach out and try to touch him. Every time he came close, she really started going crazy! Finally I made my move. While my hand was around her waist to hold her up, I positioned myself behind her, like the other couple. With my crotch right at stage level, I soon realized that my bikini briefs were so tight they were a hindrance for my full-fledged hard-on, but talk about being in seventh heaven! I was finding out how well a natural in-and-out tempo, which all males are familiar with, went with the beat of the music. For all that anyone could see us knew, we might have been getting it on. Upon reflection, I know that's what it probably looked like.

For the first time I got a little nervous and looked around to see if anyone was watching us. When I turned to the right, my head bumped into a camera that a brunette lady was positioning to take a picture of something. Probably just the band, I thought, but maybe I should give her something even hotter to photograph! Just then, the band started playing their biggest hit from the sixties and my all-time favorite song, "In-A-Gadda-Da-Vida."

My honey in front of me was definitely going to town! And since the band played a version that was much longer than the seventeen-minute version found on the album, I was going to town too. Now I had time to make things much more comfortable for myself by rearranging the position of my cock. During the long solo halfway through the song, she did something incredible. This time, as she lay down on the stage, she pulled her left knee up on top of the stage, giving me a bird's-eye view of her crotch. I could see that this natural blonde (who made my heart and my manhood jump!) was more than turned on. She was totally into it!

That sensuous odor of hers was really strong now. I was definitely grateful for the fact that her shorts were only made of a thin cotton material! She pulled both her knees all the way up to her breasts. And I thought I had seen everything before! One phrase from the sixties said it all: "Outta sight!" What I said before about appreciating a group's continuity was never more evident than now: the band never missed a beat, and neither did I! But there's one thing I truly regret I didn't do. At the moment when she first brought her leg all the way up, I had this instinctive thought to place my left hand on the inside of her right thigh and insert my thumb right into the crotch of her shorts. But, although she had allowed all this to happen, I just didn't know how far she wanted me to go, so I really didn't dare to. Instead I placed my hand along the underside of her left leg while continuing to thrust my pelvis into her.

After that real long improvised solo, the group went back to finishing the song, and I'm sure my lady finished what she had started. I know she finished, because I felt her body spasm and then go limp in my arms! I was fit to be tied! All of a sudden the song was over and the band was saying their good-byes. They mentioned the name of a club they'd be playing at a few nights later, but I didn't quite catch the name. I asked my blonde Aphrodite if she'd heard it. The brunette with the camera chimed in, while throwing me a book of matches, that they'd be playing at the club named on the cover. She said that they'd just come from there. I didn't know if she meant my blonde honey and herself or not, but I definitely wanted to see them again, and my lady indicated she planned on being there too.

I made plans to attend the show that night but, unfortunately, I couldn't make it. So now my only hope of meeting her would be if she reads this letter. Then she'll know to meet me at that club on the last Saturday of the month of the issue that this letter appears in. I'll be there wearing the same blue-and-white striped jacket, waiting to properly thank her for the fantasy that I relive every night in my dreams of that totally erotic evening!—*Name and address withheld* O⌷—

ONE MAN RECOUNTS THE JOYS OF INTEGRATED SEX IN A SMALL TOWN

I've been carrying on an affair for several months now. I live in a small, conservative Southern town, so it's imperative that we be very discreet—especially since I am black and my lover is white.

There is a saying, "Once you've had black, you'll never go back!" I think I must concur. Certainly, after Lila had had a taste of my nine-and-a-half-inch ebony cock, she kept coming back for more. We both knew we were playing with fire, but neither of us was willing to end our relationship, and it kept getting better and better. We carried on our interracial affair practically under the noses of the people in this close-knit community.

As I relived the details in my mind after each encounter, I found that words couldn't do justice to the intense feelings that we were experiencing each time we made love together during our clandestine weekly meetings. Lila's husband frequently traveled on business, keeping him away from home much of the time. This gave us ample opportunities to meet, often for extended periods of time.

At first we met in motels, changing them every so often to ensure that no one was getting suspicious. Whenever we had a liaison planned, she would either call me at work to tell me the time and place of our next meeting, or I would manage to slip over to her office to see her. We had sex in both my car and hers. Once we even made love in the parking lot of her office during our lunch break.

Once we'd decided on the where and when of our next meeting, and actually rendezvoused, our guard would let down and out inhibitions would be shed, and we would throw ourselves wholeheartedly into the lovemaking session.

Lila's favorite position for making love was her on top. She loved to straddle my large cock, then settle down on it, taking it in slow and grinding her pelvis up and down until she had it fully embedded in her pussy. On each of her downstrokes, she supported her body with her arms, allowing her big, ivory breasts to brush against my face. I generally offered verbal encouragement like, "Yeah, baby, work your sweet pussy down on my love-tool," and "Yeah, now work that hot, sweet pelvis around in circles, girl." My dick was large enough to stimulate her love-button, so it is no surprise that she experienced multiple orgasms from the very first session.

One night we even made love in her house—in the master bedroom, no less! She had contacted me at work, explaining that her husband was off at a business conference in another part of the state and wouldn't be home for a few days. She told me that I should come to her house after dark.

I must admit that my heart was thumping wildly in my well-developed chest as I casually strolled down her street. Despite the advances made in race relations, I can tell you that the sight of a black man walking down a darkened street in the white section of town is not that common. Glancing around to be sure no one was watching me, I quickly opened the gate in front of her house and walked around the the back door.

I knocked on the door. When she opened it, though the lights were all out, I could see that she was visibly excited. As we embraced there in the kitchen, I could feel her voluptuous body trembling. My hands began tearing off her dress and rolling her panties down over her wide, womanly hips. When her big, jiggly breasts spilled out, my thick lips latched onto the nipples. "I want to fuck you on your bed." I mumbled thickly, suddenly overcome by the roaring haze of lust that gripped us.

"Yes . . . yes . . . I want that too," she gasped as she unzipped my slacks and pulled them off. My massive prick was already jutting out of the waistband of my jockey shorts. As we stumbled to the bedroom, her hand was groping in my shorts and grabbing at my rock-hard ebony rod. We fell across the bed, our lips fused together in a hot, sizzling kiss, while my hands roamed all over her back, down to her ass-cheeks. Lila rolled over on her back and spread her shapely white thighs. I was poised for a quick, deep entry. As she writhed with lust, I positioned myself between her thighs and shoved my throbbing nine-and-a-half-inch cock into her cunt. From then on, it was onward to paradise. She had one climax after another. I held my thick cock deep in her cunt while she worked her ass up and down.

Hot juices poured out of her love-tunnel and ran down the cheeks of her ass. Lila shuddered in yet another climax, gripping my broad, muscular shoulders with her hands as she pumped her cunt up to meet each of my downward thrusts. We knew this time was special, and that I would joyously unload my thick, white, forbidden sperm deep into the clasping velvet of her cunt. "Aw, baby, I'm gonna shoot my load," I rasped into her ear. The bed shook as we experienced a simultaneous climax, clasping and thumping our naked, sweating bodies together.

Finally we lay still. I could feel my sperm oozing down her crotch and pooling on the clean sheets of her and her husband's bed. This turned her on so much that we made love for another hour, until I had to leave.

Such impassioned encounters help make our affair as special as it is. However, nothing can surpass what happened last night. Thinking about it has kept my dick hard all day long. Some time ago I had mailed a letter to your magazine describing my first encounter with Lila. When I opened up last month's issue, I was overjoyed to see that my letter had finally been printed. I knew I had to see Lila and share the surprise. I called her and told her I needed to see her that night. Though it was not one of our regularly scheduled meeting nights, she did agree to meet me at our usual motel for a little while after work.

At the appointed time Lila let herself in, her face showing the strain of excitement and apprehension. (She was afraid that I had called this sudden meeting so I could tell her that someone had found out about us.) Needless to say, she was relieved to see my naked body reclining on the bed, sporting an enormous hard-on. As she undressed, she got more and more into the excitement that I was conveying with my smiling face and raging hard-on. Then she noticed the copy of *Penthouse Letters* lying open on the bed. "Read the letter on that page!" I said hoarsely, as she snuggled up alongside me. My dick had never been harder. I was feasting on her nipples and playing with her wet pussy when she began to understand the meaning of the letter. She finally realized that I had sent in a letter about the two of us, and it really turned her on.

As she continued to read, I slid my body on top of hers and rubbed my cock up and down her slippery gash before entering her. The magazine fell to the floor as we consummated our passion. Lila's voluptuous body met mine in the rhythm of integrated sex. She lost track of the number of times she'd climaxed, and I thought that my load was never thicker nor as profuse as that night. Maybe we'll never surpass that moment, but I'm sure we'll try. And I have to confess that once a black man has fucked a white pussy, there's definitely no turning back for him either.— *A.J., Mobile, Alabama*

ALL IT TOOK FOR THIS WIDOW TO BE MERRY AGAIN WAS A LITTLE OF THE OLD IN AND OUT

Last spring, my next door neighbor Helen, a widow who happens to be sixty-three years old, asked if I would assist her in cleaning out her storage shed. I have lived next door to Helen for twenty-eight years, and in that time have watched her daughters grow into beautiful women. This was not hard to understand, as Helen has always been quite an attractive woman herself. After her husband died fifteen years ago, I had never known her to date or have men come to visit her. All that time I had been quietly curious about her private life, but I didn't want to pry, so I never asked her about it.

Cleaning out the shed was hard work. Helen and I spent the whole day moving all the stacks of boxes, lawn tools, bicycles and what have you, out of the shed and onto the lawn, where Helen could go through the things and decide what to keep and what to throw away. I was just picking up one of the last wooden crates from a dark corner of the shed, when all of a sudden I heard Helen scream out at the top of her lungs. I dropped the box and turned around just in time to see a huge black snake slither past Helen and out the door. Helen leaped straight for me. Instinctively, I held my arms out wide for her, and she jumped right into them. She clung tightly to me, with her arms around my neck and her legs around my waist, and continued to scream.

To keep us from falling over, I innocently clutched her ass in the palms of my hands and pulled her to me. Still whimpering and shaking, she held on for dear life and squeezed her legs tighter around my body. Well, as nature will have it, I started to pop one of those hard-as-a-nightstick boners that often come up at the most inappropriate times. However, the timing for this hard-on wasn't as inappropriate as it seemed.

As Helen's fears passed, she began to feel my hard cock pressing against her. Her cheeks turned a rosy red, but she didn't make any effort to pull away. As we lingered there, locked in our embrace, our eyes met. Beyond her embarrassment at feeling my hard-on, I sensed in Helen a need to be held. I did so without a word, until she finally relaxed her grip and allowed her feet to touch the ground. She quickly returned to her work, and I went outside the shed, found the snake and disposed of it.

After the job was completed, I went home to shower and relax. That night, with the events of the day playing over and over in my mind, I decided to grab a bottle of wine and head for Helen's place.

Helen answered the door in a white bathrobe. "I feel like socializing," I said. "How about a glass of wine?"

Helen invited me in, and went to the kitchen to get some glasses. I sat down on the large, overstuffed sofa in the den and opened up the wine. She came back in with two big water glasses, and I poured each about half full.

"I haven't had wine in years," she said as she sipped from her glass. It was only a few minutes before the wine began to affect Helen. She began to make jokes and tell me how light-headed she was feeling.

She rose to her feet, swaying slightly, and told me she had to go to the bathroom. I poured some more wine. When she returned, she sat down beside me again, only this time she allowed her robe to open slightly, just enough for me to see that she wasn't wearing anything underneath. She rested her shoulder against mine, and I felt my cock stirring the way it had that afternoon in the storage shed.

"I shouldn't have any more wine," she giggled, "but it's so relaxing! Maybe just a few more sips." As she drained her glass, I moved closer to her and put my right hand on her bare left leg.

"What are you doing?" she asked. Before I could answer, she started talking about her husband. She told me that there had never been anyone in her life but him. "He was my first, and probably my last," she said. But she did not move my hand away from her leg, and neither did I.

"I know what you want," she said, "but it's been so long."

I inched my hand up her thigh. She trembled and rested her hand on mine. I took the hint and moved my hand up higher, parting her robe and laying my palm against her cunt. Her cunt was wetter than any I'd ever touched. I pulled her robe wide open to bare her breasts. They were much firmer than I'd expected, and the nipples were full and puffy, jutting out like two ripe grapes. I wanted to feel them on my tongue, so I lowered my mouth to her left breast and lingered there, sucking the soft tit-flesh until her nipple hardened between my lips.

I moved from one tit to the other, delighted to feel her nipples get so stiff in my mouth. As they got harder, so did my prick. I had such an incredible erection it felt like it was going to tear through my zipper.

Soon my middle finger was groping and searching, prying apart Helen's moist pussy lips. She slid forward on the sofa to allow me easier access. Soon her juices began to flow like a waterfall as I pumped my finger in and out of her twitching twat.

"Please lick me there," she said in a breathy whisper.

I stood up and kicked off my shoes, then lowered my pants and briefs and stepped out of them. My wide prick was stiff and pointing straight up.

"It's so beautiful," she said with a look of pure desire. "It's so much different than my husband's was. It's so fat. Do you think it'll fit inside me?"

"I know it will fit," I said. "But first I want to get you ready for me." I sank to my knees in front of her and plunged into her fuck-hole with my tongue.

"Oh!" she cried out. "That feels so good. My husband never did that. Don't stop!" My tongue darted in and out of her. I feasted on her soft cunt lips and lapped hungrily at her clit. With a loud gasp she reached orgasm, groaning and sighing and pulling me against her so that my tongue stayed firmly planted inside her long-neglected pussy.

"I want you," Helen said after a few minutes, casting off her robe and lying back on the couch. I grabbed her ankles in my hands and held her legs up high. With one sure thrust, I sank my prick into her pouting pussy. Fully and firmly implanted in her, I released my grasp on her ankles and pumped into her. Helen met each of my thrusts with a grunt of pleasure. Her cunt began to grip and tighten around my prick and, each time I pushed into her, sucking me in. I took her sweaty ass in my hands and pulled her hard against me. "I can't hold it in!" I said aloud, and erupted inside her, the hot jets of come blasting from my cock. Helen took my balls in her hand and kneaded them as my come spewed forth. She trembled and quaked as she continued to take my hard thrusts, riding me to one final orgasm.

When it was over we collapsed on the couch. Helen was simply glowing. I knew how long her husband had been dead, and couldn't imagine how she was able to endure not fucking anyone for so many years. I was happy, though, to be there when she finally released all that pent-up lust. I looked down and saw that her pussy was a vivid pink, and knew then that I would be spending a lot of time enjoying the pleasures it had to offer.

Since that night, Helen and I get together for dinner a few times a week. We have a great meal, then retire to her bedroom where we fuck, suck and enjoy each other to the fullest. Needless to say, my desire to fuck only young women is now a thing of the past.—*Name and address withheld*

COMPUTER-ROOM RENDEZVOUS GETS THE BEST OUT OF HIS HARD DRIVE AND HER SOFTWARE

Six months ago, when Risa was first hired at our company, I could scarcely believe my eyes. Having already spent a year there surrounded by people who were at least a dozen years my senior, I was overjoyed that I would now have a golden-haired goddess of my own age working a mere two doors down from me. Immediately my mind was full of fantasies involving her: blowjobs under my desk, quick fucks in the rest room, doggie-style humping behind the hedges in the park at lunchtime.

Risa is a knockout in the truest sense of the word. She has the type of tits you dream about, big and full and never constrained by a bra, with large nipples that make themselves known through the fabric of whatever outfit she's wearing. Her legs, creamy and smooth beneath the shorts she always wears, are long and muscular. Her luscious limbs form the perfect pedestal for an ass that swishes back and forth when she walks. I must admit that I dripped my share of pre-come just from watching her, and more than once raced home after work in order to jerk off to the fantasy of her taking the hard thrusts of my cock.

The only thing about Risa that wasn't appealing was her firm belief that coworkers shouldn't date, an opinion that had caused me and my raging hormones endless consternation. But despite her steadfast refusal to have anything to do with me outside the office, Risa and I became good friends at work.

One night I agreed to stay late with her so that she could finish some work she had fallen behind on. Everyone else had left the office, except for the janitor. At about nine that night I heard Risa come out of her office, walk down the hall and go into one of the computer rooms. Soon I heard the printer spitting out paper, and assumed that she was running hard copies on the work she'd been doing all night long.

I'd noticed long before that, while waiting for printouts, Risa had a habit of leaning forward with her hands on the printer and swaying her hips ever so slightly back and forth, as though dancing to music no one else could hear. Hoping I could watch her move her butt a little, I quietly rolled my chair over to the other side of my office, from where I could see directly into the computer room. What I saw, however, was far better than I could've imagined.

Risa had wheeled over the little green chair that sits in the computer room. With her right foot on the floor, and her left knee on the seat, she straddled the back of the chair. As I watched in mute fascination, she slid her crotch forward and back along the top of the chair, humping herself silly! She did it slowly at first, but soon was jerking and wriggling and rubbing hard against the chair, bringing herself to orgasm. By the smile on her face and the quivering of her entire body, I could tell that she must have been working up quite a lather down below. For my part, my raging hard-on was a testament to the fact that I was more turned on than I'd ever been in my life.

It was obvious that Risa was feeling more than a little horny. I couldn't help wondering if this would be the night I could get her to break her vow about dating coworkers—although, as you can imagine, going out on a date with her was the last thing on my mind. What I really wanted was to slip my aching cock into her pussy and give her the fuck of her life.

Quietly rolling my chair back to the other side of my office so that she wouldn't see me if she turned around, I got up. I then made as much noise as I could, in order to alert her to my approach. Ten seconds later, I headed for the computer room.

When I got there, she was standing beside the chair she'd just been riding, watching the printer and trying her best to look nonchalant. "Hi, Robert," she said, turning to me. "I was just—" But then she stopped talking. I noticed that her cheeks were flushed red. Perhaps it was my shit-eating grin, or perhaps it was the conspiratorial twinkle in my eye. Maybe, I thought, it was the way my cock was making a tent in my pants the size of a circus big-top. In any case, it was clear that she realized I knew what she'd been up to.

Neither of us said a word. We stood staring at each other in awkward silence for a long time as I tried to think of what to do next. Fortunately Risa acted first. She reached out, wrapped her hand around my cock-bulge and pulled me toward her. Our open mouths met in a deep and passionate kiss that made my toes curl (and probably would have done the same to my hair were it not curly already). I wrapped my arms tightly around her as our tangling tongues tried to caress the deepest regions of each other's mouth. In my excitement at having finally gotten this far with such a beautiful woman, my hands roamed lower, caressing her big breasts and massaging her soft ass.

Suddenly Risa pushed me away. I groaned inwardly, thinking that I had moved too quickly or that she had just remembered that she didn't want to get involved with a coworker. Thankfully I was mistaken. She dropped to her knees in front of me, quickly fumbled with my belt and zipper, then pulled my pants to the ground. Released from its confines, my dick sprang forward and bounced a few times against the bridge of her nose.

In an instant Risa was sucking lightly on my cockhead while gently rolling my balls between her fingers. For all her hurrying to get to this point, Risa certainly took her time now. She started by pushing my shaft flat against my belly so that she could use her lips and tongue on my scrotum, licking and tugging at the sac until I was ready to shed tears of joy. The feel of her hot breath against my manhood was enough to make me shake all over. She sucked first one, then the other of my balls into her mouth. Then, still holding my dick flush against my stomach, Risa began to lick up and down the sensitive, veiny underside.

Just when her tickling tongue had brought me to a fever pitch of excitement, Risa changed her approach. Opening her mouth wide to receive me, she grabbed my ass-cheeks with both hands and pulled me in. She took as much of me into her mouth as would fit, which was a considerable amount, and began pumping her head briskly back and forth on my limb. Her tongue danced along my shaft the whole time, rolling up and down the underside and sliding to the right and left. Occasionally she sucked both balls into her mouth at once. The sensation was so intensely pleasurable that I thought for sure I was going to lose my mind!

In very short order I began to feel that glorious feeling bubbling up within my balls. I managed to gasp, "Risa stop. You're going to make me come!" before frantically looking around the computer room for someplace I could shoot my load where it wouldn't short-circuit thousands of dollars worth of equipment.

Fortunately Risa was not about to let me ruin any expensive computer hardware. She let my dick slide loose from her lips just long enough to look up and give me a wide, knowing smile, then returned to what she'd been doing with increased energy. Seconds later I wrapped my fingers in her golden hair and began to buck my hips with wild abandon. With a loud groan, I exploded inside her mouth. I could hear her take three huge, gulping swallows as all of my hot, creamy semen made its way down her throat. Risa just kept sucking and swallowing until my hips had stopped moving and my dick lay limp in her mouth.

She rose to her feet with a smile on her lips and a wild, wicked gleam in her eyes. I noticed that she had not, in fact, swallowed all my come. A thin trickle of jism ran down from the corner of her mouth, beaded under her chin for a moment and then dripped to the floor. Just before the next drop fell, she stuck out her tongue and licked most of the come from the corner of her mouth. I could already feel my cock hardening again. It was going to be some night!

"So, what did you think of that?" she asked, slowly wiping away the remains of my come with her index finger, then seductively sucking the finger clean. In answer to her question, I stepped toward her and, hooking my thumbs under the waistband of her shorts, and pushed these, along with her soaked panties, to the floor. I spun her around and sat her down on the edge of a desk. Kneeling in front of her and draping her knees over my shoulders, I buried my face in her muff.

To say Risa was ripe for the tonguing I gave her would be an understatement. Her juices were literally gushing out, soaking both the desktop and my face as I drove her wild with my mouth. "Eat me, eat me!" she said, diddling her clit with a finger to add to her pleasure. She was an incredibly hot woman, working her ass back and forth on the desk as I tunneled into her with the tip of my tongue.

I sucked her love-lips, jousted at her clit with my tongue, and thrust in and out of her deep pussy with my fingers. My hand and face were coated with her sweet nectar.

"Lick my clit," she said breathlessly. "Suck it like I sucked your dick." I went to town on her little bud, feeling it swell and throb between my lips. She rocked and rolled against my face, occasionally gasping, "Oh, Robert, that's it! Do it to me."

Sensing how hot she was getting, I planted two fingers firmly in her pussy so that my mouth could concentrate exclusively on her hard little clit. Tracing circles around her clit and plucking at it gently with my lips, I began to finger-fuck her with a steadily increasing rhythm. In no time my hand was practically drenched to the wrist with cunt juice as her rocking pelvis began to match the tempo of my busily buried fingers.

And then, just like that, she went over the brink. Feverishly bucking and thrusting against my mouth and hand, and loudly grunting out things that were for the most part incoherent, Risa came wildly for what must have been five solid minutes! It was unbelievable. She jerked backward as she came, and inadvertently leaned against one of the computer keyboards, setting off a loud series of beeps.

When the orgasm finally subsided and her breathing was back to normal, she leaned forward, planted a deep kiss on my lips and began licking her juices from my cheeks and chin.

"Fuck me, Robert," she purred in my ear. "I want your dick right now. Is it hard?"

"It's been hard since the first time I saw you," I said. I took her hand in mine and placed it on my cock, which was hot and throbbing and long as a hammer. Helping her to her feet, I asked Risa to lean up against the printer, in that pose of hers that I loved so much. She did so, with her arms placed wide for support and her ass thrusting out invitingly. I thought of all the times I'd seen her like that and dreamed of pressing my cock into her from behind. Now I was actually going to get my chance.

Grabbing her hips, I entered her pussy from the rear, burying my hungry prong in her tight, dripping oven with a single thrust. She gasped, and so did I. Soon she was meeting my every lunge with a backward surge of her own, hungry for cock and for the pleasure each deep plunge brought her.

I was pumping so hard into her that the printer, a heavy, old-fashioned free-standing model, was rocking on its legs. It looked like it might topple over, but we didn't care. The machine banged loudly against the floor to the rhythm of our fucking.

Finally, with a loud, "Oh God, Robert, I'm . . . I'm going to come again!" Risa thrust hard against me and groaned aloud. She shook all over, then went limp as she climaxed. I joined her some three plunges later, pumping an ocean of come deep inside her pussy. Then, exhausted, we sank to the cold tile floor together and rested in each other's arms.

Five minutes later I noticed that I had left the computer-room door open all that time. I had a feeling that the janitor, if he hadn't already been up to watch our show, would soon be making his rounds on our floor. I told Risa that we should go somewhere a little more private, like back to my apartment, so we could finish getting to know each other. She readily agreed.

We fucked all night long and didn't get a minute's sleep. The next morning there was hell to pay. Risa's boss wanted to know why all the work she'd stayed late to finish wasn't done. She didn't have an answer, but apologized and told him that her mind must've been on other things.

As for me, work is now more enjoyable than ever. No one at the office knows about Risa and me, but we now are together almost every night. We also come up with every excuse we can think of to go to the supply room or the basement—anywhere where we might get a few moments of privacy.—*F.A., Philadelphia, Pennsylvania* O⊢▤

IN THE GAME OF LOVE, SOMETIMES BOTH PARTNERS CAN WIN—ESPECIALLY IF ONE OF THEM CHEATS

About a year ago, I started working for an interior design company. One of the men there, Ed, had an awesome body and a great personality, and I was deeply attracted to him. We quickly became friends, and did our share of flirting with each other, but nothing ever came of it because he was married.

I left the company after six months to take a part-time job, but still did some work for them on the side. One reason I maintained my connection to the company was Ed. I really enjoyed him and had decided that, if I couldn't get him into my bed, I'd at least try to spend time with him at the office. But as time went on, my attraction to him just got stronger, and my curiosity got the best of me. I wanted to see how far I could get with him, and one day asked him flatly, "Would you like to have an affair with me?"

He laughed, but I could see from the look in his eyes that he realized I was serious. He changed the subject quickly after that, however, so I backed off.

A few weeks later, Ed announced that he was leaving the company for another job. On his last day there, I was also scheduled to do some work at the office. I wore a tight black shirt and a wraparound skirt to work that day, and Ed greeted me by saying, "You look good enough to eat."

"Well, how hungry are you?" I teased back.

Ed then took me completely by surprise by reaching out to touch one of my breasts. That simple bit of contact sent shivers down my spine and made my clit twitch. I could feel myself getting very wet as the cunt juice just poured out of me. Unfortunately, just then one of the guys from the shop, who happened to be Ed's brother-in-law, came down the hall, so we quickly separated. We were both kind of shook up, and didn't talk much the rest of the day. That night before I left, I wished him luck in his new job, gave him my phone number and told him to call me any time.

I didn't expect Ed to call, but he did, the following Monday. I was off from work that day, and he told me he wasn't starting his new job for another week. "My wife is out with the kids all day, and I'm bored," he said. "Do you want to get together for a few hours?"

My nipples tingled and my pussy sang a song of joy. I gave him directions to my townhouse and told him to be there in an hour.

When he showed up, I could tell he was nervous. He didn't seem to know what to say. I wanted to tell him, "Just relax, and in a little while we can fuck each other's brains out," but thought better of it. I poured us some iced tea, and we talked about his new job.

Soon our conversation got around to what he was doing there with me. "I've never done anything like this before," he said.

"You mean you've never fucked a woman before?" I joked.

"No one but my wife since we've been married," he said shyly.

"Well, I won't bite," I said. "Not if you don't want me to."

We were silent for a few minutes, and then Ed leaned over and kissed me. I tried to really put some wild tongue-action into the kiss, but Ed still seemed kind of shy. I knew I'd have to take control.

"I'll be right back," I said, and told him I had to go to the bathroom. Instead, I slipped downstairs, lay on my bed and put my hand down my pants. Then I called out for him to come find me. When he finally showed up in my room a few minutes later, he was greeted with the sight of me sprawled out with my legs spread and my hand thrust down my jeans as I poked at my pussy with a finger.

His cock grew before my eyes, creating a tight bulge in the front of his slacks. It looked like a meaty one, and I was dying to have it in my mouth. I had him sit beside me, then stripped down to my tank top and panties.

From all our past conversations, I knew that his wife didn't like oral sex, giving or receiving. I'd always told Ed that I was great at giving blowjobs, and now I finally had my chance to show him what I meant. I really do enjoy sucking a dick, so I pulled his shorts off enthusiastically. I looked into the full-length mirror on my wall to see his cock—huge, hard and throbbing just inches from my open mouth. It was time to suck. I was going to enjoy this. I'd waited such a long time!

I slowly circled the head of his penis with my lips and tongue. I also rubbed my clit with the fingers of my left hand, knowing he could see this in the mirror. My right hand was fondling his balls, and I started deep-throating him. He was trembling and tense, and tried to pull my head away from his dick—for the first couple of seconds anyway. But soon he was as into it as I was, pumping his hips and moaning, "Suck . . . suck it, suck it . . ." as I fed on his hard cock. I jacked him off as my tongue traveled up and down his shaft, and soon felt him shoot a thick load down my throat. I swallowed it all in a few gulps. It was sticky and sweet. God, I just love the taste of come!

It only took him a few minutes to get hard again. I laid him on his back and climbed on top of him. He grabbed my hips and pulled my pussy toward his mouth. I put my hands on the wall and rested my ass in his palms. He stuck his tongue past my pussy lips and licked around and around. He sucked my clit as wildly as I'd sucked his cock. It went on for about ten minutes. My pussy was throbbing, and I was weak from the orgasms that were bolting through me. But more than anything, I needed to feel his hard cock deep inside me.

"I need you to fuck me, baby!" I urged. I slid off his face and straddled his cock, taking its thick hardness all the way up my cunt. I wanted so badly to come with him inside me that I bounced up and down on it feverishly. I was rocking back and forth, up and down, the fire of pleasure racing through my body.

"Give it to me hard!" I exclaimed. He quickly flipped me over on all fours and entered me from behind. As he rammed it into me doggie-style, I could feel an orgasm building up inside me. I felt the walls of my cunt tighten around his cock. We were both yelling with excitement. Ed's orgasm came right after mine. He pumped out jet after jet of warm, gooey sperm until his cock was totally spent and soft.

Ed and I agreed that our affair would never continue past that day. But for the rest of the afternoon, we fucked each other all over my apartment, our sweat-soaked bodies insatiable with lust. It was the best day of sex either of us has ever had. Although he still felt guilty about cheating on his wife, I think Ed was thrilled to get into my pants. I know I'm glad I finally got into his!—
Name and address withheld

EXHIBITIONISTIC WIFE TAKES OFF AT THE AIRPORT

My husband was due back from a two-day business trip and I was planning to pick him up at the airport. As a welcome-home surprise, I wore his trench coat with nothing underneath except for a very hot, horny pussy that was ready to be fucked. I got to the airport on time and parked at the end of a line of cars that were waiting at Arrivals.

As my favorite oldies station played on the car radio, my mind began to wander. I began to fantasize about the sex games I would play with my husband when we got home. As I mentally planned the evening, my hand unconsciously slipped under the trench coat and onto my pussy. I was totally oblivious to my surroundings until I suddenly realized I was getting damp between the legs! As I shifted my attention downward, I realized I was playing with my clit and was actually quite close to orgasm!

As I got hotter, I centered my thoughts on how I would tell my husband about my plans. I decided that we'd stop at a bar on the way home to have a drink. I'd tell him what I had planned as I sat naked on a bar stool with only his trench coat on. This last thought brought on my climax, and as I began to come I closed my eyes and started to moan.

The next thing I knew, a light was shining in my eyes and someone was tapping on my window. I opened my eyes in the middle of my orgasm and saw a young, handsome airport policeman standing alongside my window. My pussy was still spasming in orgasm, but I immediately withdrew my hand from under the trench coat and rolled down my window. The officer asked me if everything was all right or if I needed assistance. In a split second, the possibilities flashed through my mind. Too horny to stop and consider the consequences, I blurted out, "Yes!"

The officer told me to pull out of the line of cars and follow him. As I did so, I felt my cunt tighten. I came again from the excitement of having been caught in the act. He moved some police barricades and I followed him into a small, deserted parking lot near the terminal.

The policeman opened the door on the passenger side of my car and got in. As he began to speak, I could feel come dripping from my cunt! He told me he was going to ask me to move my car, but when he saw the look on my face, he thought he'd better check and see if I was okay. With a smile on his face, he asked me what kind of assistance I needed.

That was all I needed to hear. I turned sideways in my seat so that I was facing him. I pulled the trench coat open and spread my legs wide apart. As I fingered myself, I said to him, "This is what I need help with! Do you need some help too?"

His eyes locked onto my crotch. Just to make sure I had him, I withdrew my finger from my pussy, slowly slid it into my mouth and licked it clean. He was hooked! I then asked, "What would you like, officer?"

He immediately answered, "I'd like to see you come and then take care of me." So for the next ten minutes I played with myself until I could no longer hold back my climax. I came so hard I screamed, and my contractions must have lasted for a full minute. Once I calmed down, I leaned over, put my head in his lap, unzipped his pants and took his cock into my mouth.

Naturally it already was hard. I didn't waste any time. I sucked him off using every little trick that I knew! He came in two or three minutes, and after I swallowed his come I sat up and thanked him for his "assistance." He smiled and got out of the car. Then he moved the barricades and directed me back to the front of the line!

Fifteen minutes later I was on my way out of the airport with my husband alongside me in the passenger seat. I told him I wanted to stop somewhere for a drink, but he said he was tired and wanted to go straight home. I looked directly into his eyes and said, "This is one night you really want to go have a drink with me." With a smile, he acquiesced.

We stopped at a bar on the way home. I ordered the drinks while my husband went to the bathroom. When he returned he found me sitting on a bar stool with quite a bit of leg exposed. Since it is normal for me to sit like this, my husband made no comment, and we toasted his return home.

Halfway through the drink, I loosened the belt on the trench coat and whispered to my husband, "Look. I've got a surprise for you." As he turned to me, I opened the coat and spread my legs to reveal my nakedness. His eyes almost popped out of his head. As I closed the coat, I noticed a few men at the end of the bar had gotten a good look too! My cunt started getting wet again, so I made sure that I left the coat open enough to expose a few wisps of pubic hair.

As we finished our drinks, I said to my husband, "Take me home and take me to bed. I want you to fuck me as hard as you can. And I have a story for you that you're going to love!"—*R.B., Newark, New Jersey*

GUY WHO LOVES BROWN SUGAR GETS AN UNEXPECTED SWEET TREAT

I'm an attractive thirty-one-year-old white male. For the past seven years I've had an almost obsessive desire to make love to beautiful black women. This obsession began after I took a trip to Jamaica a few years ago. I met a beautiful Jamaican woman while on vacation and fell in lust. I'd thought the expression "Once you go black, you'll never go back" only applied to white women and black men, but I've since learned that it also applies to black women and white men.

My most recent experience with a highly sexed black woman

occurred last month. I'd taken a trip to get my head straightened out after the woman I'd asked to marry me (also a black woman) turned me down. So I headed for our American tropical paradise, Key West, for some sun, fun and much-needed relaxation.

One restless night, with the heat of the tropics weighing heavily on my libido, I decided to stroll down Duval Street to a bar where a new friend, Toby, was playing in a hot reggae band. It was about three in the morning when I got to the bar, and the band had just finished their set. Toby was packing up to leave, and I saw he was talking to an attractive black woman. My immediate thought was how I'd love to explore this gorgeous woman's hidden coral delights. It looked like she was saying good night to my friend, so I realized time was of the essence.

I strolled over to Toby, said hello and asked him to introduce me to his friend. Her name was Wanda. After telling me she was pleased to meet me, she said good-bye and turned to leave. Something told me to be bold and not let this opportunity pass me by.

I reached out, gently took her arm and said, "You can't leave yet."

With a stunned look on her face, she replied, "Why not?"

I shot back, "Because you're going to come home with me."

I couldn't believe I had actually said this, but the next thing I knew she had moved next to me and had taken *me* by the arm. This had been much easier than I thought!

The three of us left in my car. We stopped at a store so Wanda could get some cigarettes, and while she was in the store Toby assured me that I wouldn't be disappointed. He told me that he and Wanda had been lovers ten years earlier, and that she was great in bed. Was he ever right!

After dropping Toby off at his house, Wanda and I headed over to one of the local beaches. We made love on the beach under a palm tree, which is my favorite spot to satisfy a hot, horny woman like Wanda.

She was absolutely incredible. Her soft skin and large breasts, with inch-long nipples that she loved to have sucked, drove me wild with passion. After kissing her breasts, I quickly moved down to her beautiful coral lips. In all my pussy-licking experience, I have never been more satisfied. Her beautiful quim tasted like sweet brown sugar as her juices flowed freely into my mouth.

After her first orgasm, she quickly yanked off my shorts. She devoured my eight-inch cock on one downstroke, getting me rock hard and keeping me that way without letting me come. She really knew how to suck cock. This woman had me going wild!

Finally she got on top of me and slid my cock up her incredibly tight pussy. She gave herself an incredible ride, leaning forward so I could suck on her chocolate globes. We continued to make love in every conceivable position.

When the sun started to rise, we decided to call it a night. Once back in my car, Wanda fulfilled yet another dream for me. She expertly sucked my cock as I drove her home. She also stuck her fingers into her honey-pot and fed me her nectar as we drove.

So remember, guys, sometimes you've just got to be bold and go for it!—*E.S., Chicago, Illinois*　⚬━▄

MIXING BUSINESS WITH PLEASURE WAS NEVER MORE PLEASURABLE!

I'm a thirty-one-year-old advertising consultant with an established clientele. I'm single and have never been married. I'm the proud owner of a ten-and-a-half-inch cock, and I have no problem attracting the babes. Recently I was dating a young woman with an outrageously ripe body. Unfortunately she's not very sexually adventurous. Although our sex life was interesting at first, it was primarily because of my input. Our sex life steadily declined over time.

Until last fall I had never considered having an affair with a client. I guess I followed the old adage about not mixing business and pleasure. Donna became a client a year ago. The project I worked on with her was completed a few months ago. When I first met her, I was struck by how attractive she is for a woman of her age. At fifty-three years old, Donna is a natural blonde, with a trim figure and large, firm breasts. She often wears blouses that reveal a bit of her substantial cleavage. And from the lacy camisoles that often peek out from beneath her suit jackets, I could tell she also likes to wear sexy lingerie. We met several times while I was working for her, and I noticed that her outfits, while usually businesslike, became more revealing over time. She had an excellent fashion sense, and always wore clothes that flattered her svelte figure. To top it off, Donna is one of the most successful businesswomen in this town.

As her company's sales campaign moved toward a successful conclusion, Donna became more friendly with me and even a little flirtatious. I always responded professionally, because I didn't think I was interested in an older woman. I often ignored what would have been regarded by other men as an outright invitation. My responses to her were intended to be more friendly than personal. As we got to know each other better, Donna learned that I was involved in a relationship, and probably deduced that I was less than satisfied with it, although I never came right out and said it.

On two or three occasions after the sales campaign ended, I ran into Donna and a few of her friends at a funky cafe I frequented. I had never seen her there before, but the place was a well-known hangout. Being that this was a social situation, I was more friendly and open than before. Donna respectfully inquired about my girlfriend. I learned she was in a somewhat unhappy relationship with a man who was younger than me. That night we caught a buzz together and had a great conversation, but Donna left with her friends. The invitation was now more clear, but again I didn't pick up on it.

The next morning I woke after a frustrating night's sleep and realized I had been dreaming about having sex with Donna. I was sporting a huge hard-on, and I realized that I was turned on by the thought of fucking Donna.

For the first time ever, I called her at her home that afternoon. She was pleasantly surprised by my call. We made small talk for a few minutes, then I came right out and asked her if she wanted to have sex with me. There was a long moment of silence, and I wondered if I had made a big mistake. But then she quietly said, "Yes." I added, "I really want to fuck you."

Donna asked, "When?"

I answered, "How about right now?"

She asked me if I knew how to get to her place. I told her I did and said that I'd be right over. Then I asked her if she'd dress in a silk blouse, a short skirt and high heels, with a silk bra and no panties underneath. I could hear heavy breathing on the phone before I hung up.

Donna met me at the door, dressed as requested. I told her how sexy she looked, and I planted a few kisses on her shoulders. Then I kissed her full on the lips. I had planned to be the aggressor, but Donna quickly took the lead.

She gently sat me down in her beautifully furnished living

room. She untied my shoes and removed them, along with my socks. Then she unbuckled my pants and slowly tugged them down. As I lifted my hips, I could see down the gap in her blouse. Her large breasts swayed heavily inside a lacy lavender brassiere as she moved. Her nipples were erect and huge. My cock bulged out of my tight red briefs.

Donna kissed the tip of my cock, then carefully slid my briefs down over it. My cock bobbed in front of her face, pulsing wildly. Her eyes were glued to my cock, and I could see a pink flush spread across the top of her chest. She was practically panting. She pulled my hips down so that my balls almost hung off the couch. Then she placed her hands on my thighs, opened her mouth wide and sucked in the head of my cock.

I just groaned as she thoroughly lubed the tip of my joint for a few minutes. She was making sucking and moaning noises, but she didn't say a word. I wondered which one of us was in control of the situation. She then swallowed the rest of my cock and began to gently squeeze my aching balls. She did this until I didn't think I could hold out any longer. But I knew I wanted to see her cunt, lick it, then fuck it and fill it with an ocean of jism.

I gently pushed her head away from my prick and asked her to stand up. I removed my shirt, then I leaned forward and gently parted her thighs with my hands. I lightly rubbed both thighs until she opened them wider. I carefully brushed her cunt lips with the tip of one finger. Her labia were hot, wet and puffy. I was especially pleased to see that she didn't have a trace of pubic hair. As I stroked her lips, Donna's knees buckled. Her face was flushed and she was breathing heavily through her mouth. After two minutes of this she came violently, panting and groaning as her legs quivered. And I hadn't even touched her clit yet.

She leaned against me, braced herself on my shoulder and began to tongue my mouth deeply as she caressed my stiff cock. I still wanted to see her cunt up close and fuck the hell out of it, but I wanted to give Donna more pleasure first.

As we kissed, I reached between her legs and peeled her sticky, clean-shaven lips apart. I located her clit and gently stroked it for a while before inserting two fingers into her sopping hole. Her passion had been rising all along, but Donna went out of control now. She fucked my fingers for about twenty seconds before she spasmed, bucked wildly and collapsed against me.

As she cooled down, I gently caressed her. Donna still couldn't talk, but when she caught her breath she begged me to fuck her. She started to lube my cockhead with her saliva, but at this point it didn't even need the special attention.

To intensify our pleasure, I tried to slow down the pace. I told Donna to stop sucking my cock and stand up. I asked her to take off her skirt so I could get a better look at her cunt. I couldn't believe how beautiful it was. There was a tuft of blonde pubic hair above her pussy, but not a hair on her thoroughly swollen pink lips. They were obviously more than ready to caress my shank. I told her to remove her blouse, turn around and bend over. Her nipples were so big they stretched the flimsy fabric of her delicate bra. Her breasts hung like large, soft grapefruits. She turned on her heels and bent over. As I squatted behind her, I told her to think of my cock and nothing else. Then I began to thoroughly bathe her labia with my tongue. I held her hips as she braced her palms against the coffee table in front of her. She came three times as I worked her pussy over. I didn't know how much more of a workout this woman could take or if I would just come without even touching myself.

We finally went to her bedroom for round two. She took off her brassiere. Her nipples were the thickest pair I've seen and they pointed slightly downward. We stood next to her bed. I told her that, for the moment, I would suck her nipples and not touch anything else, and asked her if she would just lightly stroke my cock and balls, smearing pre-come all over the tender tip.

At some point we just slid down onto the bed. I lifted her legs over my shoulders. Donna firmly grasped my fat tool and rubbed it along her slit four or five times, then placed it at her entrance so I could sink it all the way in.

Donna's pussy was tight, and my cock is fat, but after several strokes my penis was balls-deep inside her. I gave her long, steady, deep strokes, corkscrewing her with my dick as she crossed her legs over my lower back and pressed her hard nipples against me. I screamed as my come gushed out of me, slamming harder into her with each stroke until I realized that she, too, was screaming in orgasm.

After a few minutes I moved into a position where she could stroke my cock as I looked between her spread thighs and watched my come leak out of her hairless pussy. We watched the sun go down. I spent the night with Donna after we again fucked each other to exhaustion. It was great!

I've since dumped my twenty-two-year-old girlfriend, because

Donna requires too much of my energy on a daily basis. I just didn't see the point of continuing in a boring relationship!—*V.R., Indianapolis, Indiana* O⊢▄

SOLDIER HAS GOOD FORTUNE WHEN HE WAITS FOR AN ENCORE

I would like to relate an experience that I had a few months ago with my friend Trisha. Trisha is about five foot six inches tall, weighs one hundred fifteen pounds, and has shoulder-length brown hair, sexy hazel eyes, olive skin, long legs and an incredible bush of pubic hair that must be seen to be fully appreciated. The only thing that outshines her beautiful face is an outrageous ass.

I've known Trisha for a number of years. We've often talked about sex, but except for one time that I ate her to orgasm, we hadn't had any other sexual contact. A few months ago, though, that all changed.

Trisha is an executive secretary who looks great in everything she wears. During one of our many conversations, I discovered that she enjoys sexually explicit magazines like this one. She also likes X-rated videos. I'm presently stationed on a military base where these items are plentiful, so I picked up the latest issue of *Penthouse Letters* as a present for her and mailed it to her office. She told me later that she really enjoyed it and had even taken it into the tub with her so she could masturbate while relaxing in a nice, hot bath.

When I was home on leave, I called her to let her know I was in town. She sounded happy to hear from me, and we agreed upon a time for me to drop by and visit her. When I arrived at her apartment, she was just getting home from work. She wore a summer dress and white stockings. I sat on her couch and she sat on an adjacent love seat.

She kicked off her high heels and put her feet up on the coffee table, which gave me an excellent view up those fantastic legs almost all the way to her panties. This was enough to bolster my confidence. The conversation soon turned to sex and the magazine I had sent her. At this point she went to her desk and took it out.

As we flipped through the pages, I could see she was getting really turned on. I asked her if she was interested in repeating our sexual encounter of a few years past. She readily agreed, then got up and led me to her bedroom, where she began undressing for me.

She removed her dress, bra and stockings, and lay down on the bed, magazine in hand. I knelt down between her legs and began kissing the insides of her thighs. I noticed a wet spot forming on her panties. After leisurely kissing her through her panties and enjoying her scent, I reached for her panties to pull them off. She lifted her hips and helped me remove them. With her panties gone, I settled into a comfortable pussy-eating position. I was ready to provide some serious tonguing.

I began by slowly licking along the entire length of her outer lips. While I was doing this, she continued to look at the magazine. I next turned my attention to her inner lips, which were wet, red and swollen. Her sex was fully exposed. I licked my way up inside her and tasted that delicious box I remembered so well. I had told Trisha several times in the past that she had the nicest pussy I've ever had the pleasure of going down on. Soon she was completely drenched. I pushed my tongue as far into her as I could, licking her slick inner walls.

I then turned my attention to her swollen clit. I took the sensitive nub of flesh into my mouth, pressing it lightly between my tongue and my upper lip. She began to squirm around on the bed. She found she couldn't pay attention to both things at once, so she put the magazine down. I was sucking her clit and applying a slight tugging action with my mouth and a slow circular action with my tongue when she asked, "Do you want me to come?" I told her that I did. She then asked, "Now?" I answered by increasing the pressure slightly and speeding up my tongue action. I watched her stomach and leg muscles twitch and flutter. She then arched her back, threw her head back and grabbed my head as I ate her to her first orgasm. Her box spasmed and a trickle of warm liquid flowed into my mouth. Throughout her orgasm she bucked and writhed around on the bed. I kept my lips sealed around her clit as her orgasm washed over her.

While she was calming down, I flicked my tongue across her clit and watched her body jerk in response. This, in turn, would cause her to clamp her thighs around my head. I let her catch her breath for a moment, then I pushed her legs apart and once again dove tongue-first into her hot, wet cunt. She asked me if I wanted a towel to wipe some of her juices off my face. "No way!" I said. I then pressed my face deeper into her snatch, swirling my tongue around inside her.

She asked if we were going to do this again. I just told her to lie back and relax—round two had begun. After a few minutes she groaned, "Oh, shit," as she exploded in her second orgasm. Her fluids now covered my face, as well as her entire bush. The excess ran down her ass-cheeks and soaked the bed sheets.

After cleaning her off with my tongue, I asked her to get on her hands and knees. She did so and pushed her pussy into my face. Just then some more of her juice flowed into my mouth. I drank down every drop!

She asked me if I wanted to jack off. Although I have wanted to masturbate in front of her for a while, and would have jumped at the chance at any other time, this night I had something else in mind. I told her that I needed to come, but that I wanted to come inside her. She said she was afraid my dick might be too big for her. I told her she was wet enough for any dick.

With that I unbuckled my pants and let them fall. They hadn't even passed my knees before I was rubbing the head against her soaked slit. After getting the tip lubricated, I eased it into her velvety hole. She was incredibly tight and so wet. She felt great!

I pushed into her slowly, letting her get used to my cock. After seeing no signs of discomfort, I began picking up the pace of my fucking. Before long I was slamming back and forth into what has to be the best feeling, best tasting, best looking pussy in the world. To top it off, she looked over her shoulder and said, "You've been wanting to do this for years, haven't you?" I couldn't have answered if I'd tried!

She really must have wanted this to be special, because she told me she was anything but a passive fuck. She moved her hips and used her inner muscles so well that she had me ready to come in no time. Long before I wanted to, I shot a huge, never-ending load into her gripping, spasming pussy. The intensity was indescribable! I came so hard and for so long, she had to ask me if I was all right! All I could do was smile and continue flexing my dick within her tight confines. I wanted every drop inside that gold mine of hers!

As I started to soften, my dick slowly began to slide out of her pussy until it plopped against my thigh, coated with our juices. Her lips were swollen and red. She turned to look at my dick and just stared at it in awe. I told her that I knew she could handle it, and she just smiled.

She hurried into the bathroom to catch the flood of fluids coming out of her before anything else got soaked. Was it good? Hell, yes! Was it worth the wait? Fuck, yes!

Now I'm hoping I won't have to wait as long for the next time! Wish me luck.—*T.C., Fort Worth, Texas* ○┼▦

MARINE EXPLORES VIRGIN TERRITORY, FINDS IT'S WELL WORTH THE WAIT

I'm a United States Marine, and I've served in the Corps for four years. I'm currently home on leave after a particularly long twelve months overseas.

I hadn't been in town for over an hour when I ran into an ex-girlfriend from high school whom I hadn't seen in more than three years. Alicia looked better than ever, and I felt those old lustful feelings stirring in my cock. In all my life, no one had been able to turn me on the way she could. But no woman had ever turned me down as often as she had. After five years of dating her on and off, I had never once made love to her. As a matter of fact, the last time she turned me down (three years ago), she told me she was still a virgin.

We talked casually for a while, catching up on each other's life, and then she invited me over for dinner. After a moment of thought, I accepted.

As I showered that evening, I began to think about our last date. We had danced and drank, and ended up back at her place. After making out on her couch for a while, we were both raging with lust.

I still remember the smoothness of her breasts as I kneaded them in my hands. Her firm nipples stood up proud and erect, quivering at my every kiss. Her scent filled my nostrils as I tongued her cunt with wild abandon. She screamed in ecstasy as I brought her to orgasm with my eager tongue.

I also remember that anguishing moment—my prick was nestled against her golden bush, poised for the thrust that would send it into bliss—when she said, "Stop!" Of course, I respected her wishes.

Even the memory was too much, and I masturbated to relieve my aching cock. I told myself I didn't want to let that happen again.

I arrived at Alicia's house at seven, flowers in one hand, wine in the other. When she opened the door, I nearly dropped them both. She had clearly pulled out all the stops tonight.

Alicia stood in the doorway, her five-foot-two-inch frame stuffed into a denim miniskirt that accentuated her beautifully curved hips. Her white cotton shirt was cut low enough to reveal a hint of her firm tits, and her smile was enough to launch a thousand ships.

Dinner was perfect. She had prepared a feast fit for a king. But my appetite was reserved for my dinner companion. After we finished our meal, we retired to the den, where she had a cozy fire burning. The wine flowed freely along with the conversation. We reminisced about school, old friends and of our many escapades. I accidentally mentioned our last date, and we both got quiet and looked into each other's eyes. Unable to control myself, I leaned over to kiss her.

She was tense at first, but as our kiss became more passionate I felt her melt into my arms. As our tongues intertwined, reacquainting themselves, she let out a moan of pleasure. Our hands began roaming over each other's body, removing clothing on the way.

Soon I was completely naked, and she was down to a pair of red satin panties. Tufts of her golden pubic hair stuck out the sides. As we broke our kiss, she whispered in my ear, telling me how much she had missed me. Then she kissed her way down to my swollen cock.

Starting at the tip, she licked down to the base and then back up. When she reached the top, she parted her lips and, ever so slowly, took my pole into her mouth. She let her mouth sink slowly down, not stopping until she reached the bottom. My cock was buried completely in her throat, and it felt wonderful. She moaned softly, sending tingles down my cock and through my whole body. Slowly at first, but gradually increasing the pace, she fucked my cock with her warm, wet mouth. On each stroke she went all the way to the tip before sinking back down to the base of my shaft.

She fondled my balls with one hand while deep-throating my tool like a pro. I felt my come boiling up inside me, and in an instant my cock exploded, shooting a huge load of love juice down her throat. Alicia didn't spill a drop, but swallowed it all.

She let my spent love-stick slide out of her mouth, and sat up beside me. I gave her a long, hard kiss before I began my descent to the promised land.

I caressed her firm breasts, and her nipples stood at attention under my skilled touch. I peeled off her panties to reveal the treasure that I had been chasing for so long. I kissed my way up her tan legs to her waiting love-box.

My probing tongue sought out and found her clit. I licked it fervently and sucked it into my mouth. She moaned and squirmed on the couch. Her legs wrapped around my head, pulling me closer against her clit, and she shuddered as an intense orgasm overwhelmed her.

When her orgasm subsided, I picked her up and carried her to the bedroom. Laying her gently on the bed, I kissed my way up her body, stopping momentarily to again savor her plentiful breasts.

I positioned the head of my rock-hard cock at the opening of her cunt, preparing to claim her hole. Then I suddenly stopped. I searched her face for a sign, and asked her if she wanted it. She responded by wrapping her legs around me and drawing me into heaven.

My cock eased into the tightest hole I had ever felt. We had passed the telltale barrier of her virginity and reached the point of no return.

I began thrusting at a slow, easy pace, allowing her to get used to the sensation of my cock in her virgin hole. Each stroke sent waves of pleasure roaring through my cock as her tight cunt milked my rigid shaft.

I picked up the pace when she repeatedly moaned, "Fuck me harder!" As I pumped her faster, her ranting grew louder until she was screaming incoherently.

I was fast approaching the point of no return when her orgasm hit like a freight train. Her eyes rolled back in her head and she screamed my name. This triggered my own orgasm, unleashing an endless torrent of come.

Our passion spent, we lay alongside each other, breathing heavily from the exertion. I looked into her eyes and knew this was where I wanted to spend the rest of my days (and nights). We're getting married next week.—*R.T., Tulsa, Oklahoma*

Different Strokes

HE LOOKS JUST LIKE A WOMAN, BUT HE MAKES LOVE LIKE A REAL HE-MAN

My husband Frankie is a sissy, and I love it. We met in beauty school and, after graduation, opened our own shop. It is one of the most popular salons in town. We now have seven people cutting hair, plus four other men and women who do nails and facials.

It was during our junior year of school that Frankie and I became involved. We practiced on each other—and I don't just mean our haircutting skills. To my surprise, even though Frankie was as effeminate as any woman I'd ever met, he fucked like a stud. I would tell him how hot he looked and how turned on I was, and he would slip me the meat for hours. I used to laugh when I heard women complain that their big, macho boyfriends could only fuck for two minutes and could never bring them to orgasm. My sweet little Frankie spoiled my pussy rotten.

The first day we fucked, we'd been practicing women's makeovers. Frankie did me first, and received a B for his grade. Then it was my turn to do him. I took extra care making him look like a really pretty woman. When I was done, I got an A+. Best of all, Frankie and I went out to dinner after class, and no one even suspected he was a man.

On the way to his place, he told me how sexy he felt in the dress I'd selected for him. When we got there, we were so hot, we made love right away. The next morning we went clothes shopping and bought Frankie a whole feminine wardrobe. I coached him on his walk and talk, and how to be ladylike. We had the greatest times going out and watching guys try to pick him up. After a night of teasing all the boys, we'd run to his place and jump into bed. I'd suck Frankie's prick for as long as it took to gobble down his thick, creamy load.

The last week of school, my roommate's brother Gregg came

133

to see her. Frankie walked in, dressed like a woman, and Gregg was immediately interested. Frankie and I decided to have some fun, and kissed each other full on the lips in front of Gregg. We told Gregg I was bisexual, and that I wanted to have a threesome with him and Frankie—whom I'd been calling "Peggy" in front of Gregg.

Gregg was immediately interested, and we went to Frankie's apartment. I kissed Gregg long and wet on the mouth, and asked him to strip me. When I was naked, I told him to lay back and watch "Peggy" eat my pussy. Frankie got between my legs and bathed the folds of my cunt with his tongue. He sucked on my clit and fingered my hole until I was writhing and squealing with orgasm.

After I'd come, I crawled over to Gregg and took his cock into my mouth. He watched and cheered me on as I sucked Gregg's hard dick and played with his balls. When he started to spasm, I opened wide and took his load down my throat.

Now that he'd come, Gregg wanted to know why "Peggy" was still fully dressed. Frankie said something about being too tired to fuck him. Then I said I was tired too, so Gregg left. Frankie and I had a god laugh over this. He immediately stripped and slipped his steak into me from behind, frigging my clit as he drove into me doggie-style. "Feel my cock!" he said over and over again in his cute little girlie voice. It had been pretty interesting sucking Gregg's cock, but feeling Frankie's dick inside me that afternoon convinced me that he would always be the one for me.

To this day, our biggest turn-on is getting Frankie all decked out like a woman. We have a special harness to hold his penis snug against his body. I tuck in his dick, then he slips into pantyhose, a bra, a dress and shoes. We go out and flirt with men all night long, then return home and fuck and suck until the sun comes up and our cock and pussy are numb.

I love my sissy-boy Frankie more than I've ever loved anyone else. He may look like the total woman, but to me, he's all man.—*S.W., Indianapolis, Indiana*

LAWN-LOVING VIXEN HAS NEXT-DOOR NEIGHBOR BEGGING FOR MOWER

I am in my forties, and my wife Lena is in her thirties. I was recently unemployed for nine months, and was driving my family crazy. A young couple, Barry and Victoria, moved in next door to us. Although they were very nice, I didn't think we would have much in common. They are both in their early twenties and travel with a much younger crowd.

It all started in early July when I was cutting the lawn on our riding mower. Barry was trimming the hedges between our houses. As had become our custom, we stopped and talked for a while. Then out of the blue, Barry asked if Lena ever cut our lawn with the riding mower. I said, "No," because that was a job I always did.

Without a word, Barry pointed across his property to his wife. Victoria was riding their mower in a halter top and shorts, which revealed almost all of her ample figure. It occurred to me that for a woman who was doing a monotonous, time-consuming chore, she had a big smile on her face.

Without mincing words, Barry said, "Victoria gets off while cutting the lawn. She never lets me do it. I'll bet she's coming for the third time already."

I didn't know how to respond, but I didn't have to. Barry just kept talking. "Watch her for a while and you'll see what I mean," he said. "It's great. When she's finished with the lawn, she'll be so horny we'll have to spend the rest of the afternoon in bed."

My skepticism got the best of me, and I told him so. "That's awfully hard to believe," I said. "In fact, it sounds like the biggest line of bull I've ever heard."

"Suit yourself," he said. "But if you hear a woman's voice screaming, 'Fuck me! Fuck my pussy!' coming from my house tonight, just know it ain't no videotape."

I still thought Barry was telling me a tall tale, but I finally admitted to him that he had piqued my curiosity. In order to prove his point, when Victoria finished the lawn, he called her over to talk with us for a minute. As she walked over in her tiny little outfit, her tits practically popping out for all the world to see, he told me to pay particular attention to the crotch of her shorts.

Indeed I did, and saw that the material was darkened by considerable moisture. When Victoria headed back into the house, swaying her tight buns like a cheerleader, Barry said, "That was pussy juice. Nectar of the gods." With that, he followed his wife inside, calling over his shoulder to me, "See you tomorrow!"

With a cock hard enough to do chin-ups on, I went back to my work, still thinking of Victoria. While trimming my side of the hedges a little while later, I could hear moans and groans of joy coming from their bedroom, and knew Barry had been telling the truth.

The following week, Barry embarked on a two-week business trip to Eastern Europe. On the first Saturday he was gone, I saw his wife riding contentedly on their lawn mower, cutting the grass. I was working outside as well, doing some landscaping with my shirt off. I positioned myself so I could see Victoria without her noticing me. Every so often she would wiggle in the seat, or slightly adjust her butt and rub the front of her very short shorts.

Just as she finished mowing the lawn, I got two glasses of iced tea and offered her one. We chatted while cooling off with our drinks. I couldn't keep my eyes off her smooth body, which was almost entirely exposed by her shorts and bikini top, and covered with a thin, sexy film of sweat. The boner I'd popped from standing next to her just kept getting harder and longer.

We talked about Barry, and Victoria said, "He's never around when I need him." I asked if she wanted some work done around the house, and she said, "No, it's not that kind of need."

I asked her to be more specific, and she just blurted out, "I'm horny as hell from the vibrations of that damned lawn mower!"

I looked closely at her to see if she was asking me to fill that need, but she quickly changed the subject. We finished our drinks, and then went off to complete our yard work.

Later that afternoon, the phone rang. It was Victoria. She said she was still horny and, if I would promise not to tell her husband, she wanted me to come over and fuck her. "Come in through the sliding doors in back," she said. "Hurry!"

My wife was gone for the afternoon, doing the grocery shopping. There was no way I was going to miss out on the opportunity to bang Victoria.

I ran right over to her place and opened the sliding doors. There she was, on the floor, stretched out on her back, stark naked. What a body! My eyes were drawn to her tan lines, especially to the white triangles they left on her fluffy, round tits. As I undressed, she kept urging me to hurry up. "I want you now!"

I finished undressing and knelt between her legs, lowering my head to her pussy. I'd barely begun to lick her cunt when she exploded with a shuddering orgasm, flooding my mouth and face with her lust-honey. After I brought her to two or three quick climaxes, I switched to the missionary position and entered her.

Her cunt was extremely tight, and she continuously wiggled

and moaned as I fucked her with a slow, steady rhythm. Her hips were like a machine, the undulating motions milking a pair of orgasms out of me in the long afternoon we spent fucking. We lost track of the time, and when we checked the clock it was almost time for my wife to get home.

We hadn't spent all of that time on the floor either. Victoria was especially fond of being fucked while sitting on me—to mimic the action of the riding mower, I suppose—and for a long time she sat on my lap, her back to me, while I was perched in her rocking chair, rolling back and forth as she pumped up and down on my steel-hard erection.

The next few weeks, while her husband was away, were just as good. Victoria cut the lawn at least twice a week, giving her pussy a tantalizing workout and making her as horny as a virgin bride. Being the good friend and neighbor I am, I was always there to take care of her needs when her mowing was finished.

We discussed our sexual fantasies. I have always wanted to make love to two women at once, and Victoria has always wanted to make it with another couple. She told me that she finds my wife very attractive and sexy, and we have given serious thought to asking my wife, and Victoria's husband, if they are interested in having a foursome.

Now that her husband's back in town, Victoria and I are no longer sleeping together. But a few days ago she suggested to my wife that she try riding our lawn mower once in a while. Victoria is sure that after a couple of vibrating excursions on her mower, Lena will be so turned on she'll be ready to help fulfill our four-way fantasy.—*Name and address withheld* O�┼ ▣

EVER SINCE THIS SMOOTH OPERATOR WENT FOR THE BLADE, SHE'S HAD IT MADE

My husband is the best lover I've ever had, but lately he's really been an animal in bed! It seems that he saw a picture of a woman with a clean-shaven pussy, and it really turned him on. He asked me to shave my cunt bald for him, so I did. Well, the results have been fantastic. I've been having so many earth-shattering climaxes lately that it's been all I can do to get out of bed in the morning.

I'll admit that I wasn't eager to shave my beaver at first. The more he mentioned it, though, the more comfortable I became with the idea. Finally I decided to make it happen for him. After all, we've always tried to help each other realize our sexual fantasies, and this one seemed pretty easy.

I waited until he fell asleep one night, and I locked myself in the bathroom with a razor and a can of shaving cream. I soaked my muff with warm water, then lathered up the pubes with shaving cream. My clit became swollen with excitement. Before I even grabbed the razor, I had to masturbate to orgasm.

Then I carefully shaved my pussy hair off. The razor felt cool against my skin, and I kept bathing the area with water to keep it moist. My cunt was wet and dripping with hot juices as I stood in front of the mirror, watching the razor glide around my puffy pussy lips. I inserted my fingers in and out as I shaved, pumping myself that way as I scraped away the hair and shaving lather. I didn't want to have another orgasm until my ripe cunt lips were wrapped tightly around my husband's hard cock, though, so I held back from bringing myself to climax again.

I finished shaving and admired my cunt in the mirror. It was shiny and soft, smooth and hairless as marble. My pink cunt lips pouted out from the clean skin, and my entire body tingled with delight.

My pussy ached as I crawled into bed and roused my husband from his deep sleep. I took his hand and put it on my newly bald pussy. His cock woke up before he did. I saw it spring up, erect as a flagpole. As he opened his eyes, I grabbed his dick firmly and stroked the head against my unobstructed cunt lips. His cock was dripping with excitement, and so was my vagina.

He moaned his approval, and I pulled him on top of me. "Fuck me!" I said in a loud voice. "My pussy is so sensitive this way. I want your dick in me."

The penetration was so sweet! His cock entered me with one powerful thrust, and pumped me like never before. I could feel every vein of his hot dick, and loved the sight of the hard pole sliding in and out of my shaved, wet cave. He fucked me for a long time, and I had so many orgasms, I lost count. When he exploded, I pulled away from him and watched as his creamy white come dripped out of my bald box.

We licked, sucked and fucked all night long, and have done the same nearly every night since. I'll always keep my cunt clean and smooth, especially if it means I'll get this kind of wild cock action on a regular basis.—*Name and address withheld* O⊢

WHAT'S THE WELL-DRESSED MAN WEARING?
LOOKS LIKE A BRA FROM HERE

My wife Grace and I are both in our thirties and have been happily married for ten years. A couple of years before I got married, I sublet an apartment from a woman who was doing her two-year stint in the Peace Corps. Her dresser drawers were full of clothes, including some silky, lacy lingerie. My curiosity got the best of me, and I began to put on her frilly things when I was home alone.

Then I got a little bolder and started putting on her skirts and blouses to go shopping. I loved the feel of feminine things on my body. Wearing a pair of panty hose gave me an erection so hard that words can't describe it.

Over the years I got engaged and married, but I kept my crossdressing to myself. But one night in the hotel where my wife and I were celebrating our first anniversary, we had a few drinks and started to talk about our fantasies. I told her about my love of women's clothes, and she got a strange look on her face. I asked her what was wrong, and she said that she was very curious about how I looked dressed up as a woman. I figured, Why not let her see for herself? I excused myself and went into the bathroom with her bra, panties and makeup bag.

She giggled when she first saw me "transformed," and told me that my makeup needed a touch-up. I sat on the bed as she applied more makeup on my face, and some polish on my fingernails. After she was finished with me, we couldn't believe how great I looked—I was a different person! As she leaned in to add a final dab of eyeliner, my leg rubbed her pussy—she was wetter than I ever could remember!

I asked her if she was turned on by seeing me as a woman, and she answered me by leaning down and nibbling on my chest. I reached down to her cunt and massaged her clit. She moaned and started to grind her pussy against my hand. I played with her nipples, and she eased me back on the bed and proceeded to suck mine. I couldn't believe how good it felt to have my nipples munched.

Grace slowly worked her way down to my crotch, eventually wrapping her mouth around my incredibly hard cock and sucking it in deeply. She traced up and down my stick with her fantastic tongue, changing her position on the bed so that I could eat her as well. We spent what seemed like an eternity in a wet, noisy 69, licking and sucking each other to a pair of powerful orgasms.

I asked her afterward what she was thinking about when she went down on me. She confessed that one of her fantasies had always been to have sex with another woman, and that having me dressed up in feminine attire was the next best thing.

A couple of weeks later, Grace came home from work a little late, and said she had a surprise for me. She asked me to fix us a couple of drinks while she carried some packages into the bedroom. With drinks in hand, I went into the bedroom just in time to see her laying out the new clothes she'd bought for me.

"But you can't put these on yet," she said. "First things first."

She led me into the bathroom and had me get into the bathtub. "If you're going to dress like a woman, you have to feel like a woman." She lathered me up and proceeded to shave my legs, chest and underarms. When I was totally smooth all over, Grace dried me and put on my makeup.

Then I put on the clothes she'd bought for me. I really looked like a woman! The padded push-up bra gave me small but full tits, and my shaved legs were a pair any woman would dream of having. My wife had one more item to complete my makeover. She reached into a bag and pulled out a blonde wig for me. After she'd put it on my head, she told me to close my eyes for one last surprise.

She led me into the kitchen and told me to open my eyes. There before me stood her girlfriend Laura, smiling and telling me how good I looked as a woman.

I sat at the table with Laura on one side of me and Grace on the other. We had a few drinks and decided to go to a movie. It had been years since I'd been out in public dressed as a woman, and it felt fantastic. When we got back to the house after the movie, Laura and I sat on the couch and talked, while my wife went into the bedroom. Laura put her hand on my leg. At first she just rested it on my thigh, but soon she was slowly moving it up and down the inside of my leg. The feel of her hand moving up and down my nylon-covered leg got me really turned on.

Then Grace came back in. She sat beside Laura and put her arm around her. Grace explained to me that Laura was bisexual, and that she wanted to make love with both of us. Laura chimed in and told me how much Grace and I turned her on. As Laura worked her hand closer to my crotch, Grace lowered her hand inside Laura's blouse and started to indulge her nipples. I was really worked up by this time, and suggested we move into the bedroom.

As we were getting into bed, Laura said she wanted me to leave on my bra, panties and nylons. I took off my dress and watched as the women helped each other strip. The sight of two women undressing each other was unbelievably erotic—especially considering one of them was my wife.

We moved to the bed, where Laura and Grace leaned over me and sucked my tits. Laura's hand was between my legs, rubbing my crotch. I had one hand on Laura's clit and the other on Grace's.

Soon Grace positioned herself between Laura's musky thighs and fed on her clit. It was big, and stuck out like a tiny finger. I licked Laura's nipples until she bucked with a mighty orgasm.

When her climax subsided, Laura and I started to work on Grace. I knelt between her spread legs and lapped up her love juices while Laura played with her tits and kissed her on the lips. Grace had a monumental orgasm, locking her thighs around my neck and crying out, "I'm coming!"

Then it was my turn. Grace and Laura licked me all over, running their tongues up and down my thighs, arms, shoulders and back. Soon I couldn't take the anticipation any more and begged Grace to fuck me. My horny wife pulled my panties down and mounted me, as Laura continued to suck my entire body from head to toe with her marvelous mouth. It didn't take long for me to have a huge climax, pumping Grace's wet pussy full of my sweet cream.

Afterward, as we all lay snuggled up together, Laura and Grace decided that around them, my new name would be Margaret, and that we would all be close friends for a long time to come.—*M.O., Houston, Texas* O╾▦

MIRROR, MIRROR ON THE WALL, WHO'S THE MOST SATISFIED OF THEM ALL?

I'm a man in my early twenties. I've been away from my hometown for a couple of years now. I still keep in touch with a girl there and visit her once every few months. We're close but we still date other people.

About six months ago I went into a drug store and found myself standing for a long time in front of the cosmetics counter. An irresistible urge came over me—the urge to see myself made up as a woman. I gathered up lipstick, nail polish, eye makeup and blush, and went to the checkout counter.

It felt weird buying these things, but I realized that for many years I'd been curious how I'd look in makeup. I'd always thought I was beautiful and pretty, but I wanted to give myself the full beauty treatment.

The girl at the counter smiled at me. "Are these for you?" she teased, very innocently, I'm sure.

"They're for my girlfriend, silly," I said, blushing with embarrassment.

When I got home, I immediately put on the makeup. As I was spreading on lipstick and applying blush, my cock hardened. It got so big and rock-solid, it felt like it was going to tear through my pants. I stepped out of my jeans and underwear to give myself more room to grow.

Upon my first glimpse in the mirror of myself in makeup, I had a spontaneous ejaculation. It was amazing. My cock simply spewed out a load of come without even being touched. I pumped it until all the come had dripped out, and was amazed to see it was still hard. I kept jerking off, and soon felt another orgasm building up inside me. Fixing my eyes on the beautifully made up face in the mirror, and knowing it was mine, I pumped out another load.

Since then, I've made myself up and jerked off to my own image in the mirror every single day. I never dress in any feminine clothes. In fact, I always do this completely naked. It is very fulfilling for me, as I can have up to three orgasms before my cock goes completely soft.

If any of your other readers are wondering what it'd be like to see themselves as a member of the opposite sex, I heartily encourage them to try this exciting twist in their own lives.—*Name and address withheld*

HE JUST WANTS HIS PLACE IN THE SUN—OR ON A PLANE, A BOAT, A BUS . . .

They say there's a time and a place for everything. To me, that phrase has always been very erotic, because for me, the time is always right for sex, and anyplace is always the best place.

I have traveled a lot. Although I'm from the former Soviet republic of Georgia, where travel was very restricted for most citizens, I was involved in work that enabled me to see much of the world. I have been to many European countries, Australia, the United States and, of course, most of Russia and Eastern Europe. I am happy to say that I've seen most of these places not only with my eyes but, if I may put it bluntly, with my cock as well.

Everywhere I go I try to have a sexual experience. It's always been the biggest turn-on for me to have sex someplace new, someplace I never have been before, preferably someplace unusual, like a museum or ferry.

While I can enjoy sex in normal settings such as a bedroom, it is always much more erotic for me if I am in a place where there is the possibility of being spied on by others. My best fucks have always been on trains and in planes, cars and parks. Once I fucked a woman—a Greek exchange student I met while vacationing in France—on the beach in Nice. We were under a blanket, but it was most certainly clear to all those around us that she was enjoying the rapid, deep thrusts of my strong cock. Her sighs of orgasm aroused the interest of many of those around us. I'm sure that more that a few of them quickly retired to their own hotel rooms to satisfy their awakened libidos.

There's just something about having sex in public that I enjoy—even if no one can see me doing it. Let me explain. For many years I was a disc jockey on a Moscow radio station. I often fucked women in the studio while doing my show, pausing briefly between thrusts to change records and talk to my listeners. Many times while I was talking into the microphone, a lovely female friend was crouched between my knees, my balls in her mouth, her hand briskly pumping up and down on my shaft. No doubt I set the world record for orgasms while on the air.

And yes, a few of my listeners did know what was going on. Many times they would get in touch with me and ask if they could visit me at the station. I knew this always meant that they wanted to fuck and blow me while I was on the air. I would arrange for them to get through the radio station security, and then we'd be home free. Many times the women would simply come into the studio, strip down to their lovely, naked skin and go right to work pulling down my pants. My cock, legendary for its ability to get hard and stay hard for a long time, would welcome their soft mouths and wet pussies. I would spin records and read the news over the air while a slim, curvaceous female beauty was bouncing up and down between my legs like a horse on a merry-go-round.

Another time, I was part of a film crew that was doing a movie in one of the most beautiful caves in the Crimean mountains. I can't adequately describe the breathtaking, mysterious feeling of the total darkness, absolute silence and sublime contact with Mother Earth that occurs while fucking in such a location. We fucked standing, fully clothed, our pants lowered just enough for our cock and cunt to come together. This woman's pussy was hot as flame, and it sucked an orgasm from my body that weakened me to the bone.

Our grunts and cries echoed through the cave. These were followed by applause. It seems the other members of our crew had been watching us the whole time. Luckily this woman was no more shy than I. Seeing she had an audience made her even hornier. She turned around and bent over at the waist, inviting me to enter her from behind. My cock was still hard, and I slipped it into her with one sure stroke. I held her hips and thrust into her, fucking her soft, sweet pussy in front of the entire film crew.

I looked around to see that, one by one, they were dropping their pants, lifting their skirts and pairing off. In no time the cave was filled with the symphony of lust. People were fucking, eating cunt, sucking on cocks, to the left and right of me, on the floor of the cave, leaning against the film equipment. It mattered to none of us that we had work to do. We were all turned on to the point that nothing mattered besides the need to satisfy our carnal instincts.

That experience showed me that everyone, at one point or another in their life, can enjoy the pleasures of public sex. I am currently living in New York City, and I am lucky to have found an uninhibited American girlfriend. The day we met she told me that to be a real New Yorker, you have to fuck in Central Park. Before an hour had passed, we did just that, on a huge rock beneath some trees in the shadow of the apartment houses and hotels that line Fifth Avenue.

We've fucked all over New York, in view of all sorts of people. We even did it in the Empire State Building—although we had to do it in a stairwell, and as a result didn't have the great view we'd anticipated.

Now that I plan to stay in America, my two main goals for public fucking are the Statue of Liberty and the White House. Until then, my girlfriend and I will busy ourselves screwing in parks, horse-drawn carriages, taxis and movie theaters. Perhaps someday my girlfriend and I will be listed as one of New York's greatest tourist attractions!—*C.M., New York, New York* ⊙┤▆

WOMEN LIKE BARBARA MAKE IT EASY TO WAKE UP AND SMELL THE COFFEE

I love mornings more than any other time of day. After you read this, you'll know why.

My wife Barbara gets up earlier than I do. She's in the kitchen making coffee by five every morning. While the coffee is brewing, she hits the shower. By this time I'm usually half asleep, listening to her shower, imagining running my hands over the sumptuous curves of her wicked body. Barbara is an accountant, and those nerds she works with would go wild if they had any idea of what's under her business suit. Or maybe I should say, what's *not* under her business suit. Barbara never wears panties.

After she showers, Barbara pours our coffee and sets out two saucers on the counter. On one she pours a pile of sugar, and on the other, a mound of non-dairy creamer. Then she dips her big tits in each saucer—one in the sugar, one in the creamer—being sure to coat her dark, wide nipples with the powder. Now she comes into the bedroom.

"Wake up," she says softly, but I an already awake. My cock is bone-hard just from knowing what she's been up to. She is still naked, her tits covered with sugar and creamer. She hands me my coffee. I raise the cup to her sugar-covered tit, letting the sugar dissolve in my coffee. Then I do the same with the creamer-covered tit, jiggling it to make sure all the powder is off.

Now it's coffee time—but I don't drink from the cup. Instead, I wrap my lips around one of her big nipples, feeling it grow hard on my tongue as I lick off the sweet coffee taste.

Barbara loves having her nipples sucked, and soon she is writhing with pleasure, rubbing the wet area between her legs. She brings a pussy-drenched finger to my nose and says, "Ready for breakfast?"

Barbara lies back, spreads her cunt lips wide and gets ready for my long cock. I push it in slowly, and when it's buried to the hilt, fuck her with long, deep strokes.

We have to keep an eye on the alarm clock, as Barbara can't

miss her train. The pace of our fuck increases until we are bouncing up and down on the bed as though it's a trampoline. When I come, Barbara clenches my shoulders tightly and grinds her clit against me, rubbing herself to orgasm.

Then we both get up and head off to our jobs. As long as we start our days this way, I never mind getting up for work.—*Name and address withheld* O†—

SMOKIN' IN THE BOYS' ROOM—THAT IS, STROKIN' IN THE BOYS' ROOM

I recently had the pleasure of experiencing the most erotic encounter of my young life. I am a twenty-two-year-old male attending school in Washington, D.C., and have always considered myself straight. I am popular with women, who seem to like my intelligence, preppy good looks, sandy-blond hair and hard, gym-built body. Even though I don't pack the ten-inch fuck-tool many of your readers dream of possessing, I've never had any trouble getting my share of cunny.

It was a Sunday like any other. I was recuperating from a hard night of drinking in Georgetown, during which I'd met a rich, randy lady who picked me up in a bar, then fucked me in the limo that was taking her back home to her husband. I slept until noon, then decided to hit campus computer lab to do some homework.

After several hours in the lab, I departed for my dorm. Outside the lab I started talking with a very distinguished-looking older gentleman who appeared to be about fifty-five. Eventually we introduced ourselves, and he offered me a Cuban cigar. I never smoke tobacco products, but took him up on the offer because he'd said the cigar was a rare and excellent smoke. For nearly thirty minutes we stood outside, smoking and talking about sailing and politics, two subjects of which we were both quite fond.

It was getting near dusk when I excused myself to go back to the lab and take a leak. My new friend, whose name was Roger, said he also had to go to the bathroom, and followed me inside.

Standing side by side at the urinal, still smoking, we proceeded to relieve ourselves. It hadn't occurred to me that Roger might've been trying to pick me up, so you can imagine my surprise when he asked, rather bluntly, "Have you ever come to this men's room to jack off?"

I admitted to doing so once, after a long conversation with a beautiful young woman whose pants I'd been trying in vain to get into for many months. Roger told me that he usually went there every Sunday afternoon to jerk off while watching the hot-looking college men come in and out.

By this time, we both had hard dicks. Roger said that his biggest turn-on was to smoke cigars with handsome young men while jerking off. Although this was like no other sexual encounter I'd ever had, I was tremendously turned on. We repaired to a closed bathroom stall, and spent the next ten minutes blowing sweet cigar smoke on each other while pumping our dicks to an urgent climax. Although we never touched each other, it was some of the hottest sex of my life!

Roger eventually introduced me to a small circle of his friends who met weekly in the library of his Georgetown townhouse, where they drank brandy, smoked cigars and masturbated. I was quickly accepted into this group, and was amazed at how soon I grew comfortable with the idea of pumping my meat along with several other men. This small group includes some top government lawyers and officials, as well as many other successful gentlemen.

It's not the same as having sex with women, as none of us ever touch each other, but watching these men pump their dicks is very exciting for me. There's a real sense of community when we get together to share the basic, common interests of drinking, smoking and bringing ourselves to orgasm. I have had some excellent climaxes in this way.—*Name and address withheld* O┼─▨

THEY TACKLE BEDROOM BOREDOM BY PICKING UP A STUD IN TRAINING

After several years of marriage, sex between my wife and me became a subject of unspoken contention. I started looking for ways to bring back the romance. One evening I stumbled across some letters in *Penthouse Letters* about sharing fantasies. When it turned out later that night that Cleo was feeling sexy, I decided to give it a try. Without much preliminary action we moved into position for sex but, before we could fall into our old tired pattern of lovemaking, I began filling her ears with talk of other men sharing her body with me, and how we would take turns getting between her legs and shooting our loads of come up her pussy.

Wow! What a turn-around in sexual interest! All this smutty talk really got Cleo aroused. It was a great discovery for me too, and not just because it drove her into a fucking frenzy. I realized that releasing my hidden desires excited me as much as it obviously did her.

My storytelling became a regular part of our encounters. Instead of physical foreplay I would lie on top of her, my penis resting against her vaginal lips, half hard but making no attempt to enter her. I spun tales of me catching her in the arms of a delivery boy, or watching her blow some movie star while I jerked off in the shadows. She knew when I was excited by these stories because my dick would get hard. I knew she enjoyed them because she would get wet and open up. If we were both turned on by the same story, my dick would just naturally slip inside her without either of us moving much, and soon we would be fucking away.

While Cleo was still enjoying these scenarios as fantasies, my thoughts had already taken the next step—wanting to act some of them out. I couldn't shake the exciting idea of seeing my wife actually having sex with another man. On the one hand, it seemed like a crazy idea, and I was uncertain if it would be dangerous to our relationship. But it was also causing me incredible sexual stimulation just dreaming about what she would look like, how she would be dressed, the color of her lipstick, whether she would be driven to climax when someone else was pumping away inside her. I wondered about the sensation I would have in entering her right after some other man had come in her pussy. More importantly, I was afraid that in time my imagination would fail me, my stories would slip into the same kind of boring repetitiveness that our lovemaking had, and that would be just as bad for our marriage.

One night during foreplay we had a serious conversation about turning our fantasies into actual experiences. Cleo was very turned on to the idea, because I had explained to her that it was as much for my own enjoyment as hers that I wanted her to have sex with another man.

That night we shared some very juicy, slow lovemaking, continuing to talk until first she and then I were overcome by the throes of orgasm. Afterward, I couldn't believe how far we had already gone just to be able to discuss this so openly, especially when I consider the very conservative backgrounds we come from. It was happening, though, and for better or worse we were both keyed up by the idea.

That very weekend we decided to go to our favorite dance bar. We had been there often before, but never with the thought of picking up men. Cleo spent a lot of time making herself up in a very sexy way, with lips so thick, red and wet that no man living could possibly resist wanting to kiss them.

The place was packed with people. A live band was playing, and we had a couple of drinks to loosen up, then started dancing. Several times I walked away from Cleo, leaving her alone to accept the advances of other men. Just past midnight she started to dance a lot with one guy to whom she had obviously taken a liking. It was clear, from the way his hands kept seeking out her hips, her bottom and her breasts, that he was as horny as a bull elephant.

From across the room, lost in the standing-room-only crowd, I was thrilled by what was going on. When I saw them walk out of the main barroom toward the adjoining lobby, I pretended to head for the rest room so that I could follow them. It was lighter in the lobby, and I saw that my wife's suitor was a lot younger than I had previously realized. It was even more exciting knowing that my heretofore monogamous and conservative wife was attracting such a young cocksman.

Cleo was in the ladies' room for several minutes, and when she came back out, I could see that she had freshened her makeup. Because we had planned the evening, I also knew that the reason she had gone there at that particular moment was to insert her diaphragm. They walked outside and sat in his car, which was a good distance from the door of the club.

I probably should have been extremely patient and waited for my wife to come back to the bar, or just waited in my car for her to leave in hers, but I couldn't resist the temptation to take a walk and hope for a peek of what was happening. When I got near his car, I was gloriously stunned by what I saw.

My wife was on her back in the rear seat, and I was only able to see her naked left leg draped over the top of the seat. Her guy was butt naked. The car was rocking from side to side, and I could see the top of his ass humping up and down on her. God, I could have come right there, and I wanted so much to get closer, maybe even hear whether my wife was groaning or saying anything. After about a minute I forced myself to walk away for fear of interrupting their fuck session.

I couldn't wait to have the opportunity to get her home and fuck her myself, but it turned out to be a longer night than I had anticipated. When they were done fucking he whispered to Cleo for a minute, then they drove off! I had no alternative at this point other than to go home and wait for her to come back.

She finally rolled into our driveway at about three in the morning. Cleo was so thrilled by what had happened to her that she wanted to share every detail with me. As for me, that's exactly what I was waiting for.

She said that he had driven her to his apartment, which was very near the bar. "And it's a good thing it was so close," she added, "because his hard-on never went down after he came the first time." She was at least partly to blame for that, as she kept his dick in her mouth the whole time they were driving. He didn't get dressed for the drive, which is another reason it's a good thing they weren't going far. Cleo had gotten partly dressed, at least putting her blouse and skirt back on, though without any underwear. "It was so sexy, feeling my pussy lips rubbing together and feeling his come dribbling out between them every time I shifted my weight to get a better hold on his cock," she said with a warm smile.

I wasn't used to Cleo talking so openly about sex, even our own, and by the time she was five minutes into her story, I was so incredibly excited that I started fucking her. She continued the story, telling me that when they arrived at his apartment she had tackled him right inside the door. He kicked the door shut with his foot and just lay there on his back. Cleo took the opportunity to climb on top and slip his still-rigid pole into her cunt. "He's kind of a body builder," she said with a sexy smirk. "I loved rubbing his big chest and seeing his nipples stand out like a woman's." This little piece of information made me, if possible, harder, and Cleo moaned as I thrust into her. She continued her story.

They galloped on, with her on top of him thumbing his nipples, until they both had another massive orgasm. "Still he was hard!" she squealed, and the memory made her pussy start to contract on my cock. She went on to describe how they had moved at that point to his bed, where he made love to her much more slowly, in the missionary position. They held each other close and slid together and apart for almost an hour before he had his third, much less dramatic, orgasm.

By the time she told me that, I had held my come for as long as I could, and added my load to the three her other lover had already dumped there earlier in the night. I asked her what had happened next. "He wanted me to stay," she confided, "but I told him I had to get home so my husband could suck his load out of my pussy. You should have seen his jaw drop!" Of course, I immediately applied my lips to her cunt and did just what she had described. The combination of the two juices was indescribable, and sucking it out got me hard again. I was afraid Cleo would be too sore and tired to be happy about this, but on the contrary, she was delighted, and we fucked until almost dawn.

Your magazine, and a little imagination, have completely changed our sex lives.—*M.A., San Diego, California*   ⊖—▩

A COP'S GIRLFRIEND STOPS TRAFFIC, BUT STILL KEEPS THINGS FLOWING NICELY

My lover and I have been together for a little over three years, and our sex life has improved steadily. Our continued growth is due in great part to the openness and honesty which your magazine has fostered in us.

We are both in our mid-forties, and in good shape physically. Lee works in law enforcement, which gives him both the incentive and the opportunity to take care of his body. I was until recently an aerobics instructor, and continue to work out, which of course has kept me fit. I admit that I'm pretty vain about my looks and my body.

When I first started dating Lee, I thought it was rather perverse of him to suggest, during a warm Sunday ride in his car, that I take my blouse and skirt off and let the warm springtime sun play on my skin. The thought stayed in my mind, though, and I started to like it. Eventually I decided to try it. I was shy at first, but it felt great, and Lee was delighted.

He helped me get the seat all the way back, so that I was actually lying down, and we drove for what seemed like hours, letting the sun dance across my naked tits and pussy. I was so mesmerized that I didn't notice when a tractor trailer pulled alongside so that the driver could admire my nudity.

When I caught on I felt shy again immediately, but when Lee gently put his hand on my legs and eased his fingers into the pool of moisture between my thighs, I decided to go back to dreaming and enjoy what was happening. His artful fingers teased and played in the increasing wetness that flowed from my pussy.

I was surprised, the next time I opened my eyes, to find that our companion was still with us. Not only that, but he'd begun to signal us. He cupped one hand under his chest and pointed at me, to indicate my tits, then kissed his fingers to say that he liked them. This attention was making me wetter and wetter by the second. I began spreading my legs even further, to allow him a better view of Lee's fingers sliding in and out of me. He showed his pleasure by pulling the cord on his airhorn, letting out a long blast that was a shout of approval.

He began signaling a turn and pointing at us. Lee gave him the thumbs up. We got off the highway at the next exit and parked at a pulloff in some woods. Lee told me that he knew about this place from being a cop.

I was still naked, and he was still stroking my pussy, when the car came to a stop. I noticed that there were a few other cars around. I didn't notice that Lee had rolled down the window until I saw the truck driver standing by my side of the car, staring down at my body. I was by then writhing in a puddle on the leather seat as Lee continued to finger-fuck me.

Slowly and gently the stranger reached through the window and touched my thigh. He looked at me to see if this was all right with me, and when I just sighed he slid his hand up my thigh to my waiting pussy. Lee withdrew his hand, leaving me feeling empty, but not for long. Our new companion replaced Lee's hand, cupping my whole pussy for a moment and then softly slipping a finger inside. At the same time he pulled his stiffened cock out of his pants and began to stroke it.

Lee got out of the car and walked around to my side. He asked the stranger to step to one side for a moment. He opened the door, guided me out of the car and asked me if I wanted a good fucking from this guy. When I said yes he suggested that I bend over and put my hands on the seat for support. I did, arching my back and offering my moist cunt and ass for the stranger to enjoy.

Lee surprised me by pulling a bunch of condoms out of his pocket and handing one to the trucker, who accepted it graciously. I looked at Lee, who just smiled and shrugged at me. "I used to be a Boy Scout," he said. "I'm always prepared." Lee came back around the car, slid into the driver's seat and turned sideways to face me. He unzipped his pants, unbuckled his belt, and presented his cock to my face. In this glorious position I was able to eagerly wrap my lips around his dick while the stranger pushed his rubber-clad dickens into my cunt.

With the sun still beating down on my bare back, I started rocking back and forth between my two lovers. We got into a smooth rhythm that I wished could last forever. Nothing is perfect, though, and before too long I felt Mr. Trucker's penis pulsing inside my pussy, and felt the tip of the rubber swelling with his load. Not long after that, Lee's rod began to swell, and I knew that he was about to let go as well. I pulled his dick out until the tip just rested on my tongue, jerked him with my hand, and let him watch his sperm land all over my lips and teeth. When I had it all I licked it into my mouth and swallowed.

I assumed at this point that our afternoon delight had ended, but when I looked around I realized that another stranger had been watching from several yards down the road. He shyly stepped forward. The first stranger stepped aside, and the second guy began to feel my heaving breasts.

I stood up, turned around, and slid his sweatpants down over his hips, finding a nice hard cock tucked inside. Lee went and got his camera from the trunk of the car, and began taking pictures as I sucked candidate number two into my well-lubricated mouth. Lee stopped his camera work after a couple of minutes and handed me a condom, which I unrolled over the guy's erection. This not only protected me, but allowed me to savor his delightful prick for a little longer. Still, it wasn't long before he was close to coming, and I finished him with my hands so that I could pull off the rubber and watch his sperm spatter my breasts.

My two strange fucks thanked me very politely and went back to their vehicles. Lee and I got back in his car and headed home. I never did get dressed, though, and all the way back Lee kept fingering my cunt.

It was a glorious day, one I'll never forget. I'm so glad now that Lee suggested I start keeping a journal of our experiences, because the three years that have passed since then have been loaded with such adventures, and I would hate someday to forget a single one of them.—*L.B., Passaic, New Jersey*

SAFE SEX IS HOT SEX, ASSERTS A NEW CONVERT
TO RUBBERIZED JOY

It had been a fairly boring party. I had drifted in and out of half a dozen conversations, discussions I'd had before and will have again. Then a tall redhead spoke the magic word "sex." My brain popped back into gear and I started to listen. The word "sex" had been preceded by the word "safe." She was arguing that anyone with a little imagination can still enjoy a casual encounter and remain safe.

I must admit I was attracted by the idea, as I hadn't had any encounters, casual or otherwise, in entirely too long. I hung around to add my two cents on the topic. The party slowly died around us, and soon there were just the three of us: Tracy, her boyfriend Peter and myself.

Once we arrived, Peter and Tracy began my lessons in safe sex. I was invited to undo the zipper on Tracy's sexy dress, and she sensuously wiggled out of it while Peter went off to the bedroom. She had large brown areolae surrounding her nipples, and her breasts stood firm and high. Dull red hair showed in wisps around her cleft, and a little line of juice was flowing down her left leg.

She invited me to sit on the sofa, and moved behind me. Bending over, she nibbled at my neck while unbuttoning my shirt. Her lips were soft and her wet tongue began to explore my ear as she undid my belt. Her fingers flicked over my hard nipples, blowing cool air into my damp ear. The bulge in my pants began to grow.

Peter returned, and announced that the bedroom was ready. He came over and took off my shoes and socks while Tracy continued biting my neck, and I soon felt my pants sliding off.

With a hand from Peter and a final lick from Tracy, I rose and followed them into the bedroom. Tracy went over to Peter and began to undress him while I sat on the bed. I was surprised to find that Peter was wearing red lace panties and black stockings under his pants.

Tracy started another phase of the lesson by explaining that good safe sex was more than wham-bam-thank-you-ma'am. It's slow and enjoyable, involving the whole body. She told me to close my eyes. I felt a hot, wet tongue at my ear again, and soft fingers lightly caressing my brow. I felt my feet being grasped and firmly rubbed. My head began to spin from the warm scent of Tracy's breath. Her soft lips roamed over my face, neck and chest while the massage crept up my legs, relaxing my tensions and making me sigh.

It was a unique experience, and my penis rose under my shorts as my lovers approached it. They stopped for a prolonged kiss above my pulsing prick. Then I was rolled over, and Peter's strong hands continued rubbing upward until he could cover my ass with kisses. By the time my neck was being firmly rubbed by Peter, Tracy was circling my big toe with her teasing tongue, just like it was a cock.

Part three was a demonstration that a rubber could be a superbly sexy toy. Still on my back, now without my shorts in the way, I watched Tracy begin working on my cock, teasing with her fingernails, lightly brushing my balls. I arched up each time she fluttered over my steaming sacs.

Tearing open the package, she took the condom in her mouth, holding it in place by suction. Ever so slowly she descended toward my quivering cock. Working with finesse, she unrolled the rubber, pausing frequently to work back up to the tip, then back to the roll, licking carefully to be sure of a tight fit. Once I was securely covered, she turned to Peter and let me watch as she covered his shaft in the same way.

I was soon rolled over and on all fours as Tracy crawled under me. Propping her head on a pillow, she began to play her tongue over my rubberized rod. With an expert cocksucker, a rubber is really no barrier to pleasure. In fact it can help to make it last longer. Tracy sensed my every twitch, and her timing was incredible. I kept building up, but she kept me just this side of coming for I don't know how long.

Somewhere during this, Peter returned. I felt fingers on my ass-cheeks, followed by the sensation of warm oil being spread over my ass and up along my back. Tracy was working in perfect harmony with his stroking hands, sucking on my rigid rod as my back and butt were pleasured.

I was beginning to feel loose all over, cared for, paid attention to in a way that I wasn't used to. I felt Peter's weight on top of me, and then the hardness of his rubber-covered cock sliding between my cheeks and up the base of my spine. I clenched my cheeks to squeeze him more tightly.

It was a dream come true, with a hot and skillful redhead giving me a slow, deep blowjob, while her stocking-clad boyfriend let me feel what it was like to have a dick and balls sliding all over my lubricated fanny. Sudden hard sucks from Tracy pulled my orgasm from me, and I gasped repeatedly as I came. Peter held my hips and pressed his hardness against me, increasing the strength of my contractions.

When I finally went limp, Peter peeled my condom off and gently cleaned my softening dick with a warm washcloth. Tracy reached over to the night table and handed me a dildo. As her cunt was just below my face, I dropped to my elbows, my ass in the air, which let Peter know that his attentions had been welcome, and he went back to sliding up and down my ass-crack.

I slowly inserted the dildo in Tracy's wet and waiting slit. I was tempted to give a lick, but I stuck to the dildo for safety's sake. I discovered a button on the end, and turned on the motor hidden in that counterfeit cock. I kept it to a slow vibration at first, and used shallow strokes. My thumb would carefully make contact with her clit every once in a while, and I felt her begin to wiggle below me. Soon all three of us were moving in the same rhythm, Peter's dangling dong sliding smoothly, the dancing dildo just touching Tracy's cervix, then out and in again.

The bed was shaking, and Tracy began to move beneath me. With a cry, she bucked under me and came, over and over again, and I felt Peter speed up. Again, I clenched my muscles, giving him some friction to work with, and soon I felt the tip of his condom begin to fill with his hot spunk, his voice rising and falling in waves of ecstasy.

Sex can be safe and great, and the gender of your partner is not the only thing to be concerned with.—*R.D., Albany, New York*

Someone's Watching

BORN-AGAIN WIFE FOOLS AROUND;
HE SAYS "MORE"

My wife Sharon and I have been married for twenty years, and together for twenty-two. In her younger days my wife was very popular, and as a result had a number of sexual relationships. She was in such a relationship when we met.

After nine years of marriage I started getting restless and bored with our sex life. I started reading *Penthouse Letters,* as well as other sex publications. We both got a charge out of them and they rekindled our sex life. We started sharing our fantasies with each other. My wife's fantasies were all very laid back, while mine were a little on the kinky side.

My prime fantasy was to see my wife fuck another man. We talked about this, and it was very arousing, but the fantasy lacked details.

After a lot of discussion, Sharon said she'd like to try it, and we had to think who her new partner would be. It would have to be someone discreet and clean, maybe one of her earlier sex partners, maybe someone new.

One night, while enjoying some sex play, she shyly mentioned our friend Thom. Thom has wanted my wife Sharon from the time we first met. Thom has dated one of Sharon's close friends, and we have always talked openly about sex. He seemed a good choice.

My wife called him on the phone that same night, about nine o'clock. To our surprise he answered, as he usually goes out. Sharon asked why he was home and he said Susan was sick and he was sitting home bored stiff. My wife told him the stiff part sounded very interesting, and to hold that thought and come over. He told her, "Don't tease me; in my condition I might take you up on that." My wife responded with, "Please do. You won't be sorry," and with that she hung up the phone and unplugged it.

I wasn't sure he'd come, but he was there in about thirty minutes. My wife met him at the door in a white shirt of mine, a white garter belt, tan hose and white high heels. She greeted him with a giant French kiss that about brought him out of his shoes. A really special night followed, but my wife told me the next day that she didn't need or want any other dick in her pussy than mine. This was a letdown to me, and our sex life went back to the old routine.

My wife returned to college and graduated with a master's degree. She also started going to church, and was "saved," or born again. This in itself put a lot of strain on our marriage, as I'm the same guy I've always been.

My wife now has a job that takes her from Cincinnati to Columbus once a week with a co-worker, a two-hour drive each way.

Sharon was doing the driving one trip. They had to gas up, and my wife got out and started pumping while Eli did some paperwork. He asked Sharon a question and, startled, she bumped the hose and sent eighty-nine octane flying everywhere, including on her brand-new dress.

My wife is a natural blonde with very sensitive skin. She has a firm thirty-six-inch bustline and thirty-inch waist and is very healthy looking. Also at my request she wears only a garter belt to support her tan hose—no panties or bra—and high heel pumps. This dress code of mine is to allow me to fantasize about others maybe getting a peek of her private parts.

Well, chivalry isn't dead. Eli offered her his sport coat. Sharon still had to get out of her gas-drenched dress. To make matters worse, it was about ten at night and there was no place to buy anything new. The sport coat was going to have to do. Sharon now had to explain to the professor about her dress, or lack of, and why her kinky husband asked her to dress that way.

He said he understood and not to give it another thought. Sharon headed for the ladies' room to wash off. She was able to get quite clean and with a little perfume was good as new—or better, being without a dress. Now, my wife is only five feet tall, and Eli is himself about five foot seven, which allowed very little material to cover my wife's nakedness. The coat just barely covered my wife's pretty little pussy, and anyone close could see the naked skin above her tan hose. When she was sitting behind the wheel and shifting gears, one can only imagine the beaver shot she would be giving the young professor.

My wife said the professor about swallowed his tongue when she got back in the car, and this, while being embarrassing, was also very arousing to her. Remember, this is a church-going Christian girl of thirty-eight years of age.

My wife said that Eli could not keep his eyes on anything but her, and knowing this good-looking guy was able to see anything he wanted was making her hotter than tolerable. She told him this and asked him to turn out the map light.

Sharon said they pulled off the interstate to regather their composure. This proved to be the worst thing they could have done. Eli started rubbing himself, and this really excited my already horny wife. Soon they were both masturbating while watching one another. When Eli pulled his dick from his pants, my wife could not believe the size of his sex-root. She said that compared to my six-and-a-half-inch dick this one must be eight inches long and seven or eight inches around. The sight of this huge dick was just too much for her to let alone, so she reached over to give Eli some welcome assistance.

My wife loves to suck cock, so it was understandable that in a matter of seconds she had to have that male member in her mouth. At this point the professor leaned over and stuck two fingers in her steaming cunt. My wife informed me that his dick in her mouth was too much to let get away without being able to experience how it would feel to have this giant of a cock in her very wanting pussy, so they had to leave the car.

They went to a grassy area invisible from the road, where this guy fucked my wife's little tight pussy with that monster for what seemed to her to be much too short a time. My wife said that, even though she was very hot and wet, when he first pushed that dick between her wide-open legs it still hurt a little, but she had to have his organ inside of her cunt.

When she told me the whole story, she said she had never experienced anything as overwhelming as being filled by his giant cock. She also told me that she had climaxed three times in that short period. She has never in her life had more than one orgasm in a single fuck session.

It was good to know that we still had no secrets, or so I thought at the time. I told her I forgave her. I also found this incident to be very sexually arousing, and told Sharon I would love to hear more. The next week's trip came and I hoped to hear of some more sex advances, but when my wife came home all that was said was how much she loves me. This was nice, but I had hoped for something erotic.

A few weeks went by, and my wife was in better spirits than usual. We enjoyed some good lovemaking, her story still fresh in our minds. One Friday, Sharon told me she was going out with her girlfriends Susan and Kris. This was not uncommon, but I happened to know that Thom and Susan were going out of town for the weekend. I decided to see what was up, so I went to the local restaurant where she was supposed to meet her friends. Her car was there, so I decided to wait a while. Sharon was there only about half an hour when she came back out—not with her friends, though. Sharon was walking out with—that's right—the professor.

They both left, with my wife following him and me close—but not too close—behind them both. They drove to the country, and at that point I knew where they were headed, so I dropped a little way back.

I parked my car a short distance up his long private drive and walked to the house. The lights were on, so I started snooping around. I went from window to window until I got to the patio. Music was playing and I could hear both of their voices through the sliding screen door. I could see inside without them discovering me, as by now it was about midnight and very dark outside. There was my Christian wife in a black miniskirt, a white, translucent, criss-cross, low-cut blouse with no bra, a black garter belt, tan hose and black high heels. This is not what she had on when she left home; she had changed at the restaurant.

Through the door I could see them on the couch. He was kissing my pretty wife all over, but she would not let him kiss her on the lips. She kept telling him, "Love is for my husband, this is just sex—good sex, but nonetheless sex." Eli pushed the mini up to her waist and fully exposed my wife's pretty blonde pussy. He began probing her hole with his thumb while rubbing her clit with his forefinger. Sharon unzipped his fly and let out the biggest dick I've ever seen. I have never seen a dick so large in diameter in all my years playing sports, and now here was my wife rubbing and kissing this monster attached to another man. They were both getting hotter with every stroke. He pushed her back and planted his face in her pussy. She let out a sigh and pushed her hips solidly against his mouth. Eli then pulled back and started to shove his monster snake into my wife's hot box. I thought, There is no way all of that will fit in this little lady's pussy. Eli started going in very slowly, and as I saw the head go in, my wife's mouth dropped open and she let out a long, guttural moan of ecstasy.

I have never seen such a sexy look of fulfillment and lust at the same time, and this was my very conservative, loyal wife, not a porn queen. After about six strokes my wife said to him, "Let me on top." Sharon stood up, pulled off her blouse, stepped out of her skirt and stood in front of this guy naked, so that he could see those beautiful tits sticking straight out and that pretty blonde patch between her gorgeous legs.

She pulled him to the floor, put the pillows from the sofa under him and stood over him. Then my wife started to lower herself onto his love-pole. This was the best sight I have ever seen—my wife above this king dong, wearing only her black heels, hose, and black garter belt, and with the biggest "fuck me" look on her face I've ever seen.

As the head of his cock touched her pussy, she lowered a little more and let out another groan, then impaled herself on this man's stiff rod. I was amazed as Sharon started fucking this guy. She was doing deep knee bends on this huge cock, with every plunge a scream of joy and with every withdrawal a deep breath and a call for more cock. She was going crazy with lust and desire. I didn't know this woman, but loved her desire to be completely and totally fucked. Those deep knee bends must have taken their toll on her gorgeous legs, as my wife fell on top of this newfound fuck partner and, with a wide-open mouth, gave the professor a very lusty French kiss. So much for keeping her love for me! With all the passion I've ever seen from her, she nearly screamed in his ear, saying "Fuck me now. Fuck me like I've never been fucked before."

The professor quickly stood up, gathered up the couch cushions that were piled under his ass and put two of them in an arm chair. He scooped up my wife and laid her across the arms of the chair. Eli then put one of her legs on the back of the chair and with one thrust buried that giant, hard dick deep inside my wife's love-hole. My wife once again moaned loudly with joy, yelling, "Yes! Yes! Fuck me. Fuck me hard!" The professor was sawing in and out of my wife's cunt with fury. My wife started yelling, "Oooh, oooh, yeeeaaah!" By the look on her face and the broken words she was screaming, it was apparent my wife was coming violently and continually, wave after wave rushing through her body.

The professor just kept fucking that sweet little box for upward of half an hour before he finally moaned and started shooting his seed deep within my wife's now well-fucked pussy. Sharon told him that she had never felt so full of dick in her life, nor had she ever experienced so many orgasms during one encounter.

I hurried back to my car and then home to change my come-drenched pants before Sharon got home. She came home about an hour after I got out of the shower. She smelled fresh as a daisy. She came over to me, gave me a big, wet French kiss, and said she had danced with a guy who had a bulge in his pants. "It made me very horny," she pouted, "I need a big dick in my pussy, right now."

Being the guy I am, I gladly helped her with this problem. She was very wet and sticky inside, but had obviously taken a shower before returning home. We fucked for a while and she came only once, but while we were fucking I again mentioned how much I would love to see her with a big dick in her pussy. She told me that she had been thinking about me wanting this and was considering doing it, but not as a threesome. She didn't want me fucking anybody else if she did agree to fuck somebody for my pleasure. My pleasure, I thought, yeah. While this will give me great pleasure, I wonder if she will try to convince me that her friend the professor would be a good choice or whether she will opt for someone I know nothing about. She did admit that she has a couple of ideas, but would not tell me who until she thought about it some more.

I've just found out that I have to leave town for a few days and my wife has told me that she and her girlfriends were planning on going out that weekend, since I would be gone anyway. I wonder if it's true this time.—*W.S., Cleveland, Ohio*

DANCING, DRINKS AND DALLIANCE WHILE DADDY DIDDLES

My wife Lynn and I have been married for ten years. We have two great kids. We have never fooled around on each other, but I have often told her that it is my fantasy to watch her being serviced by a couple of well-hung studs. She always said maybe some time soon, but she also laughed and blushed, and I didn't know if it would happen.

One night we were at a dance club and ran into a business contact, Earl, who was visiting from out of town. He was there with another friend, Dryfus, and I invited them to our table for drinks. Earl is a tall, athletic black man, as is his friend. When they arrived at our table I introduced them to Lynn, we ordered drinks, and Lynn and I went to dance.

When we came back Earl invited Lynn to dance. That Lynn immediately said yes surprised me.

Lynn was wearing a tight, red mini-dress with string straps. It barely covered her tits and was short enough that it barely covered her ass. The first dance was lively, the second a slow one, and then they returned to the table. I put my hand under the tablecloth and onto Lynn's legs. I often like to play with her pussy when no one can see. When I got to her panties, they were soaked. I realized that Lynn was slightly drunk, very horny, and was staring at Earl as I stroked her thighs. I'm sure he noticed as well.

When Earl and Lynn went again to dance, I could see that Earl had his hands all over Lynn's ass and was grinding her pelvis. When they came back, Earl invited us to his hotel, and in a moment we were in a limo and on our way. In the limo, Lynn sat between Earl and Dryfus in the car and I sat across. I knew that Lynn was about to be fucked by these two black studs. In the car Earl had his hand on Lynn's thigh, and he looked over at me. I smiled, and nodded that it was all right. As he worked his hand up her thigh, Dryfus began to kiss her. She offered no resistance when Earl put his fingers in her panties and fingered her very wet cunt.

When we arrived at the hotel we all got out, and I told Lynn that I loved her and wanted to watch as they fucked her. She kissed me and we all went to the room.

I sat in a chair in the corner as Earl pulled Lynn's dress off and let it fall to the floor. Dryfus came over and started kissing her. Lynn, clad in only sheer bikini panties, was being kissed and fondled by her black lovers. They laid her on the bed and removed her panties. While Earl was kissing her tits, Dryfus stripped off his clothes and put the head of his cock in Lynn's mouth. Earl also stripped and, while Lynn was sucking on Dryfus's cock, Earl got between her legs and gently penetrated her pussy. With her legs wrapped around him, Lynn begged him to fuck her pussy hard.

After twenty minutes her studs switched positions, and Dryfus was now banging her pussy. Earl was first to come, and he shot a huge load of come in her mouth and all over her face. Lynn eagerly swallowed what she could. When Dryfus was ready to come, he pulled out of Lynn's pussy and put his cock in her mouth. She ate his sperm and licked his cock clean. Earl lay on the bed, Lynn got on top of him and put her pussy over his mouth, asking him to eat her. Lynn humped his face and had a huge orgasm.

They then positioned Lynn on her hands and knees so that Earl could fuck her cunt from the rear while she again sucked Dryfus's cock. By now I had my cock out and was masturbating. While Lynn was having her mouth and pussy fucked she was telling them how she loved having black cock in her.

After a couple of hours of their little gang bang, Earl called room service for some food and drinks. The waiter was a little stunned when he entered to see a beautiful white girl lying naked in bed between two black studs, and he watched Lynn suck cock while he arranged our food. After the waiter left we all sat around a small table and ate. Lynn sat on Earl's lap. She asked me if I liked watching her as much as she liked being fucked by her studs.

When we finished eating, Lynn told her lovers she was ready for more. She fucked and sucked her two lovers for hours, until Earl and Dryfus both said they were done. Lynn dressed, kissed her lovers, and we left.

In the morning Lynn told me that she was sore but that she wanted to be fucked by more young black studs. Since then, Earl and Dryfus have visited three more times, resulting in all-night fuck sessions, and we're looking for other black men for Lynn to bring home and seduce.—*J.C., Albany, New York* O—▪

GOOD FOR THE GOOSE, GOOD FOR THE GANDER, GOOD FOR A LAUGH

My wife and I read your *Penthouse Letters* magazine all the time. We have a whole *drawerful!* We would like to share an experience.

This past summer we went on a campout. The campsite we had in mind was only a thirty-minute drive from our home, far enough away to shake a few hassles but close enough to run home if we discovered we'd forgotten anything.

Becky and I arrived at the campground around noon. It appeared to be dead, hardly a person there. I noticed three guys in a camp across from us, and that was it.

We set up camp and went for a swim. It was already hot. It always is around here in July.

Becky stands five feet five inches tall and weighs a hundred and thirty-five pounds; it's all in the right spots too. She has long, slender, milky legs and gorgeous red hair. When we went to the water I noticed the three guys at the other camp looking at her, and of course she would occasionally steal a look at them.

After a little splashing, crotch-grabbing and other fun, we got out and went back to our camp. I took out the grill and fired it up. While I was lighting it I noticed a lot of activity on the lot next to us. I couldn't help noticing that the new recruits were all women. As it turned out, it was an all-woman campout sponsored by a local company. By nightfall there were fifty gals and bunches of tents. I tried to act cool, like I didn't even notice, but my wife didn't fall for it.

We had dinner and turned in early. I tried to sleep, but hell, there was just too much noise from the women next door. Then, as always happens when you can't sleep, I had to piss.

I felt for the door in the dark and slipped out as quiet as a mouse. I went to the outhouse, then headed back to the camper. As I passed in the shadows, one of the girls called me. For a moment I just stood there. I knew if I was caught I was dead but, like any fool who thinks with his crotch, I went into their camp.

The girls did all the intros, and I was offered a cold beer. I don't know for sure how long we sat, but I finished three or four Buds and found myself in a tent with a little blonde. She was round and soft, with skin like snow. We fucked and sucked for what seemed like hours (actually only thirty to forty minutes, but you can get a lot done in that little time). She loved to be on top, and that gave me a chance to paw her cute little tits. She had the kind on which the haloes start getting hard before the nipple and stand out like little cones from the rest of the tit. I couldn't get enough of watching them grow and then wrinkle up, and I was really sorry when she came, because her pussy squeezed me so tight I couldn't stop myself and shot up into her with everything I had.

I was pulling on my jeans, thinking, I'm dead. What a dumb fuck, going to get killed over some girl and you don't even remember her name. It was only a couple hundred feet to our campsite, but I came up with and discarded a dozen excuses over that distance. As I opened the door I thought, Fuck, this is it. To my surprise, Becky was gone.

I thought at first I had lucked out, but then I thought, You're not out of this yet, stupid. After a few minutes passed, I started to worry more about my wife than my own sorry ass, and left the camper in search of her. I checked the outhouses: no Becky. So here I am, two hundred thirty-five pounds of bull fool creeping around the shadows like some fucking commando or something, except that I kept stepping on sharp rocks in my bare feet and cursing. It was pretty funny, but I wasn't laughing then.

I had searched everywhere except the camp with the three young guys in it. I crept slowly over to their tent and looked in the side window. I couldn't believe my eyes. There on the tent floor lay my wife. One of the guys was pumping his dick in her tight pussy like mad! The other two were up at her head, one on either side. She was sucking on one and pumping away at the other with her hand. Every few strokes she would switch the one in her mouth.

Becky is a very talented woman, and she managed to calculate how close those guys were until she had them both hanging over the edge of the cliff. She then started working them both with her hands, and when she touched the heads of their two dicks together, just over her mouth, they both exploded, their jism spraying all over each other's dick and dripping down into her open mouth. She swallowed for all she was worth, but a little still leaked from the corner of her mouth.

They backed away with big grins on their faces. I looked at the other guy. I knew he was close, and when my wife moaned, "Yeah, baby, shoot me full," I knew he was done. His face looked like a devil-mask, it was so red and twisted with the intensity of his pleasure, and I could see the blood drain from it as the sperm drained from his dick.

I hurried back to our camper and waited for Becky to return. She came in and told me that she had seen me. I told her what I had seen. Mexican standoff. Then we both began to laugh. We made hot love and left before dawn. We didn't want to face anyone the next day.—*B.B., Trenton, New Jersey* ⚭

THEY WERE READY TO SPLIT, UNTIL SHE DISCOVERED STRANGERS

I'm a guy who loves to see my wife get fucked by other guys. People might be surprised to hear that it hasn't hurt our marriage—in fact, it's improved it!

Our relationship had been falling apart, and Sunny and I decided to go out for what we thought would be one last night. We were in a nice bar and Sunny, a beautiful woman, started opening up to all the guys, since she felt she was now free. She became particularly friendly with two men, and one of them invited us all over to his place, where the partying continued.

My sexy wife could always turn guys on, and she really went to work on those two fellows, probably to make me jealous and let me know she'd have no trouble scoring on her own. She was sitting on the couch with them, and all three were making suggestive moves while I looked on.

I went to the bathroom, and when I came back I couldn't believe what I saw. My wife was already naked and she was helping the two guys get their clothes off. She said I could join in, but didn't pay much attention to me as the three of them entered the bedroom.

I took off my clothes and followed, but was left watching the action as Sunny began jerking off her two new friends on the bed. She was definitely leading the way, and got on her knees so one of the guys could enter her from behind. Then she began sucking the other guy's cock. I was reduced to jacking off while I watched my wife go wild getting fucked by and sucking off strangers. The guy in her mouth shot his load, and Sunny swallowed it, something she had never really liked before.

The guy fucking her started pounding away, and I could see Sunny was in ecstasy. She came twice before he finally did.

I couldn't stand it anymore and jumped on Sunny. She came again before I shot my love-juice into her hot pussy. She got up, looked at the three of us and said, "Well, I saw, I conquered, and I came," then walked out to get dressed.

That was fourteen years ago, and our marriage has been great ever since.—*B.N., North Miami Beach, Florida*   O┼▪

I SAW BILLY KISSING LORELEI, AND THAT AIN'T ALL

Our whole family was together for the holidays, and let me tell you I have a big one: I'm one of eight brothers, two of them adopted. We also have a huge house, and some of the guys had brought home not only their wives and fiancees, but buddies as well.

On the second night that I was home I got up in the middle of the night to go to the bathroom. To get there, I had to pass the room that my older brother Eric's friend Billy was staying in. He and his wife Lorelei were the only other people in that wing of the house besides myself.

As I walked by, I noticed that the bedroom light was still on and the door was slightly ajar. I glanced in and caught a glimpse of Billy's wife getting out of bed—completely nude. She is a tall woman, with really large breasts, and dark, sexy-looking nipples. As she stood up I looked her over from head to toe, pausing to admire her neatly trimmed but still full-looking bush. The bed in the room is fairly close to the door, so I could really get a good view.

As she stood up, she was looking back at the bed where Billy lay, swinging his legs over the edge. She began running her hands all over her body, rubbing her breasts and pinching her dark, protruding nipples. She then reached down, slipped two fingers into her already swollen pussy and squished them around. After a minute of this she took her fingers out of her pussy, wafted them under Billy's nose and then slipped them into her mouth.

I heard some rustling, and before I could move I saw Billy scoot forward toward the edge of the bed, also completely naked. Now, I've seen guys naked before, but I'd never seen anyone with a hard-on. And what a hard-on this was. It must have stretched eight or nine inches away from his flat stomach, and it had a large bulbous head that had the skin stretched tight.

As he watched his wife dip her fingers in and out of her pussy, his hand slipped onto this massive cock almost by itself. In a trance-like state he began moving his hand slowly up and down the shaft. As he did this, the head of Billy's prick began to take on an almost crimson shade. I began to feel stirrings inside my own pajamas as I watched this man and his wife warm themselves up.

Well, the sight of Billy working his staff back and forth made his wife moan, and she dropped to her knees between his legs. I was frozen. I couldn't have moved if I'd wanted to. For the next fifteen minutes I watched, mouth agape, as Lorelei gave Billy the blowjob of his dreams. I could see the crimson head and moist shaft disappear into her mouth with a pistoning action. Every once in a while she would pull it out and run her tongue along the length of it, and then bury her nose in his balls until he arched his back and made guttural noises of pleasure. Then she would return her warm, wet mouth to the straining purple head of Billy's dick. She continued this intense, constant action until Billy was ready to come.

As he started to shoot, he begged her to hold on—and she kept sucking for all she was worth. With one final grunt he let his hot load go. I guess that it must have been a while, because I could see her cheeks bulge out, even though she was trying to swallow, and I could see a few streams of sticky come slipping out of the corners of her mouth.

By this time I had a raging hard-on that was begging for attention so, holding my breath, I quietly tiptoed into the bathroom and began stroking my own seven-inch member while replaying the scene I had just witnessed. Then, just like my brother's friend before me, I let out a groan and let my hot semen fly. I was so worked up that I managed to splatter the full-length mirror I was standing in front of.

As I calmed down, I tucked my spent penis back into my shorts and began cleaning up the bathroom. I got myself a glass of water and tiptoed back to my room. As I passed Billy and Lorelei's room, I noticed that the door was closed, and wondered if they had left it ajar hoping that someone would see them. With that thought in my mind, I climbed back into bed with a contented smile on my face and drifted off to sleep.—*Name and address withheld* O†—▪

HIS BRIDE SAID "I DO" AND NOW HE CAN SEE THAT SHE CERTAINLY DOES

My wife Diane is twenty-nine years old and was a virgin when we met in college. She has thirty-four-inch tits, brown hair and a great figure from working out. She gets many looks from men wherever we go. With the parties that are frequent in our community, we have had the opportunity to lead a fairly active social life, and have made some great friends.

One night Beth, one of Diane's single friends, came over after her exercise class. I overhead Beth telling Diane about the studs she'd met at the club she frequents. One guy, Neil, had recently fucked her brains out with his gigantic cock. Beth suggested that she could set something up so that Diane could also have the opportunity to experience Neil's cock. Diane laughed and said that she was happily married and could never fuck anyone else. That night, Diane woke me up and we had some really intense sex. I wondered if she was fantasizing about Neil and his big dick.

Last month we attended a party that ended up being a real blowout. There was lots of dancing and so much changing of partners that spouses rarely danced with each other. Beth and I danced together several times that night, and I also happened to see Neil, whom Beth had brought as her date, dancing with my wife as often as he could. Diane was dressed in a sexy minidress that showed off her figure. From across the room, I saw Neil running his hands over her thighs and ass. Since I was also doing the same thing to Beth, it was no big deal. Oddly, though, I felt turned on watching him touch my wife.

Beth was keeping me occupied—probably so my wife could flirt with Neil—but the more drunk she got, the more interested she became in some of the unattached single guys. By then everyone was pretty smashed, and I began to hunt around for my wife so we could leave. I was really horny from all of the flirting, and in the mood for a great fuck.

After looking around for a few minutes, someone told me that Diane wasn't feeling well and that my "friend" Neil gave her a lift home a little while earlier. I dashed home and, sure enough, Neil's car was parked in front of the house—Neil, the notorious ladies man with the really big dick. Maybe they were already fucking. Hoping to finally get my wish of seeing my wife make it with another man, I quietly entered through the back door and crept upstairs toward our bedroom.

As I peeked into my bedroom, I saw my wife and Neil lying on the bed with all their clothes still on, but engaged in a passionate kiss. My wife said to Neil, "I told you I give great goodnight kisses." Diane, although pretty drunk and very interested in kissing, was reluctant to let Neil go any further.

But soon he was running his hands all over Diane's body, eventually centering on her succulent breasts. Giggling, she said, "Come on, Neil. I'm a married woman. We shouldn't be doing this. At least not in my husband's bed." Neil just laughed as he unbuttoned her blouse and reached in to lift her left tit from its bra cup. Diane put up no resistance, sighed and closed her eyes. She pulled him down and let him take one stiff nipple into his mouth. In a matter of minutes Diane's blouse and bra were on the floor and, for the first time in our marriage, she was topless in front of another man.

Neil began to run his hands all over her legs, slowly inching his way under her skirt and up to her crotch. My wife was biting her lip and beginning to breathe hard—sure signs of arousal. She ran her hands all over his ass, thighs and crotch, but never touched his erection, which by now was visible through his slacks. She was getting off just playing with him.

After five minutes of this, Neil stood up and slowly pulled off his pants and shirt. Diane began to squirm as she gazed at his hairy chest and the huge erection that was now hidden only by his underpants. Seconds later he pulled off his shorts, revealing the biggest cock I have ever seen. It was nearly a foot long and as thick as Diane's wrist—at least twice as big as my cock. Diane was no longer shy about Neil's prick. She began practically begging him to use it on her.

But now it was Neil who was calling the shots. "You played hard to get with me," he said. "Maybe you don't want my cock after all."

"No, I do. I want to suck it and feel it inside me," Diane said sweetly.

"First," Neil told her, "I want you to put on your sexiest nightie, something real hot that'll show off your body." In a flash, Diane was going through her dresser. She fished out a red, see-through teddy. She put it on, and it showed off her hairy brown bush. Neil looked on, pumping his cock and making the head of his penis huge. I could see pre-come on the tip.

"You have the hairiest pussy I have ever seen," he said. "Come over here so I can see it better. Lay down on the bed and spread your legs wide. Play with yourself. Stick your fingers in your hole and show me how wet you are." Diane was reluctant at first, but Neil continued to encourage her. "Use your fingers to open up your cunt," he continued. "Let me see all the way in. There you go! Now give me those fingers to lick."

Diane was completely under Neil's spell and did whatever he asked. Her fingers were working busily over her squishy-wet cunt lips. She looked deeply into his eyes as she began to arch her back, approaching climax. Neil knelt over her and started to rub his cock all over her body, but when she reached for his prick, he told her not to touch.

My wife was now squirming all over the bed, begging him to touch her pussy, but he continued to tease her and stayed clear of her thatch. It was a good fifteen minutes before he finally began swabbing his dick all across her clitoris and labia.

While he was doing this, he began pumping one, then two fingers in and out of her sopping-wet twat, and my wife began running her fingers all over his cock. She said to him, "I want your rod in my cunt. I've never seen a cock that big, and I want it to fill me all the way up. Come on now, Neil, please slide that big fucking dick into me!" With these words, she jiggled her clit and came explosively. I'd been pulling at my cock while watching the whole spectacle, and suddenly I reached the point of no return, splashing a creamy load onto the wall outside our bedroom.

Diane again started pleading with Neil to slip her his meat, but he would only continue to tease her, rubbing his cock over her pussy, probing the entrance with the spongy tip but refusing to slide it all the way in. "I know how much you want my cock," he said. "Just imagine how great your pussy is going to feel all filled up with this huge pole. I can't wait either."

Apparently, though, he was willing to wait a little while longer. My wife was in a frenzy, thrusting her hips upward in an effort to get Neil's cock in her pussy. I was almost ready to come again just from seeing her so out of control with lust. Diane said, "Just don't make me pregnant in my husband's bed. I want you to fuck me, but please pull out before you come. Please do it soon, before he comes home. Come on, Neil, fuck me. Stick it in. Fuck me now!"

Neil plumbed his fingers in and out of her hole and coated his cock with her juices. All at once he drove it home. He sank in to his balls on the first thrust. I was shocked. Diane never got that wet for me. It usually takes me three or four thrusts to get it in, and my cock is only half the size of Neil's whopper.

Diane was out of her mind with sexual pleasure as Neil drove his member in and out of her grateful pussy. I had never seen her so wet and out of control. She was kissing him, thrusting her tongue in and out of his mouth as he squeezed her tits and caressed her nipples. Their pace was incredible. Neil was putting it to her with tremendous speed and power.

He talked dirty to her while they screwed. "Damn, I've never had such a wet fuck," he said. "It feels like your cunt is swallowing my cock!" They were grinding their crotches together, arms wrapped around one another, madly thrusting their tongues in and out of each other's mouth. Diane was moaning, and then she started fucking him harder than ever. With her ankles wrapped around his waist, I got a great view of his monster prong thundering into her box. In the dim light of my bedroom, his cock glistened with her juices and her wet, dark pubic hair clung to it as her pussy repeatedly took Neil's mighty thrusts.

He was pulling all the way out of my wife's tight box, then slamming back in to the hilt. Diane was nearly crying from the pleasure she was receiving. To get his cock in even deeper, she positioned herself so that her knees were resting against her breasts. Actually, they changed positions every few minutes, and she climaxed in every one of them. Her pussy was making loud slurping noises from being so magnificently fucked.

After getting this kind of fucking for ten minutes, and having enough orgasms in that time to last her a year, Diane screamed out, "Come in me, Neil! Come right now! I want to feel your sperm in my cunt. Do it harder . . . faster! God, I love your cock!" When he shot his load into her, Diane had another powerful orgasm.

Diane kept his cock inside her and, after a brief rest period and some kissing and caressing, Neil was ready for more pussy. My wife got on top of him and rode his cock. Neil played with her stiff nipples, and this time it was she who talked dirty. "I want to fuck you every day," she said. "You can come over any time and fuck me silly with that big cock. It's not only huge, but you really know how to use it. Stick it in my pussy . . . give it to me!" As they exploded together in orgasm, I splattered the wall with my second climax.

After their fuck, Neil and Diane took a shower together, and I went downstairs to get a snack. About twenty minutes later I heard Diane moaning again, getting yet another glorious fuck from her new friend. When it was over, I hid outside the house and watched my naked wife escort him to the door, sending him off with a big kiss and some dry-humping right on the porch. She was cock-crazy, and obviously didn't care who saw her.

When I came back home later on, Diane was sound asleep. I aroused her, and we had a sleepy, drunken fuck. It felt great to have my cock swimming in her come-filled pussy, and I'm sure that all the while she was thinking about fucking Neil.—*M.A., New York, New York*

WHERE DID THIS VACATION TAKE PLACE? SOUNDS LIKE CLUB HEAD

I just have to tell you what happened while I was on vacation last summer with my wife. On our first day at the beach, I noticed one of the hotel workers. His jet-black skin made him stand out among the mostly white bodies by the pool. I have, for some time now, let my wife Lane know that seeing her orally pleasure a black man would be a fantastic turn-on for me. I knew that watching her creamy white cheeks and pink lips feeding on a thick, black cock gleaming with her saliva would make me burst. She'd always been reluctant to do it, and her reaction was no different when I pointed out the fine-looking young black man working at the hotel. She just laughed and changed the subject, as usual.

The next morning I was going on an all-day fishing trip. Lane turned down the chance to go with me, choosing instead to stay behind and relax by the pool. My wife has a knockout body to begin with, but when she wraps it in a skimpy two-piece bathing suit, she is out-of-this-world beautiful. I realized that I could have more fun spying on my wife all day as opposed to being on a smelly fishing boat, so that's what I did. I told her I was going fishing, but remained around the hotel grounds, making sure to stay where she'd never see me. What I saw was beyond my wildest dreams.

After lying by the pool in the hot sun for a couple of hours, reading a book, Lane was in big need of a tall, cool one. She flagged down the poolside waiter, who just happened to be the black man I'd noticed the day before. With a big smile he introduced himself as Rob and asked how he might be of service. Lane ordered a scotch and soda. As Rob walked away to fill her order, I saw her take notice of his tall, lean build.

After several drinks, Lane was having more and more trouble keeping her mind on her book. She was obviously thinking about Rob, looking his way frequently and watching him as he served others. When she finally got too hot, she made her way back to the room to cool off a bit. I beat her to the room, hid in a closet and prepared to see what she'd do next.

First she took a shower. The water cascaded down her tan body and made her look more beautiful than ever. After she'd washed her hair, Lane turned her attention to the place between her legs. Her fingers caressed her moist pussy, bringing her nearer and nearer to the point of no return. But after a few minutes, she found that her orgasm would not come.

Lane is a practical woman, and she knew what she needed to do in order to get off. Toweling off, she picked up the phone and called the pool bar. She ordered a drink to be brought to the room and requested that Rob bring it. Lane didn't know I was hiding in the closet, but she was obviously so horny, she couldn't wait for me to come back from my fishing expedition to watch her fulfill my fantasy.

Rob arrived a few minutes later with a drink in hand. Lane answered the door wearing a pair of lace panties and a short T-shirt. Rob handed her the drink while he checked out her beautiful body. He said it was more comfortable in the room than out by the pool, so Lane invited Rob to come in for a minute to cool off. In short order, she unbuttoned his uniform shirt and told him to take it off so he could cool off faster.

Rob, now shirtless, sat in the chair by the air conditioner while Lane sat on the edge of the bed and sipped her drink. The room was practically freezing, but it did nothing to cool down these two hot, horny people. It was very easy for Rob to see Lane's rock-hard nipples standing straight out under her T-shirt. I knew he could also see the moisture spreading in the crotch of her panties. Likewise, Lane's eyes were fixed on the huge mound in Rob's uniform shorts. His broad shoulders and muscular chest made him very attractive. Rob was about six foot five and two hundred pounds. I could only imagine what his zipper kept caged up.

Lane stood up, walked over to him and said, "You'll never cool off with your shorts on." She then unfastened the button on Rob's shorts and began to pull his zipper down. Rob's face registered a degree of surprise, but he quickly got into the spirit of things and stood up to allow Lane to remove his shorts and briefs. Kneeling on the floor, she was now face-to-face with a firm, eight-inch black hose that was thicker around than the glass she was drinking out of.

Rob's huge, pulsating cockhead was leaking pre-come just inches from her nose. She kissed the head, then began to lick the entire length of his rigid shaft. She sucked each of his giant balls while his hands ran through her hair and his moaning became more intense.

When the time was right, Lane opened her mouth wide. She lowered her head, a few inches at a time, over Rob's entire cock and licked it with her skilled tongue. Little by little she slid her mouth over more of his ebony pillar. Her throat muscles soon relaxed, allowing her to take in even more of Rob's big cock.

"Let me fuck you," Rob said. But Lane told him that her pussy was reserved for her husband alone.

"But that doesn't mean we can't still have a good time," she said. Lane pulled off her T-shirt and held his throbbing cock between her tits. Having Rob's huge black club fuck her tits turned Lane on even more. She pressed her breasts tightly against his shaft, and he fucked them with fast strokes. When it seemed like he was close to orgasm, Lane began sucking him again with savage fury. She went down on him farther than I believed possible. She fondled his balls and wrapped her hand around his tight ass, squeezing his firm cheek muscles as she sucked.

Each time Lane retracted her mouth, I could see her saliva dripping off his shaft and her lips. Rob continued to thrust into her mouth as her head bobbed hungrily. Sweat poured down his muscled black chest, and his moans of pleasure were so loud, they were probably audible from outside on the beach!

And then it happened. Rob's body stiffened, his cock pulsed wildly and his thick, creamy come shot with the intensity of a cannonball into Lane's mouth. She swallowed and gulped all she could hold, then pulled away from his cock as the rest of his gigantic load shot onto her breasts.

After Rob left, I came out of the closet and told Lane I'd seen the whole thing. She was so happy to see me there that she immediately straddled me and had me fuck her against the wall, standing up. My only regret was that Rob wasn't around to watch me fuck her the way I'd watched her blow him.—*Name and address withheld* O┼_■

"CLOSET CASE" ROOMMATE LIKES BEING LEFT IN THE DARK SO HE CAN WATCH

I am thirty-seven years old and work for one of the top computer firms in the country. Two or three times a year I am sent to a week-long training seminar in Chicago to learn about the newest developments in software. During my stays in Chicago, employees from across the nation are put up in hotels and assigned to double rooms. My roommate this time was a twenty-nine-year-old black man named Dwayne. He has been with the company five years and lives in California.

Dwayne and I both arrived Sunday afternoon. We hit it off pretty good from the start. That night we went to the lounge to have some drinks and talk about work. During our talk, Dwayne asked if I would do him a favor each night. He requested that I stay out of the room from ten until one in the morning, explaining that he would use that time to find women at the bar and bring them up to the room and fuck them. "I only fuck married white women," he told me. "It's easy to find them because they're all out-of-towners here on business, and they all have a secret desire to make it with a black man. I help them fulfill their fantasy."

I told Dwayne I didn't believe it was that easy for him to get laid, especially by married women, but he said he would prove it. After dinner Monday night, he told me to go back to the room, hide in the closet and see what happened. I felt really strange doing it, but also very excited. You see, I have often talked to my wife about watching other couples make love. I also enjoy watching X-rated films showing well-hung black men fucking blondes. These films also make my wife very wet and horny. I usually finger-fuck her while watching them, and she tells me how exciting it is to watch the women in the film get fucked by these studs.

Shortly after I'd holed myself up in the closet, Dwayne came into the room with a white woman who looked to be about thirty-five years old. She immediately started kissing him all over and moaning, "Take me, take me . . ." She was in heat!

After a few minutes Dwayne pulled off her dress and went to work sucking on her breasts. Her nipples were very large, and she was going crazy. After about fifteen minutes, Dwayne took the rest of her clothes off and started to kiss her entire body from her neck to her pussy. She was moaning loudly the entire time. She went wild when he started eating her pussy. She kept telling him, "I want your black dick. I need your big black dick right now!"

After she'd climaxed from being eaten out, she stripped off Dwayne's clothes and sucked on his cock. Dwayne didn't have what I'd consider a very long cock—it looked to be seven or eight inches in length—but it was very thick. The woman sucked it lovingly, making sure she got all of it good and wet with her saliva.

Before he came, she stopped, jumped on the bed and told Dwayne to fuck her white pussy with his black dick. And fuck her he did. He pounded her pussy for a long time, fucking her in positions I'd never even seen in an adult movie. All the while he was drilling her, she kept saying, "Oh, God, I love black dick so much. I love to suck it and fuck it. Black dick is the best!" I couldn't believe it.

They kept it up for almost two hours, fucking uninhibitedly like a pair of animals in the wild. I was so horny, I jerked off three times in the closet while watching them! Finally Dwayne had to ask her to leave because his roommate would be back shortly. She didn't want to leave; she wanted more of his cock. But finally she got the point, dressed and left.

After the woman left, Dwayne opened the closet door and said to me, "Now do you see what I mean? That's the way it always is. It's a snap to pick up white married women in their thirties and forties because their husbands don't ever give them enough dick. They're hungry for it. You could even probably fuck some of these women. Just not the ones who have their hearts set on dark meat," he added with a laugh.

The rest of the week was no different. Every night he was able to score with a different white woman, and every night I hid in the closet and jerked off to fantastic orgasms watching him do his thing.

Now I'm thinking of inviting my wife to join me on my next training seminar. If Dwayne attends, hopefully he'll seduce her and fulfill her secret desires.—*Name and address withheld*   O⊢🔳

DON'T JUST WASH THE WINDOWS—MAKE YOUR NEIGHBOR COME CLEAN!

My wife had been nagging me to wash the upstairs windows all summer long, and I had been doing everything I could to keep from having to do the job. One Sunday afternoon I was in the backyard relaxing, when I looked over the fence and saw my next-door neighbor's son, Paul. He was doing some landscaping, pulling out the weeds growing along the side of the house.

I hadn't seen Paul in a long time, and went over to the fence and said hello. He told me he'd been at college, and had decided to spend the summer at home to save some money. His father was also giving him an allowance for doing work around the house.

"How'd you like to make some extra money?" I asked.

"Sure, what do you have in mind?"

I told him I'd pay him if he'd wash my upstairs windows, and he agreed. Later that afternoon I brought a bucket, some sponges, soap, a squeegee and a ladder over to his house so he'd have everything he needed. He said he'd do the windows the following day. I was tickled pink, and went back home to tell my wife that Paul would be washing our windows the next day while I was at work.

I had to leave my office late Monday morning to visit a client on the other side of town. Since I had to pass my house on the way, I decided to go home and see my wife for a few minutes. When I opened the front door, I heard the upstairs shower running, and knew my wife was up there. By the time I reached the staircase, she'd turned the water off.

I heard her go into the bedroom—and then, a second later, I heard her shriek. Then she said, "Paul, you frightened me! I didn't expect you to be washing the windows quite this early." By then I was at the bedroom door. I opened it just a crack and peeked in. I saw my naked wife covering her snatch and boobs with her hands and arms while Paul, on the ladder, looked in from outside our bedroom window. The window was open and there was no screen on it, so Paul was practically leaning into the room. My wife is very attractive, with a body like a centerfold's, so it didn't surprise me that Paul was gaping, openmouthed, at the sight of her without any clothes on.

She grabbed a pillow from the bed and held it in front of her. Although this covered her tits and pussy, it actually had the effect of making her look even sexier. The funniest thing was that, after the initial shock had subsided, she and Paul started carrying on a conversation with her still nearly nude, and him still leaning in the window, practically drooling at her nakedness.

I remained perfectly still outside the bedroom door, looking in through the tiny opening and trying not to make a sound. I don't recall exactly how he got around to the subject, but soon I heard Paul telling my wife how beautiful she looked and how he loved seeing her naked. And then, in that candid way young people have, he said, "I've turned to stone, if you know what I mean."

My wife knew exactly what he meant. She laughed and said, "Well then, I guess you'll just have to finish up the windows and go get your girlfriend to . . . relieve the swelling."

"I wish I could," Paul replied, "but I don't have a girlfriend, so I guess I'll just have to do the job myself." With that he began to unzip his pants. My wife went along with his joke and said, "You can't do that here. What if the neighbors see you?"

"I don't care who sees me," he said. "You've made me so hard, I've just got to jerk off while I look at you!"

I was shocked to hear an eighteen-year-old kid saying such things to my wife, but it was also kind of arousing. My wife doesn't get a chance to flirt much, and I knew she was enjoying herself. No doubt we were going to have a wild time in bed that night. My cock was already getting hard.

"You can't jerk off on that ladder," my wife said to Paul. "It's too dangerous. Look, why don't you come inside and relax for a few minutes."

I was surprised that she'd invited him in—but not at all surprised that he took her up on the offer in an instant. I'd been eighteen years old myself once, and would've jumped at the chance to climb into a beautiful woman's bedroom window. Hell, I'm twenty years older than that now, and I'd still do it! Just the same, my wife is usually quite reserved, so her looseness around Paul surprised me.

It was to be an afternoon of many surprises, and I saw them all from my place outside our bedroom door. The minute Paul came in through the window, my wife dropped the pillow and showed herself to him without shame or apprehension. Then she said, "Paul, I'm twice your age. I can't believe you're so turned on looking at this old body!" Of course, Paul and I—and probably she too—knew that my wife's body is stunning. It's firm and smooth and curved in all the right places. Maybe she was just playing hard-to-get.

Paul kept babbling on about her beauty until she said, "Okay, if you want, you can look at me and jerk off. Just make sure you don't ever, ever tell anyone about this. If my husband finds out, there's no telling what he'll do." I had to laugh at that. In truth, I wanted very much to watch my wife get it on with this horny young man.

He stood up, pulled down his pants and revealed a boner that, although shorter than mine, was still quite long and thick. As he stroked it, my wife sat on the edge of the bed, leaned back and spread her legs for him. "Look," she said. "Why don't you stand close to me when you do that? That way I can get a good look at your nice cock."

He did as she asked, moving right between her legs. Now his huge hard-on was just inches from her. He pulled it quickly, and soon his cockhead turned a deep purple. I could tell from the look on my wife's face how excited she was getting from watching him whack off. They were both so entranced with each other that

I probably could've walked into the room and they wouldn't have noticed me at all!

I watched and listened to their talking, beating my own meat on the other side of the door. She encouraged him to move very close, but told him not to touch her. He accidentally rubbed the tip of her pussy lips with his cock, and she reminded him that he shouldn't do that. But a few minutes later, while pulling his boner, he again accidentally touched her pussy lips with it, and this time she didn't say anything.

I was so busy pulling my own cock that I didn't realize that my wife was moving closer to him—until I looked up and saw that he was now rubbing his cock all over her cunt lips. Is she going to let him fuck her? I asked myself. Am I going to get to see my wife riding another man's hard-on?

The answer came in a matter of seconds, so to speak. My wife pulled Paul on top of her and guided his prick into her. It was a wildly sexy sight—my wife, totally naked, with this teenager, fully clothed, pants down around his ankles, on top of her. His cock sank into her with a couple of thrusts, and then they began to fuck. "That's it!" she sighed. "Just keep pumping," she told her young lover. Paul worked his prick in and out of her a mile a minute. They stayed right at the edge of the bed, not changing positions, and enjoyed a fast and furious fuck.

"I'm coming, Mrs. Nagy!" Paul announced in less than a minute. She pulled him tightly to her and let him shoot his seed into her. Her own moans soon filled the room, and from the look on her face I knew she was also having a strong orgasm! I pumped a thick load of come into my handkerchief, incredibly satisfied by the scene I'd just witnessed. I stood and watched until they both stopped writhing, then took off quietly.

That evening, when I got home from work, I asked if Paul had washed the windows. "Oh, yes!" she said enthusiastically. "And he did a wonderful job!"

"Then I'd better go next door and pay him," I said.

"Why don't you do that later," she answered, wrapping her leg around me the way she always does when she's horny. And who could blame her? Fact was, I was also still pretty turned on from thinking about watching her fuck Paul. In no time at all we were both naked on the bed, fucking up a storm.

And she was right—the windows looked great!—*Name and address withheld* O╾▪

Crowd Scenes

NEW NEIGHBOR SHOWS SHY BUT WILLING COUPLE HOW TO RISE AND SWING

I'd like to share with your readers some sexual adventures my wife Joellen and I have been experiencing recently.

Joellen is thirty-two. I'm thirty-six. We're both very physically fit and considered attractive. My wife is five foot eight, one hundred thirty pounds, with shoulder-length blonde hair, nice 35C titties, a flat stomach, a tight butt and long, gorgeous legs. Every man she comes in contact with takes special notice of her. I'm six feet tall, with brown hair, a muscular build and an average, six-inch cock. Joellen and I have been married for nine years, with a good relationship and a good, but fading, sex life. We both have a strong sex drive, but after years of monogamous lovemaking it was getting sort of old for both of us.

We've always been open with each other, and have shared our sexual fantasies with each other. Joellen always wanted to try sex with two or three guys, at once or in succession, and also with an attractive woman.

She told me of a roommate she had in college who was bisexual. Out of curiosity on Joellen's part, and to fill in between dates at their mostly female college, Joellen and her roommate had sex about a dozen times. She said she wasn't crazy about going down on another girl, but said it was well worth it to have the orgasms her girlfriend gave her with her expert tongue.

We were both heated up by talking about each other's desires and decided that our marriage was strong enough to allow us to pursue some recreational fucking.

Our wishes soon came true with the arrival of a new next-door neighbor, Liz, a single thirty-year-old with light brown hair. She is strikingly pretty, with a slender but curvy body. She wears her hair fairly short, which complements her gorgeous 38D boobs—

I've never seen any nicer that I can recall. They are nice enough to almost convert an old leg- and ass-man like me.

Joellen and I were both immediately attracted to her, and we all became good friends in short order. Liz had only moved from across town, and was dating a couple of guys. She also hinted strongly that she was bi-oriented. We noticed that a pretty girl about twenty occasionally spent the night at her house. Liz discussed sex openly, especially with Joellen, so we thought she would be receptive to us.

Joellen and I each took some vacation time to relax and lie around our backyard pool, which has a privacy fence. We invited Liz over for a swim and some sunbathing. Joellen wore her smallest bikini, one with a thong bottom and a top a size or two too small. Liz arrived in a one-piece, which was very high cut at the bottom and plunged deeply on top. How her lovely breasts didn't fall out I couldn't guess. I made a pitcher of margaritas for the ladies and made the excuse that I had to do some shopping for a couple of hours.

I got in my car and drove around for about forty-five minutes. When I returned, I parked on the street and quietly entered the house. I went to a second floor window which overlooked the pool area. My heart was pounding in anticipation of what I was hoping to see.

I wasn't disappointed. I saw my lovely wife and Liz both naked, embracing and kissing on a deck lounge. Joellen was fondling Liz's tits and Liz had a hand between Joellen's thighs. They stopped, laughed a little and Joellen lay back on the lounge. Liz immediately started to kiss Joellen's thighs. She worked her way up to her pussy and shortly had Joellen going crazy.

I tried to ignore my bulging cock, intent on watching what was happening. Joellen held Liz's head while she ate her and rubbed her breasts. I watched, enthralled by the sight, as my wife threw her head back, obviously coming hard while urging Liz on.

After Joellen came, they paused for a kiss and changed positions. Liz lay back, pulled her legs far apart and raised her knees almost to her boobs. I could see the folds of her cunt easily because she had it completely shaven. Joellen positioned her face between Liz's legs and slowly started to service her. She picked up speed as she went, and I saw her head bobbing back and forth. Joellen had her ass raised in the air, and I could see the wetness on her quim. Joellen ate her for about twenty minutes. I went to grab my video camera and got about ten minutes filmed, including Liz coming with her legs wrapped around my wife's head. They kissed again and lay back, not bothering to put their suits back on.

I waited about five minutes, trying unsuccessfully to get my hard-on to go down. I walked out onto the pool deck, and Liz made no effort to cover up. Joellen told me I had to strip to come out. I quickly obliged, and walked over to them with my cock about ninety percent hard. "Not bad, not bad," commented Liz.

"You're awful nice yourself," I managed to get out.

"Did you just get back, or were you watching us?" asked Liz. I admitted that I had seen everything. "Did you like what you saw?" asked Joellen. "From the condition of your dick, it sure looks that way!" Before I could answer, Liz remarked, "Your wife says that you would love to fuck me, and right now I could sure use some of what you have sticking in the air there!"

At that, my dick got as big and hard as it had ever been. I glanced over to Joellen, who told me, "Go ahead, Bill, you watched our show, now its your turn to perform." I went to Liz and gave her a long, hard kiss. I reached for her perfect breasts and found that they were as firm as they looked. They curved down slightly and then extended out, with her swollen nipples pointing straight out.

Liz dropped to her knees and, gently grabbing my balls, took my rigid pole in her hand and then into her mouth. She didn't waste any time taking almost all of my cock in. She held the base of my tool as she flicked her tongue around the head on the up-stroke. It felt so good, I could barely keep on my feet. I looked over to Joellen, who was sipping a drink with one hand and playing with her pussy with the other. She blew me a kiss.

Liz must have sensed that I wouldn't last much longer, because she stopped sucking me and led me by my tool to some cushions on the deck. Liz got down on all fours and raised her bottom in the air. "Please fuck my hot little pussy, Bill." I dropped to my knees and she reached back and pulled my cock to her slit.

I tried to enter her in short, easy strokes, as I usually do with Joellen, but Liz thrust back at me so that I was buried to the hilt in her bald cunt. She was very wet, yet tight, and I began to pump in and out. My first new pussy in ten years was feeling exquisite. I reached under Liz, grabbed two handfuls of tit and quickened my pace. Liz was moaning and shouting so loudly that for a second I wondered if our neighbors, two hundred feet away, could hear her. Very soon I told Liz that I was going to come. "Shoot a big load in my pussy," she urged me, "fill it with your come!" I unloaded deep inside her, grabbing her bottom and pulling her hard back against me as my hot spurts flooded her.

We lay back, exhausted, and my wife, half smashed, remarked, "Very nice, both of you guys." Liz started to pull her suit on, and told Joellen she had had a great time. We assured her that we certainly did too. Joellen asked Liz if she would like to come back again that night, and she said she had a boyfriend coming over that night, but perhaps he would like to come too, if it was okay. Joellen gave us a big smile, and remarked that she had told Liz about her desire to fuck a couple of guys. We told Liz to come over about eight.

After she left we discussed the day's sexcapades. I wanted to fuck, but Joellen told me to save it for that evening. A little while later the phone rang. Joellen answered; it was Liz asking if a friend of her stud could come over too. Joellen asked me if I minded. I assured her that whatever she wanted was fine.

Our guests arrived that evening and Joellen was primed for action, wearing a short, skimpy sundress with absolutely nothing underneath it. Every chance she got she gave everyone a view of her bare pussy. The guys, Mark and Leo, were both about twenty-five, and seemed to know why they were there.

After some smoke, Liz and I paired off in a corner and started to neck. Joellen had both of the guys stuck on her like glue, and I saw my wife drop the top of her dress down over her tits. Their hands were all over her. "Let's watch for a while," Liz said. "after all, this is for you too!"

Joellen had Mark's shorts undone and pulled down, and she was stroking his cock. It was rapidly growing to an impressive length, about seven or eight inches. Leo pulled my wife's dress off, leaving her naked as a jaybird. Leo shed his pants too, and Joellen took turns sucking them. She lay down on her back and asked Leo to lick her twat. He quickly went to work on her, while Mark straddled her face and presented his big rod to her lips. I couldn't believe what I was seeing, my faithful wife servicing two strangers at once and evidently enjoying every minute of it. She soon asked Leo to fuck her, and she let out a cry of pleasure as he sank it in her from behind. She continued to blow Mark's long tool.

I had Liz's pants down and was rubbing her twat, which was drenched with her juices. I inserted two fingers and she moaned her approval. I believe she was as turned on as I was, watching the threesome. I pulled Liz off my lap long enough to pull my shorts down and then, holding her bottom, guided her snatch down on my raging hard-on. Liz gently rocked back and forth on me as we continued watching Joellen and her friends. She stopped sucking Mark long enough to let Leo give her the home stretch, grunting as he unloaded his balls in my wife's hole.

Leo retired to a chair as Joellen pushed Mark back on the mattress. His rod seemed to tower above him like a flagpole. Joellen lowered herself on him, taking him in bit by bit until he was in all the way. She glided up and down on his cock, telling him how great it felt.

Liz's gentle rocking had me ready to blow, and the sight of Joellen starting to really ride Mark had me shooting in Liz's velvety quim. I stayed inside her until I went limp and the juices ran down my balls and thighs.

My wife was now telling Mark to fuck her harder, and she was practically howling with pleasure. She and Mark came at the same time, bucking like some lust-crazed animals.

Our guests eventually left, and we fell asleep in each other's arms. Since that night, Joellen and I make love a lot, and she has an occasional date with Mark or Leo. I still visit Liz quite often, and she spends the night in bed with us both sometimes. I highly recommend it for any horny couple with a good marriage.— *D.M., Pittsburgh, Pennsylvania* O+ ▩

PHOTO SESSION DEVELOPS INTO A MEMORABLE SEXFEST

My wife Lin and I have been married for five years and are both in our late twenties. Recently we decided that Lin should have a professional photographer take some erotic photos so that when we get older we'll have memories of just how great her body was.

We found a photographer, Tom, through a referral, and we agreed to let him do the shoot. Tom had done many nude sessions and was sure that he could get Lin to be completely uninhibited.

We met Tom at his studio on the big day. He told us he would photograph Lin for about an hour in some lingerie, then he had a professional model whom he had to photograph for an adult magazine. Afterwards, he would shoot Lin in the buff.

Tom instructed Lin to change into sexy lingerie and put on the miniskirt and sheer blouse that we had brought. I sat in a chair away from the set, so as not to be intrusive but still get a full view of the action. As Lin was a little tentative, Tom had his two assistants retire to his office for the shoot.

When Lin came out, she looked hot. Tom complimented her and started to photograph her. He told her to think about sex and look provocatively at the camera. She started to dance and wiggle her hips. She put her fingers in her mouth when Tom asked her to fantasize about sucking a big cock. Soon Lin was removing her blouse and skirt. Tom had her sit on a big sofa, and photographed her in various positions that showed off her ass and tits.

The first hour was quickly up, and Tom brought Lin a cover-up to put on. He told us we could watch, as he shot a real centerfold model.

Rhea, the girl who came in, was young and beautiful. Tom had her strip in no time down to just stockings. He instructed Rhea to spread her pussy and finger herself. Lin and I were both getting hot watching.

About halfway into the shoot, Tom's assistant Rick stripped and joined the session with Rhea. Tom instructed Rhea to suck Rick's cock while she fingered her pussy. Tom got a good shot of Rick coming in Rhea's mouth. For the rest of the session Tom had Rhea fuck herself with dildos while he got it all on film. I knew that Lin was turned on because she was fingering her pussy when Rhea was writhing in orgasm from the huge dildo in her cunt.

When the session was finished, Rhea excused herself and Tom turned his attention to Lin. Lin didn't need much encouraging this time, and before long she was flashing her pussy and tits as Tom snapped away with his camera. She moved into different positions as instructed by Tom. With only garters and a bra on, Lin was baring the insides of her cunt for Tom's camera while Rhea and Tom's two assistants stood watching. It didn't bother me and, from the way Lin was rubbing her pussy and showing her lips, it didn't bother her either. It was obvious that Lin had lost all her inhibitions watching Rhea and was, in fact, now imitating her.

Tom had already photographed her in a variety of positions when Rhea brought a dildo to Lin. Tom instructed Lin to fuck herself with the dildo. It didn't take her long to stuff the entire length of the dildo into her wet cunt. While Lin was jerking herself off, Rhea came over to me, opened my zipper and started to give me a blowjob. Rick and Pete (Tom's other assistant) moved over to Lin, and as Rick put his cock in her mouth Pete removed the dildo from Lin's cunt and replaced it with his dick.

Rhea's mouth was so good that I didn't mind that my wife was now being gang-fucked by two studs. I came in Rhea's mouth, but Lin and her studs were fucking in every position that Tom could move them into. Tom kept photographing her, one cock in her pussy and one in her mouth, asking Lin if she liked being a slut.

Rhea got up and told me it was her turn to have Lin to herself. She went over to Lin, who was still lying down, and put her cunt right on top of Lin's mouth. She told Lin to eat her cunt. This was Lin's first lesbian experience, but from the way she was eating pussy, I knew she liked it. Soon they were in a 69 and Lin had another orgasm.

After Lin and Rhea separated, Tom decided he had enough pictures. He stripped and put his cock in her waiting mouth. The other two guys also came over and Lin was now going from one cock to the other, sucking all three off one at a time. Tom was telling her how well she gave blowjobs and that he could see she enjoyed being fucked by a lot of cocks. He instructed her to get on her hands and knees so that he could fuck her doggie-style while she continued to suck off the other two guys. The whole time Tom fucked Lin he was telling her how good her cunt was. I could barely contain myself and began to jerk off from watching my beautiful wife being fucked silly by three studs. First, Rick came in Lin's mouth, then Pete shot his wad at her tonsils. Tom was still reaming her cunt from behind when she began to have a huge orgasm. She was screaming for Tom to fuck her hard. He soon shot his load in her cunt.

Lin rolled over, exhausted, her legs spread, with come leaking out of her cunt. Tom picked up his camera and snapped more photos of her, capturing the look of a satisfied woman.

After the session was over, Lin went to shower up. A few days later Tom sent us the pictures, with a note that he would like Lin to model again, but this time in his first video. Who knows?—
S.B., Flagstaff, Arizona

THE STAKES GET HIGHER AFTER THE POKER GAME IS OVER

My wife, Annie, is a big girl (five feet, nine inches, one hundred forty-five pounds) who was a high school cheerleader. She has knockout legs and a world-class butt—beautifully rounded and firm enough to crack eggs on. We're both twenty-six, and have been married for five years. When our sex life dulled I suggested swinging, but she said that, although she liked the idea, she wouldn't know how to start. Eventually, something happened that led the way.

Once in a while we make bets, with all sorts of unique rewards. Our last, over who would win the Super Bowl, had stakes that gave the winner any wish. When the 49'ers won, Annie was in my power. I told her I wanted her to serve as hostess at my next poker session. I chose her outfit: a black blouse, which I made her leave unbuttoned most of the way down the front, black bikini panties, a black, pleated micro-mini and black high heels.

As we waited for the guys to arrive, she was nervous but very turned on. I told her the outfit was only the surface of her bet payoff. The guests were Brent and Stan, both black guys from work, and Bob and Harold, who play softball with me. Annie knew both Bob and Harold from the games, but Brent and Stan were new to her. As we played, Annie served us drinks and snacks, and got plenty of attention. My pretty wife accepted all this extremely well, and even overdid the hostess bit, hovering around the table and refilling drinks and snacks unnecessarily.

When the card playing wore down, I said, "Annie, I think you'd be a lot cooler without your skirt on." A dead silence ensued, during which my wife's face went from shock to disbelief to "I'll show you" determination. While my four guests watched, transfixed, Annie unzipped the micro-mini and let it fall. The lust the guys were feeling for her was palpable, and her breasts rose and fell with her heavy, excited breathing.

"Now," I said, breathing heavily myself and barely able to keep my voice controlled, "I think you ought to spend five minutes with each of my guests." I turned to the circle of desire-ridden faces. "Make good use of your time, guys. The sky's the limit." I turned back to Annie. She looked more exited than she had in a long time. "Our room would be a good place," I said.

She turned and walked out, five pairs of male eyes eating into her bouncing buttocks and Betty Grable legs. Bob, who is only twenty-four, nearly bolted from the table to follow. After a couple of minutes I made some excuse about the kitchen and softly stole up the stairs to peek into our bedroom.

The view jolted me to my toes. Annie was lying on our bed, her panties on the floor, her blouse open, breasts shiny with saliva. Kneeling on the floor between her splayed thighs, his mouth fastened hungrily to her hairy twat, was Bob, who was eating her avidly. Unable to tear my eyes away, I fumbled my cock out and began to stroke it as I stood shakily watching my wife writhe and moan as Bob's lips and tongue assaulted her dripping quim. In less than a minute she went rigid and emitted a loud, passion-filled yell, as the bed shook with her writhing and kicking. I heard Bob slurping and swallowing as Annie's juice gushed.

As Bob rose, his face dripping sweet pussy juice, Annie slid off the bed onto her knees, taking his stiff, six-inch cock from his pants. As I watched my pretty wife suck another man's cock for the first time, my balls screamed for release, but I held off, not wanting to come yet. Bob moaned and rocked as my wife fellated him, and about three minutes later she was gulping his semen as he jetted into her wet mouth. As Annie suckled the remains of Bob's spunk and cleaned his cock with her lips, I stuffed my aching prick into my pants and stole back downstairs.

Bob entered, grinning guiltily and obviously pleased, and Harold nearly sprinted for the stairs. Again I followed a couple of minutes later. This time I found my wife and friend lying on the bed embracing side by side. Annie was stroking Harold's stiff staff; he was a bit longer than Bob and much thicker, and was also uncircumcised. Harold had his left hand down in Annie's panties, and was finger-fucking her with fervor. I had barely gotten my pulsing penis out of my pants before Annie came, and she broke their French kiss to wail yet again as her body trembled and gyrated in a powerful climax. I knew the guys downstairs could probably hear her voice, and I heard Harold murmur, "Jesus!" as his fingers were bathed in a flow of sticky, sweet cunt juice. When she finally quieted, they kissed again and she finished him off. About a minute later Harold's cock erupted in a series of powerful spurts of come that splattered over Annie's hand, wrist, arm, and panties. Again I held off my climax, though it took every bit of will to do so.

Back at the table I could tell that Bob had related his experience to Brent and Bob, for they looked at me doubtfully as Harold came down the stairs.

"Annie is an equal opportunity hostess," I assured them, and Brent quickly exited. This time, though, when I peeked into our bedroom, Annie and Brent were sitting on the bed, quietly talking. I could see from the disappointed look on Brent's face that he wasn't going to enjoy Annie's charms. Finally he stood and Annie kissed him on the lips, murmuring, "Maybe next time, okay?" He nodded and I quickly descended the stairs.

As Stan moved toward the stairs, Brent said, "She's equal opportunity all right, but I didn't get anything but a kiss." Stan was a mustached black guy in his late forties, and when I edged my eyes around the door frame, he and Annie were on the bed in the same position that Harold and she had been in. Stan's hand was down the front of her panties, his fingers working in and out. He had already come, for again Annie's hand and belly were splattered with sticky white sperm, and Stan's tongue was working her mouth as energetically as his fingers were her pussy. Annie still held his prick as she squirmed and moaned with Stan's finger manipulation. I began to stroke my tool in rhythm with Stan's arm, and when Annie came, not as strong as her other two, but still powerful, I too, exploded, my come arching out in powerful, thick streams of jism, splattering the carpet.

Back downstairs I bid the guests good-bye and rushed up to my wife. She sat on the bed, her blouse still undone, panties soaked with semen and her own juice.

"I need to fuck you," I said, ripping at my clothes. My wife slid her blouse off as I finished disrobing, and I yanked the soaked panties off. Her hands guided me expertly, and I plunged all eight inches home on the first thrust, bringing a grunt of appreciation from my wife. She was clearly exhausted, but even so, as her hips and big butt worked in perfect sync with me, she trembled in a very weak orgasm a minute later, her calves gripping my upper back as we fucked.

"Did you enjoy yourself?" I gasped.

"Yes, I did," she said, her firm butt working strongly. "Did you?"

"I . . . jerked off watching you," I admitted. She came gain, stronger this time, and that drew my own orgasm in response. As we lay resting, I asked her the big question, "Do you think you'd want to do it again?"

She looked at me for a minute, then smiled. "Wanna make a bet on something?"—*M.S., Kansas City, Missouri*   O⊢ ▪

THE GAMES PEOPLE PLAY GET SERIOUS FOR THIS BUNCH OF OLD FRIENDS

My wife Tina and I have a very fulfilling sex life, but on occasion we do like to add a little more spice, that spice being another couple we know. We have known Mike and Ann for a few years and we had all expressed our sexual interest in each other's partners many times in more or less serious ways long before anything ever happened.

Well, one night we all got together to play a sexual game that Tina and I had bought. It involved answering questions about very intimate details of our sexual psyches. The other players were allowed to challenge our answers if they thought we weren't being completely honest. In order to avoid being questioned, we became more and more graphic in our responses, and we gradually escalated from talking about our fantasies and experiences to demonstrations.

Tina, for instance, at one point had me lie on my back on the floor so that she could show one of our favorite positions, with her on top of me, facing away, so that the sensitive underside of my prick can rub against her clit as she slides her wet pussy across my pubes and belly. Although we kept our clothes on at this point, I could feel the moist heat from Tina's crotch through her panties and my pants, and she could sure as hell feel how hard I was.

Not to be outdone, when Mike got a question about the size of his dick, Ann insisted that he drop his pants and show us how he could make the head of his cock swell by contracting the muscles around the base of his dick. I know this trick myself, and soon we were trying to see who could get the best expansion.

The game didn't last long after that. The four of us went into Tina's and my room and lay with our own partners. After making out a few minutes, we decided to switch partners. Each couple got into a 69 position and got busy. The whole situation was so exciting that it didn't take me long to shoot my load, and Ann followed close behind with an intense orgasm of her own. Since we had already relieved ourselves, Ann and I went into the living room to give Mike and Tina a little more room.

After talking for a few minutes, we went to check on them. By this time Mike was pounding his dick as far into Tina as he could. Just the sight of him fucking my wife made my dick rise again, and apparently it was none too soon, because just then he blew his load and collapsed, which left me to make sure Tina got to come too. I immediately replaced Mike and went to work on my wife's smoldering-hot cunt. I worked my dick in and out, slowly then faster until finally, with a aloud moan, she reached her climax. It was one of the most fun evenings we ever had. And even though it's been a while, we are hoping one day we will get to do it again—with Mike and Ann that is!—*Name and address withheld* O†▬

CURVACEOUS CLIENTS SHOW THEIR ASSETS TO REAL ESTATE AGENT

I've been selling real estate for six years. Just recently I began specializing in the resale of larger, more expensive homes in exclusive neighborhoods.

One Friday afternoon I got a call about one of our split-level palaces from a woman with a sexy-sounding voice. She said her name was Tammy. She and her girlfriends had come into a large amount of money, had bought a disco in New England and were looking for a winter home in Florida. The particular house she was inquiring about seemed to be just what they wanted. I made an appointment to show her the home; within half an hour I was steering my van up the driveway.

There were four lovely ladies ranging in age from mid- to late twenties, I guessed, waiting to greet me. We had a round of formal introductions, beginning with Tammy. She was the eldest and the spokeswoman for her group. Her long legs and waist-length blonde hair were stunning. Then came Jill, Bev and Lisa. Jill was a knockout with a Lady Di hairstyle. Her slender frame made her tits look almost too big for her to carry. Beverly was the shortest of the four, but her figure and face were fantastic. Finally I met Lisa. She had reddish-blonde hair and the most beautiful smile you can imagine. I explained to the girls that the owners had left most of the furniture to be sold with the home when they bought a condo on the beach. They were therefore anxious to sell.

We went inside, and I began pointing out the finer qualities of the place. Tammy was asking all the questions, while the others whispered to one another and giggled.

Halfway through the tour, I realized that Bev and Lisa were no longer with us. Tammy said that they were probably getting the feel of the place.

As we were about to enter the game room, I thought I heard soft, moaning sounds. Sure enough, when we entered the room, Bev and Lisa were there, and in the nude. I felt the blood rush to my face and to my prick at the same time. Bev and Lisa had taken pillows off the couch and spread them on the pool table, and there they were, in a 69 position, licking each other's cunt like they owned the place. I was shocked, but I couldn't take my eyes off them.

Tammy laughed and said it looked as if they had found a home. Then Jill suggested we join the party and celebrate their new house. The next thing I knew, Tammy was putting a lip-lock on me and Jill was pulling my pants down and starting to lick me. I could hardly believe what was happening to me, but I wasn't going to resist. Tammy let me come up for air, and then she stripped. The two on the table were climaxing. Tammy went over and began to lick the come off their lips and help them off the table.

Jill stopped sucking me long enough to get undressed while Tammy led me to the pool table. She had me lie on my back, then got up and straddled my cock. Jill came over and began kissing me. She asked whether I could take one more. Before I could answer her cunt was spreading over my face. I began licking Jill's twat, and Tammy was still riding up and down on my shaft. With the feel, the sights, the sounds and the taste, I thought I must have died and gone to heaven.

I was zeroing in on the pussy on my face when a gentle hand took mine and directed it to a very wet slit. So, with one pumping my cock, one on my mouth and one in my hand, I wondered what the other sexpot was going to do. I didn't have to wait long to find out. I felt a hand massaging my sweat-covered nuts. My juice exploded inside Tammy. About the same time, Jill's cunt let loose with a stream of come in my mouth.

After we untangled, poor Tammy was still yearning to come, so she assumed my position on the table, and Bev licked

Tammy's cunt while Lisa sat on her face. Jill and I watched the show before us, and it wasn't too long before my rod was poking out in front of me again, like a purple pistol ready to go off. I walked up behind Bev and played with her pussy while she was still slurping Tammy. Jill took hold of my prick and masturbated herself with her other hand. Shortly thereafter all five of us were gasping in another climax.

After resting for a while, I suggested that I go get some booze and snacks to keep up our energy so we could party all night. Tammy looked me right in the cock, licked her lips and promised everyone that she was going to get a mouthful of my cream all to herself before we were done. When I got back we were all ready for action. Tammy fulfilled her promise, and the rest of that night was incredible.

They never did buy the house, nor have I seen or heard from them since. But I'm always hoping for a repeat performance when I show those big homes in the fancy neighborhoods.—
Name and address withheld O—▪

ALWAYS WEAR CLEAN WHITE UNDERWEAR SO PEOPLE CAN FIND YOU IN THE DARK

As a young New York executive, I sometimes have trouble finding time for fun. I recently had to fly down to Fort Lauderdale for a business meeting. Since the meeting was on Friday, I decided to stick around for a few days and soak up the sun.

The meeting was ten hours of pure boredom, but it finally passed. I rushed back to the hotel, quickly showered and, thinking of all those beautiful Fort Lauderdale babes, slipped on a pair of tight, shiny-white bikini briefs I had recently bought. Because I usually spend all day in Brooks Brothers suits and boxer shorts, this underwear had caught my eye in the store a few weeks before. I have to admit that after I pulled the shorts on I stood there admiring myself for several seconds. I then finished dressing and headed for the dance clubs along the beach.

I hit about four clubs, danced with about forty women in black lace miniskirts, and lusted after about four hundred more, but none of them seemed interested in me. After the fifth nightclub, and as many ridiculous cover charges, I found myself wandering down the main drag with a very good buzz but without a single phone number. It was about three in the morning, and I was in no condition to drive back the hotel, so I decided to take a walk by the ocean.

The beach was just about deserted by then, largely because a big bank of storm clouds had started to roll in. Too drunk to be daunted by a little rain, I started walking along the shore. The water looked enticing. But of course I was still in my street clothes, and even though they smelled like an ashtray full of beer, I had no desire to get them wet and then have to trudge back to the car looking like an alcoholic seal.

It dawned on me that I was wearing something that would pass for a swimsuit. Without another thought (because I knew that if I thought about it I would chicken out) I ran up the beach toward a row of wooden beach chairs and whipped off the rest of my clothes.

I plodded down to the shore, entranced by the sound of the waves and exhilarated by my own near-nudity. The breeze was really starting to whip up now, and the tide rolled in with powerful surges as I ran to greet the foamy surf. The water was warm, and I splashed headlong into the waves, enjoying the feel of the cool water against my overheated skin. I played for about half an hour, until exhaustion and the impending storm urged me back to land.

It wasn't until I had collapsed on the beach chair that I began to hear subdued but unmistakable moans of pleasure a couple of chairs away. I rolled over and peered between the wooden slats on the back of my chair. There, less than ten feet away, was the hottest, sexiest blonde I have ever seen in my life. She was lying on her back, her skirt hiked up and her legs wrapped around a dark-haired, healthy-looking stud who was still in his clothes, except of course that his blue jeans were undone at the top.

I lay there, entranced, as they humped and moaned. Through the chair I could see that he had her blouse partially undone, revealing to me a side view of her big breasts, still covered by a lacy bra. She moaned louder and lifted her feet in the air, locking them around his muscular back and opening her skirt so that I could just glimpse her precious ass. When he arched back for a particularly deep thrust, I could see the silhouette of his big, studly dick sliding in and out of view behind her firm thighs.

As they rocked I began to gently rotate my hips forward and back, pressing my crotch into the chair. In a way it was better than participating, because I could see the whole thing. I felt my cock uncurl beneath the wet material of my bikini, aching to join in the fun. I was so aroused that I almost failed to notice that the rain had finally begun.

As the storm moved in, cooling my aroused skin with huge drops of water, the couple packed up and ran for cover. It was beginning to look as if I was fated to a night of complete sexual frustration. I lay there as the rain fell, waiting for my cock to calm down. After a few minutes the rain was gone, blowing over as summer storms on the beach often do. But my erection was still there. It strained against the slippery nylon of my briefs, begging to be released.

I rolled over onto my back, picturing the woman's straight blonde hair and her round, tan thighs. I slid my hand down my stomach and across the thin wet material that imprisoned my throbbing cock. I rubbed the shaft, remembering her boyfriend's big dick sliding into her perfect, young body. I cupped my balls and thought about her moans of pleasure as he fucked her, his muscular ass sliding in and out of the top of his jeans. I looked down at the bulge in my sexy, wet, white briefs, the material so thin that my dick was clearly visible. I grasped the shaft through the thin nylon and wrapped my hand almost completely around it, tugging the material so hard that it pulled away from my body, leaving my balls exposed to the fresh sea air.

I threw my head back and closed my eyes, pumping wildly and jerking my body around. I felt my climax building, building, and then I felt something else, a presence, and I realized that I wasn't alone.

"We liked watching you swim," she said. "Did you like watching us fuck?" Her boyfriend stood a little behind her, still holding her hand. I looked at him. He looked at me reassuringly and let go of her hand.

She knelt down beside me and took both of my hands, gently moving them away from my dick so that they hung down on the cool sand. She bent over and kissed my stomach, letting her lips linger, and then slowly planted a series of kisses in a slow progression down my stomach and along the stiff shaft of my cock, still held by the wet material. She curled her hot tongue around the end, licking the drop of come that had formed there and seeped through my briefs. She leaned closer and closed her mouth around the head, right through the material, and lapped at the tip.

She brought one hand up and closed my eyes, asking me to

keep them closed. I felt her soft, pantied ass press into my face. The feel of her soft skin and silky panties was so incredible I thought I would burst out of my briefs. I realized that she was straddling the chair, facing me. As she eased her body down, I felt the warmth of her snatch against my forehead, then my nose, then on my mouth. I reached under her skirt and sank my hands into her ass, pressing my lips into her luscious, soaked crotch. I kissed and tongued her through her panties. She started bouncing and moaning wildly. I squirmed as my cock strained and begged to be set free.

Suddenly, I felt two hands grasp the sides of my briefs and pull them swiftly down my legs and off my feet. I felt my cock spring into the sea air, finally unleashed from its prison. Instantly it was submerged in warmth and moisture. I was in ecstasy. As I lapped my sexy blonde's panties, her hot young stud slurped away at my cock.

She must have sensed that I was about to lose it, because she rose up abruptly and looked down at me. I opened my eyes and looked at her. She licked her lips and smiled devilishly, then giggled and slid backward down my chest and into my lap, coming to rest against my raised knees. She lifted her feet off the ground and onto the back of the chair, one on each side of my chest. Her skirt hung open, exposing the panties I had been sucking so joyfully.

She looked at her boyfriend, then me, licked her lips again and slid her hands up her own legs and under the elastic of her panties. Slowly, enticingly, she pulled them down those gorgeous, hot thighs, letting them lie at her feet. She raised her ass and eased her perfect little muff down onto the tip of my eager cock. She smiled and gazed right into my eyes, then took a deep breath and took me all the way in.

She tightened her sweet little walls around me and worked my cock like a piece of clay. I threw my hands in the air and rolled my head from side to side, but she was relentless. Her boyfriend was enjoying all this as much as she was. He was standing next to me and slowly jerking off. The sight of his big dick and his strong muscles made me even hotter, which I didn't think was possible.

I reached over and slid my hand up the back of his leg to his tight, sexy ass, and then pulled him toward me. He lifted one leg over the chair and there it was—that big, beautiful dick I had watched plunging into this blonde beauty's clutching pussy. I was so hot I needed no further persuasion. I wrapped my mouth around his cock and slurped away while his girlfriend fucked me into ecstasy. I imagined for a moment that I was watching the action from above, and the scene was so exciting that I shot. My balls contracted and blew intense spurts of come deep into my blonde's tight little hole. She threw her head back and screamed with delight just as her stud of a boyfriend exploded in my mouth and shot wads of come down my throat.

We all collapsed where we lay. At least I think we did. I can't actually prove that this happened, because I was alone when the beach patrol rousted me out and threw me off the beach.—*Name and address withheld* O⊢▇

HAPPY BIRTHDAY TO ME—AND TO YOU AND THE STUD WHO CAME WITH YOU

The phone rang about midnight. I was already asleep, but was happy to be awakened by my new lover, Frank. Frank is married to one of my best friends. We aren't serious about each other—there is no threat to either of our marriages—but we are serious about fucking. Frank's woman is really straight. She doesn't even give head, so Frank went looking for a good blowjob and discovered that I'm the best there is. We've been playing around for several weeks, and each encounter is better than the one before.

Frank called because he was out on the town with his buddy Rick. It was Rick's twenty-sixth birthday, and they were both pretty high after a night of serious partying. Frank had spoken of Rick before, but I had never met him. Frank wanted to come over—he wanted to make sure Rick would really enjoy his birthday. I said sure. My husband travels, and is away for weeks at a time. I was so horny I would have agreed to anything. I wanted to fuck.

Twenty minutes later, Frank walked in the door. He's about six foot two inches tall, with blond hair and crystal-blue eyes. He's big and hairy—a Nordic teddy bear. He immediately opened my short silk robe and pulled a breast out of the soft beige teddy I had on underneath. He sucked my rosy pink nipple into his mouth and asked if I was ready to meet Rick. I said yes. Frank slid the robe off my shoulders and it crumpled in a heap at my feet. Then he hollered for Rick to come in.

I was standing there with one breast out of the teddy and Frank's fingers buried in my golden curls. Frank said, "Mia, this is Rick." I didn't get to say anything, because Rick immediately kissed me. What a wonderful introduction! Rick didn't *just* kiss me, he made love to my mouth. I don't think I have ever been so thoroughly kissed. I grabbed a handful of each guy's crotch, closed my eyes and turned myself over to those two beautiful men.

Rick is the exact opposite of Frank, physically. Rick is Italian, five feet eight inches or so, with rippling muscles over a flat stomach. His chest is completely hairless, and his small nipples were rock-hard. He has long, curly, black hair, dreamy black eyes, long eyelashes and a full mustache that tickled whenever it touched me. I was sandwiched between a Nordic god and an Italian stallion—I couldn't have been any happier.

Frank wanted Rick to see my body so he could fully appreciate what I was about to give him for his birthday. He left the lights on and pulled the straps of my teddy down. I wiggled and the teddy joined the robe at my feet. I'm about five feet eight inches tall and have 38DD titties with large pink nipples. I have long, curly red hair that hangs nearly to my waist and a neatly trimmed golden-red triangle adorning my full pussy lips. I have really long legs, with muscular thighs and calves from daily aerobic workouts. I'm thirty-three years old and the mother of a five-year-old and a two-year-old, but I look damn good, unlike the other computer programmers I work with.

Rick kissed me again. He slowly worked his way around to my ears and down my throat, his mustache tickling in just the right places. Frank sat down to roll a joint and told Rick to squeeze my breasts together and suck both nipples into his mouth at once. Rick did, and he had me squirming in delight. By the time Frank had the joint rolled, I had bent over and pulled Rick's cowboy boots off, gotten rid of his jeans and had his joint as hard as stainless steel.

Frank reached up, pulled me down into his lap, gave Rick the joint and told him to fire it up. Frank's hands roamed between my legs, flicked my clit a few times and gave me my first orgasm of the night. That's how hot I was already. I sucked on Frank's wet, pussy-juiced fingers until Rick offered to shotgun the joint down my throat.

We smoked two joints while I lay on the couch between my two lovers. I unbuttoned Frank's shirt and played with the hair on his chest, at the same time running my foot up and down the insides of Rick's thighs, massaging his dick and balls.

When the joints were gone, I wanted a tongue in my twat. I stood on the couch and sat on Rick's face. He was lying back on the pillows and seemed to be in the perfect position. Rick began running his tongue up and down my soaking-wet slit. I leaned forward and braced myself against the couch.

I felt Frank kissing my back. He nibbled all the way down to my firm, rounded ass, and ran his tongue all over my ass-cheeks. I don't know whether it was Rick's licks on my clit or Frank's tongue on my full moon, but I had one hellacious orgasm. I screamed in ecstasy.

I slid down on the couch between my two beautiful men and tried to catch my breath. My pussy was throbbing in time with my heart, and my legs were quivering. I was weak. Still, it didn't take me long to catch my breath and realize I hadn't enjoyed even the slightest taste of dick. But there was a problem: which dick would I taste first? Frank's throbbing pink dick is about six inches long but very, very thick. Rick's dick was much longer—probably close to eight inches, though not quite as thick—and it was a deep, almost purple color.

I couldn't make a decision, so I told them to stand facing each other and, with a dick in each hand, I licked them one after the other. I was getting all the dick I could handle, but neither of them was getting a decent blowjob. Rick could see the problem, and instantly came up with a real good solution.

He pulled away from me and sat Frank back on the couch. Frank pulled me along with him and I sucked his entire cock down my throat. I love the feel of cock in my mouth. The softness of the skin over the hardness of his cock, plus the smell of a man, is a wonderful combination—one that I never seen to get enough of. My tongue was sliding up and down, my lips progressively tightening around the object of my desire. My fingers danced over his huge balls while his fingers tangled in my hair. I licked, sucked, nibbled, and kissed his entire groin area before gently sucking one of his big balls into my hot, hungry mouth.

Rick grabbed my hips and planted his pole deep in my cunt. God, it all felt so good—two big dicks sliding in and out of my hot, wet orifices. It wasn't long before the in-and-out action sent me over the edge. I felt the orgasm begin in the pit of my stomach. Then the spasms started. My legs quivered and my body seemed to convulse. My pussy clamped around Rick's dick and I felt Frank's shaft sink deep in my throat.

I was beyond ecstasy. I couldn't think anymore. I lost all ability to function—I could only feel and smell sex. I could feel dicks in me, hands and mouths on me, legs and bellies touching me. I felt Frank's body hair on my face and the slick smoothness of Rick's chest on my back. And, oh my God! the delicious smell of sex—the freshness of Frank's deodorant and soap and the sexy aroma of Rick's cologne, all mingled with the smell of their sweat and my pussy juice. I was in heaven. I thought I had reached the height of sexual satisfaction, but I didn't know what was yet to come.

I was riding a big wave of multiple orgasms when I grabbed Frank's balls and squeezed them gently. Almost immediately, Frank erupted like a hot geyser in my mouth! He must not have ejaculated in the week since he was last with me, because he filled my mouth until the excess ran down my chin and dripped onto my breast.

I released Frank's dick in an effort to drive Rick's rocket deeper into my womb. Rick pulled me to his chest and wrapped one arm around my waist. Frank sat up and clamped his lips on one of my swollen nipples. I screamed again and ground my ass into Rick. That was all it took to cause him to tighten his grip around my waist, bury his face in my hair and fill my steaming puss with a bucket of hot, sticky jism. I could feel it oozing out of my cunt even before Rick pulled out.

I just sat there for a minute, completely happy. Frank was kissing my mouth, throat and chest, and Rick was nibbling at my neck and shoulder. Our three sweaty bodies were molded together, and I felt like a million dollars.

We pulled ourselves apart, and I fell on the couch. Frank sat up to roll another joint and Rick got up to fix us all something to drink. I put an X-rated tape in the VCR and we all piled up on each other to drink, get high and get motivated again.

After another couple of joints, we all were feeling playful again. Rick had a little cocaine, and he told me he wanted to put some on my clit. He promised it would provide wonderful sensations. I let him spread the white powder, then I lay on Frank for a few minutes while Rick did another line or two. By then my clit was tingling, almost itching, for more action.

I leaned over and sucked Rick's dick into my mouth to get him up again, and then he sprinkled some coke on the tip. Frank did the same. My Italian stallion lay on the floor on some big pillows. I straddled him and guided his big cock into my pussy. Rick reached for my tits and buried his face in then. I felt Frank's hands massaging my ass. Rick whispered wonderfully wicked things into my ear. Frank came up in front of me and wiggled his dick back and forth against my lips until they opened.

I took inventory. I could feel every inch of Rick's dick in my pussy. It was buried to the hilt. And I could feel every massive inch of Frank's dick deep in my throat. My pussy lips were buzzing from the coke Frank had put on my clit, and my other lips from the coke I had sucked off Rick's and Frank's cock.

Rick popped some amyl nitrate under my nose and I went wild. I started moving. I could feel everything with such intensity. I had an almost immediate orgasm that just didn't end. I was at a level of sexual pleasure that was completely new to me. Nothing close to these feelings had ever come my way before. It was miraculous. I was totally filled, fulfilled, satisfied and content. The orgasm went on and on, and I began to cry.

Rick stopped moving, held me, asked me if I was okay— should they stop? He told Frank I was crying, and Frank was concerned too. I told them, "Don't stop, please keep going—I'm loving it." Rick kept kissing me and talking to me and Frank, who had pulled out of my mouth when he found out I was in tears, was kissing my shoulders. I took hold of Frank's penis and guided him back into my mouth.

Frank came first, pulled out and fell on the pillows beside Rick. With Rick still in me, I leaned over and kissed Frank. Frank kissed and patted me and helped me sit up. Then I really fucked the hell out of Rick until he finally came. I lay on the pillows between them while they rubbed, massaged, and kissed my body all over. They talked a lot about how wonderful I was, and did everything they could possibly think of to let me know how much they had enjoyed themselves. We smoked another joint and all went to sleep.

They woke me up a while later, carried me to my bed and kissed me good-bye. I slept through my alarm the next morning and ended up skipping work. I couldn't imagine going back to the mundane world quite so soon. About four o'clock that afternoon, the florist made a delivery to my house. Rick had sent a dozen red roses and Frank a dozen pink ones. I put them in two vases, one on either side of the bed, lay back to smell them, and drifted back into a deep and satisfying sleep.—*M.L., New Orleans, Louisiana*

IT'S LIVE THEATER WHEN COUPLE CAVORTS AT X-RATED MOVIE

Lily and I have been married for sixteen years. One night we were drinking and talking, and I suggested that we have a threesome. We had discussed the subject before, but we'd always gotten so hot just talking about it that we ended up fucking instead of going out and looking for a companion. Lily pointed this out to me, and said that this time she wasn't going to let me get my hands on her unless we found another pair of hands to put next to them. "All right," I told her. "Put on your dancing shoes. We're going on the town."

Lily put on a black blouse and a black miniskirt, garter belt, high heels and stockings. She was a knockout. "I couldn't find any clean panties," she said, "so I'm not wearing any at all." Right. That's Lily.

We decided to go to a local X-rated movie, figuring there was no better place to find horny people. When we got there we sat in the middle of the theater. There were a few men and women scattered around.

While we were watching the movie, a guy next to my wife pulled out his cock and started to jack off. I put my hand on my wife's leg and starting rubbing her inner thigh, gradually working my way up to her pussy. When I reached her hot slot I found that she was already wet with excitement. Shy woman that she is, when I started running a finger between her lips she responded by putting her legs up on the back of the seat in front of her. While I continued to stroke her legs, and occasionally dip a finger in her honey jar, the guy who was sitting on the other side started rubbing her tits and playing with her nipples.

The three of us had a huddle. Our new friend introduced himself as Dennis, and we all decided that we should to go our house so we could be more relaxed. Like they say on the commercial, "It's just that easy."

My wife has always liked to dance and strip, so when we got

to the house she put on some music and started slinking out of her outfit. The blouse went first. She fiddled with her bra for a while, exposing her tits little by little so that by the time she exposed her nipples, they were standing at attention. She rubbed her tits real slow, then moved down to her pussy and rubbed it through the miniskirt. She slowly raised the hem of the skirt with her other hand until she was fingering her wet box directly in front of our faces. Dennis and I sat on the sideline, showing Lily our appreciation by spanking our monkeys.

After she removed the mini and let it drop, we told Lily to sit down between us. We started kissing and stroking her. She didn't want a lot of foreplay—she was screaming to be fucked. We got down on the carpet and I went right to work, sinking my sword in her scabbard with one stroke. While I fucked her pussy, Dennis was getting a hoovering from Lily's excellent mouth.

We all came quickly. I could tell that Dennis had begun to blow because he was bellowing like a moose, and I could see Lily's jaw working. It went on and on, and I watched her eyes grow bigger in surprise, but she managed to swallow each and every pearly drop. The sight was enough to send me off and, as I started to pump, Lily began to come too. We all fell down in a pile, panting. That was the end of round one.

We drank some liquor and smoked some pot. Lily started sucking on both of our cocks in turn, jacking whichever one was out of her mouth. Pretty quickly Dennis and I were ready to go again.

It was Dennis's turn to fuck her in the pussy while she gave me one of the best blowjobs I have ever experienced (and when you're married to Lily, that's saying a lot). I came first, then sat down while Dennis fucked my wife. They were rolling all over the floor and shouting with excitement. It was quite a show, and after a few minutes I was hard again. I was glad to see that Dennis was about to blow, because I was hot to get back inside my wife's pussy. They moved very slowly and intensely when he was really close, looking into each other's eyes. He held completely still when he came, but from where I was standing I could see the stump of his prick pulsing with the load it was delivering. I somehow managed to contain myself until they had rested a minute, then got down on my knees and slid into her soggy cunt.

I started off with slow strokes, but sped up with each entry. Lily started screaming, from coming so hard and so often. The more she came, the harder I fucked her, until her juices were running like water from a faucet.

After Dennis left, my wife and I were still horny, and we fucked until we fell asleep in each other's arms. Neither one of us had ever come so much in one night in our lives. We haven't repeated the experience, but believe me, we will.—*V.T., Sparta, Georgia*

THE MEMORY OF HIS GIRLFRIEND'S GIRLFRIENDS KEEPS HIM GOING

I'm a lonely inmate, and haven't slept with a woman in over two years. My only sexual encounters in these two long years have come when my right hand meets my dick in a dark place. Since I have about five more years before my debt to society is paid off, the following story will have to stay fresh in my mind for a long, long time.

My girlfriend Cecile told me on Sunday night that she had a special treat for me on Monday evening. I was to go home to my own apartment and get cleaned up after work, then go to Cecile's apartment and let myself in with my own key. She said I would know right away what the surprise was.

Monday was a very long work day, but it finally came to an end. I rushed home, washed, and ran to Cecile's. When I let myself into Cecile's apartment, the first thing I heard was a woman laughing in the bedroom. It wasn't Cecile's laugh, either! As quietly as I could, I crept over to the door. My eyes nearly jumped from my face as I looked into the room.

There were three naked women on the bed. One was Cecile. One was Cecile's good friend Simone. The third was a total stranger to me. They all had lovely bodies. Cecile's was very familiar to me. I had admired Simone's body before, but seeing her totally nude was a treat. The stranger had the most incredible body I had ever seen. My dick was rock-hard instantly at the sight of all this naked, womanly beauty.

Then I noticed what was happening on the bed. The stranger was moving around to get her pussy near Simone's mouth. Cecile was sitting at the foot of the bed, in between Simone's widespread legs, adjusting the harness of a strap-on dildo that hung from her waist.

The unknown woman looked at me as she slowly lowered her crotch onto Simone's upturned face. She looked in my eyes, licked her lips and adjusted herself on Simone's tongue. Cecile followed the stranger's gaze and saw me in the doorway. She smiled at me and nodded her head toward the chair in the room, then turned back to face Simone's splayed legs. Cecile moved up and began to tease Simone's pussy with the ten-inch dildo. When she had the fake cock covered with Simone's creamy juices, she slowly but steadily worked all ten inches into Simone's humping cunt. Cecile's thrusts matched Simone's bucking hips as they settled into a steady rhythm. It looked to me like they'd done this before, which would have been news to me.

The stranger toyed with her own hard nipples as she rocked on Simone's tongue and watched Cecile and Simone go at it. Cecile lay on Simone's body the way a man would, and breathlessly told Simone how much she was enjoying the close-up view of Simone tongue-fucking another woman's cunt, how beautiful she was, how much she liked shoving her hard dick into Simone. Panting hard, Cecile would talk, then suck and nibble on Simone's big, hard nipples, as she was trying to catch her breath.

What a scene—Cecile's firm ass humping between Simone's strong legs, and a beautiful stranger being tongued by Simone. The stranger turned to me and calmly said, "Hi, I'm Tracy, a friend of Simone. Could I suck your cock?"

As if in a trance, I stood up and slipped off my cutoffs and boxers. My dick stood straight out when it was released. My erection seemed to draw me onto the bed and into Tracy's mouth.

Cecile was behind me now, as I stood between her and Tracy, straddling Simone's chest. While Tracy took my cock down her throat, Cecile started massaging my balls with one of her small, warm hands. Tracy moaned around my dick as she started to climax on Simone's tongue. She finally had to let my prick go so that she could make more noise. Her orgasm went on for a long time, and so did her loud wailing. Then she rubbed her creamy juices all over Simone's face as she slowly relaxed again.

Tracy eased herself off Simone's face. She and I moved to the floor beside the bed, because Simone and Cecile were starting to bounce around so much I could hardly stand up. Tracy took my meat back into her mouth, slurping on the purple head of my dick.

Cecile licked Tracy's juices off of Simone's face and they shared a long, tongue-teasing kiss. Simone broke the kiss when she started to shudder into her own orgasm. Cecile kept giving it to her as she heaved and moaned and then collapsed, breathing hard. They shared another long kiss before Cecile slipped the dildo out of Simone's cunt.

Cecile climbed off Simone and crawled over to Tracy. She looked sexy as hell with a slippery dildo sticking out of her crotch. Cecile pushed Tracy's legs apart so she could get her tongue into Tracy's pussy. As she worked on Tracy's cunt, Simone removed the dildo from Cecile's waist and strapped it onto herself.

Seeing Cecile licking Tracy's pussy was all I needed to explode and fill Tracy's mouth full of my salty seed. Tracy hungrily milked my cock dry. She used her tongue to clean her spit and my come off my dick.

Tracy fell back on the bed and said she needed something bigger than a tongue in her pussy. Simone told Tracy to get on her knees and she'd give her a good fucking from behind. Cecile said she wanted Tracy to tongue her to orgasm. I was in heaven as I watched Cecile lie back and spread her legs wide so Tracy could tongue her pussy.

Tracy stuck her ass in the air as she worked on Cecile's cunt. Simone moved up to Tracy's ass and teased her cunt with the head of the dildo. Then she slowly eased all ten inches of rubber into Tracy's pussy. Tracy moaned into Cecile's cunt as Simone fucked her with the dildo.

Cecile looked at me and told me to join in wherever I thought I could fit. I walked to the foot of the bed and noticed how enticing Simone's ass looked as she humped Tracy from behind. I climbed up behind Simone and started to tease her cunt with the head of my cock. Simone told me to fuck her good and hard. I rammed all the way into Simone from behind, which in turn made Simone push the ten inches of dildo into Tracy, which pushed Tracy's face harder into Cecile's pussy. This brought Cecile to a moaning orgasm. She looked at me and humped her cunt into Tracy's face in time with my strokes into Simone.

When Cecile had calmed down some from her orgasm, she moved away from Tracy's face. She slid under Tracy so she could lick Tracy's clit while Simone fucked her pussy with the dildo. Seeing my girl eating pussy again went straight to my balls. They boiled over and filled Simone's cunt till it overflowed and ran down the insides of her thighs.

I pulled out of Simone and sat back to catch my breath and

watch my girl lick pussy. Cecile's tongue on her clit as Simone took ten inches of fake cock up her cunt brought Tracy to a screaming orgasm. Her clit apparently became very sensitive, and she made Cecile stop licking it. Cecile moved so that Tracy could lie on her stomach. Simone slowed down and gave her a last few long, strong strokes, then finally pulled out of Tracy's flushed pussy.

Cecile crawled over to Simone and said she wanted to suck my come out of her pussy. Cecile took the fake cock off Simone and proceeded to clean her vagina. Tracy crawled over to me and said she wanted to feel the real thing in her cunt. She pushed me onto my back and worked my dick with her hands until it was mostly erect again, then eased herself down on it. She rode me slowly and sensuously until we both climaxed again. Cecile and Simone had moved into the 69 position and soon brought each other off.

We were all exhausted after that. Before we went to sleep we agreed that we'd have to have another get-together real soon. That's become a little ironic, given that I'm incarcerated, but I'm still hoping that we'll be able to arrange a reunion when I finally get back in the world.—*C.C., New York, New York*

SUN, SAND, SEX, AND A SURPRISE FOR BI BODYBUILDER

My wife and I took a Club Med vacation last summer, and it was one that will remain in our minds. My wife is a beautiful blonde, with blue eyes and a body that won't quit. I love to watch her show it off. I'm a weight lifter, about five feet eleven and two hundred ten pounds. Maybe it's true, as some people say, that all bodybuilders are bisexual. I have always fantasized about watching my wife with another man and mixing in—which brings me to our vacation.

Tanya and I were on the beach. She was wearing a bathing suit that hid very little. I was wearing a pair of posing trunks cut high on the sides. Tanya took her top off to get some sun. I loved it, because she has a beautiful chest with big nipples.

We were both sitting in our chairs on the beach when a rather tall man walked by. I noticed him, but Tanya didn't. He set his chair up about twenty feet away from us. Tanya said she was a little hungry and was going to get a bite to eat. This gave me my chance. I could see from the way this guy walked that he was towing an oversize load around in his bathing suit. I wanted to get a better look. He got up and went for a swim, and I followed him in the hope of finding out just how well he was hung. While we were out swimming, he started to drift my way. The water was crystal clear and a very beautiful blue.

He had apparently noticed me too. He swam over and introduced himself as Brant. He was very curious about lifting weights and how he could build his body. I could see the outline of his cock now, and he had a big one. This made me very horny. I told Brant that I would show him a few things back at the club later in the day.

We both went back to the beach for some sun. Tanya returned shortly after. She had seen that I was talking to Brant, and asked what he wanted. I told her that he was interested in weight training. Tanya saw that I had a little bit of a rise in my trunks, and smiled at me, but with a question in her eyes. I decided to roll over and tan my butt. I looked over and saw that Brant had already taken off his suit. His cock hung at least two inches longer than mine, and it was also a little thicker.

Tanya asked if I would run up to the room and get her a book to read. From our room I noticed that Brant had walked over to Tanya. He was standing over her with his cock hanging loose. I was a little jealous, but I also developed an instant hard-on, and I had to asks myself which of them I was jealous of. I could see that Tanya was putting some lotion on Brant's back.

By the time I got back to the beach, Brant was in his chair sunning. Tanya told me that Brant had come over, introduced himself to her and asked her to rub some lotion on his back. I mentioned that I had seen them from the room and that it had made me very excited. I asked her if she liked him, and she said she had never seen a dick that big before. I quickly answered, "I know," and she gave me another searching look.

When we left the beach I decided to stop for a quick pump. I entered the weight room and saw Brant trying to lift the weights. He and I started working out together. We were still in our bathing suits. Whenever he lay down, the outline of his cock was pressed against his suit, and it got me very horny. Brant noticed this and casually said, "I'd be glad to help you with that."

I'm sure I blushed when I said, "Thanks, I'd like to take you up on that later." I raced up to the room, where I found Tanya dressed in a very sexy way. Tanya asked how the workout was and I told her, "Brant was there. We worked out together. It was pretty fair, but nothing special."

Tanya asked, "Was he still wearing those Speedos?" I said yes, and told her that by the end of the workout, Brant was coming on to me. I was spotting him, and he reached up and copped a feel. "So, what did you think of that?" she inquired.

"I don't really know. I kind of liked it, I guess."

The next day came and we decided to head down to the beach. When we got there, Brant was already sunning nude, his pecker looking even bigger than it had the day before. Tanya and I put our things down and went for a swim. When we came out of the water, Brant was standing there waiting. He asked if we would mind putting some suntan lotion on his back. Tanya grabbed the oil and started on his back, while I lay down on my towel to hide my hard-on. When Tanya finished his back, Brant came over and rubbed some oil on my back. He said, "Why don't you roll over and I'll do your front. When I moved both Tanya and Brant could see that I was very excited at what was going on.

Brant took over from there. He pulled down my shorts, put his lips on my dick and began to give me a blowjob. Tanya said, "I think it's time we moved up to our room and closed the door."

When we got upstairs, the clothes started flying. Once we were all naked, Tanya went for Brant and Brant went for me, pulling my cock into his mouth. It was a real sight to see my wife sucking a cock. Brant was not all that hard yet, but his cock was enormous. "I have never seen one that big before," I said. He asked if I would help Tanya take care of him.

I wanted to see this monster at full staff. He let my cock slip out of his mouth with a loud smack. I moved around so that I could help Tanya suck his giant cock. As I tried to get Brant in my mouth Tanya sucked on his balls. Before long, Brant was in full glory. I got up and went to get the camera to take some pictures of Tanya sucking on him. Tanya asked if I would let Brant fuck her, as she had never had such a big cock. I told her that I would love to watch and take pictures of this treat. She got down on all fours.

As Brant started to enter my wife, I crawled underneath her and sucked on her pussy lips. I was able to lick both Brant and Tanya at the same time, as he fucked her. Brant would pull his cock out and feed it to me so that I had the taste of both of them. That was the best.

When Brant was about to come, he pulled out and sprayed it all in his hand. The three of us bent down to lick it out of his palm, then started kissing each other to spread the juice around.

After that, Tanya sat on my lap and started humping me. Brant stood in front of Tanya so that she could suck on his cock and fuck me at the same time. All this was too much for me to handle at one time. It was not long before I shot my load. She hadn't gotten off yet. She moved up to sit on my face. That way, she could come and let me suck my own sperm out of her flooded pussy.

Shortly after this we all fell asleep, but we didn't stay asleep for long. I was awakened by Brant sucking my cock. Tanya woke up and asked if she could take some pictures of Brant and me doing each other. Brant and I moved into a 69, with him on the bottom. This position didn't last very long, as it became uncomfortable. I moved around so that I could take more of Brant's tool. After snapping a bunch of pictures, Tanya came over to give me an extra mouth on Brant's tool. I backed off so that I could watch Tanya suck Brant off.

The view had me hornier than ever, and I moved behind her so that I could fill her other opening. Brant and I both came at the same time, filling her with our come. She was wasted by this time, so we decided to really call it a day.

We spent a lot of time with Brant during the rest of our vacation. Now that we're home, we're looking around for a good candidate to fill his spot in our bed.—*S.P., Fairfax, Virginia* O⊢▪

HARD WORK PAYS OFF IN LATE-NIGHT OFFICE ORGY

Around three o'clock I heard my gorgeous co-worker Keri ask the clerical staff if anyone would be interested in working overtime. We had an important presentation the next day, and Keri was responsible for seeing that all the data were processed. She said that she would be staying, but needed someone else to help her. Tina, a cute little thing, twenty and unmarried, volunteered. I had my own work to finish that night, so I didn't pay much attention at the time.

That evening I got to work on my project. By nine o'clock I was almost done, but I needed Keri's final figures. I left the wife and kids and headed back to the office. The place was pretty dark. I was all ready to turn on the overhead lights when I began to hear low moans, soft passionate ones.

I crept quietly toward the sounds, where I found Keri kneeling before Tina, eating her pussy. Keri was on her knees with her rear stuck up in the air, still clothed as far as I could see. Tina was sitting in an office chair, legs askew, leaning back and looking up. Her blouse was wide open and her bra undone so that her tits shone in the dim light. Her tight skirt was unbuttoned and crumpled around her on the chair. Her panties lay on the floor beside Keri. They were both playing with Tina's tits while Keri, her face buried between Tina's thighs, rolled her head back and forth, working over Tina's cute little pussy. It was Tina I had heard, but Keri was also making ecstatic cooing sounds while she lapped away, her face thickly glazed with Tina's hot juices.

I felt funny about just standing there watching, so I cleared my throat and said, "I'm sure glad I had to come back tonight." Keri turned around, startled. Her blouse and bra were also undone. Tina sat up straight, her eyes wide. Keri got up and came toward me.

"You won't say anything, will you?" She asked. Her big tits bobbed as she spoke.

I couldn't help staring as I replied, "No I wouldn't say anything. But I would like to stay and watch, if you to wouldn't mind at all."

"Just watch?" Keri asked. She advanced and threw her arms around me, kissing me. I was already aroused, and my dick jutted against her skirt through my pants. Her tongue slid into my mouth, and I could taste Tina on her lips.

Abruptly she broke away from me and turned to Tina, who had stood up. She kissed her, eased her back onto a desk and finished undoing her skirt. As Keri started to strip Tina's blouse and bra, I reached around and unfastened Keri's skirt.

While Keri finger-fucked Tina and licked her tits, I took off my own clothes. I touched Keri's fanny, and she moved to one side. This allowed me to go down on Tina, who was already rocking through what seemed like one continuous orgasm. She groaned loudly and slapped the top of the desk. Keri cleared the desk and began kissing Tina on her pretty mouth, while I continued lapping up her pussy juice.

Eager to get in on the orgasms, Keri climbed on top of the desk and straddled Tina's face, kneeling facing me. I too wanted some direct stimulation, and stood up to sink my dick deep into Tina. God, she was hot and slick! Keri leaned forward and began kissing me again. I felt her tits, bouncing them in my palms and rolling her nipples. Keri groaned and began to come, her cunt twitching against Tina's busy tongue.

Keri couldn't take any more after a while and rolled off. I pulled them both down on the floor. Keri grabbed me around the thighs and sucked my dick. I found Tina and gently guided her head once more between Keri's legs. Lying on our sides, we managed to get everybody's genitals in contact with a warm mouth.

I began to come in Keri's mouth as she licked, slurped and sucked. I don't shoot when I'm being sucked. Instead I just ooze, but the advantage is that I can last for what seems like forever, and still be ready to fuck afterwards.

We all came, one after another. Keri was last and, when she has stopped trembling from Tina's tongue and my hands on her breasts, I asked if she wanted to fuck.

With no further ado, Keri crawled into the doggie position and I began fucking her with long, slow strokes. Keri moaned to Tina to crawl underneath, which she did. Soon I had my balls and the underside of my dick being licked as I shot in and out of Keri's clutching sheath. It was fantastic.

Keri began sucking away at Tina's pussy again. Keri's cunt was so juicy that it slurped as my dick went in and out of it. Soon Keri came again and said that she needed to rest.

Tina felt no desire to slow down, and immediately began to suck my dick for all she was worth. I got into a 69 with her and, while she continued to come, I oozed come into her mouth. I wanted to feel her cunt sloshing around me. We rearranged ourselves so that I could put it into her in the missionary position, with her legs wrapped around my back. Keri crept alongside and we all kissed at once. Finally I came, shooting a huge load into Tina's pussy. As soon as I slid out, Keri went down on Tina, licking up the come. Then she gave me a final sucking, draining me dry.

That night was without a doubt the best fucking I've ever had in my life. The women apparently felt that way too. From now on we're going to meet at Tina's apartment.—*S.O., Buffalo, New York* ○━▬

FIRST-TIME PARTNERS WASTE NO TIME GETTING INTO THE FLOW

I must say, my wife Asia is about the hottest woman I have ever known. It is hard for a man to admit that he just can't keep his wife satisfied sexually, but no man would be a match for Asia. She just loves to fuck. She is always ready. I have fucked her as many as five times a day, but there's a limit to just how many times my cock will get hard. Asia is a real beauty, twenty-seven years old, with a terrific figure, so she has no trouble finding other men to keep her happy.

Asia works with a black woman who is also a real looker, and they have become close friends. Asia's friend is named Sharon. Sharon laughed when Asia told her she'd been fucked several times by black men since we were married. Sharon invited Asia and me to be her guests at a swingers party. Sharon called it a salt-and-pepper party, as there were to be both white and black couples there. She added that there would be extra men there, so all the women would be thoroughly fucked.

We arrived at the party and Sharon led us around to make introductions. First she took us into a bedroom, where Sharon told us we could remove our clothes. She also took off her own clothes. She has big tits and her pussy was clean-shaven. She looked at Asia and said, "Wow. The guys are sure going to give those tits and pussy of yours a good working over."

I popped a hard-on. Sharon laughed and wrapped her hand around my stiff cock. She said she was looking forward to getting better acquainted with me and my friend, and she stroked my erection. Without letting go she led me by my dick to meet the others.

There were six white couples and nine black couples—all naked—dancing, eating and laughing. One couple was fucking right there on the floor. Sharon laughed again and said, "Early arrivals. They got impatient." Soon Asia and I were swept up in the spirit of the party. Sharon sat me down in a chair and started sucking my cock. Asia sat Sharon's husband down in a chair next to me and started sucking his cock. It was a super turn-on watching Asia suck him while Sharon deep-throated me.

We traded partners all night long. After the super blowjob Sharon gave me, we both wanted to fuck.

I spread the dark lips of her cunt and explored the hidden, tender pink flesh with my lips and fingers. She smelled strong, which always excites me, and soon I had another erection. I guided my cock to the opening of her cunt. I could feel the heat of her as my pale white cock slipped easily inside her. Sharon raised her hips, locked her legs around my ass, and rotated and pumped her own cheeks against the carpet, rubbing our pubic hair together. Her cunt muscles gripped my cock tightly. For a woman who has had a lot of experience, she sure has managed to keep her muscles tight. Her voluntary and involuntary contractions were working magic on my meat. I usually like to hold back for a long time, but I just plain felt too good, and soon pumped my load deep inside Sharon's pussy.

After that I rested for a while and started looking around. Sharon's husband was fucking Asia's cunt furiously, and Asia was pleading with him to fuck her hard, saying, "Yes, oh yes, fuck me. Please put that big cock all the way in me." His balls were making a slapping sound as they bounced against Asia's ass. Several guys were standing around watching and waiting their turn to fuck Asia. Sharon laughed and said, "After those guys are done with that auburn-haired pussy, she won't be able to put her legs together for a month." Since we were new, everyone wanted their turn with Asia, men and women alike. By the end of the night she got to them all.

It was five in the morning by the time most people left the party. Asia was sure she had been fucked by each guy at least twice. One guy gave Asia twenty dollars for her panties. A black man wanted a photo of him fucking Asia to show his friends. Asia invited two guys to come home with us, and they did. She fucked both of them to exhaustion, and then turned to me. Yes, I have a hot wife and I love her very much.—*L.R., Kansas City, Missouri*

<u>Serendipity</u>

WHEN SHE LANDS AT THE AIRPORT, THEY GO UP, UP AND AWAY WITH PLEASURE

I arrived at the airport in time to see my girlfriend's plane land and taxi down the runway toward the terminal. I waited impatiently, my heart beating very rapidly with excitement, for her to disembark. It felt as though we hadn't seen each other in months instead of weeks. I craved to hold her tightly in my arms, to kiss and caress her all over.

Just then they wheeled a portable staircase over to the plane so the passengers could descend down onto the tarmac. The door to the jet opened and the passengers began to file out and walk down the stairs.

As I intently scrutinized each passenger coming through the jet's door, I finally spotted my girl! She paused at the top of the staircase for a moment, as if she were making a grand entrance, and looked around. I wondered if she was looking for me. God, she looked so hot! I could hardly stand still. She was wearing high heels and a *very* short dress that hugged her body's curves perfectly. I noticed that I wasn't the only one watching her as she walked down the stairs.

I couldn't help but notice that with each downward step she took, her dress slowly crept farther and farther up her thighs. I wasn't sure if she didn't even realize it, or if she was doing it purposely because she knew it would drive me crazy!

I thought my cock would explode. As she took her final step down onto the tarmac, she stumbled forward, almost falling, causing her dress to ride up even higher and expose her bare ass to the world. At that moment I could see she wasn't wearing any panties, and no doubt so could everyone else. As she reached behind to tug her dress back down (just far enough to cover her cheeks), she finally caught sight of me, smiled and called out my name.

As she hurried over to me, we embraced passionately. I knew she could feel my hard cock pressed up against her. Just then she whispered in my ear, "I knew my little scheme would have its desired effect on you." I'd had a feeling she had planned it all from the start! God, I really love her!

I wanted to fuck her right then and there, but there were too many people around, not to mention too many security guards. As we waited at baggage claim for her luggage, she just kept on wriggling her ass at me and doing little things to tease me. I felt as though my cock was going to rip right through my jeans.

Then, as the luggage started coming around on the conveyor belt, she purposely bent over in front of me, scrutinizing each suitcase as though it were hers, just to have the opportunity to entice me again with her ass, which she knows I'm quite enamored of. I was about to go crazy!

There were a lot of other guys watching her too, and that seemed to excite her even more. Of course I wasn't worried at all, because I know that she's mine and I'm hers. However, I have a feeling that she made more than a few wives and girl-friends rather jealous and even pissed off.

As fate would have it, though, she got her come-uppance. As she bent over for the tenth time, this time to actually pick up her own suitcase, she teetered on her high heels and was thrown off balance as she grabbed the handle, no doubt because her suitcase was so heavy. I quickly came up behind her to give her a hand, but the forward motion of the conveyor belt had already caused her to fall forward. She fell over onto her suitcase, her ass up in the air and once again exposed. She wriggled around a minute, pretending that she couldn't get up. I considered rescuing her, but then thought better of it. I figured I'd let her have her fun. After she'd gone all the way around the conveyor belt once, I finally grabbed a hold of her and lifted her off. By the look on her face, I knew she was really excited and had enjoyed the hell out of it!

By the time we got to the car, we were both raring to go and ready to fuck. I was all set to pounce on her in the backseat when security drove by, and we decided it would be prudent if we waited until we got home. But of course I couldn't even wait that long.

On the way home, I decided to pull over onto the shoulder of the freeway. I pretended there was something wrong with the car and told her I needed to check under the hood. I asked her to get out of the car and hold the flashlight for me. I positioned her so that she had to stretch way over the engine compartment, knowing her dress would again creep up her ass! I quickly moved behind her and stuck my throbbing cock into her awaiting bare pussy. As I reached around to caress her tits, she dropped the flashlight and yelled, "Yeah! Fuck me hard!"

As I came, I thought she was going to go crazy. She exploded in a paroxysm of pleasure. Needless to say, this was the start of a wild sexfest for us!—*W.B., Palo Alto, California*   O⊢ ⃞

HE LOVES TO STUFF HIS ITALIAN SAUSAGE INTO HER FRENCH ROLL

After a failed marriage of fifteen years, where oral sex was considered dirty and lovemaking was passionless, it's so wonderful to be engaged to a sexy, voluptuous, hot-blooded Frenchwoman who oozes with eroticism. This fiery-eyed nymph loves to suck my cock and can never get enough of it inside of her.

Though I was completely faithful in my marriage, I had been around the block a few times before I got married, so I've made love to numerous women. Although most of my wild oats were sowed during the wild and crazy free-love sixties, no woman I've ever been with compares with my current fiancée. I can't tell you how wonderful it is to finally have a partner who has a similar sex drive.

I am a handsome forty-year-old Italian who loves sex. I am especially fond of big breasts and having my cock inside a wet and hungry mouth. My fiancée and I have been together for one and a half years. Last year we were both unemployed for five months, and we made the most of it sexually. We would make love all day and all night long.

Often, after an all-nighter of hot and sweaty lovemaking, my woman would wake me up, her head under the blankets as she licked and kissed my cock. It didn't stop there, though. My pretty babe of thirty-two, with her long eyelashes and dark hair, would lay her head by my crotch and passionately suck my sleepy love-tool until it stood up proud and tall. Groaning softly, she'd tell me how much she loved having my cock in her mouth. She would lie naked for hours in this position, moaning in complete satisfaction, while her big, luscious lips were wrapped around my Italian sausage.

I love watching her put on her makeup while she's sitting at her vanity in panties and an overflowing bra. I also love burying my face in those 40D boobs. I could get lost in her cleavage. I often suck and caress her tits for hours. Sometimes I'll try to squeeze one of her luscious breasts into my mouth, but that's always impossible because of their size! Her nipples are the size of silver dollars, but are worth their weight in gold to me. She loves when I straddle her while she's lying on her back so I can slide my throbbing love-pole through her cleavage. No silicone here—just two natural and beautiful mounds that I can squeeze together while slowly tit-fucking her. Every time I expose those love-pillows, I'm amazed at my Amazon woman's natural resources.

She gets excited and soaks her panties with her sweet juices whenever I surprise her with a can of whipped cream, because she knows she can anticipate hours of good eating before a very special dessert. Of course, a full-course meal always starts out with an antipasto. Her favorite is sucking on a couple of ripe, dark, oval olives. She loves to *mangia* on my Italian-style delicacies, whether served plain or in a creamy sauce.

After the first course, my lusty lover is famished and panting for seconds. I slowly shimmy my cock almost within reach of her hungry lips as her tongue attacks the sensitive tip. With one hand on my rear, she pulls me into her desirous mouth. Noisily sucking and devouring me inch by inch, her head madly bobs back and forth, sucking me deeper and deeper till nothing is visible but my pubic hair and a very satisfied lady with a mouthful of cock.

Then it's my turn to lie on my stomach while my busty babe straddles me. She gently massages my back, rear and thighs with her warm breasts, sending chills through my body. As a finale, she kisses my balls and inner thighs from behind.

We then continue making love. On all fours, she waits anxiously for me to penetrate her. I slowly put my cockhead in her slit and then withdraw, repeating this motion to make her even more horny. She whimpers, "How do you do that?" before she pleads for the whole length. After hours of teasing each other, with hormones raging and juices flowing, we ride to the finish. At these times an almost religious fervor takes over my sexy nymph, and she begs me not to withdraw my blessing, but to leave it in that sacred place all night.

Whenever we drive anywhere, the first thing she does, whether I'm in jeans or a suit, is unzip my pants and devour my cock. Eagerly she clamps down on my stick shift, and there's no way I can put on the brakes!

One time the air bag opened by mistake while she was sucking me and, with her mouth stuck on my cock, she couldn't move. An hour later help finally arrived. My lusty lover never once complained, and even wanted to know if we could try it again! Another time I gave a stranded motorist a lift. He sat in the backseat, and I told him my girlfriend was lying down, taking a nap up front. He and I chatted, and he was completely unaware that my sweetie was actually savoring every inch of my throbbing cock. With her lips locked on my erection, she tamed the wild beast with oral persuasion, but refused to put it back into its cage until she was done playing with it.

When we talk on the phone, she tells me the sound of my voice gets her panties soaked. Whenever we don't see each other for a few days, my woman lets me know that my meat's in for a treat when I bring it home. When I walk in, a dozen roses in hand, she French-kisses me, puts one hand on my bulge and the other on my zipper, then leads me to the bedroom. She immediately disrobes me and whispers that we have hours of catching up to do.

I can't imagine any other woman fulfilling my needs like she does. My woman is all woman! She's a total woman, and I'm proud to be her man!—*A.M., New York, New York* ○┼▄

THINGS DEVELOP QUICKLY WHEN PHOTO LAB CLERK EXPOSES RACY PICTURES

For the past two summers I have worked at a photo developing lab where the unofficial policy is, "The pictures you take are your own business." This is unusual in my small, somewhat conservative hometown, so we get a lot of what I'd call "alternative" pictures.

When I'm alone in the store, I've gotten into the habit of masturbating in the darkroom while looking at some of the racier pictures. One day it was my turn to stay at the store during lunchtime, while everyone else went out to eat. I was amusing myself in the darkroom when a customer rang our service bell. I sighed—I had been really close to orgasm—and quickly made myself presentable.

When I opened the door and stepped out to the counter, my jaw dropped. A gorgeous woman was standing there. Her huge breasts swelled within her tight, white shirt, and I swear I could see her nipples harden as her eyes caressed my muscular body.

What was most shocking was the fact that I had masturbated to pictures of this same woman just the day before! I couldn't believe my luck. Her pictures had really stood out. In most of them, her beautiful, tan body was pressed up against a stunning blonde woman. In others the two were writhing in passion on black satin sheets. I remember being extremely envious of the photographer.

Now here she was, standing right in front of me in the flesh. I cleared my throat and tried to regain my composure. "Ummm, may I help you?" I stammered. She looked slightly impatient as she told me her name and waited for me to locate her pictures. I did my best to hurry, but I was nervous and I dropped the pictures. They spilled all over the floor. I tried to pick them up without looking at them—I knew my erection was evident enough already. When I stood up, blushing, she smiled, her impatience suddenly gone. "So, did you see anything?" she asked coyly.

I said, "Well, I developed them."

She leaned over the counter and examined my engorged cock. With a big smile, she said, "I see you liked what you saw."

Tongue-tied, I couldn't think of anything to say, so I just stared at her cleavage. I felt my cock throb as I imagined sliding my pole into that deep chasm. The woman stood up straighter, throwing out her chest, and seductively licked her lips. I thought I was going to pass out. It seemed as if all the blood in my head had rushed to my dick, making it even bigger than before.

She grabbed my hand and pulled me into the darkroom. She saw the pictures I had been masturbating to earlier and laughed. "And what were you doing with these, you naughty boy?" she asked with a smile.

I quickly grabbed the photos and shoved them into an envelope. As I put them back into the file I had taken them from, I felt the woman's hand on my rod. She stroked it as she pressed her breasts against my back. Then she turned me around and took my pants off. I leaned against the file cabinet when she dropped to her knees and began to suck me off.

Her soft lips circled my cockhead and her tongue teased my slit. I begged her to take me all in. When she did, I nearly lost it right then and there. She didn't let me come, though. She knew exactly what she was doing. She brought me to the brink several times with her talented mouth before she took off her shirt. "I saw you looking at my chest before," she said. "Do you want to fuck it?"

I was delighted to plunge my cock into the soft depths of her cleavage. Sliding in and out between her tits was sheer heaven! All I could think of were the pictures of her I had developed the day before. The image in my mind of this babe with her friend was enough to make me shoot my load all over. I collapsed to the floor, completely spent.

She stood up and put her shirt back on. I sighed when her beautiful breasts were covered again, but she ignored me. I was too tired to care. It was all I could do to get dressed. In fact, I was still in the darkroom when my coworkers returned. I tired to act normal but, evidently, my condition was obvious to the other guys I worked with. They looked at each other and laughed. "She got you too, didn't she?" one of them asked.

I looked at them in bewilderment, not understanding. Then they explained. Evidently this woman always came in during lunchtime, and managed to get away without paying for her pictures everytime. I laughed sheepishly with the guys about it, but the truth is, I would pay *her* for another experience like that one. If it was up to me, she could have all the free pictures she wanted! The blowjob she gave me was the best I ever had!—
T.K., Detroit, Michigan ⊶▣

TRADE SHOW LEADS TO FUTURE BUSINESS—AND PLEASURE—EXCHANGES

I am a twenty-four-year-old retailer. I often work a booth at trade shows, and at a recent show in a luxury hotel I met a salesman from New York City named Noah. I could tell from the way he looked at me that he was interested. Whenever my boss walked away, Noah would come over and talk to me for a few minutes.

When the show was over, Noah invited me to party with him and some of the other fellows from the show. We all headed for the hotel bar, and it was soon very obvious that Noah and I were going to end up together.

Noah is thirty-two, stands about five feet eleven inches tall and has a very nice build. I've always been attracted to dark-haired guys, so his Jewish heritage helped a lot.

I am five-seven, weigh one hundred twenty-five pounds and wear my hair short. To stay in shape, I work out three times a week. I get many compliments on my looks and have never had any problems attracting a man.

After several drinks and a lot of talking and laughing, we went to his room. At that point I was beginning to have second thoughts about getting involved with a man I might never see again. But I ultimately decided he was just too hot to pass up. I finally gave in, and it was definitely the most sensuous and erotic experience of my life—until last night.

Yesterday afternoon he called me unexpectedly. He told me he had flown into my city for the night and asked if he could see me. Of course I said yes. I quickly dressed in one of my favorite outfits: a silk sarong miniskirt and a matching tank top.

I met him at his hotel and we went to a romantic restaurant for dinner. We were totally caught up in each other. As we reminisced about our last meeting, I was getting extremely turned on, and I guess he could tell. My breathing was getting heavier and my nipples were trying to poke out of my shirt. We were sitting next to one another in a cozy booth, and he started licking my ear and the nape of my neck. He put his hand on my knee and started slowly working it up my thigh. He pushed my skirt up and discovered that I wasn't wearing any panties. He began teasing my clit with his thumb while he inserted a finger into my extremely wet hole. He slid it all the way in, and started massaging me in the most wonderfully pleasing way I had ever felt. It was as if my pussy was molded just for his fingers. At this point I was totally into it and I didn't care if anyone was watching. My head was thrown back and I'm sure I was moaning a bit.

When I felt an orgasm approaching, I grabbed the tablecloth and held on tight. I sensed it was going to be a big one, and I was right. When I finally came back down to earth, the waiter was standing there with a big grin on his face. I was a little embarrassed, but it had been such a great orgasm I really didn't care.

The waiter told us that, if we were interested, dessert was on the house, but we declined. I just needed to have Noah's beautiful, soft skin next to mine as soon as possible.

We went for a walk along the beach and started kissing very sensually—the kind of kisses where you suck on each other's tongue. Soon he began to lick my ears and neck. We sat down on a bench, and I pulled his cock out of his pants. There wasn't anyone else around, so I went to town on him.

Noah has a very nice penis. It is probably about seven and a half inches long and very thick. I've often been told that I give a great blowjob, so I decided to go for it and pull out all the stops. I slowly licked his cockhead and teased the shaft with my tongue.

Then I grasped the base of his dick and engulfed his entire tool in my mouth. I slid my mouth up and down his shaft, simultaneously jerking him off with my right hand. With my left hand, I fondled his balls. Either he hadn't had sex since the last time we'd met (which had been two weeks before), or I am really talented, because he came in about ninety seconds.

On the way back to his hotel room, he told me that he was going to make me come at least a dozen times.

While in the elevator on the way up to his room, we basically undressed one another. We passed a few guys in the corridor who grinned at us and gave Noah a thumbs-up sign. Once in the room, we finished undressing and I put on his condom for him. I opened it with my teeth and slowly slid it on his hard cock.

We started in the missionary position, with my legs wrapped around his waist. As he was driving it home, I could feel his balls slapping against my ass. We then shifted so that I was on top, straddling him. I could feel his entire cock deep inside me. We were fucking so hard that the headboard of the bed was banging against the wall. I was real surprised that the people in the next room didn't call the front desk to complain.

After a few minutes, Noah had the strangest smile on his face. I knew he was going to come. His body tensed, and I could feel him shooting his load. We fell asleep in each other's arms.

I woke up in the early-morning hours with the sensation of someone caressing me. Noah was definitely up, in more than one sense of the word. I was still tired, so I just gave him another blowjob. Around dawn we showered and said our good-byes. We made plans to see each other again at a national trade show in a few months. Noah already told me not to bother getting my own room. I can hardly wait!—*P.R., Baltimore, Maryland* ⊶▥

HIS HALLOWEEN COSTUME IS UNFORGETTABLE WHEN HE WEARS HIS BIRTHDAY SUIT

I still can't believe my good luck! The costume I wore last Halloween got me the best blowjob I ever had in my life! But let me start at the beginning.

I was at a singles' bar when I ran into Katrina, who works at a bank I go to. She's married, but I've always had the hots for her. Luckily her husband wasn't there. She was dressed for the occasion as a flapper, and her costume only emphasized her beauty. She was with her friends, Stephanie and Eve. Stephanie was dressed as a witch, and Eve as a vampire. They are also married, but the three were having a girls' night out. I wasn't wearing a costume because I had worked late that night and at the last minute had decided to stop at the bar for a drink. I ended up dancing and partying with the girls all night in the club.

Katrina kept saying that I should be wearing a costume too. I finally told her that I would go home and get one if she would come with me. I had just talked her into it when Stephanie and Eve came over. Since the bar was about to close, I invited them all to my place for a drink. Stephanie and Eve were feeling pretty good and agreed immediately.

When we got to my place and settled down, Katrina kept pestering me about a costume. I said I really didn't have one and didn't know what to wear. Everyone started making suggestions about what I should be, and someone mentioned "X-rated movie star." I think one of them had spotted an adult movie in amongst my videos.

I asked what an X-rated performer would wear. Katrina quickly said, "Nothing," and the girls started giggling. As I was feeling no pain, the idea seemed appealing to me, so I told them I'd go in my room to change into my "costume." Katrina yelled out, "All right!"

I didn't really know if they were serious or just teasing me, so when I got to my room I wasn't sure what I should do. But then I just thought, What the hell, stripped off all my clothes, took a deep breath and walked back into the living room.

Eve gasped and Stephanie looked shocked. I could hardly believe it myself. There I was, standing totally naked in front of three women. Then I looked at Katrina and saw a big smile on her face. "Oh, cool!" she said. That made me feel a lot better.

I walked over and sat down next to her on the sofa. She started giggling, saying that she loved my costume and joking that I should have entered the contest at the club. Eve calmed down too and started joking with Katrina. But Stephanie the witch still looked disgusted.

After a while, with music playing on the radio, Katrina asked me if I wanted to dance. Eve said, "Yeah, I'd like to see that!" so Katrina and I got up and started shaking it up. Eve was clapping and hooting, while Katrina was chuckling and dancing with me. It was only a matter of moments until I got a raging hard-on.

There was no way to hide it. Katrina seemed pleased. Eve pretended to be embarrassed. I purposely turned toward Stephanie, my erection just inches from her face. She got up in a huff and stalked off into the kitchen. Katrina laughed and said, "Well, now, you look like a real X-rated star!"

I told her I thought I should change my outfit, and walked back into my room. I figured the joke had gone far enough. To my surprise, Katrina followed me into my room and closed the door. "Let me be your X-rated starlet," she said, and we started kissing.

Soon Katrina was stroking my hard cock, and my dream was coming true. She kissed my neck and chest, and nibbled her way down to my belly, falling to her knees. She showered my aching hard-on with kisses. Then she licked up and down the shaft, and finally began sucking it. She was an absolutely superb cocksucker, and I envied her husband, though I was getting Katrina's full attention and tender loving care now. As she slowly glided her lovely mouth up and down my swollen member, she started rubbing her hands up the backs of my thighs, then grasped my buttocks and squeezed them while she sucked.

Her expert tongue felt so good. She sucked faster and faster, and I began pumping my cock in and out of those warm lips while I held her head in my hands. I was fucking her mouth harder and harder. I soon felt myself nearing the point of no return. Since she had been so nice to me, I told her I was about to come so she could pull away if she wanted. But she held my stiff penis in her mouth as I exploded my hot semen down her throat. As I pumped spurt after spurt of come, I heard her gulping it all down. She sucked me until I was completely dry. Then she turned her head up toward me and smiled. I told her, "That was the best blowjob I've ever had in my life." She answered, "I'm happy to oblige."

Then I got dressed. When Katrina and I walked out, Stephanie had already left, but Eve gave Katrina a grinning look, as if to say, "What have you done to this poor boy?" But I certainly wasn't complaining!

I still see Katrina when I go to the bank. Every once in a while she'll wink at me and ask me what I plan to wear next Halloween. Last time I told her I'd be wearing something exciting, and she licked her lips and said, "I can't wait to see." I sure hope this turns out to be an annual event!—R.L., *Fort Lauderdale, Florida* ⚬╼▪

DOLLAR NIGHT PAYS OFF FOR MAN OUT ON THE TOWN

Last weekend I decided to visit a new nightclub that had just opened in town. It was "dollar night," so every drink in the house was only a dollar. As I walked through the crowded club and checked out all the foxy ladies, my expectations of meeting someone soared.

I walked up to the bar and ordered a beer. That's when I noticed a woman dressed all in red. Out of all the women in the club, she literally stood head and shoulders above the rest. This Amazon was at least five feet eleven inches tall and as sexy as could be.

I immediately walked over to her and asked her to dance. To my disappointment, she said she didn't like the song that was playing. But I don't give up that easily. I sat down and introduced myself, hoping to eventually win her over. She told me that her name was Belinda and that this was her first time there. She mentioned that she had noticed me walking into the club. Just looking at her made my hormones sizzle.

As the night progressed, we danced several times and really began to get friendly with each other. After a particularly fast song, I asked her if she wanted to take a walk outside to get some fresh air and cool off for a few minutes. She agreed, and off we went.

Before I knew it we were at my car, kissing passionately. I started to gently caress her breasts. To my surprise they were huge and firm, with large, erect nipples. I began to feel my slacks get very tight as my cock swelled, so I decided to make my move. I asked her to come home with me. She agreed, and I drove to my place like a bat out of hell.

As soon as I opened the door, Belinda began ripping my clothes off. I led her to the bedroom and stripped off all of her clothing. Her skin was so soft and silky, and her pussy was so wet and juicy. We lay down on the bed and I began to devour her juicy melons. They tasted so good and sweet. She moaned with excitement the whole time. Every time she moaned, my dick grew longer and thicker, and more and more pre-come leaked out.

Without any hesitation she wrapped her ruby-red lips around my swollen dick. As she worked my dick over with her soft lips and expert tongue, I began to fuck her face. I just love getting my dick sucked. But even though I enjoy it immensely, I have trouble reaching orgasm like that. The warm juices of a hot pussy caressing my cock is the only thing that will make me spill my protein.

As I stretched her out on the bed, I began to gently caress her cunt lips with the head of my dick. She began to squirm and moan. This was the moment I had been waiting for. I slid the full length of my cock inside her and she let out a loud scream of pleasure.

Belinda was so soft and tender that I wanted to be real gentle with her, but she obviously had other things in mind. I slowly worked over every crevice of her steamy pussy. She began to buck and grind against me. I soon felt two warm hands clamp down on my buttocks and shove me in even deeper. I knew then what she wanted. I lifted both of her long legs, put them over my shoulders and began to fuck her with long, slow strokes. She loved every bit of it and started humping me furiously.

As we bumped and ground, I noticed that the frenzy of our fucking had moved the bed away from the wall. By this point we were fucking like there was no tomorrow. She soon was fast approaching a climax, loudly crying out, "Oh, yes! Yes, baby, I'm coming! Oh, yes, yes!" I continued to pound away, and her body began to spasm as she had one orgasm after another.

When I began to climax, there were no words to describe the intensity. I felt drained, but she begged me not to stop, and her wish was granted. Her moans were so deep and sensual that my love-pole just stayed at attention. As we fucked on, sweat began to drip from my chin onto her chest.

After about an hour of hot, steamy fucking, I came for the second time and collapsed on her chest. I was exhausted. She got up, went into the bathroom and brought out a damp washcloth. She tenderly began to wipe me off. She started kissing and licking me all over, telling me how good I tasted. In no time at all she had me as hard as steel, and I wanted more.

I lay flat on my back, and she straddled me and slowly impaled herself on me. It felt so good as she rotated around and around on my love-pole. Belinda was so horny that she was flooding hot come all over my bat and balls.

I asked her if she wanted to do it doggie-style an she said sure. As she positioned herself on all fours, I inserted my rod of steel. With my left hand I reached around and began to caress her clitoris and swollen cunt lips. She was clearly very aroused by this sensation. She began to wiggle and twitch as I shoved every inch of my prime tubesteak into her hot, steamy snatch. Soon we both exploded in orgasm.

We both had outdone ourselves that night, and soon fell into a deep sleep. When I woke up the next morning, she was gone. Unfortunately I never heard from her again. But what a night it was!—*Name and address withheld*

GUY'S IN FOR A SHOCKING WHEN HIS EX-WIFE COMES A-KNOCKING

I was married for about four years to my first wife, Nicole, but we've been divorced for six years now. Those four years of marriage led me to believe that Nicole was one of the most old-fashioned, straitlaced, sexually hung-up females on the planet. When we had sex (once a week, on Saturday afternoon) the lights were always out. The only position she would permit was the missionary position, and she thought oral sex was absolutely disgusting. She dressed like an old lady and never wore any makeup. After four years I just couldn't hack it anymore so I asked her for a divorce. Thankfully she agreed.

I remarried about four years later. I never heard from my ex, nor did I ever give her a thought. I basically tried to forget about her.

Then, last fall out of the blue, she called me at home one day. My wife Terri answered the phone, and Nicole told my wife that she was a coworker who needed to talk to me about an important project. When I got on the phone, she told me that she needed to speak to me in private. She said it was very, very important that I meet with her, and she assured me that she had no intention of getting me in trouble with my wife. I told her to call me at work the next day and we'd arrange something. She called the next day as planned, and I agreed to meet her one Saturday evening in a large city about sixty miles from where I live.

On the prearranged day, I arrived at the downtown hotel dining room where we'd planned to meet. The maître 'd seated me at a table in the back corner of the dining room. I ordered a drink while I waited for my ex to show up and clear up all this mystery. I had absolutely no idea why she wanted to see me. My mind wandered as I considered the possibilities.

Suddenly I heard a familiar voice say, "Thanks for agreeing to meet me, Charlie." I glanced up quickly. Nicole was standing right next to me. As I looked her up and down, I could hardly believe that this was my ex-wife. She had bleached her hair platinum blonde and was wearing a skintight orange dress that looked as if it had been sprayed on. Her tits appeared to have grown a few sizes since I'd last seen her. My eyes wandered down past the hem of the dress, which was a good six inches above her knees, and fixed on the outrageous shoes Nicole had on. They were white leather platform shoes, but they had no buckles or ties. A single strap crossed the top of her foot just below the toes, and another strap ran up from the outside of the shoe and wrapped around her ankle and lower calf about five times before running down across her instep. As she walked past the table to hang her coat on a wall hook, I got another jolt when I saw the back of her dress. Plunging from her shoulders to below her waist, it was completely backless. There were metal rings down each side, and they were laced with orange material that crisscrossed her back. The dress was cut so low that an inch or more of her ass crack was plainly visible. I still had no idea what was going on, but I was aware that my dick was starting to get hard.

She sat opposite me, giving me a good view of her tits, which were popping out of the top of her dress. After suggesting a round of drinks, Nicole said I was probably wondering what was going on, and she promised she'd do her best to explain.

She told me that, after our divorce, she'd dated a lot of guys, and most of them seemed to like the same things I'd liked—eating pussy, getting my cock sucked, talking dirty and so on. When they saw how straight she was, most of them didn't bother to ask her out a second time. She added that most of the guys were either cheap, weird or not too clean. About two years ago she'd formulated a plan. She'd had her breasts enlarged with silicone implants to a 36D. She'd completely revamped her wardrobe, and set about learning all the sexual variations that I had liked but she would never take part in.

By this point my mind was reeling, and I began to wonder if this was all a dream. After our drink, we had some dinner, and then Nicole hit me with a stunner. "I have a suite on the twentieth floor," she said. "Could we continue our discussion in private?" I was so intrigued I had to agree.

As soon as the elevator door closed behind us on the way up to her floor, she took out a cigarette case and lit up. Damn, I thought, she smokes now too! Then I smelled a familiar sweet odor and realized she was smoking reefer. I almost died of shock. She just smiled as she took another hit, then passed the joint to me. She didn't even care if anyone saw us when the elevator door opened on her floor. Nicole led the way down the hall while I admired her swaying ass, her fuck-me shoes and her backless dress. My dick was hard as nails and leaking come into my jockey shorts.

Her suite was large and lushly furnished, with a thick, soft carpet and soft lights. Nicole poured us each a drink, and we sat down on the sofa to talk some more. Then she excused herself to the bathroom and told me to answer the door if anyone knocked. Sure enough, in just a minute there was a knock on the door. I got up to answer it as Nicole had requested. My mind was spinning out of control from the booze, the pot and the whole situation in general, which was still hard for me to grasp.

When I opened the door I got yet another shock. Standing in front of me were two girls in their early twenties. One of them informed me that Nicole was expecting them. They introduced themselves as Barbara and Debbie. Both wore a lot of makeup and basically looked like hookers. Barbara, the blonde, had on gold, high-heeled, open-toed sandals, a white micro-miniskirt and a white crop top that hung out over the erect points of some rather large boobs. Debbie was dressed in black spike heels, black shorts and a black halter top. Her hair was raven-black and she had smooth, mocha-colored skin.

The two newcomers proceeded to make themselves at home. They poured themselves drinks, rolled up a joint and turned on the radio. As they passed the joint back and forth, they danced to the fast beat, shaking their tits, wiggling their butts and making all kinds of lewd gestures. The next song was a slow number that the girls danced to in typical boy-girl fashion, arms wrapped tightly around each other.

Their wild gyrations had exposed Debbie's ass-cheeks, and Barbara rubbed and squeezed them as if she were in heat. Barbara soon discarded her crop top, baring her beautiful titties, which jiggled and shook in her half-cup bra. When the song ended, Debbie discarded her halter top. Then the girls lay on the rug and began to suck on each other's tits and caress each other's ass-cheeks.

By now come had soaked through my briefs and my pants, leaving a wet spot on my crotch. I was in heaven. At this point I didn't give a fuck what this was all about as long as it continued.

I wondered what had happened to Nicole, but I'd really lost track of time, so I wasn't sure how long she'd been gone. I suddenly had a feeling that someone was watching me. When I turned around, I saw my ex-wife standing there. My cock pulsed and more come leaked out. Nicole had changed her outfit and now resembled an image out of some sex dream. She wore black open-toed high heels, the likes of which I'd never before seen. The shoes basically comprised her entire outfit. The black straps wound around her ankles and then continued in one unbroken sweep up her calves and thighs, criss-crossing first in front and then in back. They wrapped around her waist and then ran down across her crotch and up the crack of her ass. Continuing up her back in a crisscross pattern, they ran over each shoulder and wound around each tit, squeezing them into cones that stuck straight out from her chest in a lewd and obscene manner. Her nipples resembled the rubber erasers on pencils. Not even in an X-rated video or in any men's magazine had I ever seen anything so slutty.

Nicole had put on loads of eye shadow, mascara, blush and lipstick to complete the whorish look. She had even colored her nipples with red lipstick and shaved her pussy to silky-smooth perfection.

She strode over to the radio and changed the station to something with a hard, driving beat. She lit up two more joints, handing one to me and toking on the other as she began to dance in front of me. The girls on the floor were still sucking and fingering each other, but my attention was riveted on Nicole, my personal go-go slut. Allowing the joint to dangle from her ruby-red lips, she danced quite suggestively, practically rubbing her bald twat in my face. She spread her cunt lips open to show me she had reddened them with lipstick too. She then grabbed each tit by the nipple, tweaking them as she cried out loudly in pleasure.

Nicole told me to stand up, and she proceeded to strip me naked and sit me back down. She got on her knees and began to suck and fondle my cock, which was now harder than it had ever been in my whole life. Before I could shoot off, she moved away and lay on her back on the rug in front of me. "Okay, girls," I heard her say, and Barbara and Debbie crawled over to her. Spreading my ex's legs wide apart, Barbara began to suck on Nicole's beautiful, bald, dripping wet pussy. Debbie positioned her mocha body near Nicole's head, facing her feet, leaned over and began to suck and squeeze my ex-wife's tits and rock-hard nipples.

Debbie's brown boobs hung right over Nicole's mouth, and

she did a wonderful job rubbing and licking them. Barbara stopped eating Nicole's cunt just long enough to grab a two-headed dildo and impale herself on it. Then, with the dildo sticking out of her as if it were a penis, she slid the other end up Nicole's gaping love-hole. They went crazy banging their boxes together, fucking that dildo as if there were no tomorrow. Each woman began to finger her own clit, and I'm sure their screams of pleasure must have been heard out in the hall. Debbie inched forward and settled her gash on Nicole's face for some oral attention. They all orgasmed as I watched, jerking my cock to the best orgasm of my life.

As we sat around talking afterward, Nicole told me more about her new lifestyle. She explained that she had discovered she was an exhibitionist. She also enjoyed lesbian love, but she still craved cock on a regular basis. Since the AIDS epidemic scared the hell out of her and most guys she met were losers anyhow, she had hit upon the idea of getting me back as a part-time lover and had set out to turn herself into the woman I had wanted her to be. She drinks, smokes and dresses like a slut all the time now, and she absolutely loves to show off her new tits in public. She's addicted to giving head and swallowing come. She even keeps her pussy shaved. She claims she cannot go more than a couple of days without a hard cock in her pussy. She is desperate to have me now and will do just about anything for me. These days she lives with Barbara and Debbie in a lesbian love nest. The three of them suck and fuck each other every weekend.

Nicole and I see each other two or three times a week now. I have fucked and eaten both Barbara and Debbie while Nicole watched and talked dirty to me, egging me on. Two black male friends of mine recently joined us for an evening, and Nicole took them both on at once while I watched. Glenn fucked her doggie-style while she sucked Troy off, then they switched places.

Because my job requires many business meetings and out-of-town trips, my wife has no idea that anything is going on. The new, improved Nicole is now thirty-six, and I am thirty-nine. Things are so perfect that I hope it goes on forever. If Terri should ever find out, I've already decided what I'll do. I'll tell her she can either join us or hit the road! It would be excellent to have the five of us living together.

Now Nicole wants me to take her on a trip to Europe so she can shop for sex items we can't get here in the States. She also wants to live out a fantasy of selling herself as a whore in Amsterdam, then having me eat the john's come out of her pussy.

How can you beat this kind of life? Never again will I doubt any of the things I read in your magazine. After my experience with Nicole, I know that absolutely anything is possible.—*C.S., Philadelphia, Pennsylvania*   O╾▣

NEPALESE NATIVE RAPIDLY ADJUSTS TO LOVE AMERICAN STYLE

I am twenty-seven years old and five feet six inches tall. I have dark hair and brown eyes. Most people mistake me for a Mexican or an Indian, but I am actually from a small Himalayan country called Nepal, which is located between China and India.

Nepal is sometimes called the Roof of the World, because of its tall Himalayan mountains. Although Nepal draws a melting pot of tourists from all the over the world, it is considered a third-world country and its people are very poor.

Regardless of the poverty, the mountain range that surrounds the valley is as beautiful as the morning sun. The snow-covered mountains look like silver at sunrise and gold at sunset. Beneath the magnificent snowy mountains lie foothills with endless varieties of wildflowers. The mountains, the foothills and the valley combine to make this place resemble paradise.

I worked as a tour guide in Nepal. My responsibilities included taking tourists to various historic sites as well as guiding them on expeditions into the mountains. Most of my clients were Americans.

It never occurred to me that some day I would end up in the United States. One day a tourist, who was the dean of a college in the States, asked me if I wanted to go to school there. Never being one to pass up an opportunity, I was quick to respond that I would love to. A few months later I was on a plane for the first time in my life, heading toward my dreamland—America.

I have been living here ever since. After I graduated from college, I got a job as a computer specialist at a nearby university. I thoroughly enjoy my new life in the United States.

Ever since I started to work at the university, I've had a burning desire to make passionate love to this blonde who works in the same department as I do. Her name is Jennifer. She is thirty-two years old and had recently been divorced. She is a little taller than I am, and she has the prettiest legs in the world. I especially love seeing her in a miniskirt. Just looking at her long, shapely legs turns me on, and I always wonder about that secret spot where her legs meet.

For many months I dreamed of making love with her, but things were not looking too good for me. I asked her out a few times, but for some reason she always turned me down. I never thought I'd have the opportunity to bed her. I always made it a point to smile at her, and she always smiled back, but I wanted more than a smile. I never would have guessed that, deep down inside, she wanted me as much as I wanted her.

Recently, on a Friday afternoon as I was passing by her office, I noticed she was staring at me intently, a curious look in her eyes. I stopped and chatted with her for a few minutes. As I was about to leave her office, she softly whispered that I should call her on Saturday afternoon. I was shocked. I could hardly believe my good fortune. The woman I had been lusting over for months actually wanted me to call her!

Little did I know, but she later admitted to me that she had had an extremely erotic dream about me the previous night. She'd dreamed of me grazing at her pussy and sucking on her perfect, round breasts. Completely unaware that I had been the subject of one of her dreams, I called her on Saturday and invited her over to my place for dinner. She was quick to accept, so I told her to come by around seven that evening.

I spent the afternoon shopping and preparing specialties from my homeland. Everything was ready when she arrived, and she was very impressed by the fact that I had gone to such trouble to prepare a nice meal for her. We drank a few beers and decided to watch the movie *Basic Instinct* while eating dinner.

At eleven o'clock the movie ended. I asked her if she was interested in shooting a game of pool. She liked the idea, so we headed down to the basement where my pool table was.

I didn't expect anything to happen, but as the night progressed it became more and more evident that lust was in the air. After a game of eight ball, which I won, Jennifer suggested we play strip pool, adding that the rules were similar to strip poker. Whoever lost a game had to take off one item of clothing. The catch was that the winner would decide which item came off. That sounded fine to me.

As the play progressed, it soon became quite obvious that

Jennifer was a real pool shark. I lost four games in a row and was down to my underpants. I finally won a game and requested that she take off her shorts. Her million-dollar legs were perfect. They were firm, well-toned and could practically make a man come on the spot.

We talked a lot as we played, and she told me a number of things that really surprised me. She admitted that she had not had sex for almost a year. She also mentioned that her ex-husband only made love to her every few months, if she was lucky. I could understand the sexual frustration she must have been experiencing. It had been almost six months since I'd last had sex, so I could certainly empathize with her situation. She told me that their sexual frequency—or infrequency—was the main reason she'd gotten a divorce.

As I leaned against the pool table to make a shot, she gently massaged my back with her soft hands and thanked me for listening to her problems. When her firm, tight legs pressed against mine, I felt a shiver run up my spine, giving me goose bumps. I slowly turned around and saw that her lips were only inches from mine. I could see the desire in her eyes. Gently she made the first move. She leaned over, kissed me on my cheek and gave me a big hug. I knew that I wanted to make slow, passionate love to her, and I sensed that she wanted the same. I didn't think that either of us was willing to settle for a quickie. I had a feeling that she wanted to feel every inch of me in her.

I was beginning to feel a little nervous about the situation. At the same time, though, I was loving it. Nothing like this had ever happened to me before. I kept thinking to myself that I couldn't make love to someone whom I barely knew, but my cock was telling me otherwise. I tried hard to control myself and concentrate on the game.

A few minutes later she kissed me again to thank me for inviting her over for dinner. This time she kissed me right on the lips. The moment just seemed right. I couldn't control myself as her tongue met mine. We both began to moan as I laid her down on the carpet next to the pool table. While I sucked on her nipples, causing them to protrude out at least half an inch, she revealed the details of the erotic dream she'd had about me.

I gently caressed one breast with my hand while sucking the other into my mouth. At the same time I slowly let my other hand creep inside her panties. I felt her quiver and moan with pleasure as I touched her sensitive spot. "I can't take this teasing any-more," she said. "Please give me your cock."

I was still trying to control myself. I probably would have been content to just have oral sex that night. I wasn't sure if I wanted to end our very first date with sex. I guess I'm just old-fashioned. However, the temptation was so strong that I couldn't refuse her. I knew that she was more than ready for sex.

As we lay on the floor, playing with each other, I eased my face toward her. I ever so gently ran my tongue all over her body, trying to build up the anticipation. "Oh, yeah, baby!" was all I heard. I kept working my tongue toward her crotch. I moved her panties aside so that I would have access to her pussy. She cried out loudly as my tongue met her sensitive vagina, which was about to explode. I kept teasing and teasing her until I couldn't control myself any longer. Hearing her moans of pleasure made my penis harder than it had ever been. Finally I suggested that we go to my bedroom, where we'd be more comfortable.

Once we were situated on the bed, she took my underpants off and started to suck my hard penis. I asked her to get into a 69 po-sition. I was close to shooting a load, and her juices were copiously flowing into my mouth. We both felt a need to let ourselves go.

Repositioning ourselves, I lifted up her legs and put them over my shoulders as she eased my prick into her vagina. It truly was the best and most sensual lovemaking session I have ever expe-rienced. Even though she was older than I, her body was in great shape. Her pussy felt very tight as it engulfed my cock, and we had an excellent fuck.

We have agreed to see each other at least once a week so that we can relieve our sexual urges. I would like to start a serious re-lationship with her, but I don't quite know what she wants from me yet. Nevertheless, my fantasy surely came true, and our first encounter will always be a memorable night for me.—*Name and address withheld*

COWORKERS GIVE HIM A VERY WARM WELCOME ON HIS FIRST DAY AT THE JOB

I'm a young woman who recently gave birth to a beautiful baby boy. Although I don't usually read *Penthouse Letters* myself, it's one of my husband's favorite magazines. So I'd like to dedicate this special letter to my husband Larry. He often masturbates while reading the letters and looking at the pictures, and I know he'd get a real kick out of seeing this in print.

Larry has a slim build and mischievous, sparkling brown eyes. His hair is black, and he wears it feathered back. His ass is skinny and his chest is hairless. Besides being really handsome, he's also an all-around great guy.

Recently Larry applied for a job at a magazine distributor. The secretary at the front desk gave him a big smile when he arrived for his interview. He was dressed all in black, and he looked really sexy. She pointedly looked him up and down, and he told me his face turned red from embarrassment. The boss hired him on the spot after only a brief interview and told him he could start immediately.

As it turned out, Larry is one of only a few male employees. The women who work there are all young, attractive and unmarried. Evidently these women viewed Larry as a new challenge and began to flirt outrageously with him, vying for his attention. We've always enjoyed an open marriage, so I didn't have any objections to him having a little fun at work. Occasionally I get a little jealous, but it always excites me to know that other women find my husband attractive.

A woman named Dawn was the first sassy slut to directly approach Larry. She is thirty-five years old and seems to be constantly in heat. Larry says she's always complaining that she's tired. Just before the morning coffee break, she told Larry her department was a little behind schedule, and asked if he would help her out. She said she needed help stacking pallets. He felt sorry for her because she looked so tired, so he said he'd help her while he was on break. She told him to meet her in the warehouse.

The warehouse seemed deserted when Larry walked in, but he found Dawn out of sight in a back corner. With a sigh of exhaustion she carelessly threw a sweater onto one of the pallets and lay down on it with her legs sprawled open. Larry later admitted to me that he thoroughly enjoyed the sight. She asked him to give her legs a massage, but he was afraid to get too close. He knew he had a huge hard-on and he didn't want it to get worse.

She shimmied around, causing her breasts to fall out of her skimpy top. This temptation was more than he could resist. Throwing caution to the wind, he threw himself on top of her and slowly massaged her tits. Her nipples were rock-hard as he sucked on them. She sighed heavily and thrust her crotch upward to make contact with his huge bulge. Taking the hint, he pulled down her skintight jeans and fucked her. After they both exploded in orgasm, they went back to work. Larry said he could hardly believe what had happened.

Amazingly, Dawn wasn't the only coworker to show Larry the ropes on his first day. Later that day he met another attractive coworker named Megan. Megan is a beauty, with long, raven-black hair, a pale complexion and ruby-red lips. She was wearing a skimpy red miniskirt and a satin bustier. She was tall and very nice-looking. Her ass was a little plumper than Dawn's, and she had breasts that rounded into bulging softballs. As she passed him in the hall, she winked and suggestively licked her lips. Larry had a hard time paying attention to his work after that. He finally arranged to meet her in the lunch room for a late lunch date.

When he walked in, she locked the door behind him. She ran her hands up and down his slender body, finally stopping at his bulging crotch. She knelt down and slowly unbuttoned his tight jeans. When she discovered he was wearing a pair of cutoff sweatpants underneath his jeans, she giggled and said, "You'll be sure to work up a sweat now." She quickly pulled them down and sucked his cock into her mouth. She sucked and licked until his cock was purple and very hard. Then she stood up and bent over in front of him. Wiry black hair covered her muff, which smelled sweet, like cherry pie. He fingered her until she begged him to fuck her from behind. He slid into her doggie-style and pounded her until she couldn't take any more. Then he licked up her flowing pussy juices for dessert.

The final surprise of Larry's first day at work came when it was time for the afternoon break. He met another coworker named Nancy, who works in the returns department. She's a woman in her forties who'd never been married. Like the rest of her female coworkers, she loves to flirt with men. This rather top-heavy lady wore a low-cut blouse that displayed her merchandise each and every time she bent over. Larry could tell by the look in her eyes that she was attracted to him.

She told him that she was a nymphomaniac who needed a lot of sex. Larry said he was game if she was. Of course she was—that's what being a nymphomaniac is all about. When no one was looking, she leaned over and kissed him passionately. She whispered to him that she hadn't had sex in a long time (actually, just a couple of days) and that she really needed it badly. She added that her cunt was already dripping. They arranged to meet after work. She told him she wanted all the semen he had left.

They met at her car in the parking lot after everyone else had gone home. She had changed to a tight, black, low-cut dress. With it she wore sexy black stockings that had sparkly gems running up the sides, and purple pumps. She really looked hot. Larry admitted his eyes and dick bulged out at the same time.

After a bit of foreplay, he finally thrust his dick into her pussy. While he fucked her, he tweaked her nipples, causing her to cry out in ecstasy. He humped her hard and fast, and was soon on the brink of shooting a hot wad of sperm into her. He kept from coming as long as he could, but finally couldn't hold back his orgasm any longer. He exploded wildly into her hot, clenching pussy.

She panted madly for more. "Screw my tits, my pussy, my mouth," she said. "Oh, please, Larry, do it to me again."

But as he put on his jeans he said, "Sorry, I have go to home now and take care of my beautiful wife. She'll be pissed off if I don't save some for her. I know she'll greet me with open arms, a glass of wine and a gourmet dinner."

He came home that night with a dozen red roses for me. He told me all about his incredible day, being sure to elaborate on all the juicy details. He knew it would turn me on. Later that night we made wild, passionate love. And on Friday, when he received his first paycheck, he brought me home a beautiful gold ring. So please dedicate this letter to my husband. He's a wonderful man, and I love him. As long as he comes home to me, I don't mind if he has his little fun.—*J.W., Albuquerque, New Mexico* ○⊢▪

MIDNIGHT BEAUTY BLOWS AND GOES—A TALE TOLD WITH DISPATCH

It all started when I was working dispatch for a small-town fire department in southern California. It was about one in the morning, and there wasn't anything going on. There was a knock at the door, and I was quite surprised to see a young woman, about twenty-five years old, looking into the lens of the security camera.

When I asked her what she wanted, she told me she had hurt herself trying to change a flat tire on her car. I naturally let her in.

She said that the lug wrench had slipped, making her fall against the car. She had a small cut just above her left breast.

When I came back with the first aid kit from one of the engines, she had taken off her blouse. This took me a little off guard, because she was wearing one of the sexiest see-through bras I had ever had the pleasure to lay my eyes on.

I couldn't think of anything else to do, so I introduced myself. I told her that my name was Stanley and that I was a paramedic. Then, with a completely straight face I added, "As soon as I take care of that laceration on your chest I'll have to do a primary survey to make sure you don't have any other damage." I waited to see if she picked up on the innuendo or ignored it.

She said, "My name's Brenda, and I'm not sure that a light, superficial survey will be enough. Shouldn't you probe a little more deeply? What if I have internal injuries?"

After hearing that, I did the best I could to keep my hands from shaking while I cleaned and bandaged her. I couldn't wait to get to the rest of the physical. It didn't help that I had to watch her pretty tits rise and fall with every breath, or that she was starting to breathe harder. "We'd better start in the vicinity of the initial wound," I told her. I reached behind Brenda and unsnapped her bra. The most beautiful pair of little cupcake tits popped out of that black lace restraint. They were capped with munchable, upturned nipples. I leaned over to take one in my mouth, and Brenda just leaned back against the counter and moaned. I pressed my crotch against Brenda's to let her feel the effect she was having on me, and she immediately reached down and unzipped my pants to release my erection and give her room to work on it.

Brenda began to masturbate me, running her hand up and down in long strokes that had me gasping and panting. I worked my hand under her skirt and into her panties. I applied a finger to her creamy cunt, sliding it back and forth until it was good and wet, then settling down to slowly circle her clit. We looked into each other's eyes, only occasionally leaning forward for a soft, wet kiss. We went on like this until we were both near the edge of great orgasms. Brenda suddenly dropped to her knees and slipped my cock into her mouth. I watched it disappear to the root, then reappear. She wrapped her hand around my shaft again and resumed jerking me off, at the same time applying her tongue to the head of my dick. This didn't go on for long before I spurted my sperm into Brenda's luscious, waiting mouth.

I wanted to show her my appreciation, so I lifted Brenda up on the counter, lifted her skirt and slid her soaking panties off. I got down on my knees and started slowly licking my way up her leg until I was at her sweet-smelling pussy. I caressed her lips and clit with my tongue. I started with long strokes, but soon settled in on her clit, as I knew we couldn't go on forever without some-one else coming in, and I wanted to get my dick into her snatch. My attention to her button was quickly rewarded as she began drumming her legs against the counter in an extended orgasm.

I stood up and finished taking off my pants. Brenda took hold of my prick, which was hard again, and guided it into her pussy. I began stroking, and she started working her internal muscles, mak-ing it feel like I had dozens of little hands massaging my penis.

I couldn't take too much of that without coming, and when I told Brenda I was ready to shoot, she just clenched all her mus-cles so that I couldn't move, and I went off deep inside her.

When I pulled out, Brenda bent over and started to clean my dick with her mouth. Just then there was a 911 call. She let go of me, but the second I had dispatched the engine company and hung up she was glued to my cock again. I finally had to tell her I just couldn't get it up again so soon. When I said that, Brenda stood up, turned away, and left without another word. It was a weird ending to a strange story, but it was definitely the most fun I've ever had at work.—*S.B., Berkeley, California* O╾▪

HE STANDS IN FOR AN OLD FRIEND TO KEEP YOUNG GIRLFRIEND HAPPY

An old friend of mine recently moved back into the city, about three blocks from where I work, bringing with him his girlfriend, Jill. Jill is petite, not more than five feet tall, and nineteen years old. She has jet-black hair, full, red lips and deep green eyes.

I had given Royce and Jill a ride home from my place a few times, when they'd had too much to drink. The conversation was always the same. Jill complained to me that Royce was an old fart (he and I are both thirty-two) who wasn't fucking her often enough. I would just laugh at Royce and say that I should be so lucky as to have a girlfriend who was so horny. Royce would make some comment about being tired from work and the conversation would stop, but you wouldn't see me neglecting the needs of that young beauty.

About two weeks ago I phoned Royce to shoot the shit. During our conversation Royce said that he was going out of town on business for the next three days. He had started to tell me about his trip when Jill told him to ask me whether I was interested in coming over for lunch the next day. I quickly said yes, trying not to sound too eager, and could feel both my pulse rate and cock begin to rise at the idea of lunch with Jill.

Still, I wasn't sure that Jill was thinking along the same lines I was. I decided to play it by ear during lunch. That night I had a dream in which Jill was sucking my cock and begging me to fuck her. After that dream there was no question that I was going to try to fuck Jill the next day.

My morning at work was a blur of anticipation. I left for lunch fifteen minutes early and practically ran all the way to Jill's apartment. When she opened the door I knew that the gods were smiling on me. Her hair and makeup were perfect. I hadn't thought that she would go to so much trouble for me. She had on a purple halter top and black stretch pants. Her flat tummy seemed to beckon me, and her breasts pressed against the material in a way that told me she had no bra on.

She invited me to sit down, and we started eating right away. I was barely able to eat, but did, if for no other reason than to see what was on her mind. Jill told me that she had to work for the next two days, so this was to be my only lunch with her that week. After we ate she went over to the couch to get her cigarettes, and I suggested we move over there to be more comfortable. As she enjoyed her post-lunch cigarette she started to tell me about the places in the apartment where she had fucked Royce.

I didn't wait for her to hit me over the head with a club. As soon as she had put her smoke out, I made my move. I put my arms around her and kissed her full on the mouth. Her tongue immediately responded by probing my mouth. As I started to remove her halter top she stopped me and asked whether I thought we were doing the right thing. I told her I didn't care whether it was right or wrong. I wanted her so much that I couldn't control myself. She started kissing me again.

Jill's top came off, and I got to see the pinkest nipples I have ever gazed on. I couldn't wait to suck on them, so I didn't wait. They were firm and had a slight taste of baby powder. As I sucked on her tits she started to remove my shirt and undo my pants. Again Jill asked me if this was what I wanted. When I said yes, she lay back on the couch, spread her legs and told me to kiss her pussy.

My first look at Jill's pussy was a sight I'll never forget. The hair was shaved into a very small, black triangle, through which I could plainly see her pussy lips. I didn't waste a second before approaching her with my tongue. Again the faint odor of baby powder tickled my nose. I kissed her cleft until she started moaning and twitching involuntarily. Jill reached down and took hold of my shoulder.

My chin was dripping with Jill-juice as she pulled my mouth up to hers. Her tongue probed my mouth, as if I were hiding something from her. As I lowered my head to her tits, Jill said, "I love the taste of my pussy. Kiss me again." I pressed my mouth against hers and ran my tongue all over her face.

When I could no longer taste pussy-juice in the slippery mixture that covered both our faces, I put my head down and started to kiss her cunt again. Jill stopped me, saying, "No, I want your cock in there." My prick felt as if its skin was stretched to its limits. Jill lay back on the couch, and I knelt on the floor and positioned my cock against her pussy lips. I rubbed the head of my cock against her clit, wanting to tease for a little while, but she grabbed my dick and guided it into her pussy. She let out a sigh of relief, and started moving her hips to meet my thrusts.

After a moment she let out a small cry and her body shuddered. Jill grabbed my ass and pulled me as deep inside her as possible. I was just about to come when I pulled my cock out.

I asked her if she would like to taste her pussy again. As I stood up, she grabbed my cock and started sucking it as if it were her last meal. My dream had become a reality. She paused for a second and asked me not to come in her mouth, I said okay, and she went back to work. I knew that my moment was at hand, and I tried to postpone it by thinking of the federal debt crisis. That soon failed, and I pulled back and let go. It was the most come I had ever seen.

Jill laughed and said, "All that, just for me?" I laughed along with her. As we dressed, she told me to stop shaking or everyone at work would know what had happened to me at lunch. I told her that was easier said than done. I kissed her at the door and ran for work, arriving only fifteen minutes late. I spent the rest of the day dreaming about what had happened and thinking what a shame it was that I would probably never get to fuck her again.

Three days later my phone rang at work. Jill was calling. She asked if I could drop by the apartment after work and lend her a few bucks. She added that Royce wouldn't get home from work until eleven.—*C.C., Albany, New York* ⚷

A SIDETRIP TO A MODEL HOME BRINGS HER A BIG SUR PRIZE

Before last summer, I didn't believe in sexual chemistry or blind lust or whatever else you want to call the hot urge that leads to random fucking. Don't get me wrong: I'm no prude. I'm twenty-eight and have enjoyed plenty of stiff, horny cocks in my life, but I always thought in advance about when and where I was going to play with them.

Anyway, I was cruising along a twisty coastal highway one Friday, after a tough week at the store where I was a lingerie buyer. I wore my shortest white shorts and a yellow silk shirt with the tail tied at my midriff. I didn't have on panties or a bra. By Friday I'm sick of underwear.

I was enjoying the way the cool wind whipped around my bare thighs and under my shirt, tickling my tits and my pussy. I was thinking how much I love the coast and how someday I want to live there, when I spotted a sign that pointed toward a housing development.

Pure impulse made me stomp on the brakes and spray gravel. I had just made the turn onto a road that led up a hill toward a model home. Dust was still settling when I hopped out of the car and stepped onto the porch of the place. I was too late. The model home was closed. I was bent over, trying to peer through a window, my round ass-cheeks sticking out of my shorts, when I realized there was someone behind me.

I spun around to see a guy looking me up and down. He was tall, dark-haired, with white teeth that gleamed in the sunset light. A mesh tank top stretched over about a half acre of bare chest, and the jeans that rode low on his slender hips strained to contain the massive bulge that swelled out where his legs joined.

I couldn't believe the tingle that was starting to grow in my pussy, or the dampness that began to gather there. I had to say something, do something, find out what had caused this sudden reaction.

"Guess I'm too late to see the house," I said to the handsome hunk, whom I took to be a security guard. Something told me that he was feeling the same magnetic attraction that I was. Something behind his eyes.

"Yes," he said. "Sales manager locked up and went home fifteen minutes ago."

I'm sure I looked very disappointed. He spoke slowly, as though in a dream. "There's another model up the hill. Be glad to show it to you."

He turned without another word, and I followed him up the hill, watching the swing of his shoulders and the thrust of his buns as he walked in his tight jeans. Even the smell of him, like warm honey and bitter almonds, made my pussy drip. I caught up with him and gave him my hand. Without thinking or commenting about it, he took my hand and held it, and we walked along like teenagers in love until we reached the house.

We arrived at the terrace of the house, and I turned to watch the view of the sunset over the ocean. I could feel the heat of him standing close behind me. I couldn't believe how hot I was getting. It still felt like everything was in slow motion.

I said something about the beauty of the sunset, and he said he had never seen anything as nice as the curve of my buns a few minutes ago when he walked up behind me. It seemed like a natural thing to thank him for the thought, so I turned and stretched up to give him a kiss. Just like that, the feeling of slow-motion shattered. I gave him another kiss. He gave me one. And another. My lips parted to let his tongue explore my mouth.

I pressed my tits hard against his chest while our tongues played, and I felt the bulge in his jeans thrust against my belly. My hands flew to untie my shirt so my hard, bare nipples could rub across the rough mesh and soft skin of his chest. I felt his hands on my ass as he lifted me up, and wrapped my legs around his waist, pressing my pussy against the throbbing bulge in his pants. I relaxed as if we'd known each other for years.

He carried me easily to a lounge on the terrace and laid me down. He never took his burning eyes off me as he peeled off his mesh shirt and jeans. Then he pushed his briefs down and his thick, brown cock jumped up like a powerful spring.

I reached for it, but he gently held me back. Slowly he pulled my little white shorts down my legs and dropped them on the terrace. He gave me a look that seemed to smoke with desire. He put his mouth on my swollen tits, licking, sucking and nibbling my hard nipples. My pussy was so wet, it oozed onto the lounge pad. My hips thrust up toward his rigid cock.

I gasped, begging him to let me have that monster, but he just moved his mouth slowly down my belly until he reached my close-cropped bush. He licked all over the top of my mound, along my thighs and all over the outside of my leaking pussy lips, while I ran my fingers through his hair.

I was twisting uncontrollably when his big hands took hold of my ass-cheeks and he began to run his tongue up and down my burning slit. He lapped me and gave my whole pussy big, open-mouthed kisses, raising me to a higher and higher pitch of ecstasy. When his wet, hot tongue finally reached my rock-hard clit and circled it again and again, I lost control completely. I came, my thighs clasped around his head. I pressed my throbbing cunt against his mouth as hard as I could.

I could hear my own voice, hoarse and demanding, telling him to, "Fuck me! Fuck me! Fuck me now!"

He didn't delay any longer. He jammed that beautiful tool into my steaming pussy in a single thrust. The wonderful friction stretched the walls of my cunt and the length of my orgasm. Just when I thought I had peaked, his thrusting raised me still higher, until I felt his powerful cock jerk uncontrollably inside me and he cried out hoarsely with pleasure.

I think I passed out for a minute. I had never come like that before. I lay limp and sweaty. But this guy wasn't through with me. His lips traveled over me again, waking my nipples. His tongue found my pussy and we were off again.

We were delirious with the wild sensations we shared. After the third incredible peak, we lay quiet for a time, until I finally eased my lips and tongue over the head of his thick cock. Amazingly, it rose again, thick-veined, velvet-ridged and ready.

This time I lowered myself on top of it and rode him slowly and steadily, his great knob buried deep inside my juicy pussy walls. He reached up to play with my nipples and then down between my legs to stroke my swollen clitty.

After that, I lost track. All I know is I never had such a wild fuck in my entire life. It wasn't until I was crouched over him doing a lazy, sleepy 69 that I thought to take my lips away from his juicy cock and ask, "What's your name?" I could feel his warm breath against my lower lips as he laughed.

"I was taught that it's impolite to talk with my mouth full of pussy," he said. It was only when I threatened to stop that he told me his name was Enoch. It turned out that he wasn't the security guard for the model homes. He was the builder. His terrace was the one where I had the greatest fuck of my life.

I'm going back next weekend. Maybe this time I'll see more than just the terrace. But I really don't care.—*D.R., San Francisco, California*   O┼▪

THEY'RE ROLLING ALONG SINGING A SONG, BUT NOT SIDE BY SIDE

One weekend last year my girlfriend Bernice and I decided to take a three-day vacation. We just wanted to escape from work and worry for a little while. We settled on a little town in Nevada, a pretty spot on the Colorado River. We planned to take old Route 66.

I told Bernie that I'd pick her up after work and we'd shoot off into the night. Her shift ended at eleven at night, so we wouldn't arrive before three in the morning. All our bags were packed, and I loaded them into my red Chevy pickup. I drove over to pick up Bernie. Bernie's a perky woman, a real beauty and full of fun and fire. She finished her work, threw her arms up and said, "Hallelujah! Let's get in the truck and go."

We jumped into the truck and headed off. It was a clear, dark night and the stars were exceptionally bright. Bernie and I had not been dating long, but we had quickly learned to trust one another. We were both divorced, and she had just suffered a hard breakup with a boyfriend, so we were both a little gun-shy. Nonetheless, our relationship had soon become sexual, and we had already enjoyed some great sex.

As we drove through Twenty-nine Palms, Bernie began to tell me about her previous lovers. I found it very exciting to have her tell me about how she used to call her recent lover on the phone and talk dirty to him while he was at work. I tried to imagine what he must have been going through listening to her describe what she had on and how she was going to make him feel when they got together.

Bernie told me that this lover, Frank, was the first man who had enough skill and stamina to bring her to a multiple orgasm. Then she inflated my ego by telling me that I had as much skill and had lasted much longer than any of her other lovers. She said I was definitely her marathon man.

Our conversation continued on about past relationships and what we had done with our previous lovers. I told her how my ex-wife Louise and I had fulfilled Louise's fantasy of fucking in a public telephone booth. While we were in Germany, Louise commented that the telephone booths were large enough to fuck in and still leave room for someone to place a call. One night we got dressed and drove to a phone booth, where I hiked up her dress and drilled her until I shot my load.

After that story, Bernie asked what else I had done, and I told her that I had had sex in a car. She said, "Everyone has done that."

I responded. "While the car was moving?" That surprised her. She asked how we kept from crashing. I told her that we weren't on a road and were only going maybe ten miles an hour.

Bernie asked, "How fast are we going now?" I told her we were going about seventy. Bernie undid her seatbelt and laid her head in my lap. She slid her hand inside my short pants and found that I had no underwear on. I told her that I never wear underwear. She said, with a sly smile on her face, "Let's see what you have in these shorts." She grabbed my half-erect cock and began stroking. Soon I was quite hard.

Bernie pulled my pants aside to expose my erect cock. She lowered her head and gently kissed the tip. She darted her tongue out and flickered at the tip and sensitive underside of the head. After a few minutes of indulging me that way, Bernie looked up at me with her big, brown eyes. She smiled, lowered her gaze again, parted her lips and eased her mouth down the entire length of my shaft. Her tongue stayed glued to my column, slithering all the way to my pubes.

It would have been great to explode right then, but I would have missed what was coming next. Bernie continued sliding up and down my dick at an agonizingly slow pace. All the while we sped alone across the open desert on Route 66. I really wanted to spill my seed, but Bernie had something else in mind. While she sucked my cock I fingered her clit and wonderful, tight hole. Bernie's pussy was hot and buttery.

I was disappointed when she sat up, until she told me to set the cruise control and proceeded to work my pants off. Then she took off her top and bra, exposing her beautifully matched breasts. They may not be huge, but those boobs are perfect. Her nipples

are as big as the first knuckle on my little finger, ideal for sucking on, and her tits are as round as they can be. She pulled off her
pants and showed me her panties, which tied at the sides. I untied
them with my free hand and pulled them off. Bernie had neatly
trimmed her pubic hair.

She was so hot that I wanted to pull over and take her right then,
but Bernie said, "Keep driving." She moved over and mounted my
lap while I was driving down the highway at seventy miles an
hour. Her butt fit right into the bottom of the steering wheel.

I said, "Hey, we're going to have an accident."

She looked into my eyes as she lowered her hot, wet pussy
onto my cock and whispered, "There's not going to be any accident. Your cock is going to spray come inside me on purpose."
With that she began to fuck me while I tried to drive. She was
amazed that I was able to keep the truck steady while she
pounded away, and so was I.

Occasionally another car would pass us going the other way,
and Bernie would push all the way down on my cock and hold
me tight, hoping the other driver wouldn't see. The other cars
passed by so fast that if they did see anything it would have been
an unrecognizable flash. She began to bounce rapidly up and
down, grinding her tight little cunt against me. After a while
Bernie began to take long, high strokes, going all the way up to
the tip of my cock and then slamming down so that my balls
would slap against her ass.

It was wonderful. Bernie came repeatedly. Each time she climaxed, she arched her back against the steering wheel, her body
would become stiff as a board and then she'd shake convulsively.
Her pussy was dripping juice down to my ankles.

Bernie was so hot and tight and wet that I could only hold out
just so long. Bernie knew it from the swelling of my cock. She
said, "My God, your cock gets so hard and so big just before you
come. God, this is the biggest your cock has ever been." I was so
close to coming, and I knew I was going to shoot like never before. Bernie started to coax the come out of my cock. "Give it to
me, baby. I want every last drop."

I could barely see by then because of the climax building in
my balls. She gave one last downward slam and a rocking wiggle, and my cock exploded. I felt the first rush of come shoot up
my cock, slam open the head of my shaft and spurt deep into
Bernie's cunt. Then the second rush of sperm darted up my dick
and splashed into Bernie. Now Bernie's cunt was filled with

steaming come, but I wasn't finished. Bernie rocked back and forth on my cock, drawing another jolting load of semen into her belly. There was so much come, and so much pressure, that it began to spurt out the sides of Bernie's cunt, down my cock and onto my tightly contracted balls.

It was magnificent, the most extreme orgasm I had ever had, and still another spurt came from my cock, and then another. Come was running down my cock, over my balls and down the crack of my ass. My cock spasmed and twitched from the greatest ride of my life.

Bernie wiped the sweat from my eyes so that I could see the road clearly. I began to pull myself together to keep us from being killed. Bernie waited just a few seconds, then lifted herself off my cock and collapsed across the seat, her back against the door. Droplets of sweat glistened on her breasts and jism oozed out of her dripping pussy. She was beautiful lying there in the moonlight, as we flew across the desert. For the rest of the trip she sat against the passenger-side door, idly massaging her cunt-lips and nipples, keeping herself hot and ready without pushing herself to another orgasm.

We reached our destination safely. Don't ask me how. I think the desk clerk at the hotel knew that something had been going on. When Bernie stepped out of the truck, all anyone could see was her high heel shoes, stockings and her full-length fur coat, which showed lots of cleavage. As soon as we got to our room, we were all over each other. Bernie kept the coat on, only opening the front to expose her nakedness to my touch. We rolled on the bed, enveloped in the fur and in each other, kissing and licking each other's face. I slid my dick into her and we fucked like we hadn't touched each other in two weeks instead of two hours.

We had a great vacation. That was the first time I had ever climaxed while driving, but it wouldn't be the last load I would shoot on the highway—especially now that Bernie and I are married.—*Name and address withheld* ○⊢▦

SHE CAN'T RESIST A MAN IN UNIFORM, SO SHE DOESN'T

Damian is gorgeous. He is Puerto Rican, with thick, dark hair and big brown eyes. He's absolutely irresistible in his navy whites.

The first day I saw him I knew I had to have his cock deep inside me. I was positive that he could make me feel and do things I had never dreamed of before. However, both of us are married, so over the next several months we played with each other only verbally, each trying to outdo the other, the sexual tension between us constantly increasing.

The phone rang one day when my husband was out of town—it was Damian. He said he would be over that night to tuck me in. At first I thought it was his usual teasing, but he had never called me before. I spent the whole afternoon fantasizing about what might happen.

When he arrived, he came into the hallway, pushed me up against the wall and kissed me hard, his rigid tongue probing my mouth. He tasted so good, and the feel of him nibbling on my neck sent shivers of excitement through my entire body. I reached down and felt his engorged rod straining to get out of his shorts. My cunt was dripping and aching to have his Puerto Rican kielbasa in me. Damian wanted me to wait just a little longer.

Damian led me into the living room, where he quickly removed both his and my clothes and thrust the head of his massive, thick tool into me, spreading my pussy lips farther apart than they ever had been before. He continued fucking me with just the head of his dick, until I pleaded with him to fuck me deeper. He looked me straight in the eye, stopped moving and asked, "Are you absolutely sure you want it?"

My pussy was throbbing, and I was dizzy from wanting to have his cock fucking me deep and hard, and I said, "I've never wanted anything more."

At that he slid his incredible thick cock all the way in, pounding his hips against me. We both groaned, and I rocked my own hips against his, grinding my pussy on his cock, his shaft rubbing my clit. At last he exploded in an incredible orgasm. I could actually feel him pumping his sperm inside me, and that sent me over the edge as well.

When we both stopped moaning he pulled out, his cock glistening with come, both his and mine, and told me to clean it off. He said he was sure I would love the taste of pussy as much as he did, and he went down and sucked my clit, slurping up all my pussy juices while I hungrily licked every drop off his cock. Then he told me to get on my hands and knees so he could fuck me from behind, his favorite position (and ever since then one of mine too!) His cock plunged into me deeper and harder than the first time, his balls pounding against my clit. His strong hands rubbed up and down my back, grabbing my hips and encouraging me to thrust them against him harder and harder. I threw my hips back against him, squeezed the muscles in my cunt and we both came again.

After a brief respite in each other's arms, we realized that he had to go home. We got dressed quickly but reluctantly. I walked him to the door and he kissed me good night.

That was eight months ago, and we've arranged a great many erotic rendezvous since. One of our most spectacular episodes took place in his office on the naval base.

I told Damian that I wanted him to take me to his office, dressed in his whites. He told me that someday we would do it. One afternoon we'd planned to meet, and when Damian appeared at the door in full uniform I knew the day had come.

As soon as we got into his office I asked him to sit down in the chair he always phones me from. I knelt in front of him, unzipped his pants and started licking his cock all over. My tongue lingered on every inch of his shaft, my mouth sliding up and down until he couldn't take it any longer. I saw Damian grab the desk, his knuckles tensing as he tried to hold back his come. His face was red with the effort. I continued, thrusting his cock deeper down my throat, ticking the little hairs on the backs of his thighs. I reached up to rub his nipples and he let go, filling my mouth with his come.

At that point Damian picked me up and pushed everything off the top of his desk. Laying me on the bare desktop and spreading my legs apart, he ran his tongue over my pussy, darting inside me, then circling my clit. He slid two fingers into my cunt, while I ran my fingers through his incredibly soft, thick hair. Just when I was about to come, he stood up and started fucking me, his cock reaching onto the deepest parts of my body. He fucked me slowly and tenderly, then hard and fast, until we both climaxed together, as we often do.—*L.S., Fairfax, Virginia*

<u>Girls & Girls/</u>
<u>Boys & Boys</u>

THREE GUYS GET AWAY INTO THE WOODS AND COME BACK TRANSFORMED

One of my best sexual experiences occurred the summer after my senior year in high school. My two best friends and I went on a camping trip for a few days. We were at my parents' cabin in the mountains, and it was a hot summer day, so we got our beer and headed for the river to go skinny-dipping. After about an hour in the water we decided we would get out and lie on the river bank to dry off.

Our talk turned to blowjobs. It was obvious we were all getting horny. Wayne said he wished his girlfriend was there to take care of his prick. Terry asked if we had ever thought about fooling around with other guys. Wayne said that he'd always been curious about it. Terry leaned forward and took Wayne's thick cock in his hands and started slowly jacking him off. I was getting very aroused, so I reached over, grabbed Terry's huge prick and started to stroke it.

We decided to go to the cabin before anyone caught us. When we got there, we all got into the shower and started washing each other's body. I felt Wayne's hand playing with my dick and balls. My cock was so hard I thought I would get off right then. I started to play with Terry's cock. I felt Wayne licking my stiff rod, then felt his warm lips wrapped around me. It felt wonderful. Terry got on his knees to suck Wayne. Wayne started to take my cock down his throat. My girlfriend loves to suck my cock, but she doesn't come close to Wayne's expertise. It didn't take long before my nuts were tingling. I warned Wayne that I was going to lose it, but his lips started pumping me faster and faster until his mouth was filled with my semen. Wayne must have shot his load at the same time, because Terry had sperm on his face.

Wayne and I started to take turns sucking Terry's cock. I loved the way the head felt as Wayne slid his cock back and forth along my tongue and the roof of my mouth. I felt his dick throbbing, so I started sucking faster and he unloaded his balls down my throat.

We decided to put an X-rated movie in the VCR and watch it in the nude. Soon we were in a circle giving each other blowjobs. Terry was sucking me, I was sucking Wayne and he was sucking Terry. Terry was taking my cock all the way to the base. I sucked Wayne's cock faster and faster, and he was soon blasting me with another load of slippery cream. I had never experienced anything like it before in my life. I could feel Wayne's cock getting harder and thicker as he released his load. It seemed to go on forever. I couldn't hang on any longer, and shot my load off into Terry's mouth.

We were all worn out. We fell asleep in each other's arms. I have never told my girlfriend what my friends and I do on our monthly weekend getaways. I just tell her that we give male bonding a new meaning. We couldn't be closer friends.—*Name and address withheld* ⊶▪

BI BABE PROUDLY KEEPS THE BUNNIES HOPPING IN BIKINI-LAND

I am an ardent bisexual woman who is wild about young beach bunnies. Five years ago I divorced a wealthy man and used the settlement money to open a bikini boutique in Miami. It's a position that puts me in close contact with thousands of girls each year.

I think of myself as an attractive woman, thirty years old and lean. I wear my blonde hair short and my nails long. Recently I had an experience that I'll never forget.

It was Spring Break week, and the bars and beaches around here were crawling with beautiful young women. I had just closed shop and was sipping a glass of Chablis, when a couple of girls peered through the front window. Naturally I unlocked the door and allowed them in. After thanking me for reopening, the girls eyed the open bottle of wine. I laughed. "Well, as long as I'm technically closed, would you two care to join me?" The girls helped themselves to the wine while I discreetly locked the front door.

My young friends introduced themselves as Sue and Angela, both nineteen and down from Santa Barbara for the week. Sue was pretty enough, but I could not take my eyes off Angela. Full-figured and deeply tanned, with sparkling green eyes and a long, thick mane of chestnut-colored hair, Angela wore a pair of denim cut-offs and a T-shirt tied in a knot above her bare midriff. My mouth was dry with desire.

I was cooking up ways to seduce Angela, when Sue suddenly leaped up as if she'd been shot. "Oh my God," she cried, "I was supposed to meet Timmy downtown an hour ago!" What luck! As sincerely as I could, I commiserated with Sue for having to leave so suddenly, but I insisted that Angela stick around and try on a bikini or two.

With Sue out of the picture, I stood up and took Angela by the hand. "Let's see if we can find the right bikini to show off that lovely body of yours," I purred. I plucked a particularly racy peppermint-striped number off the rack and handed it to her. "This will bring out your tan," I suggested. Angela looked around for a dressing room.

"Oh dear," I laughed, "I've got a million things for you to try on. If you keep going in and out of that dressing room, we'll be here all night!" Without waiting for a response, I crossed the room and drew the shades. When I turned, Angela had disrobed and was standing there completely naked.

I caught my breath. She was even more beautiful than I had imagined! Her breasts, luxuriously full and minus even a hint of sag, were tipped with the biggest, most beautiful bubble-gum-pink areolae I have ever seen. Her nipples, thick as gumdrops, jutted out a good three-quarters of an inch. Angela's waist was thin and elegant, her belly fine, round and deeply tanned, tapering down to a luxuriant mass of chestnut-colored pussy hair. Her pussy itself was ravishing beyond description. The lips were luscious, fat and rosy, peeking out from beneath her thick bush.

Fighting to keep my voice from trembling, I asked Angela to bring over the measuring tape I'd left on the counter. This gave me a chance to drink in that magnificent tush, white as snow and so full that it jiggled as she walked. Angela turned, and I stared in open admiration. "You're quite a catch," I whispered. Angela said nothing, but she blushed deeply. In that instant I knew she would be mine.

"Lift your arms for me," I told her gently, approaching from behind with the measuring tape. "I may need to alter the top." With Angela's arms upraised, I cupped the bikini top under her overripe titties, mischievously running a thumb along one of those big nipples as I did. "You ought to carry insurance on these," I teased. Angela giggled. She was aroused, and I knew it. Pressing my advantage, I slid my hands down her smooth belly and whispered hot into her ear. "Have you ever made love to a woman, Angela?" Again Angela said nothing, but her nipples suddenly popped fully erect.

"Oh, darling," I murmured, "they're so beautiful . . . and so big!" Cupping my hands under her breasts and caressing the fat nipples with my thumbs, I began grinding my pubis into her baby-soft ass in the eternal dance of love. Angela moaned and turned to kiss me. Gently but firmly my roving hands took possession of her beautiful pussy. She was soaking wet!

Something about the smell and feel of her young body triggered an animal frenzy in me. I captured first one and then the other of her big nipples in my hungry mouth, sucking and slurping across her tender belly, tonguing the deep cleft of her navel, burying my face in her thick bush. Dropping even lower, I attacked her pussy, teasing erect the head of her large clit and devouring it mercilessly, until Angela came in a series of hysterical spasms.

Eventually Angela and I adjourned to my beachfront apartment, where she spent the night in my arms. I could not get enough of my ravishing young playmate, stirring her frequently in the night for more loveplay. Angela left town at the end of the week, but I got a Christmas card from her reminding me that she'll be in town for Spring Break again this year. I'm already making plans!—*M.V., Miami, Florida*

FUTURE LAWYERS FORGO THE GLORY HOLE AND LOOK INTO EACH OTHER'S BRIEFS

Ten years ago I had an evening that was the height of my sexual history.

Luis and I had become fast friends in our last year of law school, and hung out together frequently. I was married at the time, but my wife had her own agenda, and I didn't see much of her.

In any case, Luis and I had numerous conversations about women and sex. He told me stories of his past conquests. To hear him tell it, there had been a lot of them. I didn't doubt it, as Luis was a good-looking, intelligent guy, and not shy about telling people what he wanted. He was also well endowed. I had seen his cock once as he came out of the shower when I was in his room, and was impressed by its size. Even in its flaccid state, it appeared to be about five inches long.

One night we were at my apartment, smoking some interesting weed and, as usual, looking at men's magazines. At Luis's suggestion, we decided to go to a local adult bookstore to pick up some fresh stimulation.

On the way, we discussed our current sexual dry spells. He was between girlfriends and I, as I have mentioned, had a wife whom I rarely saw. He said that he would probably go into one of the video booths in the back of the store to see whether they had holes to the adjacent booths. He was hoping to get a blowjob. We sat in silence for a moment while I thought about this, knowing that, as a rule, only men went into the booths. "Have you done that before?" I asked. "I mean, with a guy?"

"Yeah," he said, "I like it. I mean, to me, sex pretty much all feels good."

I thought about that for another few silent moments. Then, almost to my surprise, I said, "You know what? That's pretty much what I think, too. I fooled around a little bit with buddies when I was a teenager. It was never a problem for me."

Another long, awkward silence ensued, then he said, rather quietly, "So, would you be interested in doing something like that?"

"Sure," I responded matter-of-factly, almost without thinking.

We changed course for his place, not knowing when (or if) my wife would get home. After riding quietly for a few minutes, he swallowed audibly and said, "I'm getting real turned on here, thinking about this."

I gently reached over and put my hand on his upper leg, feeling around. I didn't have to feel far. Down the inside of his left leg, seemingly halfway to his knee, I felt his thick cock, hard as stone. I rubbed it for a minute through his pants, then gave it a squeeze, feeling it throb slightly. He licked his lips, his mouth as dry as mine was.

When we got to his place, he pulled the blinds and sat on his bed. Without a word we took off our shirts, shoes and socks, and sat there looking, but not looking, at each other, with our pants on but unzipped.

"This is hard," he said, pulling off his pants at the same time, which made it unclear whether he was referring to what we were doing or to the incredible cock I saw bounce up in front of him. It had to be eight inches long, with a pronounced downward curve. The tip seemed to glisten. I pulled off my remaining clothes and stroked my own rock-hard cock, breathing heavily at the thought of what was to come.

He sat on his bed, and I sat on the chair next to it, both of us slowly masturbating, our eyes riveted on the other's dick. His had a steady stream of clear liquid running from it, which he spread around its massive surface. After a few minutes his eyes glazed, and he said, "Come feel this."

I slowly moved over and took his heavy, hot cock in my hand, gradually jacking it up and down. "That feels real good," he said sleepily. I was mesmerized by the size of what I was holding, and marveled at the continual pumping of clear come from the tip.

I leaned over and took the swollen head in my mouth, swirling my tongue around, and slowly moved down his shaft, taking as much in as I could before backing off again. His hips began to pump rhythmically, and I could taste the salty sweetness of his fluid. I became aware of an incredible heaviness between my own legs. I felt his hand caress my balls, then move up along my shaft. I began to tremble slightly, and sucked his cock with increased fervor. As if reading my mind, he said, "That feels amazing. Let's do a 69—I want to suck you too."

We lay on our sides, next to each other, and examined and played with each other's genitals for a while. Almost simultaneously, we each took the other's shaft in our mouth and began to suck with abandon, feeling each other's swollen, heavy balls with our free hands.

We began fucking each other's face like jackhammers, grunting and moaning with the effort and the ecstasy, and about a minute later I felt the unmistakable tremble and twitch that meant I couldn't stop myself from coming. The entire Bar Association could have walked in at that moment, and I wouldn't have cared. At the same time I felt his cock grow, impossibly, even bigger in my mouth, and the stream of fluid increased to a flood. Then the pulsing began, and jets of come splashed into the back of my throat. It was easy to fight the gag impulse, because right then I felt my balls tighten and begin to squirt. When we finally stopped emptying ourselves, we rolled apart, breathing like we had just run a marathon. We looked at each other for a moment, then began laughing so hard we almost rolled off the bed.

"That was great!" he said, and I had to agree. We got together a few more times after that, then Luis moved away. I haven't been with a man since, but sometimes, when I think about that night, I wonder why not.—*Y.L., Minneapolis, Minnesota*   O⊦▄

AFTER MONTHS OF WARM-UP ON THE TELEPHONE, AT LONG LAST LOVE

In the past couple of months I have become extremely attracted to one of my close female friends. Her name is Faith, and she is one of the most beautiful women I have ever met, both inside and out.

Faith and I speak to each other on the phone every day. Every once in a while we talk about what arouses us. Faith has a very sensual voice, and whenever she talks about what excites her, I imagine myself doing what she's describing. While we're just talking on the phone, I often become so turned on that if she were to say one more thing, I would have an orgasm. Sometimes I can't wait until we get off the phone before I have to rub my clit to a quick, intense come. I always tried not to make any noise that would tip her off that I was whacking myself off, but she somehow got the idea that I was attracted to her.

One day Faith called me at work. She said she was watching a friend's house and wanted to know if I would like to come over for a visit. I've been to the house before, and I said, "Sure, as long as we can go in the Jacuzzi."

She said, "Fine, be over by six o'clock." For the rest of the day, all I thought about was Faith. I imagined a million possibilities for what might happen when I got there, and I had to stop at my apartment and change my soggy panties before I met her.

When I got to the house that night, every room was dark except the living room. There I found a fire in the fireplace, several lighted candles and Faith, who walked up and greeted me with a passionate kiss on the lips.

The kiss ended. We looked into each other's eyes and I felt my knees weaken. Faith took me by the hand and led me to a sofa by the fire, where we sat down. After about a half hour of small talk, I said that my back was getting a little stiff. Faith knew what I meant and suggested that we hop into the Jacuzzi for a bit. I told her that I wanted to, but I didn't have a bathing suit. She arched her eyebrow and purred, "That won't bother you, will it?"

My knees were rubbery again, and I admitted, "I hoped you would say that." I modestly undressed in the bathroom. When I came out, I walked around to the Jacuzzi. All the lights were off, so I could only find it by the sound of the jets making the water bubble. When I got to the edge I could just see Faith's shadow in the water. I took off my towel and climbed in.

It was as if I was in a trance. I felt Faith's hand caress the inside of my thigh under the water. "Your legs are so soft, and they feel so good," she whispered. As her hand gently moved up my inner thigh, she turned to face me. Her lips met mine, first just brushing them, then pressing more insistently. I could feel her body press against me as we kissed, and I wrapped my arms around her neck, wanting her even closer. I was unbelievably aroused by the feeling of her nipples hardening and pressing against mine.

I started kissing her neck, and made my way up to her ear. Faith let out a soft moan as her hands explored my body under the water. Faith's fingers touched my pussy. She slipped one finger in between my lips and slowly moved up and down. I shivered at her touch and sighed, "Faith, please, please put your finger in my vagina. I want to feel you inside of me."

Faith kissed me passionately, and I felt her penetrate my hole. Her finger moved in and out of my slippery box, slowly, almost too slowly for me to bear. I started grinding my hips in rhythm with her movements. I could feel my pussy starting to throb, and I knew that I was already close to exploding. "Oh, my God," I said, "it's even better than I imagined. Please don't stop!"

"Don't worry. I'll never stop," Faith said. When she said that, I wrapped my legs around her body, trying to pull every inch of her inside me, and my whole body went numb as my muscles started to shudder. I could feel my pussy squeezing Faith's finger in quick, hard contractions as my orgasm exploded. It was like my vagina had a mind of its own. It was the most intense orgasm I've ever had.

After a few minutes, even though my pussy was still throbbing, I gently moved so that I was on top of Faith. I kissed her lightly on the lips and ran my fingers through her hair. Faith said that she thought we should get out of the Jacuzzi, as we had been in there for quite some time. I'm glad she said something, because I had no sense of time having passed at all, and I certainly didn't want her skin to get all dry and puckered. I had other plans for it.

We got out, wrapped each other in towels, and went to lie down on a blanket in front of the fire. As we lay there, we just held each other for a while.

When I thought Faith was starting to fall asleep, I decided that I was going to give her a full body massage with my tongue. I started with her toes. I kissed and sucked each one, running my tongue up and down the arches of her feet. "That feels really wickedly great," Faith murmured. I licked my way up the insides of her legs, then moved from leg to leg, making sure I didn't miss a single spot, wanting to taste every part of her body. When I reached her inner thighs, her pink pussy lips were swollen and spread. Her clitoris was peeking out, and I just wanted to flick my tongue across it for a small taste. Not yet, I told myself. I wanted to finish my tongue-massage first.

I licked my way up to Faith's belly-button and slid my tongue in and out of it. I then kissed her entire stomach while slowly moving upwards.

When I reached her breasts, the sight of her beautiful, rock-hard nipples made my juices overflow. I slowly circled the tip of my tongue around one of her areolae, slid across to her other breast and did the same thing. I didn't touch her nipples yet, just moved back and forth in lazy figure eights, my tongue circling her dark plums.

Faith was moaning loudly now, and kept begging me to suck her nipples. Finally, not wanting to tease her forever, I pushed her lovely breasts together with my hands and moved from nipple to nipple, fucking each one with the end of my tongue. Since I had her breasts pushed so close together, I started to suck gently on both of her nipples at the same time. She grabbed my hand and hugged me as I sucked on her nipples. She was coming just from my attention to her chest, and I had another orgasm from her reaction to what I was doing.

When Faith let go of my head and her breathing returned to normal, I started kissing my way back down her stomach. I stopped when I reached her pussy and just stared at it. Her sticky nectar was making it glisten, and I couldn't wait to taste it. Her erect clitoris seemed as hard as her nipples were a few moments ago. I wanted her so badly it made me dizzy.

I put the tip of my tongue in between her pussy lips. As I did this, I heard Faith softly croon, "Oh, my God!" and I pushed my tongue in further so I could taste her sweet honey. I moved my tongue up and down between her swollen lips, kissing them tenderly between licks. I was careful not to touch it yet, as it looked like it was ready to explode at any second. I just wanted to make her wait a little longer, because I knew it would make her orgasm more intense.

I blew softly on her clit and felt her tremble. I started to circle it with the tip of my tongue. I did this slowly. Faith started moving her hips against my tongue. That was when I put my lips lightly around her button, but still moved my tongue around in circles. After only about fifteen or twenty seconds of this I felt her start to throb against my tongue as she came to a powerful climax.

When her contractions finally subsided we kissed again, very gently and sweetly, and fell asleep in each other's arms. We haven't gotten together since, except by telephone. When we do, we'll both be ready to go off like a couple of oil wells.—*Name and address withheld* O⊢▪

IT TURNS OUT HIS OLD COACH REALLY MISSED HIS TIGHT END

I'm twenty years old and have known I was gay ever since high school. I have an androgynous look about me that a lot of men find attractive. Many people tell me I resemble Prince. I've had so many offers to have sex, it's not even funny. From football players to nerds, everyone wants to fuck me. And that includes women. About half the women I meet want to get me into bed. I never take any of them up on their invitations, though, because it's really only men that turn me on.

I left my home three years ago after graduating high school. However, I often return to visit friends and family, and to watch my hometown team play football. At one of these football games I met up with Dave, my old high school football coach. He's a big Prince fan—in fact, he was the one who turned me on to Prince's music when I was a freshman. Dave was real nice to me and was always a lot of fun to be around. All the girls in school had a crush on him, and why wouldn't they? He was fine!

The best way to describe Dave is that he looks a little like President Clinton. He's in his early forties, graying and attractive in a clean-cut way. He's about six feet tall and must weight two hundred twenty pounds. He has that classic stocky build I love, and his arms are so big and muscular that just thinking about them gets me hard. When I used to pass him in the halls between classes, my eyes would go straight to his dick. He wore these tight gym pants and, believe me, his package really showed through in those things. I often wanted to drop to my knees and suck the hell out of his dick right there on the spot.

Anyway, I was watching my old high school team play football. They won by a landslide. Just seconds after the game was over, Dave spotted me standing by a fence. He jogged over to me, gave me a great big hug and started asking a lot of questions about what I'd been up to for the past three years. We got caught up in conversation and, the next thing I knew, I was walking into the locker room with him and the rest of the team.

I took a seat in his locker room office while he gave his players a pep talk about how well they played that night. He then returned to his office. I couldn't believe he was so excited to see me. After we'd talked awhile, I saw that the football players were clearing out of the locker room. Soon they were all gone, and Dave and I were the only ones left.

Our conversation was still going strong, but I couldn't take my eyes off Dave's dick. He was wearing jeans and a T-shirt with the name of the football team in big letters across his well-built chest. I couldn't stop thinking about having sex with him, and how badly I wanted to suck his cock and swallow his come. After Dave closed up the locker room, we walked out to his car. He asked if I wanted to go with him to pick up some fast food. I said yes right away, since I didn't drive and could've used a ride home anyway.

There was a lot of traffic on the streets, with all the high school students driving around and blowing their horns after their team's big win. After we got our food, we drove around a little more, and our conversation took a different turn. "So, you must have a girlfriend," Dave said to me.

It hit me that Dave didn't know the truth about me, but I didn't answer him at all.

He persisted. "What? No girlfriend? You must not be getting any, then!" he chuckled. I laughed along with him. He paused for a while, then said, "If you don't have a girlfriend, you must have a boyfriend. A guy as good-looking as you shouldn't be alone."

I was shocked by what he said, and didn't know how to respond. Finally I replied, "Sorry, no boyfriend either." We were silent for about two minutes, and then I became bold and asked, "Why, are you interested?"

Dave looked me up and down from the driver's seat and replied, "Yeah, sure, I'd fuck you."

"Are you married?" I asked.

"No," Dave said. "I've been divorced for about six years."

"Are you seeing anybody now, Dave?" I asked. Not that I cared. It was just my way of trying to find out if he wanted to fuck me right away, or sometime in the future.

Dave softly said to me, "We can go back to my apartment." I was feeling even more bold by this point. I could see Dave's cock begin to swell in his jeans. I unsnapped his pants, undid his zipper and slid my hand in for a fistful of dick. It was the huge cock I'd always dreamed he had. Dave's tool was massive—a full ten inches long, as I was soon to find out. It felt strange to me at first, covered with a lot of soft skin. Then I realized he wasn't circumcised. I'd never touched an uncut cock before. It was very exciting.

Moans and groans started coming from Dave's mouth as I stroked his penis. All the times I'd fantasized about having sex with him, and now it was really about to happen! Never in my wildest dreams did I think such a wish would ever come true. I'd never been with a man, but I knew it was time to explore my homosexuality, to take it beyond mere fantasy. I felt safe with Dave. He was older, more mature and more experienced than I was. It made opening myself up to him in this way so much easier.

"It feels so good to have you stroking my prick," he said. "But if you keep it up, I'm probably going to drive off the road and get us in a wreck." I took the hint and backed away.

Within a few minutes we were at his apartment door. He had a beautiful place. I took a seat on the couch, and noticed that Dave had converted one of his bedrooms into a weight room. "That's how I keep in shape," he said proudly. Dave poured us some fruit juice, then sat on the couch with me. He put his hand behind his back and yanked his sweaty T-shirt off. He kicked off his shoes, then rolled off his pants and socks. He was hairy from head to toe—especially across his broad chest. It was like a jungle. This is a man, I thought.

Dave suggested we take a shower before we had sex, but I was able to talk him out of it. I told him that the hot sweat of a real man after a hard day's work was a big turn-on for me. I told him

I'd been dreaming of licking the sweat off his body since we were together in the locker room earlier that day.

Dave smiled and asked if I still wanted to go through with it. I said, "Let's cut out the bullshit, Dave. I'm not a kid anymore. I want you to fuck me."

I also told him he would be the first person I'd ever done it with. "A virgin!" he said excitedly.

I poured some of my fruit juice on Dave's big, strong, hairy chest, licked it off and then walked to his bedroom. "Are you coming?" I asked. I stood there and watched him take off his underwear. Oh, that cock was magnificent! He then followed me to his bedroom. He was so well hung, his dick actually swung back and forth like a vine as he walked. I got undressed while Dave sat on his bed and watched. There was no doubt which roles we would play out in this sexual encounter. He was going to be the man, I was going to be his little girl for the night.

Dave's dick was somewhat soft yet, but mine was rigid and sticking straight up in the air. I threw my legs across his lap. We began to French-kiss for a few minutes, and then I pushed him back onto his bed. He folded his hands behind his head and said, "Make me come fast. If you do that, I'll be able to fuck you all night long."

At first I thought that was a strange thing to say, but everybody has their own special way of having sex. I started by kissing his chest with soft little pecks. Then I used my tongue to glide over to his armpit. I inhaled deeply and licked up the warm sweat that lingered under his arms. I worked my way down his belly and soaked his thick stomach hair with my tongue. I then grasped his penis, took a deep breath and . . . boom! Before I knew it, I was sucking him like an old pro. I had him moaning and grunting and thrusting hard into my mouth. I swirled my tongue around his cockhead.

Dave grabbed the back of my head roughly and started pulling me against his groin, really feeding me that big pole. Deeper and faster I sucked, listening to the slurping sound of my mouth as it moistened his dick. Dave tightened his ass up, bit his lips and squeezed his whole face into a funny expression. A few grunts later, his hot jizz erupted all over my face. Two things I learned about come that night: it's very hot, and it smells like swimming-pool chlorine.

Dave got up and went to the bathroom. I listened to him while still tasting the hot come dripping down my face. Dave returned with a tube of lubricant. He told me to turn over, then spread my legs open with his manly hands and spread globs of K-Y all over my asshole. I could feel his semihard dick brush up against my body while he did this to me. I was thinking, Damn, I wish he would be rougher with me! I wanted him to use that studly body of his to throw me round a little. I wanted him to take me brutally.

I knew it was up to me to get him to be more aggressive, so I placed my foot on his stomach and pushed him away with great force. He went flying to the floor. I sprang up off the bed and said, "If you want it, you'll have to take it."

Dave got up off the floor. He responded, "So, you want to play! You want it rough, do you?" I smiled. He was experienced enough to read my mind. I dashed out of the bedroom and into the kitchen. Dave caught me in a split second. He snatched me by the arm and pushed me back against the refrigerator. It was just the sort of lusty treatment I wanted. Dave grabbed both of my wrists and bent me over on his kitchen table. "You want it rough? I'll give you rough!" he growled.

He proceeded to kick my ankles apart with his foot, the way a police officer would prepare to frisk a criminal. Before I could even think of what it might be like to have my first dick in me, Dave rammed it home, crunching his full ten-inch cock into me without warning. My hips jerked forward and banged against the table. I lost my breath for a minute and wanted to cry from the pain. But after he'd pumped my asshole a couple of times, it didn't feel bad at all.

Dave had his hands on my waist and was sliding my ass onto his steel-hard prick. I didn't think he should do all the work, though, so I started moving my ass up and down, harder and faster and with power. I was gaining experience with every stroke. Dave was pleased that I was moving my ass now. He took his hands off my hips and let me wiggle my ass back and forth.

Twenty minutes went by and I was still doggie-styling Dave with my ass. He began to breathe harder, and I knew it was time for him to come again. He forcefully took my buttocks in his hands and began to hammer the fuck out of me. He was moving like a wild rabbit in heat. I swung around and slapped him across the face with the back of my hand. Then I disengaged and raced to the weight room. I turned around to slam the door behind me, but it was too late. Dave grabbed the door just before it shut.

"Shit!" I screamed. I knew I was in for it. Dave was mad because I didn't give him a chance to come.

I backed up against a wall in the corner of the room. Dave stroked his dick to keep his erection, and pointed a finger at me. With an evil grin on his face he said, "You're going to get it now! You've teased me for the last time, bitch, and now you've got to pay." Yes, he was angry! The sweet, innocent football coach from high school who used to joke around with me had a nasty side after all.

He walked over and stood face-to-face with me. Just then we both noticed a jump rope on the floor. We looked at each other, thinking the same thing. We both lunged for the rope and, after a scuffle on the floor, Dave came up the winner. He yanked me by the hair and dragged me back to his bedroom. He slammed me facedown on the bed. I must have bounced three feet off the mattress, but I was loving the abuse!

Dave started pacing in front of me while I lay on the bed, nervous with excitement. In one hand he had the jump rope, and in the other hand he was stroking his prick. "You're going to get it now," he said. "I'm going to fuck the taste out of your mouth." He'd raised his voice and was yelling at me now. "You're going to get fucked hard this time, baby," he yelled. He started using his coaching voice as though he was yelling at one of his football players for messing up an important play in a game. "You're going to get it!" he screamed as he crawled across the bed toward me.

I lay back and let him lay on top of me. He grabbed me by the back of the head, pulled me up against his face and said, "I'm gonna fuck the shit out of you." I started to French-kiss him in order to calm him down a little. After a couple of kisses, I pushed him off me and onto his back. What a sight—little one-hundred-pound me, overpowering this he-man! I took the jump rope out of his hand. Managing to get his arms above his head, I tied his wrists together, then used the remaining rope to tie him to the bedpost. He smiled with amazement and said, "You're just not going to give up, are you!"

I hopped off the bed, ran into the kitchen and grabbed a large jar of honey I'd seen in there while we were fucking. Then I went back into the bedroom with the honey. I picked a towel off the floor and wiped the globs of lubricant off his soft dick. Dave grinned when he saw me open the jar. I emptied the sticky honey all over his dick, and in no time it grew back to its full size. It was like pouring water on a thirsty plant. The honey oozed down Dave's hard pole and coated his fat, sagging balls. The sticky honey made a nice lubricant. I knew this was going to be the best dessert I'd ever tasted.

I said, "Have you ever had this done to you before, Dave?"

"No," he whispered, so softly that I knew I had him right where I wanted him. I started sucking his dick and balls like a madman. I even nibbled on his scrotum a little. I had sticky honey all over my face from rubbing it against his private parts. His dick was so hard, every pint of blood in his body must have rushed to his incredible cock. Veins were popping out everywhere. After a couple of deep-throat plunges, he came in a gush. "Oh . . . yes!" he moaned as he released several thick ropes of come. I was pleased to lick up every drop.

After Dave came, I continued sucking him off, but he told me to stop. He said his cock was too sensitive and it it didn't feel good to have his dick sucked after he'd just come. But I didn't listen. I just kept right on sucking.

"Stop! Stop!" He yelled again. His body was flopping around, as he was still tied to the bed. "You bitch! Get the fuck off my dick!" he cried.

Suddenly, with a great burst of strength, Dave broke free of the jump rope. He pushed me off him, and I fell to the floor. His big body followed mine, and he landed right between my legs. His hands were flat on the floor and his arms where straight, as if he was doing a push-up. "Don't fucking tease me anymore," Dave said. "When I told you to stop, you should have stopped."

"Come on, let's do it again," I said. I started stroking his hard penis. I guided his dick, solid as stone, inside my asshole and moved my ass up and down.

"Damn it," he cried, "that feels so fucking good!" I had him horny enough to go another round. He put his elbows to the floor, pressed his body against mine, grabbed the back of my head with both hands and moved up and down with the rising and falling of my body. Before I knew it, his whole body was off mine, and just his hands and toes were holding him up over me. Then his hips came down crashing against my bottom.

After about fifteen minutes of very hard banging, Dave arched his head back. His body froze up, his face turned bright red as sweat dripped off of it. Then he let out a load roar and let it rip! He shoved his dick into me three or four times, draining all the spunk out of it, then he collapsed, out of breath, on top of my body.

"Are you happy now?" he asked. "There's no more come left inside me."

Dave didn't even have enough energy to take his dick out of me. I reached down to slide that monster out of my ass, and we both lay there with him between my legs. After about five minutes I could tell Dave had fallen asleep on my shoulder. I could feel his heart beating slower, and his breathing was more controlled than when we were fucking. Shit, I thought. I could go a hundred more rounds. Now I know what women feel like after sex, and why they always want more.

We stayed on the floor the whole night in the same position. I didn't fall asleep at all. I just stared into space the whole night, playing the encounter over and over again in my mind. When day broke, I got up, took a shower and got dressed. I left Dave face-down on the floor, still sleeping soundly.

I got the remaining honey, poured it up and down his ass-crack and began to lick out his ass. He awoke at once and flipped over. I tried to give him a blowjob, but he was just too tired to get a hard-on. "I can't . . . I don't have anything left," he mumbled. Oh, well. You can't blame me for trying.

I got up and let Dave fall back to sleep. On my way out, I wrote him a note and told him I hoped we could see each other again. In all, I was quite surprised by our encounter. Not only did I lose my virginity and have my long-awaited first homosexual experience, but I also found out that appearances can be deceiving. Dave drank beer, played sports, coached a football team and watched wrestling on television—a real macho man. If only all those girls at his high school knew what he liked to do between the sheets! I'm sure glad I found out.—*G.A., Austin, Texas*   ⊶▄

TWO HEADS ARE BETTER THAN ONE—AND THAT'S JUST THE DILDO!

I've just lived through the most fulfilling forty-eight hours of sexual excitement that I ever could've imagined. My best friend John had come over to see the master bathroom my wife and I had just finished working on. As part of the project, we built a sunbathing deck off the outside shower. The deck got full sun throughout the afternoon. Since we enjoy nude sunbathing, we installed a seven-foot wall for complete privacy.

John was impressed by what he saw. When we left the deck and walked back through the master bedroom, he spotted our collection of X-rated tapes and expressed interest in seeing one. I asked if he'd ever seen a threesome with two men and a woman. He said no, so I popped in a film I thought he'd like. It featured two men servicing a beautiful lady, as well as each other. John watched the film, and I watched him begin to squirm. He fidgeted around quite a bit during a scene when the two guys went down on each other. I knew he was getting hard, and I loved it.

I asked John if he'd ever handled another guy's hard-on. He admitted he'd only thought about it, but was not sure how to approach a man for sex. I dropped my pants, yanked out my tool and said to him, "Consider yourself approached."

I coaxed him into showing me his cock. It was splendid. Eight and a half inches long, cut, and a good four inches in diameter. I dropped to my knees and slowly fondled his balls and massaged his pole. He was pleased. My lips slowly encircled the massive purple head. A drop of pre-come oozed from the tip. As I rolled my tongue over and over his head, it really began to stiffen. Pressure was building up in my cock too. I was going to need some relief before long.

John reached for my chest and played with my nipples as I sucked. He began to groan and moan, rotating his hips into my vacuum-like mouth. I could tell it wouldn't be long before he spewed his goo. I took his dick all the way down my throat. He exploded furiously. I kneaded his balls and scrotum as his semen pumped out. Spurt after spurt shot down my gullet, his balls spanking my chin. I, too, had climaxed, my come oozing all over myself and the carpet. I couldn't ever remember my dick being so hard—it redefined the word "stiff"!

John got close to my balls and inhaled deeply. "I love that smell," he said. He licked my shaft slowly with long, smooth strokes of his tongue. Against my will, I erupted instantly. It was my second orgasm in about three minutes! I'd never done that before.

"Let's sunbathe on the deck," I suggested. We rushed to the deck, spread out a couple of cushions and began to talk about what had just happened. I told him I wanted more. I told him I wanted his dick up my ass. John admitted to having had some pretty wild fantasies about butt-fucking, and said he'd do it to me.

We were both stiff again, despite having come only ten minutes earlier. I went to my wife's nightstand and took out her K-Y jelly. I said to John, "It's now or never." I dropped to my knees and licked his cockhead. "What a beautiful dick," I said. "I want to take you up the ass." John soon was crawling the walls with desire. He was mine!

I spread jelly on my anus and on his prick. As I knelt in front of him on the deck, I felt the sun shining on us. His cockhead popped into my asshole, and the rest of his seven inches soon followed. In no time at all he was nuts-deep in my butt. He reached over and grabbed my dick. "I want us to fire our loads at the same time," he told me. His rhythm was steadily increasing, and his hand was getting coated with my pre-come. He stroked my dick and banged my rear over and over again.

I moaned with passion and lust. "Give it to me, John. Dump your load inside me!" I gushed just as he shot his load up my rectum. My fanny ground into his groin. I wanted to feel all of his come-coated cock in my slimy ass. We were covered with sperm. Everything smelled of sex!

As we pulled apart, I heard a female voice behind me. "You guys do this often?" It was my wife Sami!

She'd caught the last ten minutes of our act. I didn't know what to do. She finally said to John, "I think you might want to leave now. My husband and I have quite a bit to talk about."

After John had left, Sami asked me why we did it. I told her I'd wanted to experience another man in my mouth and in my ass. I was curious, and John was too. We hadn't planned it, but it did happen. She hugged me, but said she had to give it some thought. Then she went for a ride.

As part of our remodel, we'd installed a sunken tub. My dick, which was still semi-erect and covered with sperm, needed a bath, and so did my ass. I filled the tub with hot water and bubbles and relaxed for a half hour or so. I thought about my marriage and how it was probably over. I dressed, put on some music and had a couple of beers. When Sami came back three hours later, I was very happy to see her, and tried to give her a big kiss.

"Not so fast, buster," she said. "I'm going to punish you for your behavior. Do you remember when your dad caught you smoking, and he made you smoke so much it made you sick?"

"Yes," I said.

"Well," she went on, "I'm going to ream your ass until you never want to see another dick again as long as you live!" She then pulled out an eleven-inch, double-headed dildo, grabbed me by the hand and dragged me into the bedroom. My dick was showing signs of excitement again. Sami, who I think is the most beautiful woman in the galaxy, tore open my shirt, ripped off my jeans and demanded to know if I liked boys and not girls. My stiff dick pointed directly, in answer, at Sami. She took some jelly and smeared a handful on my cock. She wanted to know how John and I started, because she'd only seen our finale. When I told her about dropping to my knees and popping John's dick into my mouth, she lubed my ass. When I described the feeling of his balls against my chin, she lubed the dildo and gently stuffed five inches of it up my backside. When I told her how good his prick felt in my butt, she pushed me to the floor, doggie-style, and pushed the dildo in to the hilt.

Now Sami was getting pretty hot herself. I could smell her cunt juice, and saw it running down her leg. "Why don't you ride the other end of that thing, Sami, and really ream me good," I suggested. When the dildo made contact with her moist pussy, I could hear her breath stop. I think she wanted to fuck herself more than she wanted to see me squirm!

I leaned back into the dildo and could feel her trembling. She quivered and shook. We began to rock back and forth, faster and faster, fucking each other in a way I'd never dreamed! She climaxed violently, three, four, five times in a row! In all my years she'd never come that much. Never. We finished off with me sliding my cock into her asshole and pumping her ass full of spunk.

It seems Sami no longer cares if John and I get it on. In fact she wants to hide in the closet the next time we do it. I just hope she comes out to play when the action gets hot!—*H.D., Los Angeles, California* O┼▄

A TWO-WAY SUCK-OFF IS JUST WHAT THE DOCTOR ORDERED

I am a college senior, and run a cleaning service to help pay for my schooling. About a year ago, one of the doctors at the medical office that I clean got a divorce. When he bought his new townhouse, Doc—which is what everyone calls him—asked me to clean it.

One day at Doc's place, I found a copy of your magazine on his bed. It was open to the "Boy Meets Boy" section. I had no idea that you printed such letters in your magazine! The title grabbed my interest, so I sat down on the edge of Doc's king-size waterbed and began reading. It wasn't long before I had a lump in my shorts. I was glad to see other guys talking about their gay experiences with enjoyment.

As I turned the page, I looked up to see Doc standing in the doorway with his shirt unbuttoned. He was massaging his dick through his trousers. He had a lot of body hair, and his muscles were clearly defined. Doc walked into the room and toward the bed. By the time he reached me, he had unhooked his belt and unbuttoned his trousers. I lowered my eyes to his zipper, then pulled it down. Much to my surprise, his cock instantly sprang free. I love it when a man doesn't wear underwear. I continued pulling his trousers down until they were at his knees, revealing his sculptured, hairy thighs.

I stuck out my tongue and played with the slit of his cock. He let out a soft, approving moan. His legs were far enough apart to allow his low-hanging nut sac to swing free. With one hand I began to massage one of his thighs. With the other, I gently massaged and pulled his two large nuts. I stroked his cock, sucked his balls and then tickled his anus with the tip of my tongue. Doc moaned once again and began to run his fingers through my hair.

Pulling on his nut sac firmly, I closed my lips around his cockhead and began my slow decent down his shaft. As I did so, I slid my hand to his ass-cheeks, which were also covered with hair. I had to have at least eight inches of hard-as-stone-cock in my mouth! I relaxed my neck muscles and was able to take all of Doc without any difficulty.

Doc moaned louder this time and held my head in his grip. I squeezed his nuts and ass at the same time, and he began to rotate his hips. He would pull his cock out of my mouth just enough to breathe, then thrust it back in again. With each thrust he would moan a bit louder and fuck my mouth a bit harder.

"Oh, God!" he shouted as he pushed his hips forward forcefully, plunging his cock deep down my throat. "You're a damn good face-fuck!" he said. With those words, several thick squirts of sperm shot down my throat. I swallowed all of his huge load without spilling a drop. Then Doc released his grip on my head, and I loosened my hold on his nuts.

Doc removed his shirt and trousers. He knelt back down and, pulling my shorts to my ankles, he pushed my tank top upward. He explored my smooth body with his hands, then began to work my cock with his mouth. We both groaned with delight. He would bring his lips to my cockhead and run his tongue all over it, while pulling the skin back as tight as it would go. Doc was able to engulf my cock with ease and great skill.

In less than two minutes I felt my nuts getting ready to explode. I grabbed the back of his head with both my hands and pushed his face all the way into my crotch. I then thrust my hips upward and shot my load down Doc's throat. He grabbed my hips with his hands and rocked us back and forth as he swallowed.

As soon as I'd pumped the last of my sperm down his throat, he jumped up on top of me, straddling my waist. He grabbed his cock and began to beat it with great fury. I immediately grabbed his nipples and squeezed as hard I could. In just about ten quick strokes, Doc shot his second load all over my chest. As the sperm dripped down my chest, Doc released his cock and licked his sperm off me. As he licked, he purred with contentment, like a cat lapping up warm milk.

When he finished licking my chest clean, he lay his head on my chest, between my pecs, and massaged my biceps with his strong hands. We lay there, kissing and touching, communicating without a word the enjoyment we'd just shared.

I had given and received my share of blowjobs, but I can't remember any man giving me head with as much enthusiasm and enjoyment as Doc.—*B.M., Chicago, Illinois* ○┼▪

THE OBJECT OF HIS DESIRE GETS THE MASSAGE, BUT NOT THE MESSAGE

I'm a twenty-year-old physical therapy assistant at a hospital in Seattle, where I've learned an assortment of treatment techniques. Among other things, the hospital has taught me about different types of massage.

I'm strongly attracted to my best friend Mickey. He's basically straight and is unaware, as far as I know, that I'm not. This twenty-year-old stud is about five feet eight inches tall, weighs a hundred and thirty pounds and has short brown hair. Mickey has hazel-brown eyes, a thirty-inch waist and a bubble butt that is to die for. His square jaw is complemented by a sexy mustache.

All right, you can see I've been looking at him pretty closely. We've been friends for a long time. I often sleep at his house. We usually pull a spare mattress out from under his bed and put it on the floor right next to him.

One night, as we were pulling out the mattress, Mickey complained, "Damn, my neck is stiff tonight. It's bothered me all day. I have no idea what I did to it." I offered to massage his back and neck, and he was delighted.

He lay on the bed, and I started to work his trapezius muscles, which stretch down from the back of the upper neck to the deltoid muscles of the shoulders. They were very tense, but after a while started to unclench. Mickey began to moan, "Ah, that's great, Aaron." I really hadn't set out to get something sexual going with him, but a moan is a moan, and the sound got me hot. My cock began to swell with excitement. I thought of kissing him, but chickened out. After about a half hour of being worked on, Mickey said he was ready for bed.

Any thought of putting the moves on him evaporated. I slipped down onto the mattress on the floor, and Mickey rolled over onto his back. After he settled, he said, "Good night, Aaron, pleasant dreams." It was a tremendous disappointment, but after a long time my cock softened, and I eventually dozed off. This is what I dreamed.

I was straddling Mickey as he lay supine on his bed. I was massaging him. My cock grew hard once again. Mickey raised his head and said, "Has that big bulge in your pants got anything to do with me?" I was appalled at what he'd said, or rather at his catching me with a hard-on. I couldn't answer or move. "I guess I'll have to see for myself," he said. His hand darted down my sweats and pulled at my throbbing cock. His fingers felt soft. I closed my eyes and leaned my head back.

He removed his hand from my pants and pulled me close to him. Before I knew it, his tongue was exploring my mouth. I ran my hands through his hair, my heart pounding. A warm glow flowed through my whole groin. We rolled over so that Mickey was on top of me. "Aaron, I want your dick," he growled, kissing my neck.

"It's yours, all yours," I sighed. He was sucking my right nipple. The feeling was indescribably intense. As he worked from my nipple to my cock, he pulled my pants down to my knees.

"I've waited way too long for this," he said, smiling. He lifted my pole to his mouth, taking only the tip at first. He slowly eased my whole length into his mouth and throat. The warmth and wetness of his mouth, and his obvious pleasure in sucking my dick, sent powerful sensations flying back and forth between my cock and my brain. I could feel the juices stirring in my balls, waiting to be sprayed onto his waiting tongue. The sounds of Mickey's sucking made me even hornier.

He turned around so his crotch was over my face. I removed his jeans and put his dick in my mouth. Mickey began fucking my face—in and out, up and down—moaning in complete ecstasy. I was close to coming even before he touched me. Once he started groaning, I couldn't hold back any longer. My cock spewed love juice like never before. It seemed like I'd never quit. Mickey just kept lapping it up. Soon after I started spraying, Mickey also exploded. His sperm had a delicious, salty-sweet taste.

We both collapsed. Mickey turned around and kissed me on the lips. There were still gobs of come in our mouths and our tongues mixed it around. Mickey lifted his mouth from mine, smiled and said, "Thanks for the massage."

The next thing I knew, I was wide awake in my bed and drenched in my own come. I went to the bathroom and cleaned up, then lay awake in disappointment because it never happened.

But Mickey, if you read this (and I'm sure you will), look for the bulge the next time I massage you. Yes, it's there for you.—*A.R., Seattle, Washington* ○┼▪

PATIENCE PAYS OFF IN A PECCADILLO WITH A PEDALING PROFESSOR

I've had a lovely encounter that I want to tell you about. My name is Maria. I'm a natural blonde, with brown eyes, and stand about five feet two inches tall. Three years ago, while in my first year of college, I was on the pep squad. The faculty adviser was named Judy. I used to watch her in the hallways and classrooms. She always said hello to me, and sometimes we would stop long enough to have a good talk. I started falling in love with her.

One day we were showering after a pep squad workout. Judy walked by as I was stepping out of my stall. She looked me over, as though surprised to run into me, and asked me to see her in the gym teacher's office. I got dressed and went to see her. She asked me whether I would mind giving her a ride home, as her car was in the shop. I said I'd be glad to.

I was very excited and giddy when we got in the car, because this was as close as I'd ever been to her. I asked how she would handle a situation in which one person wanted to show how much that person liked another person. I'm pretty sure Judy could see right through my intentions. She said to just kiss the person. My face flushed, and I was glad we pulled into the parking lot of her apartment building, because my feet were trembling too much to drive.

Judy started to get out of the car, but I put my hand on her sleeve and said her name. She turned to look at me and I kissed her on the mouth. It tasted wonderful—warm and soft. Shocks of electricity raced through my body at the soft touch of her lips.

She pulled back from the kiss and told me to come with her into her apartment. We needed to talk, she explained. My legs were so shaky I could barely get out of the car, and I was frightened that she would be angry. We got inside and she helped me with my coat. As I turned round and looked up into her face, she said, "If that kiss was an indication of how much you like me, then maybe you really don't like me that much." My heart just soared.

We embraced and kissed again, this time for much longer. Her body was very different from the high school senior boys I'd kissed, firm in different places, soft and conforming in others. I was becoming dizzy, and my body started to feel hot. I was just getting into kissing her when she started to use her tongue on me. It felt as though somebody had pushed me into a red-hot cauldron of lust. I started to moan and grind my hips against hers. She started to do the same to me, almost frantically grasping my body.

We came up for air, literally panting from desire. She took my hand and we went into the kitchen of her apartment. We poured some iced tea and she told me to wait a moment.

She went to the bathroom, not returning for several minutes. It was obvious, when she returned, that she'd been crying. Judy told me her marriage was breaking up and it was a terribly difficult time for her. She said that what she had done, both leading me along and finally kissing me, was wrong, and that we shouldn't meet anymore. I pleaded with her, begged her not to cut me off. "You didn't lead me along," I wailed. "I wanted this as much as you did." She refused to listen, and insisted that she couldn't see me anymore. I was heartsick and confused, but I assured her that I would do as she said and not try to see her again.

At the end of the year I transferred to a different school just a few miles away, though not because of Judy. I had decided to become a teacher, and the second college had a better program. After transferring, I had two excellent male lovers, and my feelings for Judy were put away.

During the summer break, I went back to my old school to take a class that I had missed. Every day I rode my bike between the two campuses. One day I saw a woman who looked very familiar riding a bike ahead of me. It was Judy! I caught up with her, and we started to talk. She gave me her address and asked me over to her apartment for a glass of wine that afternoon.

After class I went home, showered and changed, all the time thinking about what might happen. My boyfriend asked me where I was going, and I told him I was having dinner with an old friend.

I arrived at Judy's place and knocked on the door. She opened it wearing a pair of denim cutoffs that showed a peek of cheek, and a new, snowy-white T-shirt with no bra. We drank some wine, talking about college classes and riding bikes. I couldn't stop looking at her nipples and full breasts, swaying under the fabric with every gesture. She noticed that I was staring, and smiled, asking, "Do you like what you see?" I looked into her eyes and just nodded. I confessed that I hadn't thought about her much since our one encounter, because I'd had several lovers.

"But," I immediately added, "I've been thinking a lot about you since we met up again earlier today. All day I've been getting more and more excited."

Judy looked pleased, and responded, "I've been getting turned on too, thinking about you coming over." We moved closer on the couch and started to kiss. She moaned as we continued kissing, our lips and tongues sucking and licking. This time she didn't pull away. We held each other, running our hands over each other's breasts. I could feel her nipples getting hard with desire. We rolled sideways on the sofa, with her on the bottom and me lying on top. The tip of her tongue poked between my lips, which eagerly parted to encourage its entrance. As our tongues met, we began grinding our hips and breasts into each other. I could feel my pussy getting wet and hot. I put my hands on her ass-cheeks and held her as I rubbed and pushed my pussy against hers.

We stopped kissing for a moment to catch our breath, and she looked into my eyes. It was the critical moment and I had a little twinge in my stomach at the idea that she might call a halt to what we were doing. Instead she kissed me on the cheek and, with her mouth very close to my ear, said, "Why don't we go into the bedroom?"

We got up and walked hand-in-hand through the door. Judy started to lift her T-shirt but I stopped her, turning her slowly so her back was to me. As her shirt came off, I ran my hands and fingers along her ribs and smooth stomach, eventually moving up to her breasts. They felt wonderful as I cupped them, running my thumbs over the nipples. She turned, dropping her cut-offs, unbuttoning my jeans and taking my T-shirt off. We were both nude, almost touching. I could feel the heat from her body, and my own body felt flushed and hot.

She took my hand and we went to the bed. Judy pulled the covers off and lay on the cool sheets. I eased down next to her. No words were spoken. Our lips met again, and we lay back on the bed. Kneeling next to her, I moved down to kiss and suck her breasts, not believing how good it felt. Now I knew why my boyfriends liked doing it so much! My hand inched its way down to her pussy, past her pubic hair, and I lightly ran my fingers along her slit, parting her swollen labia. She shuddered, pushing against my hand with excitement. I wanted to taste her pussy, but she pulled me back on the bed next to her.

Judy started working her way down the front of my body, and I found myself holding my breath. She kissed the lips of my pussy, and I felt like I was going to melt. Her tongue went deep inside me, and I let go of my breath, arching my back and pressing my hips into her face. She held my thighs open and managed to keep contact with me as I bucked under her. She reached a place deep inside me with the end of her tongue, then wiggled it back and forth. Every muscle in my body jerked at once. My clitoris was rubbing against her face, and when I came I felt like a weight was being lifted off me. My pussy juices were all over Judy's face. I took her face in my hands and licked off the shining drops. I've always liked doing that, even when my boyfriends go down on me. Judy obviously liked it too.

Judy lay back on the bed with a sigh. I really wanted to taste her. Without any preliminaries I kissed her pussy, which was shining with moisture. My new lover's pussy tasted a little salty, but wonderful. As my tongue slid up and down, occasionally diving into her vagina, Judy reacted like someone was shooting electricity through her. Her clit was standing up like a little light switch, and I was flicking it on and off with my tongue. Everywhere I touched with my tongue I got a reaction, and I loved it. She became more and more tense as her orgasm built. The lips of her pussy and the muscles in her legs were quivering. With a final tremor, Judy came, crying out my name, her legs flying in the air as she let go like an uncoiling spring.

I moved up the bed, kissing her face and mouth as she caught her breath. After that we must have dozed for a while. When we woke up we switched positions, arranging ourselves on our sides for a hot 69. We started licking each other's pussy. If felt so exquisite that I was having difficulty concentrating on eating her out. But as we got into the groove of the sex, I could feel our rhythms blend and mesh, pushing and receiving, sucking and licking. We bucked as though riding wild horses.

Judy came first, then guided me over her. I was actually sitting on her face, looking at her body on the bed, running my hands over her stomach and thighs. She pressed my pussy against her face. I wiggled and twitched, which only made her lick and suck deeper and harder. I came so hard that I thought I was going to faint. The strength just ran out of my body.

Exhausted, I lay down on Judy, our sweat making our bodies slippery. I looked at her and said that I was glad I had come over for that glass of wine, and she told me that I was welcome any time.

It was time for me to leave, so we put our clothes on and I went back to my own place. I was still really turned on, so my boyfriend and I made love before falling asleep.

I went to Judy's apartment several times while she was in class that summer, and we made love for hours. She went back to Denver in the fall, but has visited me since. We've been on skiing weekends, since it's winter now. Where it goes from here we don't know, but come what may I'm certainly glad we've had the chance to explore each other.—*M.J., Denver, Colorado*

SOUTHBOUND SAILORS HITCH WITH OUR HERO, IN MORE WAYS THAN ONE

I drove south in my pickup to get some furniture I'd left behind when I moved recently from Florida to Virginia. Midafternoon found me in South Carolina. I was getting stupid from boredom, and still had a long way to go, so I stopped at a roadside restaurant for a cup of coffee.

Two young sailors, nineteen or twenty years old and dressed in whites, were sitting at the counter. We started talking. The guys, Tommy and Bo, were hitchhiking to Daytona. When I offered them a ride through Georgia, they eagerly accepted. They threw their bags in the back and crawled into the cab. Tommy sat in the middle. We drove along at a steady pace, talking about the navy and other things. After a while we just listened to the music on the radio. Bo dozed off.

A little later Tommy nudged me and pointed to Bo. "He must be having a heck of a good dream. Look at that trouser snake running down his leg." I glanced over and, sure enough, Bo's cock was very obvious, pressed against his leg in his tight pants. It grew longer and thicker as we watched.

"That's some weapon," I said.

"You ought to see it. It's huge. Eight inches at least." Tommy punched Bo and he woke up. "That's quite a slab of meat there, Bo. Shame it's wasted. Some girl'd fall in love with you in a heartbeat," he joked. Bo blushed and covered his crotch with his hands.

We laughed, and took turns telling dirty jokes for a while. I enjoyed their company. It made the boring drive much more pleasant.

I was really starting to nod—understandably, as I'd been driving for about ten hours. Around nine, I suggested we stop for the night. They wouldn't be able to catch a ride that late, so I asked if they'd like to share a motel room. I agreed to pay the single rate if they would pay the additional charge for a double and share a bed. We found a motel on the edge of a small town and got a room with two double beds.

Instead of going to a restaurant, we bought hamburgers and several six-packs of beer and took them to our room. After eating, and drinking several brews, I took a long, hot shower and stretched out in just my undershorts. Tommy and Bo decided to clean up also, and went into the bathroom. I turned the TV to an adult movie channel. I heard the guys laughing and joking around. Were they showering together? In a few minutes they came out, put on clean boxers, and sprawled on their bed. They watched the movie and made lewd comments about the action on the screen.

Tommy suddenly exclaimed, "Damn it, Bo, you're getting a hard-on."

"So what? Aren't you? You're just jealous." I looked over, and indeed Bo's prick was poking up.

"Jealous of what?" asked Tommy. "I've got enough to satisfy you." Bo laughed and playfully pushed at Tommy. That started them tussling about on the bed, then rolling on the floor in a tangle of arms and legs. Their lean bodies were twisted around each other like pretzels. Bo grabbed the waistband of Tommy's shorts and pulled them down to his knees. Tommy quickly kicked them off. He reached for Bo's groin and yanked down his boxers. The two naked guys wrestled playfully, each sporting a full erection. Their game became more and more sexual, as they rubbed together and reached for each other's dick.

Tommy finally just lay on his back. Bo crawled to him and held his cock straight up. "Go ahead, Bo," Tommy whispered. "Blow me. That's what you were dreaming about this afternoon, isn't it?" It sounded more like a challenge than anything else, and I wasn't sure how Bo would respond. Bo didn't answer, but lowered his open tongue to Tommy's prick. I watched as he sucked it greedily. He sank more of it in his tongue with each stroke, until his nose was buried in Tommy's wiry, blond pubic hair.

It may not have started seriously, but neither one of them was laughing now. Bo's head rose and fell. Tommy's whole body twisted and bucked. Bo removed his tongue and sat with his eyes glued to Tommy's throbbing cock. He pumped it with his hand until it spurted globs of come onto Tommy's belly. Bo traced patterns in the pond of come with his fingers.

When Tommy recovered he looked at me, and said, "You liked watching that, didn't you? Well then, watch this." He led Bo to the bed and began to lick him from head to toe. Bo moaned with pleasure. Tommy finally sucked in as much of Bo's eight inches as he could without gagging. Bo was so aroused that he was quick on the trigger and shot his wad. Tommy took a mouthful, but some drooled down his chin.

Seeing these guys eat each other had made me horny as hell. I covered my engorged cock with both hands and tried not to jerk myself off.

"Let's see what you're hiding there, sport," Tommy teased. "Come on, Bo, let's see if we can't get some of that."

They crawled onto the bed on either side of me. Four hands roamed over my body. They pulled down my short and my cock sprang free.

"Really nice, really very nice," commented Bo. They each wrapped a hand around my prick. They licked my nipples, cupped and fondled my balls, and took turns sucking my willing unit. My cock went from mouth to mouth, and I found it impossible to decide which I liked better. Damn, they were cock-hungry. I tingled all over and humped upward to meet the mouths that took turns vacuuming my tube. They were each rewarded with a couple of big spurts of come, some of which fell on my stomach and pubes. When I finally stopped pumping it felt like my insides had been sucked out.

After breakfast in the morning I took the guys to a big intersection and let them out. I wondered if I would be lucky enough to spot another hitchhiker on the way back home.—*S.D., Winston-Salem, North Carolina*   ⊙⊢▥

LIFELONG FEAR OF QUEERS STARTS TO CRUMBLE IN THE BACK ROW

A few years ago I went on an extended business trip to a midwestern city. I had been away from home for several weeks and felt quite horny, so I decided to go to an X-rated movie.

I took a seat in the back of theater. When my eyes became accustomed to the dark, I was surprised to discover that most of the men seated near me had their pants unzipped and were masturbating. What the hell, I thought. When in Omaha, do as the Omahanians do.

I suppose that every man who has ever attended an adult movie has fantasized about some gal coming in and sitting down next to him, looking for some intimate contact. Well, that didn't happen. What did happen was a guy sat down beside me and whispered in my ear, "Can I jack you off?" I was speechless. Since I didn't answer, I guess he assumed that I didn't object. So he reached over and started pumping my prick. It didn't take me long to start imagining that the beautiful blonde on the screen had hold of my dick.

No one around me was making any noise. The silent intensity of all these guys pumping themselves off without a sound was much more erotic than the exaggerated moans and groans of the actors. I found myself straining to hear the soft gasps that were released around me each time one of my fellow masturbators started to come. I thought I could actually hear the sound of a guy in the row in front of me stroking himself. I saw him ever so slightly lean his head back, a look of concentration on his face. In the next second I saw all the tension drain out of his features, and I knew he was dumping his seed on the concrete floor. That was enough to give me my release.

After I shot my load, the guy who had been doing me got up and left—to wash his hands, I suppose.

I've always had nothing but contempt for queers. I wasn't sure whether a guy who went to adult theaters to jack other guys off was homosexual, but I knew he sure as hell wasn't normal. Still, I had to admit I had enjoyed my little adventure.

A couple of months ago my wife went to visit her parents down south. After sleeping by myself for several nights, I decided to go see a dirty movie. I picked out a seat that wasn't near anyone else, and after a while I had my dick out of my pants and was rubbing it.

I had been enjoying the movie and my masturbation for a few minutes, when a man came and sat down a row in front of me. I put my dick away and zipped up my pants. But after a few minutes the man in front of me unzipped his pants and started fondling himself, so I pulled my dick back out and resumed my penile massage.

After a few minutes I noticed the other guy glancing over his shoulder and looking at my dick. This gave me a weird, tingling feeling, but instead of stopping, I started kind of showing off for him. I cupped my balls with one hand and circled my cockhead with one fingertip of my other hand. With that finger I smeared the drops of pre-come that had gathered on the tip of my dick. He turned around and whispered, "Want a hand with that?"

"Help yourself," I murmured.

That was the night I discovered there is more than one masturbation technique. He had some twists and turns that made it supremely enjoyable. By the time I blew my wad, I was twitching all over the place. I knew that several pairs of eyes were watching us in the dark, silently cheering on our progress. My come finally flowed down over my partner's hand. He lifted it to his lips and licked it off. I'm sure that more than one of guys around us got off when they saw that happen.

I've been back to the same theater several times, and have gotten a handjob almost every time. Most of the guys have their own technique, which gives each episode the excitement of variety.

The anonymous nature of these liaisons makes the adult theater situation perfect. I feel like I've discovered a precious national resource that's been going largely untapped.—*Z.R., Chicago, Illinois* ⊙╾▦

HIS MARRIAGE IS BEHIND HIM, BUT SO IS A NEW ROUTE TO PLEASURE

Last year after my divorce, I moved into a new apartment in a different neighborhood. My neighbor Ben and I quickly became good buddies. We would often get together after work, have few beers, talk, shoot pool or watch television.

I quickly got the idea that Ben was interested in being more than just a friend, as he often touched me when we talked, and seemed comfortable saying things to me like, "You're a very attractive man." I'd never had a gay affair before, but I must admit I'd often thought about it. I decided that I would not make the first move—but if Ben did, I'd go along with it.

One Friday night Ben stopped by my apartment. We had a couple of beers and smoked a joint, and then Ben broke out a gram of coke. When I saw the coke, I was sure he was going to seduce me. We did a couple of lines, after which Ben started talking about sex. We sat up half the night, doing blow and talking about the women we'd screwed, the different things we liked to do in bed, and the fantasies we had that had never been realized. As the night went on, I kept waiting for him to make his move, but he never did. He finally left at about o'clock in the morning. I was surprised by how horny I was when he left, and had to jerk off a couple of times before I could fall asleep.

The next night, I fixed myself dinner and took a shower. It was a warm night, so all I wore when I got out was a tank top and a pair of beach pants. Ben stopped by about seven o'clock. He brought a bottle of Jack Daniel's and a bag of pot. After a couple of joints and a few drinks, I was again ready for anything. Most of all, I was ready for Ben. We were sitting on the sofa, and I scooted over next to him. I accidentally bumped his foot with mine. He bumped back, and before I knew it we were playing footsie.

Finally he made the move I'd been waiting for him to make. He put his hand on my thigh, slid it up to my crotch and started stroking my cock. I instantly got a hard-on, which was obvious through the thin material of my pants. Ben undid the buttons of my fly, took out my cock and started jacking me off. After a few minutes of this, we moved to my bedroom, got undressed and got into bed together.

We lay on the bed in a 69 position for several minutes, both of us silently working up the courage to bring our cocks and mouths together. At last, I took him into my mouth and started blowing him. A few minutes later he did the same. Ben had a beautiful cock. It was long and slender. He was circumcised too, and I was grateful for that. I could never have gone any further if I had been confronted with anything as hideous as a foreskin.

I shifted to a more comfortable position and began sucking his dick in earnest. At first I could take only a few inches, but after a few minutes my jaw began to relax and I found I could fit most of his cock in my mouth with no discomfort. After a few minutes of sucking him, I could tell he was close to orgasm. I wasn't comfortable with the idea of him coming in my mouth, so I was almost grateful when he told me he wanted to fuck me in the ass.

I got a towel, a condom and some lubricant from the bathroom. I lay facedown on the bed while Ben greased up his dick. He spread my ass-cheeks and shoved his cock up my ass, simple as that. The penetration was quick and easy. It was a little painful, but it was a pleasant kind of pain, a taut sense of fullness. After only a minute or two of thrusting the entire length of his cock up my ass, Ben shot his wad. I went into the bathroom to clean up. When I came out of the john, Ben was gone.

We avoided each other for almost a week, but after a while I couldn't stand it any longer. That Thursday, I waited until Ben got home from work, then went over to see him. He had just gotten out of the shower and answered the door wearing only a bathrobe. We didn't say a word, we just walked into his bedroom and got undressed. His body was still moist and steamy from the shower.

He sat on the edge of the bed and I knelt between his legs. His cock was still limp, and I could easily take the whole thing into my mouth. With my lips and tongue I worked him to a full erection so that his dick filled my mouth. I began bobbing my head up and down as I slid his cock back and forth across my lips. He begged me to use long, slow strokes to make it last, but I was eager to make him come. I wanted to know what semen tasted like.

I picked up the tempo of the blowjob, working his dick in and out of my mouth as fast as I could. Suddenly his cock swelled and seemed to explode. As he dumped his load and shot stream after stream of thick, rich come in my mouth, I paused to swallow it down, then licked his penis clean.

We got dressed, went back into the living room and smoked a joint, and soon I went home.

The next night I had just gotten in when the phone rang. It was Ben, inviting me to party at his place. It turned out to be a party for just the two of us. We had pizza and beer, smoked a couple of joints and then went into his bedroom, got undressed and got into bed. Ben already had a hard-on, so I went down on him. He was so turned on that he came fast. It really took me by surprise to have his sperm spilling across my tongue after only a few moments of sucking.

I put my hands on his head and guided his mouth to my cock. He hesitated before taking me in. It was obvious that he was still uncomfortable giving me a blowjob, and I had to coach him along. He soon got the idea and began sucking my dick with style and enthusiasm, keeping it nice and wet with long slurps of his tongue. Unfortunately the moment was somewhat ruined when I came in his mouth. He jumped up, slapped a hand over his lips, ran into the bathroom and spit my jism into the toilet.

After brushing his teeth, he came back into the bedroom. We huddled together in bed and smoked another joint. I teased him about not swallowing my come, and stroked his cock until he was hard again. I ran my tongue from the base of his dick to the tip. Then I took his balls into my mouth one at a time and rolled my tongue over them. It was a long, slow blowjob. I deliberately took my time, bringing him to the edge of orgasm several times before finishing him off. We then fell asleep in each other's arms.

The next morning we woke up, had breakfast and took a shower together. I squatted down in the tub and sucked Ben off. Then I put my hands on his shoulders and pushed him down. He got the idea, squatted down, took my cock into his mouth and blew me. This time he got right into it, sucking me dry in record time and even swallowing my come!

After we dried off, we moved to the bedroom. Ben asked me to butt-fuck him. He got down on his hands and knees, and I greased up his asshole. Fucking his ass was pretty much like fucking a pussy, although it was much tighter and drier. Ben and I both took a long time to come. It was a long, slow process. We started out slowly and built up the tempo and rhythm of our fuck. Ben cried out that it felt like he was being split in half, but he didn't want me to stop. I shot my wad deep into his bowels just as he sprayed the sheets with his own spunk.

Ben recently moved out of town, but I will never forget the good times we had together. It was an unexpected introduction to single life, but one I do not regret.—*B.T., Maui, Hawaii*   O+▪